To Northumberland – huge skies, great views, big hearts

The First Time I Saw Your Face

HAZEL OSMOND

Quercus

First published in Great Britain in 2012 by

Quercus
55 Baker Street
7th Floor, South Block
London
W1U 8EW

A CIP catalogue record for this book is available
from the British Library.

ISBN 978 1 84916 419 1

10 9 8 7 6 5 4 3 2 1

Typeset by Ellipsis Books Limited, Glasgow

Printed and bound in Great Britain by Clays Ltd, St Ives plc

CHAPTER 1

Yes, the statue was definitely winking. Down came one of the Roman centurion's silver eyelids and there was a twist of the head which made the plume on his helmet ripple. The little cluster of tourists gathered nearby gave a variety of squeals before they went back to taking photographs, snapping indiscriminately at the statue, the front of the Abbey, a guy hanging about with a dog on a piece of string and, sometimes, themselves.

Mack, sitting a few yards away on a bench, felt a small finger poke his leg. 'Why is that silver man winking at you?'

He turned to look at the girl attached to the poking finger.

'Don't know, Gabi,' he said with a shrug and went back to trying to work out whether under all that silver paint there was someone he knew.

He was not surprised when his answer proved to be nowhere near good enough for Gabi and the poking finger was in action again.

'Come on, Uncle Mack,' she said, in a voice that reminded him very much of a talk-show host's, 'you can tell me.'

'OK, I'll come clean.' He leaned into her. 'He's not really a Roman centurion: he's a spy and I'm a spy and this is how we pass messages.'

'Don't fib. You're not a spy, you look after Granny and you write particles—'

'Articles.'

She patted his leg, but did not acknowledge the correction. 'Besides, spies have posh cars and lots of girlfriends.' That seemed to conclude the debate as far as she was concerned, and he didn't know if he felt like laughing or becoming intensely depressed about the way she had, with a four-year-old's clarity and cruelty, boiled his life down to 'Granny' and 'particles'. That did just about sum it up. She was definitely spot on about the lack of posh cars and girlfriends.

He looked over at the centurion again and got another wink. There was a further wave of Euro squeals from the tourists who, Mack guessed, from the cut of their jeans and general glossiness, were Italian.

He was mulling over how bizarre it was that a group of Italians was staring at a man pretending to be Roman, when the statue not only winked at him again, but did a little jig, which sent the tourists into giggling, retreating clumps. As they drifted back and regrouped, Mack wondered where they were off to next: Oxford? Stratford? Would all the places merge into one long blur of history and fiction when they got home? Jane Austen mixed up with Inspector Morse and Anne Hathaway?

'Come on,' he said, helping Gabi down from the bench, 'let's go and see what Silverus Maximus is up to. Your mum will be back soon.'

'Mum and Fran and Granny,' Gabi corrected him, and then added as if enthused by the idea, 'How many teeth do you think Fran will have left?'

'All of them, it's only a check-up.'

'And Granny, will they be able to mend the broken one?'

Yes, ready for her to break a different one next time.

'Should think so. Now, can I put your mittens on?'

'They won't fit you.' She waved her hands at him to make sure he got her joke. With the chubbiness of the very young child still about them, they made him think of little, fat starfishes.

He decided to drop the mitten idea and, as they set off over the flagstones, braced himself for the tide of questions that would be coming. It was one of the many things he loved about Gabi, her ability to ask questions that made him look at the world in a new way, but sometimes they fried his brain. Particularly the animal-related ones. Today she was interested to know whether the dog on the piece of string knew it should really have a lead and if it did, how would that make it feel – sad? Or free? And that pigeon with a ring round one leg, did that mean it was married? And if it was, where was Mrs Pigeon?

Mack knew it could have been worse: she could have asked him why some of the angels on the front of the

Abbey were falling from the ladders they were meant to be climbing. He didn't want to think about that. Every time he passed them they reminded him of his own spectacular fall, although that hadn't been off a ladder; more off a career, out of a revolving door and on to a pavement.

Leaving the marital status of pigeons behind, they reached the makeshift plinth, mingled with the Italians and looked up at the centurion. There had been a certain amount of artistic licence employed in the creation of his uniform, which not only featured the regulation breastplate and a sword held aloft in a 'Forward to victory' way, but also something that in a previous life had probably been a tigerskin rug, but was now a cloak, thanks to the addition of a gold-coloured chain and clasp. Mack hoped it provided some protection from the cold bite in the air, otherwise under all that silver it was probable that the centurion's legs were blue. Hard, standing on a wintery plinth in Bath, when you were used to the seductively warm breezes of Rome.

He saw the centurion's eyes shift his way, the whites looking sludgy against all that silver. Yes, definitely something familiar about the face.

'Worked it out yet?' the silver lips whispered, barely moving, and then the centurion jumped down off the plinth, causing a huge flurry of excitement. The sword was lowered on to the flagstones, and Mack felt Gabi cling on to his hand more tightly and tuck herself behind his legs.

'Show over, show over,' the centurion said loudly,

making clapperboard motions with his silver hands and using the 'for the deaf' tone that has endeared the British to other countries for centuries. The Italians slowly peeled away, some dropping coins in the tub at the base of the plinth, others pointedly looking anywhere but the tub.

'Peter Craster,' the centurion said with another of his winks before taking off his helmet. Bizarrely, the hair under it was also sprayed silver. He handed Mack the helmet and then stooped down to pick up the plastic tub, and Mack saw that Peter was from the Roman legion that favoured Y-fronts over boxers.

His mind scrambled to fit a character to the name and came up with a rather posh boy from school, one of the rugger crowd. Ten years ago, which was probably the last time he'd seen him, the guy had been heading for an economics degree at Warwick.

'Of course,' Mack said. 'Sorry, didn't recognise you, what with all that paint and the um . . . the uniform. It's been a while.'

Peter Craster was picking through the coins, transferring them from the tub to a leather purse he had produced from under the tigerskin cloak. 'Recognised you straight away.' There was the wink again. 'Bet you're surprised to see me like this?'

What, painted silver and dressed as a centurion? No, natural career progression for an economist.

Mack was failing to come up with a polite reply when Peter said, 'Of course you're surprised; to tell you the truth, so am I. Went to Warwick, got a job in the City afterwards, but you know . . .' Mack guessed his wasn't the only career that had taken a nosedive.

'Thing is,' Peter lowered his voice, 'only got the bullet a few months ago and decamped back here, but it's turned out to be a godsend. Bit of a goldmine.' Mack looked at the leather purse, and Peter must have got his meaning because, stowing it away, he laughed. 'No, no. I don't mean standing here like a tit. I'm just filling in today: one of my lads is having his varicose veins done. Plays havoc standing up on one of those things for hours not moving.'

'One of your lads?'

'Yup, collective noun really – I have women too. About twenty people in all on the books now.' Peter's silver hands were constantly moving as he described the building of his own little Roman empire. 'They were just crying out for someone to lead them, you see. I mean you can make little bits and pieces standing around all day, it's still a steady earner, but the real money's in events. Getting hired out for parties, book launches, that kind of thing. Not just centurions, of course.' He laughed as though such a narrow specialisation was ludicrous. 'Got all the Regency period covered, tourists go mad for that, and Mr Darcy's a huge hit at weddings.' Mack had a vision of Fitzwilliam Darcy appearing in a wet shirt just as the vicar said, 'Does anybody know of any just cause . . .'

'Tudors, Normans, Victorians,' Peter enthused, 'and now we're branching into lookalikes. Film stars, pop stars.' He whistled. 'You should see my Gaga.'

Mack felt rather than heard Gabi giggle and said

quickly, 'Glad it's turned out well for you . . .' He trailed off as he became aware that Peter Jordan was frowning at him in a way that threatened to make his paint peel.

'So, you just back here on holiday?' he asked. 'Went into journalism didn't you? London? My mother said something about showbiz gossip? Must be—'

'That didn't work out. Just freelancing now.' Mack handed the helmet back to Peter, hoping it would serve as a full stop to the conversation.

'Didn't work out?' Peter asked, hint untaken.

Mack wondered what would happen to Peter's paint job if he told him the truth.

It's like this, Peter; I came home early to find my editor, a bastard called O'Dowd, in bed with my girlfriend. So, in revenge, I dropped his home phone number into an article about a man who was impotent. No one spotted it until the next day, when prank callers began making obscene phone calls to his wife, and the other papers took to calling him 'Mr Floppy'. That's when he went ballistic, threatened to remove my testicles with a hot spoon and made sure I would never work on a national paper again.

'Artistic differences,' Mack settled for, easily fudging the truth. When Peter looked as though he might have follow-up questions Mack added in a weary tone, 'Happened about three years ago.'

'Oh, that's hard.' Peter was all concern now. 'Especially when you've got little ones.'

'No, Gabi is my sister's – Tess – remember her?'

'All the same.' Suddenly Peter's arm was round Mack's shoulder. 'Might be able to help: you'd be a shoo-in for a pirate lookalike. Earring, eyepatch, let your hair grow longer. Can you do stubble?' Mack was unable to confirm what his achievements with facial hair were before a business card was produced. He lifted it from silver fingers.

DOUBLE TAKE
Let us be the still life and soul of your party

Peter's face brightened as much as a face already painted silver could. 'There's plenty of work out there, especially if you're prepared to do hen nights.' He darted a look towards Gabi, who had partially re-emerged from behind Mack's legs. 'You're a good-looking guy. The women would want to know where the silver paint ends, if you get my drift.' The wink got another outing before Peter was all businesslike again. 'And now, if you'll excuse me. Got a call earlier from Lord Nelson. Coachload of Scandinavians heading this way, stopover en route to Stonehenge.' The helmet was hurriedly rammed back on. 'Need to mop them up before they get to that Ancient Briton in woad round by the Parade Gardens.' His paint puckered. 'Not one of mine.'

Within seconds, the fierce centurion on the plinth was back, only unfreezing for one final wink and a mouthed, 'Give me a call,' before the sword was once more brandished aloft.

Mack imagined himself standing up there like a metallic, ersatz Johnny Depp and remembered the day he'd actually interviewed the real one. He expected some form of intense emotion to sweep over him at that: regret possibly, or the urge to rip Peter Craster's business card into pieces, knock him off his plinth and beat him with one of his replica sandals.

'It's a very kind offer,' he heard himself say. 'I'll have a think about it.'

He was uncertain whether his response was due to a gradual mellowing over the last three years or the worry that he was up to his ears in debt and a job offer was a job offer.

He was stuffing Peter's business card in the pocket of his jeans when someone said 'Boo!' behind him and, as he turned, he felt Gabi let go of his hand.

'Mummy,' she yelled, a whirl of arms and legs as she threw herself towards Mack's sister, 'we've been talking to this statue and he wants Uncle Mack to be a pirate and show hens where his silver bits end.'

He wished he could have got his phone out in time to capture his sister's expression. His mother simply looked at the centurion, looked at Mack and said, laconically, 'A pirate? How lovely, you could use some of those skills you picked up on that paper.'

He felt his mouth already forming the shape of some cutting reply when the pleading look on Tess's face held him back. Instead, he turned to Fran. 'So, Frangipan, how are the teeth?' In reply he got a thumbs-up and a huge smile that suggested she still had a full set. There was a sticker saying 'Star Patient' on her coat.

'Mum's are OK too,' Tess said, looking nervously at Phyllida. 'Temporary crown. So . . . everyone set? Let's go find the car.'

Slowly they cut across the Abbey churchyard, along the front of the registry office and the Market before reaching the underground car park. Later in the year, they would have heard all the world's languages on their journey as the tourists descended on Bath to pick it clean of Roman and Austen memorabilia, but today it was mainly English, and much of it had a soft, Bathonian burr.

The girls walked ahead, and as he looked at them, Mack felt that he was seeing time-lapse photographs of the same person: blonde hair, wise blue eyes, a lower lip that was slightly fuller than the upper one. Whereas he and Tess looked nothing like each other, hadn't even done so when they were younger. He glanced at her now as she walked, letting Phyllida lean on her arm. She had their mother's blue eyes and fair skin tone; he had their father's brown eyes and darker looks. He'd also got his father's messy hair gene, whereas Tess's blonde hair, a shade or two darker than both her daughters', stayed exactly where it was put. In fact everything about Tess was neat – even the green scarf she was wearing today did not hang like some kind of forgotten piece of lettuce in the salad crisper, but was tied in a just-so, loose knot.

At the car park, the ever-practical Tess got Phyllida settled in the front seat of the car and the girls strapped in the back before even attempting to pay at the machine. Or perhaps she wanted to talk to Mack on his own. He followed her.

'Did Phyllida get a "Star Patient" sticker too?' he asked with a sardonic laugh.

He was pleased to feel Tess link her arm through his and give it a squeeze. 'Not quite, and anyway, I'm thinking of awarding you one for not rising to her "pirate" comment.'

'But she did behave herself?'

'Uh huh. Told the dentist she'd broken her tooth on a piece of hard toffee.'

'Not on a piece of hard pavement after five hours in the pub?'

'Well, it's one way to kerb her drinking.'

'Yeah, at least falling on the pavement keeps her out of the gutter.'

They were employing the light and cheerful tone they habitually used when talking about their mother, but Mack knew that if he turned and looked at Tess closely right now, she would have the same expression on her face as he had. They called it their 'standing by the gallows' look and Mack was certain it got handed out to anyone with a heavy drinker in the family, along with buckets of patience and an endless supply of hope.

They had reached the head of the queue and Tess fed the ticket into the machine, followed rapidly by a stream of coins. Mack added one or two as his contribution. When Tess had the ticket back in her hand, they walked as slowly as possible back to the car and, because Tess looked uncharacteristically morose, he gave her a playful nudge with his hip.

'Look, I know we're in another one of her dips, but she's always pulled herself round before; she'll do it again. And at least this time I'm here, just upstairs. It's not like before when you and Joe had to keep going round to check on her.'

'I know, I know. But it's hard on you.'

'My turn, Tess.'

'That's what Joe thinks,' she said with a grin, and Mack had no problem imagining just what the straight-down-the-line Joe would have said. The phrases 'Now he's stopped skulking around' and 'Pulling his weight' would have featured largely. There was no dissembling with Joe, what you saw was what you got. Hard to remember that when Tess first took up with him, the all-knowing, arrogant Mack he was then figured she could do a lot better than a guy learning how to be a joiner. Now Joe had his own business and had proved to be a bit of a star on the husband-and-Dad front, while Mack had what? Granny and particles.

'Sensible guy, Joe,' he said.

'That's why I married him.'

'I thought that was because you were pregnant.'

Tess cuffed him on the arm and looked covertly towards the car. 'Shh. That's why I married him *then*. Not why I married him at all.'

'OK, OK, and mind the writing arm, will you? Anyway, what's all this about it being hard on me? You still do too much. I'd have made her sort out her own dental appointment.'

'Oh really, tough guy? Who was it got her glasses fixed when she sat on them, and remind me, how many times in the last week have you cooked for her, hmm?'

'Yeah, well, it keeps me busy.'

Tess gave him a disbelieving look and he took the point that they were both as bad as each other. Phyllida had them on the rack again with her drinking, and all they could do was keep her on her feet as long as possible and ensure everything jogged on around her.

When they reached the car, Mack sensed Tess was back on an even keel, even though there was still a ring of hiked-up brightness about her voice as she opened the driver's door and said, 'Right ho, everyone. That's sorted.'

On the way home, while playing 'I Spy' with the girls, Mack studied Phyllida's profile. At first glance, she didn't look bad for a woman in her sixties. Up closer, though, the texture of her skin was like sucked paper and the whites of her eyes had a jaundiced look to them. She was dropping too much weight as well. Phyllida turned her head as if she was aware he was studying her and he pretended to immerse himself in the game of 'I Spy' again, but he was still thinking about her.

When he was growing up, he thought all mothers smelt of alcohol, just as his father smelled of the little Turkish cigarettes he'd taken to smoking since his stint reporting in the Middle East. The pair of them joked that they were 'work hard, play hard' journalists, with Phyllida swearing that she wrote better with a drink inside her. Hard to pinpoint when her ability to drink heavily had tipped over into something else. Five, six years after his father had died, he guessed.

After Phyllida, Tess and he had left London things had, despite the odd hiccup, got a little better, but since he'd been exiled back to live with her in Bath this time, the general trend had been mainly downwards. He wondered from time to time if that had something to do with him.

'Phone box begins with an "F" doesn't it?' Gabi asked, pulling him out of his thoughts. He set her right before dipping back in.

Things might have been different if Phyllida had ever admitted that things were as bad as they were, gave what she was its proper name. Not a hope; too proud to say, 'I spy something beginning with A.'

As they pulled up outside the house, Tess said, 'I could just pop in and get Mum settled,' and he answered, 'No need,' and was out of the car and round by Phyllida's door before Tess could argue. Phyllida was getting some packs of chocolate buttons out of her bag and twisting round to give them to the girls. He heard her tell Fran how proud she was of her for being brave at the dentist; how grown-up Gabi had been staying with Uncle Mack. He saw the little hands extended and his mother's smiles and felt a rush of compassion. After Tess had hugged Phyllida goodbye, he helped his mother from the car, but she insisted on walking up the garden path unaided.

Tess wound down her window. 'All that pirate stuff back there?'

'A job offer. Nice of the guy really—'

'It hasn't come to that, surely? I mean, I know the free-lance work's been a bit slow recently.'

'Slow as in none at all?' He was trying to make light of it, but once he'd let that thought out, he couldn't stop the other ones. 'Never mind, still got my short stories . . . that's if I could actually sell any of them. And then, hallelujah, there's my ground-breaking novel. Any year now I'll get off Chapter Five and move swiftly on to Chapter bloody Six.' He heard the girls' chocolatey giggle at the swearword and it made him pause. 'Sorry, Tess, swearing and self-pity in one speech – you won't let me have that "Star Patient" sticker now.'

He turned to see if Phyllida had reached the front door and immediately felt his arm being tugged.

'Listen, you,' Tess said, giving his arm a real seeing to, 'you're allowed the odd bit of self-pity, but things are going to get better, I can feel it. No, don't laugh at me.'

Mack never would understand how Tess, despite the trials of Phyllida, had retained an optimistic outlook on the world.

'And however bad it is now, it can't be as terrible as when you were working for O'Dowd,' Tess went on. 'We got the "nice" you back when you lost that job. I'd rather have that one, even if he has to paint himself silver.'

'Thanks, Pollyanna.' He stepped back out of range of her hand and gurned at the girls to cover up the emotion he really felt.

When they had driven off, Tess shouting that she'd give him a ring tomorrow, he walked back up the path. Tess was right: working for O'Dowd had been the worst experience of his life and in the end he hadn't been up to it, but at least he'd felt alive. Now the 'nice' Mack was bored out of his mind and drifting God knew where.

He turned and looked at the row of Bath Villas opposite and the streetlights coming on. You could almost hear the sedate hum of Bath life and the solid assurance that tomorrow would be very much like today.

There was no sign of Phyllida when he reached the front door, nor inside, and he went along the hallway and rang her bell. Nothing. He put his ear to the door. No sound. Looking through the ribbed glass of the door was useless: it made whoever was on the other side look distorted and wavering. Mind you, with Phyllida, that was often what she looked like after you opened the door.

'Can I get you anything, Phyllida?' he shouted.

A faint, 'No, thank you,' drifted back and he wondered what she was up to. He suspected it would involve a bottle because getting up and out this morning, being charming to the dentist – it all told him that Phyllida had squirrelled some drink away in the flat again and had a good stiffener as soon as she'd woken up. She would be desperate for a top-up now. Tess would know that too, but that optimism of hers often allowed her heart to overrule her brain and she would be hoping that maybe, just maybe, Phyllida was showing iron self-will and keeping her promise to drink only in the pub. It was a promise they wrung out of her regularly, figuring that in the pub she'd get less alcohol for her money and at least they'd eventually turf her out.

But ... perhaps he was wrong to be so cynical about what she was up to right now. Perhaps the half-bottle of vodka gaffer-taped to the underside of Phyllida's bed that they'd found last week *was* her last attempt at smuggling and hiding. After all, both he and Tess had double-checked all the usual and unusual hiding places regularly since. Only this morning, while Tess was putting her in the car, he'd swept the place again. It was a mad game of hide-and-seek and he wanted to shake Phyllida and say, 'Even when you win this, you're losing.'

Suddenly weary of the whole thing, he walked back along the hall and upstairs to his flat. Without even bothering to remove his jacket he sat on the sofa and must have dozed off because he woke to hear his mobile ringing. By the time he had extracted it from his pocket, the call had gone through to voicemail. Perhaps it was someone wanting him to write a 'particle'.

He laughed at that thought, but the laugh became a kind of strangled cough as he retrieved his message. It was short and brutal, very like the man who had left it.

'O'Dowd here,' it said. 'Meet me at the Stairbrook Hotel, Paddington, two p.m., Friday. Room 751. As they say in all the best spy films, I've got a little job for you.' There was that nasty, raspy laugh Mack hadn't heard for three years. ''Course, you could stand me up, my son, it's no odds to me. It won't be my mum's name splashed all over the papers. Won't be my windows getting smashed by bricks.'

CHAPTER 2

Mack had tried to prepare himself for this moment ever since that phone call, and now, seated in the dull-brown chair drinking his dull-brown coffee, he watched the man opposite as you might watch a wild animal, in the hope that you could spot the moment when it was going to spring at your throat.

There he was, his ex-boss and everlasting bastard, Gordon Edward O'Dowd.

Before he had worked for the old slug, Mack had suspected that a lot of things about O'Dowd were constructed to mimic every hard-nosed newspaper man he'd ever seen at the cinema. There was the way he sprawled back with his hands behind his head, his suit looking as if it had been slept in and his tie always askew. There was the brutally cut hair; the Mockney growl. All he needed was an eyeshade and a curl of cigarette smoke to complete the picture.

Mack knew now that none of this was merely affectation. Gordon O'Dowd was a hard-nosed newspaper man right to the bone, one of the last, great, grubby dinosaurs, and there were journalists walking around with 'QWERTY' indented in their foreheads to prove it. Mack was sure his own backside still bore the imprint of one of O'Dowd's size nine lace-ups.

Out in the wider world, anyone with a cupboard holding a skeleton took a deep breath when O'Dowd's name was mentioned: ferreting out skeletons was what made O'Dowd happy; that he got paid for it was a bonus.

The important thing was not to show him how much he intimidated you. Which was why Mack, even though his heart had been on double-quick time since walking into the room, was not jumping straight in to ask why he was there and what the hell had Phyllida and bricks through windows got to do with it?

But whatever the reason he'd been summoned, it was huge. He could still smell a big story in the offing.

'You listening, or am I just blowing hot air out my ass?' O'Dowd snapped from the sofa.

Mack tried not to let that image burn into his brain and steadied his breathing so that when he spoke his voice sounded untroubled.

'Yup, listening, but not sure why. What are you playing at? First-class rail fare up from Bath, all this secrecy? You've even got your Hobnobs out.'

O'Dowd glanced down at his flies before the realisation dawned that Mack was talking about the plate of biscuits on the low table in front of him.

'Very funny,' he said, 'but let's leave the small talk. You heard of Cressida Chartwell?'

'I've been in Bath, not on another planet.'

'Well then, you know about the feeding frenzy stirred up by her move to America? "English Rose, national treasure and hottest actress on the planet leaving us to live amongst the savages" – that kind of thing?'

Mack nodded, his brain now whirling around, wondering what the stellar Cressida Chartwell had to do with him.

'So,' O'Dowd continued, 'what do you think I do when every man in Hollywood with a pulse and a penis starts sniffing around her?'

'Send her a load of condoms?'

O'Dowd moved his jaw about as if he was chewing something particularly bitter. 'Thanks, Oscar Wilde. What I do is I play it cool; I don't go hurtling to the US or hire some cut-throat, paparazzi scrotum. I sit tight. I watch the other papers chucking any name into the mix to see if it sticks. She's already knocking off her pool boy and the guy who delivers the groceries. Allegedly. Only a matter of time before they rope in the dog-walker.' O'Dowd smirked. 'If she had a dog.'

There was a long pause during which Mack felt like a gasping fish on a hook.

'I get it, you're just sitting tight,' he said to fill the silence.

'Yeah, because with Cressida you have to play slowly, slowly catchee monkey. The long game. Know why? Because for one, she has class.'

O'Dowd reached into the shabby briefcase by his feet and pulled out a thick wedge of magazines, before fanning them out, almost reverentially, on the low table next to the Hobnobs. Cressida stared up, beautiful and serene from the covers, working her 'brainy totty and serious actress' image.

'Look at her. She's done Shakespeare, Chekhov, Shaw.'

In O'Dowd's mouth it sounded as if Cressida had been sleeping her way through the world's great playwrights.

'For two, our Cressida's in no rush to hook up with anyone new; she's just come out of that really bad break-up with Alistaire Montagu . . . that git who's been playing that bloke in that Russian thing about those fruit trees.'

'*The Cherry Orchard*?'

'Exactly. Him. So I know I've got a bit of time to play with. And four—'

'Three, you'd got to three on your list.' Mack knew it was risky to correct a man who usually channelled Genghis Khan, but it felt like a small victory before whatever was to come.

'And for three,' O'Dowd agreed begrudgingly, 'Cressida's bloody bright: we're going to have to be crafty.'

O'Dowd was staring at the magazine covers again and it was obvious that, like most males in the country, he had a bit of a thing for Cressida Chartwell. Still, that wasn't going to save her from having her private life pawed over. She was a celeb, ergo, she was fair game.

Letting O'Dowd drift off into whatever obscene daydream he was having, Mack gnawed away at why

O'Dowd was telling him all this rather than someone who still worked for him?

Like Serena.

He leaned forward and poured another cup of coffee, trying to stop Serena Morden escaping into his brain. It didn't work; there she was: beautiful face, wonderful body, personality of a hired assassin. A light-fingered expert at turning over stones and seeing what crawled out from underneath. For five wonderful months and twenty-three editions of the paper, she'd been Mack's. Out of his league one minute, in his bed the next. He and Serena had been going places; a tight little hit team. Mack, poor sap, had thought love was involved somewhere.

That had ended the afternoon when he'd found her and O'Dowd trying to swallow each other's body parts. That they were doing it in Mack's flat, in his bed, was a nice little touch on O'Dowd's part, akin to a dog marking out its territory.

He'd backed out of that room like some chastened schoolboy trying to get away from the noises they were making and the realisation that he'd been dumped for someone higher up the food chain. As Serena had said, 'An editor is an editor.'

Or 'predator' in O'Dowd's case.

Mack felt the old anger spiralling up again, not buried as deep as he'd thought. He was back to wanting to shove bits of people into a shredder.

'You were saying?' he asked quickly.

'I was saying, because I know these things about

Cressida, I decide –' O'Dowd gave a little 'Ta-da' flourish with his hands – 'to get to her through her Achilles' heel.'

Mack blinked rapidly, shocked that O'Dowd even knew who Achilles was, let alone that he had a heel.

'Her Achilles' heel?'

'Yup. The lovely Cressida's cousin, one Jennifer Roseby. Her mum and Cressida's mum were sisters.'

Was that really O'Dowd's master plan, to doorstep this cousin and her family? Pretty run-of-the-mill stuff. Mack had done it often enough, sniffing out the weak link who would dish the dirt for a nice, fat cheque and then beating the other papers to a buyout.

A buff-coloured file placed on the sofa cushion next to O'Dowd distracted him from those thoughts.

O'Dowd nudged the file. 'Now, in case you're not up to speed down there in Yokel land . . . Cressida's father died when she was twelve, blah, blah, usual heartache stuff, and Cressida and her mother used to spend the summer holidays after that with Jennifer's family. Since Cressida's mother died, the Rosebys are her only family really. There's two years between Jennifer and Cressida, but they've always been close. Get together whenever they can. Doesn't make much sense . . . Jennifer's a farmer's daughter, gave up on a drama course and works in a library, still lives at home, while her cousin . . .' With one hand, O'Dowd did an impression of something exploding. 'But that's women for you. On the phone to each other for hours. Jennifer's the one person Cressida trusts.'

'And how would you know that?'

O'Dowd looked particularly feral. 'Don't know what you're getting at. Hacking and bugging, things of the past. Haven't we all had the backs of our legs slapped soundly? Even if someone was still trying it, making out what these two are on about is a nightmare. More often than not they just start wittering on about people from their past ... and our Cress is on the ball – doesn't use voicemail, often resorts to pay-as-you-go phones. Means we need someone on the ground, if you get my drift.'

Mack had a horrible feeling he did.

'The other papers have already drawn a blank with the Jennifer link. All they got to show for it was the local police buzzing around them like flies round shit. Jennifer's brother threatened to feed Clive Butler to the pigs.'

'Even pigs would draw the line at eating Clive.'

'Right enough. Besides, Jennifer's family don't keep pigs. The Rosebys are into sheep.' He picked up the file and chucked it at Mack. 'It's all in there.'

As if O'Dowd knew that Mack had no intention of opening the file, he reached across and flipped it open. Mack saw the words 'Lane End Farm, Brindley, Northumberland.'

'Northumberland?'

'Yeah, as far north as you can get before the men start wearing skirts. Better take your thermals, my son.'

Mack closed the file again. He needed to nip this conversation in the bud, not get into discussing types of livestock, parts of Britain, thermals.

O'Dowd went careering on; his eyes alight as if scenting his quarry.

'My old guts are never wrong. When Cressida scores a Yank, Jennifer will be the first to know and we'll be the second because by then we'll have become Jen's very special friend.'

'You don't mean "we", do you?' Mack said.

'No, well done. I mean "you".'

'Forget it, give it to someone else.'

'Can't,' O'Dowd shot back, 'you've got the perfect qualifications. You know how these things work, but you've slipped off the radar, no one remembers your name or your face. And as for some big-shot freelancer? No way. One of those suddenly goes haring off, it's going to make the rest suspicious about what they're working on. Whereas you can get yourself up there, and who's going to miss you? Mack Stone . . . my little "Mack the Knife".'

Mack flinched as much at the chummy tone as at his old nickname.

'Don't be modest, my son, before you screwed your career up big time, those brown eyes of yours used to really get people to open up. You'll get this Jennifer to trust you.'

'No.'

'Really? Got so much work on you can afford to turn this kind of money down? Heard you spend your time on little bits and pieces for the local rags – "George and Rita Celebrate their Golden Wedding" stuff.'

O'Dowd made it sound as if that were akin to peddling heroin.

'And you're in debt; cards maxed out, the lot. Think about it, Mack. You'll be well paid for this job . . . I've

written the figure down in that file. Plus expenses on top
... and if you pull it off, who knows where your career
will go – you'll be back in demand. You'll have struck pay
dirt.'

'I'll also be dragged through the courts, might even get
put away.' Mack got to his feet. 'So stuff it, and stuff all
that threatening garbage about Phyllida. If that had been
real, you'd have hit me with it straightaway. It was just
bait to get me here, wasn't it? I wish you luck with your
shitty little plan. I hope her brother tears your head off
just before Cressida's lawyers rip your liver out, or what's
left of it. I can't believe after all that *Sunday Screws* stuff
you're still playing this game. Well, I'm not. I don't grub
about in other people's lives. I'm not a bloody saint, but
I'm not going back to that.'

Mack moved to the door and already had hold of the
handle when he heard O'Dowd get off the sofa and come
up right behind him. He could feel his breath on his neck.

'You sanctimonious little shit,' O'Dowd whispered,
'what – you're suddenly above all this? You used to lap up
all that stuff: the backstage passes, the inside stories.'

Mack forced himself to turn around and look right into
O'Dowd's face, smelling the coffee on his breath.

'I should never have worked for you or this paper, I—'

There was a moment when Mack thought that O'Dowd
was going to headbutt him, but he simply jammed his
face right up close to Mack's.

'You're not going to ruin this for me. Cressida Chartwell's
got it all. Box-office gold, real talent, heart-shredder. If we

break this story before the rest, it'll be worth whatever anyone chucks at us, whatever Cress and her lawyers heap on our heads. I can think about retiring. Get myself somewhere hot.'

'That'll be Hell, will it?' Mack said, his neck aching from the effort of keeping his face from touching O'Dowd's. 'I'm going. Get someone else's nuts in the vice this time.'

It would have been a great parting shot if O'Dowd hadn't said softly, 'You heard of Sir Teddy Montgomery, my son?'

That was when Mack knew this was going to be very, very bad indeed. He watched O'Dowd saunter back to the sofa.

'You should have agreed to this when I was trying to be nice,' he said, 'when I thought we should bury the hatchet because of how we're going to have to work as a team.' O'Dowd patted the cushion next to him. 'Now you're going to have to let Uncle Gordon tell you a scary story.'

Without registering having moved, Mack was sitting next to O'Dowd. The room seemed overheated suddenly, devoid of air. He was in a beige, carpeted, airless trap and Phyllida had put him there.

As O'Dowd himself would say, 'I've found your Achilles' heel, my son.'

His insides felt as though he were about to be dropped down a well.

O'Dowd was leaning back again, his groin thrust forward as if demonstrating he was the dominant male. 'Hear old Phyllida has good days and bad days. Real shame.' There was a theatrical sigh, 'Your mum was a belter of a journalist in her day. Hell of a looker too. This Sir-Teddy thing will probably be the final straw.'

Mack was frantically leafing through all he knew about Sir Teddy Montgomery, personal friend of the Windsors and regular visitor to No. 10. Until his death six months before he'd been seen as the archetypal Establishment gentleman. Except that papers found after his death proved that for all of his fifty years in the public eye he'd been passing defence information to the Russians.

The country had been apoplectic with rage and the media had thrashed about trying to find someone they could blame for him getting away with it scot-free, but it was beginning to look as though good old Sir Teddy had been acting alone. With his wife long dead and no children, the public couldn't even lash out at them.

There was a dangerous vacuum of retribution out there, just waiting for someone to fill it.

'Hey. Quit dreaming,' O'Dowd said. 'Turns out that during the summer and autumn of 1982, good old Sir Teddy Montgomery had a hot and heavy affair with a woman and kept quite detailed diaries about it. Called this other woman his soulmate. Said he trusted her with all his secrets. When this woman ended the affair it left him brokenhearted – so broken-hearted that he couldn't bear to throw the diaries away.' O'Dowd shook his head. 'Silly man. Never know where they're going to end up if you do that.'

'With a scumbag like you.' Mack swallowed down the disgusting taste that was suddenly in his mouth.

'Correct. And you know what? As I read old Teddy's diaries, I started to wonder whether he told this soulmate of his about those jolly Russians. That would make her as big a traitor as he was. *Her* life wouldn't be worth living if the story got out.' O'Dowd made a mock-sorry face. 'Of course, when I say "her", I mean Phyllida.'

Mack could feel the edge of the well through the soles of his shoes.

He tried to make the accusation go away, juggling dates and probabilities in his head to prove to himself that O'Dowd was wrong. But Phyllida was out of the same mould as Montgomery: Home-Counties family, good boarding school, Oxford. Their paths would have crossed.

'You're lying. You're a lying, fat, bastard,' Mack said, more vehemently because he knew he was on shaky ground.

'I'll admit to the "bastard" and maybe the "fat", but in this particular case, my old son, I'm not lying and I can prove it.' O'Dowd paused. 'There are some lovely intimate bits about his lover in the diaries; old sod waxed quite lyrical about her appendix scar—'

'Lots of women have those.'

'And another quite distinctive scar low down on her back from landing on some corrugated iron when she was a girl.'

Mack thought of the wavy scar to the left of his mother's spine.

'Then Teddy, the old goat, gets a bit naughty. Lots of details about how she could never keep quiet when they were—'

No. No. No.

When Mack and his sister were young they had giggled over the sounds their mother made in the bedroom with their father. Later, it had become a huge embarrassment; particularly when the noise had been lavished on a succession of 'uncles' who had passed through their lives.

Tess said Phyllida sounded like a particularly leaky lilo and someone was trying to pump her up.

O'Dowd laughed. 'Sir Teddy said she sounded like a particularly leaky lilo and someone was trying to pump her up.'

Mack felt himself falling, could see the fetid water at the bottom of the well.

'You're a liar,' he said, louder this time. 'You're telling me Phyllida worked alongside the best journalists in the country and nobody noticed this affair?'

'Takes a person who knows all the tricks to be able to play them herself. You know how bright and devious your mum can be. And we know Sir Teddy could keep a secret, sneaky sod, he took his to the grave.'

What have you done, Phyllida, what have you dragged us into, Tess, Joe, the girls, me?

'Of course, you could ask her about it, but I doubt you'll get a straight answer, even if you get her on a day when she can talk sense. And remember, once I fling the mud, it'll stick.'

Mack was flailing around in that stinking water.

O'Dowd bent down and fished out an A4 brown envelope

from his briefcase before placing it delicately on Mack's knees.

Mack looked down at it as though it was a piece of excrement: brown envelopes, unless stuffed with cash, were never good news.

'Romantic Sir Teddy Montgomery also kept a rather lovely photo of him and the woman. Have a look at it, Mack . . . though really no son should have to see his mother doing that to a man.'

Mack pushed the envelope off his knees and heard it land on the floor.

'You liked my mother,' he said. 'How can you do this to her?'

'All's fair in love and circulation wars. And I have a duty to inform a betrayed public of my findings . . . unless –' O'Dowd bent and picked the envelope off the floor – 'unless I decide for some reason, not unconnected with a famous actress, to spike this story. Think about it, Mack, what Cressida gets up to is of global interest; it'll make you, me, the paper, big money. The Montgomery story's just a little domestic something that'll soon be old news – except for Mongomery's lover and her family, of course. No one will ever let them off the hook.' O'Dowd did a shifty little side glance. 'How old are those nieces of yours now?'

'OK,' Mack said, slipping under the water without any more struggle. 'This Jennifer woman. Where do I start?'

CHAPTER 3

Jennifer tried to concentrate on what Mr Armstrong was saying and filter out the muffled laughter coming from the poetry section. Luckily Mr Armstrong was fairly deaf and would not realise that it pinpointed exactly where two other members of the library staff were hiding to enjoy another classic Armstrong performance.

'Also, pet,' he said, leaning against the counter and wetting his forefinger, 'as well as the bad language, there are some scenes of a sexual nature on page thirty-four.' He turned the pages of the book with the specially wetted finger until he reached the offending passage and began to read in a wavering voice: 'Pulling her to his chest, he placed her hand on his iron-hard member thrusting against the confines of his rough, calico breeches and suddenly the two hard nubs of—'

'Yup, that's definitely sex,' Jennifer cut in, and looked towards the poetry section, where Auden through to Coleridge was actually shaking.

'Aye,' Mr Armstrong said eventually, 'shocking.'

He glanced down at the piece of paper in his hand covered with faint, spindly writing, and, as he did so, his stick fell off his arm, causing him to lean more heavily against the counter.

'Would you like to sit down, Mr Armstrong?'

'Aye, I would.'

Jennifer fetched a chair and settled him in it, lifting his carrier bag up off the floor and placing it gently in his lap.

'So what's next?' she asked when she was back behind the counter.

'Page one hundred and eighty-four – blasphemy.' Mr Armstrong turned the pages torturously slowly, referring to his list from time to time, and Jennifer looked at the library clock, hoping that somebody would come in and give her an excuse to call Sheila and Lionel out of hiding. Not much hope of that: late-night opening and only an hour until closing time. The graveyard shift. The only voices Jennifer could hear were coming from the children's section, a woman and a little girl by the sound of it. They must have come in when she was up in the office.

It was always a mistake, one way or the other, to come out of the office.

Mr Armstrong found the offending page and held the book up for Jennifer to read, obviously deciding that the blasphemous passage would sully him further should he reacquaint himself with it.

Jennifer scanned the words. 'The character just says, "God's Blood", Mr Armstrong. He *is* a pirate.'

Mr Armstrong sucked his teeth. 'Then, on page two hundred, more sex.'

The torturous finger-wetting and page-turning recommenced until he found what he was looking for.

'Lord Percival Dennison feasted his eyes on Lady Cranleigh's voluptuous form, from the milky mounds of her breasts to that place where he longed to plunge his . . .' Mr Armstrong stopped and tutted and there was more pained sucking of teeth before he passed the book to Jennifer. 'I'll not read the rest.'

Jennifer glanced at the page and snapped the book shut. 'Yes, easy to see where that's going . . . so, anything more, then?' She nodded at his carrier bag, hoping there was nothing else he considered improper lurking within it.

'No, not this time. You'll send a letter to the council?'

'Of course. Would you like to see it before I send it?'

'Why no, pet. I trust you.'

'Fine, and you know, Mr Armstrong, what I was saying last time, about you perhaps being a bit more careful concerning the books you choose if strong language and, um, physical interaction offends you?'

Mr Armstrong looked up at her from under his brows, and she ploughed on, picking up the book he had just laid down and looking at its cover.

'For example, the title of this one – *Plundered by Pirates* – it should have warned you off really.'

'Warned me off? How?'

If it had been anybody else, Jennifer would have thought

they were pulling her leg, but Mr Armstrong's eyes were devoid of humour. A faint tang of soap and toothpaste lingered about him.

'Well, "plundered", particularly in historical novels, is often used to describe the act of –' Jennifer had another run up at it – 'when a man forces himself, um, upon a woman.'

Mr Armstrong studied her intently and then shook his head.

'Well, I dare say it's a modern thing. We never had that when I was young. We were Methodists.'

In the poetry section, Jennifer heard several books thud to the floor.

'Why not try some poetry, Mr Armstrong?' she said, very loudly.

'Ooh, no,' Mr Armstrong's eyes were wide. 'Poets. They're the worst.' He looked down into his lap, rummaged about in his carrier bag and then produced two more library books. A little more scrabbling and he had a library card in his hand. 'Put these new ones through for me, will you?'

Jennifer took the books: *Lust for the East* and *The Hidden World of the Victorian Gentleman*. She might as well have the chair permanently bolted to the counter ready for his next visit.

'You'll tell them to reply directly to me. The council?' he said, getting slowly to his feet.

Jennifer nodded and handed him his books and his ticket and, when he was ready, his stick. She wondered which poor soul at the county council got the job of answering Mr Armstrong's complaints.

'Right, I'll be away then.' He moved slowly towards the exit.

Jennifer followed him and pressed the large button on the wall that had been fitted to make it easier for the old or frail to open the door. It had not been an unqualified success, even in this, its second incarnation. The first button, simply round and black, had flummoxed most of the older users, who had viewed it as some kind of knob that had to be turned. Consequently it had only lasted a matter of days. The council had dispatched another mechanic with a new button, square this time, and with the word 'Press' upon it in large red letters. This had solved the problem for those whose sight was still good, but it was not unusual to find some poor soul looking wistfully at the door and waiting for somebody else to get it open for them.

Mr Armstrong's approach was to jab the button with his stick.

'I forgot to ask,' he said, pausing on the threshold and causing Jennifer to leap for the button to stop him getting battered by the door as it tried to close. 'That brother of yours, Danny, how's he going on?'

'Not getting a lot of sleep. Louise's teething.'

'And your dad?'

'Fine, he's hoping to get some good lambs through this year, off one of his new tups.'

Mr Armstrong's laugh was wheezy. 'That'll give those

Lambtons a run for their money.' He gave Jennifer a sly glance. 'You and young Lambton back courting?'

'No,' Jennifer said, more quickly than she would have liked. In the past it had always irritated her when people assumed that she and Alex Lambton were naturally destined for marriage, as if, like both families' sheep, putting them together would make a stronger breed. Nowadays there was a new set of reasons why putting Alex and her together made her irritable.

'We're friends these days, that's all, Mr Armstrong.'

'Aye, well, you don't want to leave him waiting too long. Not with your . . .' Jennifer felt that he was rummaging around in his mind as he had rummaged in his carrier bag, looking for something that he knew was in there, but he couldn't quite grasp.

Eventually his face brightened. '. . . affliction,' he said, catching hold of the word and bringing it up into the light.

Jennifer put her head down, took a deep breath in and then looked back up at Mr Armstrong. He appeared oblivious to how she might feel about what he had just said.

She was tempted to take her hand off the button so that he would have to make a quick exit. Instead she just waited and watched and waited as he plodded off.

When she got back to the desk, Sheila had reappeared, along with a shame-faced Lionel.

'Thanks,' she said and hoped they wouldn't notice that she was genuinely upset under her playing-to-the-gallery eye-rolling.

Sheila was picking bits of fluff off her cardigan, her massive chest still wobbling with laughter. 'Sorry, Jen. It was just too good to resist. Although, next time, could you get him to speak up a bit when he's reading?'

'Next time, I'll be the one hiding behind the bookshelves laughing loudly while you have to listen to him read. And, Lionel, I'm surprised at you. Aren't you meant to set an example?'

'Completely unprofessional behaviour,' he agreed sadly. 'Would it make amends if I got the last cup of tea of the day?' He gathered together their three mugs. 'I'm sure we could all do with something warm inside us.'

When Sheila told him not to be such a dirty devil, he looked appalled and scurried off in the direction of the kitchen.

'Poor Lionel,' Jennifer said, 'he'll be reporting himself for making an inappropriate comment.'

'Speaking of inappropriate, ever think old Armstrong's getting his thrills by reading you those bits that shock him?'

'No. Wouldn't occur to him, he just sees it as his duty. Thinks he's all that stands between civilisation and the ravaging, sex-starved hordes.'

'If I'd known they were coming I'd have worn a shorter skirt,' Sheila said, looking excited.

Jennifer didn't want to think of Sheila's large hips in anything shorter than she was wearing now and turned quickly to the shelf holding the reserved and requested books. She picked up one and wondered why anybody would read it, let alone reserve it. 'Thought Mr Armstrong looked a bit tired today, though. I'll mention it to Mum; get her to ask him if he's getting enough rest when she's on the lunch deliveries next time.'

Sheila hefted a pile of sorted books into her arms and propped them against her chest. 'Forget him; I see Cressida's fallen for her pool boy.'

There was a barely interested look on Sheila's face, but Jennifer was not fooled. From time to time Sheila would embark on these little sessions, which Jennifer secretly called 'fishing trips'.

'Really?' Jennifer matched Sheila's innocent look. 'Her pool boy? She never mentioned it.'

'Not that you'd tell us if she had. It's like trying to prise open a whelk.'

'I thought you got whelks out with a pin?'

'Don't try and distract me. What's the good of me having direct access to Hollywood when you won't pass on anything juicy?'

Jennifer picked up one of Mr Armstrong's books and balanced it carefully on the pile Sheila was carrying. 'Here you go, I'm passing this on. Mr Armstrong reckoned it was juicy and completely . . .'

Sheila's expression made her stop talking.

The woman and the little girl in the children's section were having an argument. Jennifer half-turned to watch.

'No. You are not having a DVD, Araminta, no DVD,' the woman was saying, pulling on one end of the DVD case that the little girl had shoved under her arm. 'You can have as many books as you like. But no DVD.'

'Want-it-want-it-want-it.'

'No.' One massive tug got it safely into the woman's hands, and she strode over to the shelves holding the DVDs and put it back on the highest one, way beyond the girl's reach. 'And why they have these in a library, I don't know. It's like sweets at the checkout in a supermarket.' This last statement was delivered loudly enough to ensure it reached the librarians and the tone was particularly admonishing.

'New people,' Sheila said out of the side of her mouth. 'Moved into the barn conversion over at Johnson's.' She hefted the pile of books up higher against her chest and added, 'Southerners.'

'Ah,' Jennifer grinned. Sheila was into pigeonholing people, so anybody a bit posh was a 'Southerner', difficult men were 'sexually frustrated' and almost everybody else was a 'tosser'. Her tetchy performances at the county's 'Opening Books, Opening Minds' staff-training courses were the stuff of librarian folklore.

Lionel came back with the tea and they tidied up a bit more, pretending not to notice how the argument in the children's section was escalating. The little girl was now trying to drag a chair towards the shelves, presumably to retrieve the coveted DVD, and the woman's studiously reasonable tone was slipping to show the steel beneath.

Jennifer took a sip of her tea and positioned herself where she could watch, but not be seen. The fight hitched up a notch as the woman sat down on the little chair before the girl could climb on it.

Lionel rolled his eyes. 'The poor mite's picked loads of books. What harm is one DVD going to do? We always let our kids watch cartoons and films.'

Sheila gave him a little push. 'Go and tell her then, Lionel. Tell her your kids both got to Cambridge and a few DVDs didn't hurt them.'

Lionel shook his head. 'Wouldn't listen. Know the type.' He hesitated. 'Sorry. That was prejudicial stereotyping.'

Lionel always emerged from 'Opening Books, Opening Minds' with a pat on the back.

'Stop it, Araminta. Stop it now. I will tell Daddy when he gets home. He will be very cross. Very cross. Privileges will be withdrawn. Withdrawn, Araminta.'

Lionel took off his glasses and started to clean them with his tie. 'Storing up all kinds of problems with that autocratic parenting,' he said bleakly.

They all watched, pretending not to, as the little girl tried to push her mother from the chair. She would have succeeded if her mother had not been hanging on to the seat. It was one of those scenes that might have been comical had it not been so emotionally raw.

'Oh, I've had enough of this,' Sheila said and went and deposited her pile of books on the little reading table in the children's section. Both mother and child stopped fighting.

'There, Araminta,' the woman said, 'the lady has come to tell you off for being naughty.'

'No, I came to ask you not to sit on that chair.' Sheila crossed her arms; an exceptionally tricky manoeuvre given the size of her chest. 'They're meant for children and we tend to find that even the lightest adults –' the pause might as well have had 'of which you are definitely not one' embroidered on it – 'even the lightest adults, tend to buckle the legs.'

'Oh dear,' Jennifer said. Lionel busied himself with the stapler.

There seemed to be a stand-off, but the woman was only regrouping. She stood up, catching the girl by the arm just as she made another attempt to climb on the chair and said, 'May I just observe, it is not particularly helpful of you to put DVDs out in a library. Not for those of us who believe in the beneficial effects of reading.' There was a sniff at the end of the speech which served both as punctuation and a mark of cultural superiority.

'I think you'll find,' Sheila retorted, 'that a balanced intake of different forms of stimulation produces a wider vocabulary in pre-school children and prepares them for participating in a range of multi-media learning scenarios.'

'Well, look at that,' Lionel said, 'she *was* listening in those training sessions. And she's using verbal reasoning instead of barely sublimated aggression. That's a good sign.'

'Possibly. But how is she standing, Lionel? Is she doing that jutting-out-her-chin thing?'

'Oh,' Lionel said and went back to checking his stapler.

Sheila reached for the offending DVD. 'Ah, *Bananas in Pyjamas*,' she said, smiling at the little girl. 'My kids loved them when they were your age.'

'Really,' the mother retorted, snatching the DVD back

and replacing it on the shelf, 'and, don't tell me, they're all brain surgeons now.'

For a moment, Jennifer thought Sheila was going to lie, but when she chanced a quick look, she saw Sheila's shoulders sag. 'Fair point,' she said and, bending down to the little girl's level, shouted, '*Listen to your mother and do exactly what she says at all times!*' Then, picking up her pile of books again, she walked quickly towards the kitchen.

Jennifer felt Lionel move behind her. 'Has young Reece got a court date yet?' he whispered.

'Friday. Sheila's convinced he'll get a custodial sentence this time, even if she does the pleading-mother act.'

Sheila did not reappear.

There was no more noise from the children's section after that – the little girl was now meekly holding her mother's hand and casting nervous glances around as if she was afraid that scary woman was going to return and shout at her again.

Lionel went upstairs to the gallery, climbing the spiral wrought-iron staircase and Jennifer heard him huffing at the mess the high-school kids had left in the quiet study area. She counted up the money they'd taken in fines and placed the returned CDs back in the secure cabinet until, just as the clock said half past six, she became aware that the posh woman was standing right by the counter in front of her. She had her head down and was looking in her bag.

Worst possible scenario.

When the woman looked up she would see Jennifer for

the first time. Cold. Jennifer knew how the script would go: a couple of seconds of silence; the usual unguarded look of shock and then some determined, frantic attempts at direct eye contact and a cheerful, breezy tone.

'Just these books . . .' the woman said, lifting her head, and everything spun out as Jennifer thought it would.

She was pretty good, though, the woman, only missing a beat before changing her shocked expression into a mask of forced brightness. She studiously stared Jennifer straight in the eye.

Funny how the 'Let's pretend nothing's out of the ordinary' approach is worse than unashamed gawping.

Jennifer did what she always did in these situations, smiled vaguely and pretended she was up in one of the top fields at home, looking down on the river. If she concentrated hard she could imagine a flash of iridescent blue kingfisher.

Breathe in. Breathe out. It is the other person's problem. It is not your problem. You have come a long way. They are only looking.

'Good series, this,' she said and reached out and picked up one of the books.

'Yes. Yes. Very good. Oh, yes. We love them. Absolutely. Love them.' The woman was almost hyperventilating with the effort of not letting her gaze fall from Jennifer's eyes.

Silence again.

'I'll need your card, then,' Jennifer prompted.

There was a flurry of activity, and more desperate bag-searching. The little girl wandered over.

Oh dear.

'It's here somewhere, I had it just now. I can't think what I've done with it.'

There was nothing covert about the way the little girl was staring at Jennifer.

Here it comes.

'Mummy, Mummy, that lady's got a horrible—'

'Noooooo,' the woman shrieked, rounding on her daughter. 'No, no, no. No talking now, Araminta. No.' She caught hold of the girl's arm. 'You will help Mummy look for the library card. Come on. Now.'

She all but rammed the girl's head into the bag.

'But, Mummy . . .'

'Araminta,' snapped the woman. 'I will not tell you again. You have been naughty today. So naughty.'

'But what's she got on her face?'

'Right, that does it,' bellowed the woman, her own face becoming redder and redder. 'No books today. No books. Naughty girl. No books.'

Jennifer was half-tempted to lean across the counter and just explain everything. Children were brilliant, asked sensible questions, sometimes wanted to touch and then moved on to the next thing. That moment had passed with Araminta, though; she started to cry loudly.

'Not fair. You said if I didn't understand something . . .'

The rest of Araminta's plea bargaining was lost as her mother began hauling her out of the library in a flurry of bag-rearranging and scolding. There was a final clumsy scene as they tussled with the door button, and it was then that Araminta's voice drifted back over the library, tearful and high-pitched, 'But she's got a horrible scar, worse than Harry Potter. It's yukky, all down her face.'

The door closed and there was silence.

Jennifer took a deep breath in and let it out slowly before picking up the books that the girl had chosen and taking them back to the children's section. Finding their correct homes on the shelves, the Rowling after the Reeve, the Higson before the Ibbotson occupied her mind and slowed her pulse.

When she returned to the counter, Sheila was back and she and Lionel were standing very close together. Sheila coughed.

'You know, Lionel and I were thinking of going for a drink after work.'

Jennifer looked at the united little front of support.

'You're awful at telling lies,' she said. 'I'm fine. Really.'

'Yeah, like I'm Angelina Jolie. Really,' Sheila said and, despite all the other emotions swilling about in her, Jennifer couldn't help laughing.

'Go on, keep us company,' Lionel said. 'Get your stuff and we'll meet you out front. I'll lock up.'

'Besides,' Sheila said, 'if you don't need a drink, I bloody do. I've got one son who's buggered off to Ibiza and can't even talk in a straight line when he rings ... which is barely ever, and only when there's a Z in the month. Then there's Reece, can't see a car without wanting to drive it. Even if it belongs to the police.'

Jennifer gave in. A drink would take the edge off things.

First Mr Armstrong and then Araminta; please God, it wasn't the start of a whole alphabet of awkward incidents lined up for the rest of the week.

She went off to the staff toilets (a rather grandiose name for the one cubicle space used by all the female employees of the library) and gave her hair a brush. When she had been growing up, she'd coveted her cousin's hair with all that bounce and curl, the kind of hair that always looked winningly dishevelled, but now she was content with how hers fell straight to her shoulders: a thick blonde curtain she could withdraw behind simply by dipping her head.

Ignoring the large mirror behind her, she got out a small one from her make-up bag and used it while she smeared on coloured lipgloss. Then she repositioned the bag on the windowsill, next to Sheila's deodorant and celebrity magazine. On a whim she picked it up and flicked through it, shaking her head at the rubbish in it about Cressida. Nice photograph, though. She was putting the magazine back on the windowsill when the phone rang in her bag and she jumped. It was the ringtone she had picked out for Cressida's latest number, and she felt as if somehow looking at her cousin's photograph had prompted her to ring.

'OK, what's new?' she said as she brought the phone to her ear. There was no reply and Jennifer stayed silent too, just listening to the breathing.

'Would it help if we talked about the weather?' she said after a little while. 'It's blummin' cold here, and a frost on the car this morning. I suppose it's warm there?'

There was a rushed 'Uh huh' in reply.

'Cress,' Jennifer said softly, 'what's wrong? Homesick?'

Another grabbed 'Uh huh'.

'And I'm guessing you're a bit nervous about that tricky scene in the lagoon tomorrow?'

When there was no reply at all this time, Jennifer leaned against the wall and said very distinctly, 'OK, now listen to me. Look on this as some free therapy. You're doing what you love. You're brilliant at it and that's a fact, not flannel. For goodness' sake, they've given you those hideous bits of metal and Perspex to prove it. This is a doddle, just another aspect of the craft to conquer. No, no, don't interrupt, Cress, I haven't finished yet. You will repeat this after me until all that fear's banished.' Jennifer looked at the door, feeling faintly foolish, but then went on, 'Here we go – I'm talented and clever and beautiful and I'm going to rock them back on their heels with what I can do. Go on, let's hear it.'

There was a pause and then she heard Cress say, 'I can't remember all that.'

Jennifer snorted. 'Who are you kidding? Of course you can remember one simple line. And, what's more, I bet you've got yourself in front of a mirror so you can watch yourself saying it.'

There was a little squeal from the other end of the phone.

'Yeah, thought so,' Jennifer said, transferring the phone to her other ear. 'Just like the time when you had that terrible thing to tell Mike Egan and you acted the whole thing out.'

'There's no fooling you.'

'Nope, so let's hear it from the top . . . I'm talented and . . .'

Jennifer closed her eyes and listened to Cressida repeat word for word what she had told her. At first there was a slight waver in her cousin's tone, but soon the old, assured Cressida was discernible.

'OK, OK, that's enough,' Jennifer said finally, 'otherwise that head of yours won't fit in any of your hats.'

Over the top of her own voice, Jennifer could hear the sound of Sheila's footsteps, so she leaped to the door and opened it before Sheila could. Hiding the phone behind her back, she said, 'Out in a minute. Sorry, didn't realise I'd taken so long.' Sheila grumbled something about Jennifer needing to eat more roughage and it being perishing outside and could she hurry up?

When Sheila had gone, Jennifer said into the phone, 'Got to go, Cress, are you feeling better now?'

'Much. Thanks Jen; just needed you to get me back in off the window ledge.'

'Any time. Now go . . . go on. And if it happens again, you know where I am. Bye, sweetheart.' She was just about to switch off the phone when Cressida spoke again.

'But are you OK, Jen? Everything all right?'

'Of course,' Jennifer said, brightly. 'I'm fine, absolutely fine. I'm always fine; no need to ask. Scram.'

When Jennifer had replaced the phone in her bag, she

stayed propping up the wall for a while, her mind over the other side of the Atlantic, but then the need to meet Lionel and Sheila roused her and she stood upright. Moving her position seemed to whisk Cressida away from her completely and the memory of Araminta and her mother took her place.

If Cress was homesick, she was just sick.

She lifted her chin. 'Come on, it's their problem, not yours.' But no matter how many times she said them, the words just sounded like shiny, happy counselling-speak to her. It *was* her problem.

Carefully she dipped her head so that her hair fell forward and then opened the door.

CHAPTER 4

Mack sat on the train heading north and fought the desire to fall asleep. If he did he'd probably shoot past Newcastle and end up in Scotland, and he hadn't had the inoculations for that.

Hardly surprising he was tired. Since O'Dowd had handed him this poisoned chalice, he'd lied to his sister and her family; had a disturbing showdown with his mother; buried his old identity and got himself a new name.

He stared out of the window, not registering the view skimming by, but then the thought that he'd left Tess to cope once more with Phyllida on her own made him turn away, just in case he caught sight of his own reflection in the glass. Breaking the news to Tess that he was going away had been horrible, and thinking of a reason to explain his departure had taken all his story-telling skills. But telling her the truth, all that stuff about Phyllida and Sir Teddy Montgomery, had never been an option. Along with her optimistic nature, Tess had the kind of soft heart that would have turned itself inside out to find a way out of this mess that did not involve deceiving someone else. Whereas Mack knew that was pointless. Once O'Dowd's teeth were clamped on, you either gave him what he wanted, or waited for the death roll.

He had carefully chosen his moment to lie to Tess. They had taken themselves out into the garden, Tess sitting on one of the patio chairs and him on the low, stone wall with the lawn stretching away behind him. Even in the sun, sheltered from the wind, it was what Phyllida called 'bracing'. Mack had his hands in his jacket pockets and Tess had poked hers up the sleeves of her coat. Cold as they both were, it was good to be outside while Phyllida slowly resurrected herself; a nice break from peering in bins and feeling under furniture.

The chat at first had been about his old school friend Bob, the one he'd used as his excuse for going up to London. Telling Tess he was going to see O'Dowd would have been akin to saying he was off to see the Antichrist. Bob stumbled from one carcrash relationship to another and it was perfectly believable that, yet again, Mack had been called to help Bob sit up all night and vent about the female of the species.

After that, he and Tess moved on to chatting about the garden: how the lawn was more moss than grass these days, which shrubs were looking a bit leggy and whether it was a healthy sign that Phyllida had been out and cleared the dead herbs from the oversized terracotta pots and filled them with compost ready for planting up when spring came round.

At the first lull in the conversation, Mack said, 'Remember you felt there was something good just around the corner? Well, didn't want to get your hopes up before it happened, but I wasn't only seeing Bob in London, I was seeing a publisher ... about writing a travel book.'

He had seen the enthusiastic questions lining up to come out of Tess's mouth, and rushed on, telling her it was a small outfit called Sidecar Imprint round the back of Vauxhall, and that one of the guys there had once worked on a travel magazine (now folded) and been impressed by some articles on Cornwall Mack had submitted to it – that year he went just as the heatwave broke.

Tess had nodded slowly. Sprinkling big lies with little bits of the truth was something he'd learned working for O'Dowd. Do it right and people would gobble up the lies quite happily. In reality there was no travel book, no Sidecar Imprint, no magazine that had folded. He had been to Cornwall, though.

'A whole book,' Tess had almost cooed before he dropped the big bomb.

'They're sending me north, to Northumberland, in fact. I'll have to stay up there. Couple of months at most, and of course I can come home like a shot if there's an emergency ...'

He had seen the happiness drain from her, could almost see it leave, muscle by muscle. He let her absorb the news, trying not to stare as she composed her face into one that didn't look as if it was melting.

'I'm really sorry, Tess, leaving you to mother Mum again, but you know how I need the money.' He had watched her hands moving inside her sleeves.

'I thought you hated the North,' she'd said at last, and then, 'it's a bit of a bombshell,' and finally, 'I'm happy for you, 'course I am. It won't make any difference here.'

Mack had wondered how Tess was such a bad liar and he was such a good one. Probably because he got so much practice. He was about to get a lot more.

The train was coming into Peterborough Station and Mack stopped thinking about Tess and watched the man opposite stand up, wrestle his way into his coat and weave down the train ready to get off. He waited to see whether anyone would get on and come and sit with him, but when the train pulled out again, there was just him and the three empty seats round the table. The carriage was barely half full. Why should that surprise him? Who in their right minds would be travelling north in February unless they had a gun at their head?

He suddenly had an image of O'Dowd with a revolver. Well, it certainly wasn't going to fire blanks; he knew that after his showdown with Phyllida, hot on the heels of his conversation with Tess.

She had appeared inside the back door as he and Tess had been discussing how soon he had to head north, and Mack had known from the neatness of her navy skirt and gold blouse, to the way her hair was actually brushed, that she must have had a drink.

She had levered herself over the doorstep and walked

towards them with a slow, deliberate gait as if she had to concentrate on replicating what normal movement looked like. He remembered how, when he was little, she used to stride out and he'd had to look sharp to keep up with her.

Ignoring Mack, Phyllida had wished Tess 'Good morning', and an embarrassed Tess had leaped up and offered Phyllida first her chair and then a cup of tea.

Phyllida's only words until Tess returned had been a pointed 'Such a good child', and Mack had seethed quietly. He'd seethed some more when Tess had passed the fine bone-china teacup and saucer to Phyllida – it was another fancy prop Phyllida used to convince herself she was still in control. They had all ignored the way Phyllida's hand had shaken as she took it.

He'd said nothing as Tess had told Phyllida in a shamingly proud way that he'd landed a job writing a travel book. Her reply, accompanied by a graceful ascent of her eyebrows, hit too many nerves.

'Not your usual area of . . . expertise,' she had said, 'or will you be snooping on the locals too?'

Even Tess's pleading look couldn't keep him sitting down.

They had then had the same fight they'd been having since he had gone to work for O'Dowd, the one when he told her he knew he'd taken a wrong turning and she gave her view forcefully that he had wasted his training: O'Dowd was the worst kind of journalist overseeing the worst kind of journalism.

'Sloppy, nasty, pandering to the basest instincts of the public.' Her voice had grown harsher and harsher. 'And you, you developed the morals of a hyena.'

Tess had said 'Mum' sharply at that point, and Phyllida had stopped talking while Mack returned to his seat on the wall, outraged at the injustice. His morals! Wasn't it her messy morals that had catapulted him back into O'Dowd's world?

That anger had still been there when Tess had gone off to see if she could find the article on Northumberland she'd seen in one of the magazines in Phyllida's bathroom.

Mack had moved towards Phyllida as soon as Tess was out of sight. There had been more coldness coming off her than the breeze. He saw the way she drew back from him, something she had always done, even before his spectacularly disastrous attempt to follow her into journalism. All of it stoked his anger further so that although he had little hope that he would get a straight answer, he decided to ask her about Sir Teddy, if only to see some of that haughtiness come crashing down.

'You worked on the Arts pages at the *Echo*, didn't you?' he'd said conversationally. She nodded.

'Must have been fascinating, being there right at the heart of London in the eighties.'

Another nod.

'Hard to remember all the faces and the names, though?'

'A little.' There had been uncertainty in her voice.

'Remember anyone called Teddy?'

It was what he called a 'softener' question, preparation for hitting her with the name 'Montgomery,' later, and he'd expected some kind of guarded look in response. Instead she had turned her beautiful, ruined face towards him and panic had slewed across it, widening her eyes and making her mouth dip.

'Who told you about Teddy?' she had said, her voice low and intense. 'Who told you?'

Mack had felt the shock roar through him. It was true . . . jeez, if he'd opened that brown envelope . . .

When he'd managed to reply that O'Dowd had told him, her hand had gripped his. 'The swine, why tell you? It was madness, a stupid passion. Nobody knew. Nobody.' With horror he had seen tears in her eyes, and it was such an un-Phyllida type of thing to happen that he could still remember, sitting on this train miles away from her, how breathless it had left him.

'What exactly did O'Dowd say?' she had asked almost frantically, her hand now clutching at his sleeve and managing to catch some of his flesh.

'That you'd had an affair.'

'That's all?'

He'd wanted to shout 'That's all? That's bloody well enough!' but instead had got down on his knees and tried to soothe her, enclosing both of her hands in his.

When she'd seemed calmer, he had suggested she went for a lie-down and, as he'd helped her from the chair, asked her to take it easy while he was away, pointing out that Tess couldn't pop in all the time like he could, and if she did drink in the flat on her own and something happened . . .

'There you go again,' she had replied, but without her usual exasperation. 'I don't drink on my own any more. Just in the pub, in company. It's not a sin.'

He hadn't argued, and just before she had stepped into the kitchen, she'd done a clumsy little turn and given a smile. It had missed him and landed somewhere among the flowerpots, but it had buoyed him up, made him hope she might be trying to pull herself around.

Minutes later, when Tess returned with a pink hot-water bottle in one hand, that buoyant feeling had been punctured.

'Take a sip,' she had said tersely.

In many other families, being asked to taste the contents of a hot-water bottle might have seemed bizarre, but Mack had upended it and felt the vodka with a hint of rubber burn its way down his throat.

Fooled again . . . but not about Sir Teddy Montgomery, of that he was sure. That naked anguish had been Phyllida telling the truth.

Tess had taken the hot-water bottle from him and, shaking it as if she wanted to break its neck, said, 'So, that's what she's decanting the drink into, but where are the bottles?'

Mack had thought back to Phyllida's departing smile and walked over to the nearest plant pot. Digging his hand down into the cold compost, it had connected with something hard and smooth and he'd pulled out a full bottle of vodka. Presumably there would be others – some empty – in the rest of the pots.

'Well done, Phyllida, you're growing the stuff now,' he'd said, but he'd been thinking: *Is this how devious you were about Sir Teddy Montgomery? Fooling everyone, leading them in a dance?*

The train gave a jolt, and above him in the luggage rack, a dark red rucksack shifted. It lay on a fleece and he gave both items a sour look. Never in his life had he expected to own either. But then he'd never expected to become Matt Harper, travel writer and, he grimaced some more, keen walker.

Finding his new name had taken best part of a morning in front of the computer. On page thirty of the search engine's results for 'travel writer' he had spotted it and knew it was perfect. There were no photographs and only a tiny biography saying: 'Twenty-nine, born in Weymouth, author of two books on walking in the West Country. Currently lives in Bristol.'

He'd have no problem remembering to answer to that brilliant first name and good old Matt didn't even appear on any social networking sites.

Big, anonymous Bristol was perfect too. Mack knew it almost as well as he knew Bath, and unlike Bath, nobody in the frozen north would have visited it looking for bloody Jane Austen and want to talk to him about it.

The only thing that would scupper everything was if low-profile, low achiever Matt Harper suddenly embarked on some publicity-grabbing behaviour such as running naked through a load of nuns. On a chatshow.

The buffet trolley started its lumbering journey along the carriage and he got out some cash from his wallet. That was all that was in there since he'd emptied out anything with his real name on it. The one thing he'd hung on to was his passport, currently safely locked away in his suitcase. O'Dowd would have a fit if he knew, but Mack would need it if he had to fly home quickly.

He flicked through some of his guides to Northumberland laid out on the table, but his brain couldn't take any more forests and castles and miles of sodding coastline. He opened up one of Matt Harper's West-Country walking books unearthed in a bookshop in Bath. Fortunately *A Guide to Dorset Coastal Walks* and *A Walk Around North Somerset* were slim little volumes he could easily read and more or less memorise, not some five-hundred-thousand-word tomes on kayaking in the melt water of the Himalayas. Also, not once did the words 'Because I am six foot seven and have bright ginger hair' appear. The writing was nicely anonymous too, but skull-crackingly dull – if Matt Harper had been walking the Hanging Gardens of Babylon he would have spent half an hour describing the soil.

Putting down the walking books he opened O'Dowd's file, skimming through the details on Cressida Chartwell yet again – a BAFTA and Olivier Award; what the bookies were giving as odds for her winning an Oscar within two years of arriving in Hollywood; past lovers. There wasn't so much on this Jennifer, and what he did know depressed him – particularly that she was secretary of the Brindley and Yarfield Drama Club. Great, the north, the country-side and amateur dramatics; throw in a bit of morris dancing and he'd be reet ecstatic, pet.

The only other facts were about her schooling (bright girl), her gap year (VSO in Botswana) and the drama degree at Manchester University (dropped out a couple of months shy of graduation). Silence for twelve months before she'd gone to work in the local library in a place called Tyneforth. Been there ever since.

No significant boyfriends among the guys she'd dated at university and a complete drought since. After reading that, Mack had invented himself a girlfriend. If this Jennifer was desperate for a man, it was best to get it clear from the start that he wasn't offering anything more than friend-ship.

There was no photograph of Jennifer in O'Dowd's file and somewhere in the back of Mack's brain a question formed about that before he shrugged it off.

Mack felt the train start to slow again as they came into some godforsaken place called Doncaster, and he looked up at the luggage rack again. The rucksack and fleece were just two of the things he'd bought during a depressing afternoon kitting himself out for a 'holiday in Scotland'. Among his other purchases was a thing called a 'wind-proof, waterproof outer shell', but which looked suspi-ciously like a cagoule to him, two pairs of heavy-duty walking trousers and some thick socks. The fact that the things made him look like a twit and were either itchy or slippery wasn't mentioned in any of the sales patter.

By the time he was looking at walking boots he wanted to run out of the shop screaming.

Thinking about Phyllida had brought him to his senses. Neither Tess nor he had told her that her potted-drink supply had dried up, but she had obviously discovered it herself, as she'd left the house in a door-slamming tantrum. Mack had felt the walls vibrate in his own flat.

With the sound of that slamming door still in his head, Mack had settled on the pair of walking boots that hurt him the least. He was a keen walker, he had to remember that. My how he loved walking – preferably from a car to a house. In a small act of rebellion, he had added a bright bandana to his pile of purchases and, when he had got back to the flat, relished making all his outdoor gear look used. He had especially enjoyed going over the walking boots with sandpaper: giving them a taste of what they would be doing to his feet.

The rest of the shopping trip had been occupied with buying the other props that would help him play the character of Matt Harper. Even though it pained him, he had bought a sludgy-brown cord jacket that he thought said 'author' better than his leather one; a selection of hearty jumpers to replace his normal slogan-bearing T-shirts and a couple of pairs of hideous jeans. Next stop had been a 'gentlemen's shoe shop' for a pair of brogues that made him depressed just looking at them.

He had also bought various pairs of spectacles off a stand because they made him look more studious and could be left on tables and in bars in a forgetful, vague way. Being absent-minded was a character trait he had observed made others drop their guard as they kept an eye out for you, rather than on you. For the same reason he bought a load of notebooks and put his name in all of them.

He had only just got his coffee and a bar of chocolate from the trolley when his mobile rang and, seeing it was O'Dowd calling, he went and sat in the loo.

'Listen,' O'Dowd said, plunging right in without any pleasantries, 'a Third Party's going to meet you at Newcastle Station with a key to a rented house in Brindley – No. 3 Brindley Villas. It's just up the hill from the Rosebys' farm. He's got cash for you, too, whenever you need more just call him; he'll give you the number. Don't worry, he can keep a secret or I'll drop him in a bigger load of shit than the one that's waiting for you. He'll give you a mobile phone as well.'

'I've already got one.'

'Really? I thought we were talking via cocoa tins and string. Listen, turnip head, the new phone is the only one, from here on in, that you use. And no phoning my office and leaving a message. There are just three people who know what you're up to: you, me and the big bastard upstairs, so keep it that way or everything will leak out like an incontinent nun's knickers. Anything else?'

'Yeah, those diaries and that photo.'

O'Dowd just laughed.

Mack struggled back to his seat and drank his luke-warm coffee, but stowed his chocolate bar away for later.

He was tempted to ring Tess. That last view of her, waving him off at Bath Station with Gabi up in her arms and Joe and Fran by her side, had cut deep. Especially the way Joe had looked at him as though the travel-book story had stuck in his throat.

Hard when someone you admired smelt a rat and that rat was you.

He had to keep reminding himself he had no choice and once it was over and O'Dowd was off their backs, he could pay off his debts, even get some help for Phyllida if she'd agree to it. Although more likely he'd be standing in a courtroom while Cressida Chartwell's lawyers tore him into little pieces.

Him in the dock or his family in purgatory? Bit of a no-brainer and if he played it right, he might get away with it.

With that thought he looked defiantly out of the window and was aware of a new feeling stirring within him, one he hadn't experienced for quite a while. He certainly hadn't expected to experience it now.

There it was, though – the thrill of the chase, no mistaking it.

CHAPTER 5

Jennifer drove off the main road and down the track, bumped over the cattle grid and stopped the car. There were snowdrops here, but the daffodils were still cowering, barely out of the soil, as if saying 'You're joking, we're not going out there yet'. She turned off the engine and listened. Nothing.

Here, on this small road looking out on the hills and down to the river, she felt the embarrassment and anger that had stayed with her since yesterday's Armstrong and Araminta incidents seep away. Thank goodness for half days. Sometimes she just needed a rest from pretending everything was fine; from that new tendency she had to want to smooth over any unpleasantness as though it was somehow her fault and not the other person's.

She reached for her jacket, aware that the hard brightness in the sun gave a false impression of how warm it would be, and got out of the car to look at the sheep. It was the Bluefaced Leicesters up here, heavy with lambs.

When she was little, she had thought them ugly, all

bony-nosed and arrogant. Now, if she heard anyone else say that, she bristled. They were pedigrees, beautiful in their own way and the farm's reputation as well as her family's was bound up with them.

Besides, these days, who was she to call anything or anyone ugly?

'Not long now, ladies,' she called and laughed at their complete lack of interest.

The wind was picking up, whipping the little bits of wool caught on the fence and, down by the river, she could see the branches of the trees swaying. Up here the trees had long ago been moulded into shape by the prevailing winds and now gave the impression that they were leaning forward as a preamble to setting off for a walk, the wind at their backs. The lichen on them made them look as if they were already in strange, fluorescent bloom.

Everything was simpler out here: sheep, earth, grass, trees, sky. She could usually stay here for hours just breathing great lungfuls of the purity, but not today: the wind had ice in it and despite her jacket she was starting to feel chilled. Back in the car, she turned up the heater.

Passing the large Suffolk ram, she slowed the car and wound down the window. He was a big-shouldered lad who, despite looking chunky and cuddly, could break the neck of a more delicate Leicester in a scrap.

'Hello, Winston,' she shouted and the ram took a few steps back, havered from side to side and then turned and ran.

All mouth and trousers.

Reaching a fork in the road, she hesitated and then turned left. The track here got bumpier and narrower until it ended in front of a small stone house with a green door. Right now the door was open and a young woman was struggling to peg out a variety of baby clothes on a rotary dryer. As she waved, the babygro she had been hanging out flicked up and over her face before she slapped it back with her hand.

'Good drying day,' she said as Jennifer got out of the car, 'if you've got the strength to get the stuff hung out.'

Jennifer knew that in a straight fight between the wind and Bryony, her sister-in-law, the wind might possibly lose. The Suffolk ram definitely would. Bryony was a 'direct from central casting' farmer's daughter and filled the role much more ably than Jennifer ever could. Hearty, a good rider, only ceding a few inches in height to Jennifer's brother who himself was a big man, she approached everything with gusto, including motherhood. But today her eyes had a redness about them that Jennifer knew was not due to the wind.

'How's Louise?' Jennifer asked, and as if on cue there was a loud bellowing wail from inside the house.

Bryony flicked her eyes skywards. 'Teeth still giving her jip. There she blows.' She hared off into the house, returning with Louise still bundled in her quilted sleeping bag. She was struggling and crying, her face pink and wet.

'Now, look,' Bryony said, leaning her head back to avoid Louise's flailing fists, 'what's Auntie Jen going to think of you?'

Louise obviously didn't give a damn and both women watched her continue to try and fight her way out of her sleeping bag and her mother's arms. As Bryony was used to handling appreciably bigger livestock, Louise was wasting her time.

'Oh, for goodness' sake,' Bryony said wearily after one particularly bolshy struggle, and Jennifer wondered how much worse this would be for her when lambing was properly underway and Danny too busy to take some of the strain from her at night.

'How about I take Louise for a couple of hours?' she said. 'Mum would be delighted, and you can have a sleep.'

'No, no. I can't let you do that.' There was something in Bryony's tone that told Jennifer she could be persuaded.

'Come on, I'll take your car with the seat; you can bring mine along later when you come and collect her.'

Jennifer was amused to see that once the decision was made Bryony set about getting her daughter bundled away with her customary vim, wrestling Louise into the car seat and pinning her down expertly with the straps. Louise looked outraged and reapplied herself to trying to make everyone's eardrums bleed, but as Jennifer set off the crying lessened and when they reached the fork in the road, this time Jennifer taking the road on the right, it had stopped. Jennifer saw Louise's hand go to her mouth. By the time Jennifer got her first glimpse of home, Louise was asleep.

Set down in the fold of the valley and surrounded by fields on all sides Jennifer likened Lane End Farm to a big stone ship that had come to rest in a sea of green. The farmhouse itself was the bow, albeit a blunt one; the wide yard was the deck and the clutter of barns and sheds forming a U-shape on the other side of the yard, was a stern of sorts. With a stretch of the imagination you could see the sheep dotted over the fields as white flecks of foam.

In the yard, Jennifer stopped the car and gently lifted Louise out. A quick fluttering of her eyelids was her only response and as Jennifer manoeuvred past the coats and discarded wellingtons in the porch, she did not stir again.

'Brought you a present,' Jennifer said pushing open the kitchen door and her mother, putting a plate high up on the dresser said, 'If it's anything else that wants feeding, you can take it back,' before turning and seeing it was her granddaughter. She took Louise into her own arms eagerly, a smile transforming her face. It was a face that, with its aquiline nose and high cheekbones, Cress always joked belonged to a duchess, but had ended up on a farmer's wife. Her mother's way of carrying herself too, with her back very straight and her chin lifted, added to the impression that she was slightly superior and not to be crossed. Mostly this demeanour was saved for those who angered her; with those she loved she was as warm as any apple-cheeked farmer's wife, and with children she was a thing of putty. The only time that the family had to be wary was if she had on what Jennifer's father Ray called her 'lemon-drop look'. Then you'd best keep quiet, find something that needed doing elsewhere and hope that it wasn't you that had displeased her.

As her mother settled down with Louise in her arms, Jennifer took off her jacket and wandered over to the cake tin. Coffee and walnut today, the icing thick and studded with nuts. 'This looks good,' she said, cutting a slice and bringing it over to the table.

'You'll not have bothered with lunch before you left, I suppose?' her mother asked.

'Did, but wished I hadn't. Thought I'd give that new shop round the back of the hospital a go. Sandwich tasted a bit weird though, left a lot of it.'

Her mother screwed up her face. 'Meant to tell you not to go there. You know Craig who helps with the silage?'

'Craig with the long nails who keeps ferrets in his kitchen?'

Her mother nodded. 'His daughter's bought that shop.'

Jennifer almost spat her cake out. 'Lovely, ferret-meat sandwiches.'

'Don't be daft,' her mother said seriously. 'You can't eat ferret meat, it might even be illegal.'

Jennifer went back to eating her cake with slightly less gusto. As she chewed she watched Louise's hand curl itself around one of her mother's fingers and felt again that sense of peace she had experienced on the drive home, even if she couldn't go so far as to call it contentment. Everything was safe and familiar here in the kitchen with the clock ticking, the Rayburn pumping out the heat, the big wooden table solid with memories of family meals.

'Alex rang again,' her mother said and Jennifer's sense of peace withered. There were all kinds of things lurking under her mother's statement: the hint of disapproval that Jennifer had not returned his earlier call and, most gut-wrenching of all, the inference that she should get on the phone right now because Alex was obviously still keen on her and how much longer did she think she could leave the poor man dangling?

'He mentioned something about a dinner with the Henshaws? Carlisle on Wednesday? Said he'd pick you up at seven.' Jennifer couldn't bear to see that awful optimism in her mother's eyes.

'Let's have a look at the lamb-cam,' she said, almost sprinting towards the small television perched on the worktop by the window and knowing her mother wouldn't have been fooled by the unsubtle change of subject. Installed with great fanfare, the lamb-cam relayed images from the four CCTV cameras fitted in the lambing barns and enabled her father to see at a glance what was going on. With the sound turned right up, it was easy to hear the distinctive bleat and blare of a ewe about to give birth. Though it was rarely on during the day, at night it enabled her father to simply tumble out of bed at regular intervals and check what was going on rather than having to go out to the barn in the dark and cold.

Jennifer switched on the monitor, turned up the

volume and waited for the screen, split into four, to settle. Lambing had barely begun yet, and she did not expect to see much happening, but in one of the quarters she could see her father and brother bent over a ewe. She fiddled with the volume, but could not pick up what they were saying.

'Hear the cottage next to Mr Armstrong is rented out,' she said back over her shoulder, 'Sonia mentioned something about a writer?'

She realised it was a mistake as soon as she'd said it. There was the lemon-drop look.

'Just a writer, Mum, not a journalist,' she said hurriedly, but her mother made a little 'humph' noise and Jennifer knew it would be a good idea to retrieve her jacket and pop out and see how Ray and Danny were doing.

In this mood her mother reminded her of a particularly ferocious lioness protecting her cubs.

Outside the light looked fragile and the cold hit her after the warmth of the kitchen, but inside the smallest of the rooms in the barn the lamps used to warm the lambs gave everything a comforting glow. The combined smell of sweet hay and warm sheep was one that reached down deep inside her to tell her everything here was safe, like when she was a child. The old Jennifer.

She had a quick look in a couple of pens and the knobbly-kneed lambs stared up at her and bleated; a high, thin noise. They had that shell-shocked look they all had at being born, and tottered about on their spindly legs, their wool still yellow from the afterbirth.

Her father and her brother were further down the barn, her father watching as Danny tried to push a tiny lamb under a ewe whose head was restrained in a wooden clamp. The ewe was becoming increasingly agitated about not being able to turn her head to see what was going on.

'Hello, love,' her dad said, with a quick smile. 'You look nice.'

She saw her brother gently show the lamb where it was meant to be aiming while trying to stop the ewe from kicking out. It was a delicate operation and it always surprised her how her large, often clumsy brother, could exhibit such co-ordination when necessary. After a few false starts the lamb started to suckle, its tail wriggling excitedly, and the ewe gave one more indignant shuffle and then stood still. For the moment the ewe, which had lost its own lamb, was accepting this one as hers.

Danny straightened up and smiled, but it was a smile that morphed into something more mischievous and Jennifer knew that someone, some time today had been on the receiving end of a practical joke and Danny wanted to tell her about it. Ray had always been fond of a little gentle leg-pulling and Danny, the more robust variety. Jennifer took it as a sign of the rude, often extremely rude, good health of their relationship.

'Go on,' she said. 'What was it this time?'

Ray frowned. 'Not sure we should tell you, Jen.'

Danny grinned down at the straw.

'I'll just go and ask Mum then,' she said pretending to

move away and heard her Dad's quick, 'Best keep it between the three of us.'

'It's about Mrs Chambers, see,' Danny added.

Jennifer felt her curiosity sharpen. Mrs Chambers was fantastically efficient, like some particularly virulent weed-killer – no piece of church brass was polished, no jumble sale hosted, without her being there to keep everyone right. Her behaviour as chair of the Luncheon Club made Jen's mother and the rest of the committee feel as if they had been serving up swill to the local OAPs before she'd arrived.

'Mum was hosting the Luncheon-Club meeting, see,' Danny said, 'so I'd kept out of the way until all the cars had gone and then nipped in to get a handful of biscuits. Turns out Mrs Chambers was still waiting for one of those daft sons of hers to pick her up. I just did a quick in-and-out, like, but not before I heard Wifey lecturing Mum on the proper way to cook beef. Should have seen the way Mum was pleating the edge of the tablecloth. Then I noticed the monitor for the lamb-cam was on.'

'I'd been looking at it over breakfast with the sound down. Forgot to switch it off,' Ray added helpfully.

'She had her back to it, Mrs Chambers, and Mum was busy with the tablecloth,' Danny's eyes were twinkling at the memory, 'so I came back out here and—'

'He . . .' Ray could not finish the sentence for laughing.

'What? What?' Jennifer said.

'I mooned her.' Danny was looking very pleased with himself.

'Buttock-naked,' Ray confirmed.

Jennifer felt the laughter bubble up through her.

'More a half moon really,' Danny said in all seriousness, 'it was that quick.'

This set Ray off again and he had to go and sit on a straw bale.

Their laughter had just died away again when there was a commotion at the door of the shed and Jennifer's mother appeared, eyes blazing and a wide-awake Louise on her hip.

Ray stood up abruptly.

'Hello, pet. Jen didn't say Louise was here.' He tentatively raised his hand and waved at the little girl.

'Never you mind Louise,' Jennifer's mother snapped, shifting her gaze to Danny and then back to Ray. 'It's very interesting what you can pick up on that lamb-cam.'

'Oh bugger,' Danny said, 'the monitor's on in the kitchen again, isn't it?'

'Yes it is, and the volume was up nice and loud too.'

'That was me,' Jennifer said. 'Sorry.'

'Now, Bren,' her father started, 'it was just a bit of fun, no harm done.'

'No harm done? She could have had you both for sexual harassment.'

They were all waiting for the lemon-drop look, but it didn't come. What came was laughter, quiet at first and then louder and more wholehearted. It set them all off again, even Louise.

Jen wanted this moment of laughter and new lambs to

go on forever. 'You should be really grateful Mrs Chambers didn't turn around,' she said to Danny. 'She was bound to have found fault with your buns.'

'Aye,' Danny agreed, just managing to get the words out, 'but I'd have got a winner's rosette for me sausage roll.'

CHAPTER 6

As Mack struggled to stand upright in the wind, clinging on to the door of a taxi, he found it hard to recall that thrill-of-the-chase moment he'd had on the train.

'This is it,' he asked, looking around, 'the whole of Brindley?'

'Divvn't be soft,' the taxi driver replied. 'The opera house is down that hill and the casino's round the corner.'

Mack didn't laugh, but even if he had, it would have been torn away in the wind. There were no streetlights, but he could just make out a row of squat, stone cottages which he supposed was Brindley Villas. Turning his head to the left, he saw a couple of larger, detached houses, also built in stone. He looked off to the right. Nothing, just a signpost. He guessed it would say 'Civilisation: 350 miles this way'.

He knew the North would be like this. Bring on the cloth caps and rickets.

As the taxi driver struggled round to the boot and started to get out his case and rucksack, Mack turned to see what delights lay behind him. A low tin hut, a couple of cottages and what might be the shop.

He registered that there was also a play area with some swings being bullied by the wind and a well-worn slide.

'You all right there?' the taxi driver asked.

No, put my stuff back in the boot and drive away like a bat out of Hell.

'Yes, lovely place. Away from everything; just how I like it. No distractions from thinking and writing. Looks like there's plenty of good walking to be had.' He waved his hand towards the black nothingness.

'Not a great walker myself,' the taxi driver said, starting to close the boot and then stopping. 'Hey, I keep a shovel in here, do you want a lend of it?'

'For any snow that's on its way?' Mack squinted at the sky in what he hoped was a knowledgeable, country manner.

'Why no, to beat off the locals.' The taxi driver shut the boot and walked towards Mack with his arms outstretched as if he were a zombie. 'Saw some of these curtains twitching when we pulled up. Best watch yourself.'

'Ah, yes. Funny, very funny,' Mack agreed, wishing he could club the man with his own shovel, if only to stop the incessant flow of humour. It had started when he got into the taxi at Tyneforth, after a jarring, bouncy ride on the little train out from Newcastle where he'd morosely watched the view out of the window get greener and greener with every mile. He wasn't even going to think about the earlier, shabby little meeting with the so-called

Third Party in Newcastle Station. Even now it made him want to wash his hands.

The taxi driver's merry chatter had been kept up as they'd driven out of Tyneforth on the dual carriageway and then along little roads that wound past streams and down into valleys and through villages until for a long while there was nothing and then there was Brindley.

'How much do I owe you?' Mack shouted into the wind once the zombie impersonation was over.

'Forty-five pounds. Want a receipt?'

Mack paid and acted as a windbreak while the taxi driver struggled to write out the receipt and then, because it was O'Dowd's money, he handed over a large tip.

He regretted it when the taxi driver raised his eyebrows and said, 'Last time I got a tip like that it was one of them journalists. Could charge the silly buggers anything you liked. They'll have your knadgers off round here if they think you're one of them.'

'Do you really think I'm a journalist dressed like this?' Mack kept his voice level and his delivery slow despite the surge of adrenalin he'd just received.

'Aye, crackers idea,' the taxi driver said looking him up and down and hastily pocketing the money.

After executing a showy three-point turn he was gone, and Mack stood in the road and wondered whether he should just wait for the four-times-a-week bus service to run him over. The wind was trying to tear off his fleece, and even with one of his new jumpers on, he felt chilled. Little pricks of ice in the wind were numbing his face.

'So, let me guess,' he said, walking towards the cottages, 'which one of these delightful residences is mine?'

Each of the four cottages in front of him had a gently sloping front garden bordered by a path, which culminated in a run of little steps, at the bottom of which was a decorative wrought-iron gate set in a low stone wall. Only one had an overgrown garden, a door faded to a faecal brown and a dry-looking creeper hanging on to the stonework for grim death.

'Ah, that'll be mine, then,' Mack said and that fact was confirmed as he drew nearer to the gate and saw a battered number '3'. On his journey to the front door he tried to look as if he was not trudging in case he was being watched. Retrieving the keys from his pocket, he opened the door.

A smell of damp dog, or possibly dead dog, came out to greet him and another gust of wind propelled him through the door. He was standing at the bottom of a flight of stairs, in a cramped space only just bigger than he was. To make enough room to close the front door, he had to balance his suitcase on the end of the banister, with the rucksack on top, and, steadying both with one hand, reach behind him and give the door an almighty slam. Alone at last, he lowered his head, let the luggage fall where it could and ripped into the world, Northumberland, O'Dowd and Phyllida using every swear word he knew. If he hadn't, some valve or artery would have spontaneously burst. He finished with a venomous, 'And there isn't even a sodding pub. That's because it's not a village, it's a hamlet. And we all know what a bloody depressing play that is.'

Feeling only marginally better, he reached out and pushed on the door to his right. It swung open to show a small, shabby sitting room. Brown walls, brown carpet, brown curtains. He flicked on the light. Brown lampshade. Presumably *Beautiful Homes* had only just finished their photo shoot.

He shivered. It seemed colder in the house than outside and he'd need to find the controls for the central heating. That's when he realised there would be no controls for the heating because there was no heating to control. He looked at the tiled fireplace, its mouth filled with some broken bits of wood and newspaper. This wasn't the twilight zone, it was the Middle Ages. In frustration he gave the nasty brown sofa a kick and watched a puff of dust bloom out of it. He was seriously cold now and he could see his breath as clearly as the dust from the sofa. He wanted to lie down on the floor and never get up again. He had no heart for this 'thing' he had to do. How could he possibly have imagined he could pull it off? This wasn't his world. He'd already nearly blown it with that tip for the taxi driver.

He reached into the pocket of his jacket for his mobile. No signal. He got out O'Dowd's phone. Nothing there either. Probably no Internet coverage either. He looked around. No telly.

He wrenched open a door to what he presumed was the kitchen. Battered units, an old gas cooker, Formica-topped table and possibly the smallest fridge he had ever seen. Why had he assumed someone would have stocked it? Although now he'd met the Third Party he wouldn't have wanted to put anything he'd touched near his mouth anyway.

Returning to the sitting room, he plonked himself on the sofa, reached in his pocket for the chocolate bar he had stowed away earlier, and morosely started to unwrap it.

Jennifer switched on the printer in Ray's office, or to give it its proper name, the 'Oh-Bugger Room' – which was what Ray shouted at frequent intervals when he was stuck at the desk doing the farm accounts or completing the welter of Ministry forms needed for just about every activity on the farm.

The posters for the Drama-Club meeting started to print just as her mobile phone rang, and she got it out of her bag and made sure the office door was firmly shut before answering it.

'Greetings there in little old Engerland,' a mock-American voice shouted into her ear and she laughed out loud.

'Cress, that's dreadful, I hope they're not paying you for that accent?'

'Pound a word and cheap at the price. Serves them right for inflicting all those Cockney chimney sweeps on us. So ... what's new?'

'Just printing off the posters for Finlay's Drama-Club

meeting on Thursday and, oh yes, Danny flashed Mrs Chambers. Not to her face, but via lamb-cam ... we are verrrrry sophisticated over here.'

There was a prolonged period of giggling from Cress and Jennifer let it wash over and around her. It seemed to bring the Californian sunshine along with it.

'Anyway, enough of flashing,' she said when the giggling had lessened. 'You sound back to your normal obnoxiously enthusiastic self – not feeling homesick any more?'

'No, your therapy worked marvels. Cheque's in the post.' There was a pause. 'Thank you, Jen, I'm not sure I could do this without you . . .' Cressida's voice powered up again. 'So, knocked them for six, like you said. Saw the rushes yesterday and boy, even though I say it myself, I'm amazing.'

'And why, Miss Modesty, aren't you in make-up having your slap and lippy trowelled on?'

'There's been a teensy technical problem—'

'Teensy?'

'I'm working that "upper-class English girl" thing and it's going down a storm. Complicated underwater scene and something's gone awry. They did explain it and I pretended to understand. Now I get to have breakfast by the pool rather than pretending to fornicate by a lagoon in the studio.'

Jennifer got up and twitched aside the curtain on the window and looked out at the darkness. It was hard to imagine Cress sitting in the garden of her little pink bungalow, the sun glinting off the water in the pool.

'Not tanning that peaches-and-cream skin of yours, I hope,' she said.

'Bog off, Jen. It's not that warm today, only in the high sixties, besides I have minions to hold a parasol over me.'

'Ah, didn't take long for you to go Hollywood. I'm going to send out those overalls Dad used to lend you during lambing.'

More laughter and then Cress said, 'Hang on a mo, Jen,' and there was a clunk and Jennifer presumed the mobile phone had been put down. A couple of minutes passed with vague sounds of talking going on, and then Cress was back.

'Sorry about that.' She sounded embarrassed. 'Met Rory Sylvester for the first time last week, kind of pre-shoot get to know each other, and he's just sent me a car.'

'A whole car? To keep?'

'Mmm. And the maid doesn't know what to do with it as it's my driver's day off.' There was a pause. 'Oh God, Jen, send those overalls right away.'

'So . . . Rory . . . he obviously . . . thought you were very . . . nice.' Jennifer was aware that she was veering off into the kind of territory that Cress preferred not to talk about on the phone.

'Rory's a generous man, Jen.' Cress sounded guarded too. 'Very charming and more handsome in the flesh than on the screen.'

Jennifer couldn't imagine how he could look *more* handsome without things bursting into flames as he walked past. Rory was all dark hair and dark eyes and a body that was just the right mix of lean and muscled. Such attributes had allowed him to corner the market in action heroes with a sensitive side and Cress landing a role as his love interest was probably going to be her big Hollywood breakthrough. After a few more pleasantries and clichés, Cress said, as if changing the subject, 'You ever hear from that boy with the dog who had a black spot right in the middle of its back?'

'No, shame that.'

'I'll bet,' Cress said with a snigger, and Jennifer knew that her cousin was telling her Rory Sylvester was cast in the same mould as Josh Brewers, a good-looking lad who had turned out to be vain and spoiled and quite happy to invite Jennifer and Cressida to join him in a threesome on the sly while he was dating one of their friends.

'I believe he got married, that boy,' Jennifer added, wanting to know what Rory's wife was like.

'Yes, someone very like that Biology teacher I had.'

Mrs Ravenscroft had married a very much younger man, and whenever she was seen out with him, had him clamped to her side as if under arrest. So, Rory Sylvester's wife was obviously insanely jealous and kept him on a short leash.

'So, you and Alex, out tonight then?' Cress asked unexpectedly and Jennifer felt a little bit of gloom push its way into the room.

'Mmm. Didn't see how I could wriggle out of it.' She heard Cress take a breath. 'And don't start, Cress. I know what I've got to do, don't go over it again.'

'I know Jen, it's just I can't bear—'

A sound of water splashing suddenly drowned out what Cressida couldn't bear, and then Jennifer heard her shout very distinctly, 'Oh my God, you stupid great idiot', in a most un-English-rose type of way, and, just before the phone was either put down or dropped, Jennifer heard, 'One of them has only gone and fallen in the pool!'

The noises that followed sounded as if all Hell had broken loose. There was the pounding of many feet, and a great deal of loud but indistinct yelling from a number of different voices, and above it all that weird sloshing noise.

'Cress, Cress, are you all right?' Jennifer kept asking over and over.

What's fallen into the pool? A statue? A bird? A member of staff?

Cress was back, breathing heavily as if she had been running.

'What fell in the pool, Cress? What?' Jennifer asked again.

'One of the paparazzi. Little shit. Climbed up the tree that overhangs it. I heard this whirring noise just now, when we were chatting and just thought, "Blimey, those crickets are loud." Then there's a splash and he's in the pool.' There was an exasperated sigh. 'Stupid bugger was convinced I had a man here with me. Only just got him out before he went down for the third time, all that camera stuff round his neck.' Cress suddenly sounded weary. 'My

God, Jen, is there nothing this lot won't do to get some dirt on me and a man? Is my sex life really worth that much?'

CHAPTER 7

Jennifer glanced at Alex as he drove them back from dinner at the Henshaws', and as the miles flicked by her mind churned through what she had to say to him. He was trying to turn the clock back on their relationship and if she didn't call a halt now, she'd look as though she was letting him.

Why couldn't she come straight out and tell him?

Because you're afraid that this might be the best it's ever going to be, and if you don't have him, who do you have? But how many more of these evenings can you take?

The people sitting round the Henshaws' dining table had been the friends Alex had known since he was a child. She'd had nothing in common with them when she was seventeen and that hadn't changed. Even their conversations were the same – beef and lamb prices; hunting, shooting and fishing talk; the absurd amount of government legislation they had to deal with and county gossip.

At several points Alex had mouthed 'Are you all right?' and she had made an effort to join in, offering up her views on subjects as scintillating as the windows in the new swimming pool and the chances of it being fine for the county show.

It felt like she was acting, although what part she was meant to be playing she wasn't certain. She had a creeping suspicion that Alex thought it was 'straying girlfriend returning to the fold'.

When the conversation spiralled, tipsily, into who was sleeping with whom, Alex started making 'What can you do with this lot?' faces at her, but she felt it was because he could see she was uncomfortable, not because he was. She excused herself and went and sat in the downstairs toilet for a while. When she returned, they were still on the same subject and she looked at Alex laughing away, and wondered what had happened to that rebel who had turned up in Sixth Form refusing to go back to his boarding school to do his A-levels.

She had been too young to realise that this rebellion was mainly directed against his monumentally snobbish father and did not represent the flowering of a free spirit. At the time though, with his blond hair, tanned skin, washed-out shirts and worn-down cords, he'd had a touch of the wild frontiersman about him and by autumn half-term Jen and he were a couple.

His skin was more weathered now from being outside all day, with a slight rosiness to the bridge of his nose and the top of his cheeks and he'd filled out a bit across his chest, but physically he did not look that different from the sixth-former he had been. So Jennifer could not quite explain how, in the years since they'd split up, he had begun to turn into a less tweedy version of his father. It was discernible in his gestures and speech patterns, even that way he had of standing, feet slightly apart as if there was a sergeant-major in his head shouting 'At ease'.

Jennifer had another go at practising what she had to say. Whatever she did, she mustn't think of all his visits to Manchester to see her in the hospital straight after the accident. All those little kindnesses since. That would only intensify the guilt she felt at being so spectacularly ungrateful about it.

But this gratitude of yours, if you're not careful, you know where it could lead.

As they passed through Brindley, she noticed there was a light on in the cottage next to Mr Armstrong's, but no smoke coming out of the chimney. Bit of a cold welcome to Northumberland.

When they pulled into the farmyard and Alex turned off the engine, she knew he would say 'Not a bad run back', just as she would reply, 'No, not bad'. She saw him unbuckle his seat belt and his hand moved gently to her knee, to land half on and half off her skirt. She hoped no one had heard the Land Rover pull up.

'Alex,' she said quickly, 'it was ... interesting to see everyone tonight, but I'm really—'

'Tired. I know.' He frowned as if that thought pained him. 'I'm sorry. It's a strain for you, meeting people.'

'No. No. It wasn't a strain, not in that way. I'm fine with people I know. Who know me.'

His hand patted her knee and settled completely, this time, on flesh.

'It's all right, Jennifer, you don't have to pretend with me – everyone else, but not with me. I could see it was a strain.'

'Only because,' she said, trying to get back on track, 'I felt everyone was assuming we were back together again. And that's not how I feel.'

He removed his hand from her knee and switched on the light.

No, no. These things are easier in the dark.

'Well, I haven't said anything to give them that idea,' Alex said defensively, and the hand that had been on her knee was now resting on the steering wheel. She looked at it warily, feeling that, like a large flying insect, it might at any moment settle on her knee again.

'I'm not accusing you, Alex. I'm just worried that since you split up with Felicity, which I somehow feel was to do with me, you're starting to hope we could pick up where we left off.'

There, the hand was no longer on the steering wheel, but it did not land on her knee. She felt him take her own hand.

'Jennifer, I can't help how I feel about you.'

There was such tenderness in his eyes and in his tone that she was tempted to reel in the rest of her speech – until she remembered her time spent in the loo at the Henshaws', reading *Horse & Hound* and feeling like an alien.

'Alex, I'm sorry.' She was as gentle as possible. 'I don't have the same feelings for you, and if we keep going out to places together, I'm afraid it looks as if I'm leading you on.' She intended to pull her hand from his after that, but the command did not appear to travel from her brain, so she stumbled on. 'You're the last person I want to hurt. Not after you've been such a very kind friend.' She saw his face undergo a subtle change with the word 'friend' as though she'd insulted him, but still he held her hand. She was very afraid that if they sat any longer like this she would sugar-coat things.

'My feelings haven't changed since we were at school,' he said, his gaze lingering on her. 'I've only ever wanted to look after you. Protect you. I know this is difficult for you, Jennifer, coming to terms with how your life has changed. But the people who really love you don't care. We still love you, just want to keep you safe.'

She couldn't put into words why that made her feel so trapped.

'And ... don't take this the wrong way –' he gave her fingers a hearty squeeze – 'but the Drama Club, Finlay, even Cressida, they're not helping by reminding you of what you've lost and can't have back. Whereas,' he lifted her hand to his mouth and gave it a kiss, 'you *can* get "us" back.'

She didn't know if it was that kiss or the way he was talking about Cress and Finlay that gave her the strength to get her hand away from his.

'Alex,' she said forcefully, 'I know you have deep feelings for me, but I can't return them. It's not just about now, it's about the future too – we want different things.' She waved aside his attempt to interrupt. 'I know that what I intended to do with my life isn't going to happen, but that isn't a good enough reason for me to cling to you.'

She undid her seat belt and tried to gauge from his face how he felt about what she had said. No clue. She got out of the car and was closing the door when he leaned across and pushed it back open.

'Give it a few more months, Jennifer,' he said, 'I can wait.'

Had all her words simply slid off him as if he were coated in Teflon? The cheery wave he gave her before he drove off did not suggest a man who was now driving his crushed spirit back home.

She went into the house, thankful that there was no sign of her mother, and as she reached her bedroom her mobile rang.

'Jen?' Cressida's tone was urgent. 'How did it go? Can't stay long – had to throw a prima-donna to come off the set, they're all running round like headless chickens trying to wrap it up by tomorrow. So, Alex?'

'Felt like I was kicking him in the teeth.'

'You wouldn't know how to be brutal. I should give you lessons.'

'He thinks I've just got to come to terms with everything and when I do, I'll realise I want him. Says he wants to keep me safe.'

There was an impatient noise from the phone.

'Listen to me, Jen. Don't get sidetracked here. Yes, he's

been great since the accident. But remember how he used to sulk when you had Youth Theatre? That time he didn't want you to be in the play that was going to Edinburgh. He's always tried to keep you to himself.'

'I know, I know.'

'Oh damn, look, I'm going to have to go, there's someone here tapping their watch. Very bloody subtle. But you've done the right thing, Jen. There's a part of you Alex just can't fathom, never has. Hold on to that.'

Lying in bed afterwards, Jennifer thought how weird it was that Alex believed he was the only one who understood her properly, whereas in reality it was Cress. She had been spot on about there being a part of her Alex couldn't fathom; the part of her that needed something 'other'. Acting had given her that. When it went well, she felt like she was flying.

She turned over and got comfortable. So, with acting gone, what was she waiting for? In all honesty she didn't know, but there had to be some way of moving forward again, didn't there? Of shaking off this feeling that everything had ground to a halt on that slip road back in Manchester. If she couldn't believe that she might as well give up now.

She expected to lie awake for a long time feeling guilty about Alex, but she was already more or less asleep when her mother came in and as she always did, kissed her pointedly, lovingly, on the scarred side of her face.

CHAPTER 8

'All right, time to meet the locals,' Mack said, with the kind of grim expression that only a man who had slept dressed in all his clothes in a clammy bed, missed out on supper and breakfast and washed in cold water could muster.

Brindley didn't look any better in daylight. Everything around it was either green, green or more bloody green. Except for the brown mud and the bare trees. Oh, and if he really peered into the distance, it looked as if there was snow on some of the hills. The silence made his ears hurt and the cold was finishing off all the other bits. He had spectacularly, among his purchases, forgotten to buy gloves.

He remembered the day when he had failed to get Gabi to put on her mittens. Well, he wasn't that guy here. He wasn't doing 'nice' until Gabi and the rest of them were safe.

He walked over the road, across a muddy piece of grass and ended up in front of 'H. Schofield. General Stores'.

There were the usual postcards to be found in any shop window, although he was slightly worried that the ones for stump removals might refer to limbs.

As he pushed open the door, a bell pinged and he had a moment to register how neat and well stocked the shelves were before a woman shot out from behind a bead curtain as though she had starting blocks back there.

'Hello, you,' she said.

Mack was good at reading the clues people gave out without even knowing: the style and age of shoes and watches; the amount of eye contact; an accent that slipped under alcohol; even the Pantone reference of a tan. What Mack saw was a woman in her forties in a tabard that showed a lot of flesh, nails that were painted, a well made-up face and hair that was coloured. Her clothes weren't cheap, but they were too tight and short for her figure. He clocked the way she looked at him: a quick up-and-down and then a return linger over his thighs and groin.

All of that said she was a game girl, a woman who'd lived a bit and wasn't planning on putting on her slippers and drinking her cocoa just yet. He noted the open gossip magazine on the counter and wondered if she might be a good source of gossip herself.

'Hi, nice to meet you,' he said, offering his hand. She took it with a widening smile. 'I'm—'

'Matt Harper, come to stay over at the Villas.' Her eyes had a mischievous sheen. 'Yes, I know, pet. Good journey yesterday, was it? Well, don't suppose it would worry you if it wasn't, what with being a travel writer, like.'

So, nosy, game girl who likes you to know she's well informed. Careful, Mack.

He clocked her wedding ring. 'You're well informed, Mrs . . . Mrs?'

'Sonia,' she twinkled back at him. 'Not Mrs Sonia, just Sonia.' Her eyes did another quick tour of his groin. 'I didn't know you'd be this young.'

'Sorry.'

'Oh, don't apologise. I like them young. So, heard you got off the King's Cross train. That a connection? Or did you start in London?' She tilted her head slightly. 'Recognise the accent, just can't quite place it.'

Mack admired her questioning technique and normally would have strung her along, but he didn't want to give the impression he was hiding anything.

'I come from Bristol.'

'Ah, West Country. You've not got much of a burr.'

'Can 'ave if Oi want,' he replied before feeling that was a bit too flirty and throttling back to studiously businesslike. 'So, I'll need one or two things.'

He saw her dip forward in an extravagant, cleavage-revealing way to haul a cardboard box on to the counter. It was filled with an assortment of packets, jars and tins.

'Bread, coffee, tea,' she said, lifting up the items to show him, 'some eggs and bacon and a couple of tins of beans. I put in low-fat spread rather than butter, but I can swap it if you like, and a couple of pints of milk. We have a milkman delivers to the village, so if you want him to include you, let me know.' She looked over the things in the box. 'And there's matches of course, washing-up liquid, cleaning stuff, some pasta and a jar of pasta sauce.' There was a flash of amusement in those eyes again. 'Nice soft toilet rolls too.'

'Wow.' Mack was genuinely surprised. 'How did you know what I wanted?'

'Not much I don't know about round here.'

Yeah, I'm starting to understand that.

'Well, that's just brilliant.' Was he being too gushing? 'Now, about the fire—'

He was interrupted by the door opening, and a man of about sixty walked in as though his feet were hurting. Following him was a much younger man, probably only in his late twenties. The eyes in his handsome face were startlingly green, and with his trendy padded jacket open, it was possible to see that his T-shirt was tight across his substantial, toned chest. Mack saw Sonia's smile.

Ah, her husband and son. Husband's a bit old for her.

'How did you get on, Hal?' Sonia said to the older man.

'Oh all right, did a good job. Got out the corns.' He sounded as though the 'r's were rolling around on the back of his tongue.

'Go and have a rest then.' Sonia touched his arm lightly, and he headed for the bead curtain. The instant he had gone, something happened to the atmosphere in the shop. The young man stepped towards Sonia, and it was a wonder Mack wasn't scorched by the sexual charge between the two of them. Her 'Hello' was deep with meaning, all of it dirty.

'Hello,' the young man replied, the foreign accent obvious even in that one word.

Oooh no, definitely not mother and son . . . although it is the country . . .

Sonia reached behind her, located a chocolate bar by touch alone, and placed it in the young man's hand, not once taking her gaze from his face.

The young man, with a quick look towards the beaded curtain, put the chocolate bar in his pocket, patted it suggestively and left.

Well, well. Here was me thinking I'd come to Nothings-happeningville. Perhaps her husband is the old one, because those two are definitely having it off and they don't want the older one to know. File that away.

Sonia made absolutely no comment about the men; it was as though Mack had dreamed the incident.

'You were going to ask me about the fires?' she said. 'I dropped a couple of bags of coal and some firelighters into the bunker in your back yard. If you prefer logs, I can arrange that too. Must be cold over there.' She frowned. 'That guy who rents it out is a slob.'

'How much do I owe you?' he said taking out his wallet.

'Open an account if you like. I know where to find you if I need to.'

Mack decided that Matt Harper would look a bit nervous about the double entendre in that sentence. He put his wallet down on the counter and lifted up the box.

'Can't interest you in any shampoo for that lovely thick

hair?' she said as she came round the counter. 'Toothpaste, toothbrush?'

'Thank you, no. Brought them with me.' He moved towards the door.

'Disposable razor?' She followed him.

'No, brought that too.'

She had her hand on the door handle.

'Condoms?'

He had to swallow down a laugh. 'No. No ... um ... don't think my girlfriend would approve.'

'Ah, all the best ones are taken. Still, if you get lucky ...'

He brought out his nervous-rabbit impression. 'Uh ... yes, well ... and, about my girlfriend, I need to—'

'Down by the bench, come out of your front door, turn left and keep walking, it's on the brow of the hill. Only mobile reception in the village.'

He must have looked dumbstruck because she said, smugly, 'Told you, I know everything around here.'

She had opened the door for him, but then abruptly closed it and led him by the box over to a noticeboard wedged between two of the cold cabinets. 'Nearly forgot, Jen told me to point this out to you.'

She was tapping a poster with the headline: 'Twelfth Night' on it and he must have appeared as if he was casually reading it, whereas like a heat-seeking missile he had locked on to the words, 'Meeting', 'The Roman Sentry', 'Thursday' and 'Brindley and Yarfield Drama Club'.

'Get yourself there,' she said, looking at him under her

lashes. 'I can see you in a nice pair of tights and they're always desperate for young men to act. Just ask for Jen. Lovely is Jen.'

He was afraid that Sonia's expression was the kind people normally had on their faces when they said a woman had a 'nice personality'.

'Well, I could,' he said in a 'slightly doubtful but prepared to be persuaded' tone. 'This pub, the Roman Sentry, it's—'

'Yarfield, the next village. Not sure why they've always called it the *Brindley* and Yarfield Drama Club, nothing ever happens here. The Drama Club hold all their meetings in the pub in Yarfield and perform in the big village hall down there too. It's about three miles away.'

'Just a stroll then,' he beamed.

Jeez, three sodding miles.

'I'll think about it,' he said, heading back to the door. She opened it for him, and he slowly walked away.

It was only seconds before he heard the ping of the bell as the door of the shop was opened again.

'You forgot your wallet,' she called, running after him to stuff it into one of the front pockets of his jeans.

'I'd forget my head if it wasn't screwed on,' he said with a laugh and ignored the way her hand lingered before she withdrew it.

Back inside the cottage he put his shopping away and struggled with the bags of coal and then with the fires in the front room and bedroom, eventually managing to produce a lot of smoke and not much heat. He left them flickering pathetically while he followed Sonia's directions to the bench. Still no signal. He walked around it ('In memory of Peter H. I. Clarke. Not just sitting: Contemplating'). Still nothing. He held the phone up high in his freezing hand and the bars on the screen immediately pulsed into life. 'Sorry, Pete,' he said, climbing up on the bench and punching in Tess's number. He was relieved she wasn't in because he wasn't sure he could carry off the lie that everything was fine. He left a message saying he'd ring back soon and told her his address, which actually belonged to another empty property the Third Party owned way over the other side of Northumberland.

Reluctantly he got out O'Dowd's phone.

'Anything to report?' O'Dowd said when he answered.

Mack looked around before speaking, but he didn't really know why. He hadn't seen anybody all morning and there wasn't much passing traffic.

'Everything's either green or brown or dead. The shop's run by a sex-starved Miss Marple; the curtains in the next door cottage twitch whenever I walk out of my front door and—'

'I meant about our Jen.'

'Seeing her tonight, some Drama-Club meeting in a pub, next village. But listen, Miss Marple said they're always looking for young men to act. What do I do about that? Prancing about on stage, it's not exactly low profile.'

'You're not in the West End, Dame Judi. Do what they want, whatever gets you closest to Jennifer. If you can stay backstage, fine, if you can't, tough. Besides, if you pull your finger out, you'll be gone before long – Cressida starts filming *The Unfeeling* with Randy Rory next week and my guts tell me it's all going to kick off then. Now get lost.'

Back in the cottage he wasn't surprised to see that the fire in the front room had died in his absence. He went and got the duvet, noticing that the bedroom fire had extinguished itself too, and wrapped himself up to lie on the smelly sofa.

Everything about the cottage depressed him, from the way you could only get enough hot water for a bath that barely covered your legs, to the dark-wood wardrobes in the bedrooms that looked like coffins. It felt like the kind of place lots of people had died in, and when he looked at the lumpy single bed in the spare room with its crocheted cover, he wondered whether one of the bodies was still in there.

At least that would explain the smell.

By the time he laced up his walking boots that evening, he had worked himself up into a nasty stew of bitterness and when he arrived outside the Roman Sentry in Yarfield he wanted to punch something or someone. Preferably a northerner, or failing that, O'Dowd.

It hadn't just been three miles through enemy terri-tory; it had been three miles and then another foot-chewing extra half-mile. He was sure he had blisters coming.

He'd felt horribly exposed walking through all that green, sure that out there in the dark there had been something, or more likely lots of somethings watching him. If the torch went out would they move in for the kill? His heart had been permanently thudding at every rustle in the long grass, every weird cry from God knew what. Once, the torch beam had picked out two horrible shining eyes by a fence and he'd yelped and stumbled on to his hands and knees. When he'd retrieved the torch there had been an indignant baa and a sheep had peeled away into the darkness. Not far from the pub, something white had come out of the sky towards him before veering away. He was convinced it had been a vulture.

His hands were frozen, but his body was sweaty from walking in his jumper, fleece and cagoule with his bandana wrapped round the lower half of his face. Fantastic, now everyone's first impression of him would be of a cold-handed, sweaty, smelly, wild-eyed nutter.

He reached out for the handle on the pub door, his determination to get the job done the strongest it had been since O'Dowd had blackmailed him into doing it. If he had to be especially sly or even hard-hearted, so be it. Get the job done and bugger off back home.

He stuck a hearty, slightly gung-ho expression on his face and walked into a large room with sepia views of the countryside on the whitewashed walls and a healthier fire in the grate than the ones he'd managed to get going. A group of men sitting round a table turned to stare at him.

'You here for the Drama-Club meeting?' the barman called and Mack heard one of the men at the table tut.

When Mack admitted he was, the barman said, 'They're out back. Sonia said you'd be coming. Get you a drink?'

Despite desperately wanting a vodka and tonic, he bought Matt Harper a pint of something called 'Sheep's Tackle' and headed towards an archway at the back of the room, aware that the surge of adrenalin now roaring around his body was taking his mind off his sore heels. He glanced at his watch. Only five past seven, she might not be here yet.

Under the arch he went and had to conclude that no, she definitely wasn't here yet, unless she was an old lady of about eighty dressed in a lilac suit, one of two men or a full-sized snooker table jammed up against the far wall.

The man facing him with a pinched little face and a turned-down mouth had given him an unfriendly look when he'd walked in, but the other bloke, the one with his back to him, had turned and smiled. His eyebrows were so thick and dark, Mack had thought for an instant that he had black masking tape stuck on his face, and those, along with his short, closely cropped hair, should have made him look threatening. Instead the open face and that broad smile suggested a child's drawing of a big, friendly clown without the make-up.

'Are you him,' the pinched-looking man said, 'the writer guy from Brindley?'

'Yes, yes I am. Matt Harper, pleased to meet you.'

'Sonia said you were young.' The man reached out for the glass of red wine in front of him and sipped it as if he was swallowing down vinegar.

Before Mack could apologise for his age, the friendly-looking clown stood up, 'Hey, give o'er, Neale, divvn't start all that.'

Mack wasn't sure the guy was talking English, but as he was coming towards him with his hand out he guessed he was introducing himself. It was the roughest hand Mack had ever held, like the coarsest sandpaper. 'I'm Doug,' the guy said, 'this here is Neale and this is Marjorie.' The woman inclined her head graciously.

'Divvn't be hard on Neale,' Doug said, letting go of Mack's hand, 'he's just papping himself that you'll muscle him oot.'

Mack must have looked confused or deaf because Marjorie leaned forward.

'Doug is from Ashington originally,' she said as if that was explanation enough.

'Aye, I'll gan more slowly,' Doug nodded. 'Forgot you were a southerner. Sit down.'

Mack sat down, taking a sip of his beer to give himself a little breathing space.

OK, nobody here to worry about – happy idiot, old woman and sulky saddo.

As if he'd heard his opinion of him, Neale said, quite aggressively, 'I suppose you've done lots of acting?'

'No,' Mack lied, having done quite a bit of acting at school and a lot more as a journalist. 'And I'm not looking for a part in your play. Just happy to help backstage out of the limelight. Never done this kind of thing before, but it seemed a good way to meet people. It can get a bit lonely, you know, walking, writing and living alone.'

Had that last sentiment been a bit too much? Well, that was Matt Harper for you: earnest and enthusiastic.

Neale looked sadly at his wineglass. 'You might not want to act, but when Finlay sees how young you are . . .'

'The important thing with Shakespeare,' Marjorie butted in, 'is speaking the verse properly. So few people can. Clear enunciation, feel the rhythm, don't gabble. Feel, feel, feel.'

'Aye, Marjorie, you're not wrong,' Doug said earnestly, but he winked surreptitiously at Mack.

At least the happy idiot looked like a bit of fun, even though his inability to speak English might be something of a barrier.

'Many more to come?' Mack asked, taking his cagoule off and bundling it up so that the Ordnance-Survey map in the inside pocket was visible.

'Oh aye, standing room only when they all get here.'

Mack took a sip of his drink and moved his stool a little so that he had a view of the archway: always better to see the target before it saw you. Two middle-aged men appeared. The one in a suit had very little hair; the other had a lot of it, ginger and tied back in a ponytail.

Ah, something office-based and ageing hippy.

They were introduced as Gerry and Steve and after shaking hands they commented on how young he was.

'Says he hasn't done any acting,' Neale got in morosely before Mack could speak.

'That won't matter when Finlay sees him,' ginger-haired Steve said, and both men went and sat on a different table and started to discuss him in low voices.

So, not making any enemies and just fitting in. That's going well.

'They'll get o'er it,' Doug said with a little laugh, 'divvn't sweat.'

'Oh Doug.' Marjorie had a pained expression on her powdered face.

Doug grinned. 'Apologies. I meant, divvn't perspire.'

Mack hid his smile at that and took off his fleece, trying to ignore the whiff of his own sweat. He placed his glasses on the table.

'Nice jumper,' Doug said.

A few more men arrived, all older than him and all shook his hand warily. 'Sodding Hell,' a particularly dissolute-looking guy called Angus said, 'you're no more than a baby.'

After that, women started to arrive and with each one Mack felt his heart speed and then slow as it became obvious it was not Jennifer. Doug kept up a stream of introductions: 'This is Susan, she's our stage manager', 'Here's Lydia and Wendy, they're Costumes', 'Say hello to Pamela'.

Mack gave up trying to remember names as it got closer and closer to half past seven and he felt more and more jittery. A young woman walked through the arch and his anticipation peaked and then fell away as Doug said, 'This is Jocelyn.' The woman slid her gaze over him, and Mack decided that he didn't much care for her. Despite her vitality and shiny, bouncy hair, there was something mean-looking about her face.

'Jesus,' she said, plonking her bag down on a table, 'you'll have this lot booking in for Botox.' She finished off with a snide little laugh and just on the edge of his vision he saw Doug make an irritated movement of his head.

Right, so, you don't like her either.

'I hear,' Jocelyn said, 'that you're from Bristol. And what is it you're writing? Something about Northumberland?'

Answering that was easy, he'd rehearsed it enough. People nodded as they listened, and he waited for the next, inevitable question about whether he'd written any other books.

'Yes, about walking . . . in Dorset and North Somerset.'

Jocelyn smirked. 'How many did you sell, three, four?'

There was that irritated movement from Doug again.

Another little rush of people came in before a woman walked under the arch whom Mack sincerely hoped was Jennifer. With everything pushed up and pert, her tiny waist accentuated by a wide belt, she was gorgeous. Ripe, one might even say. Her brown, shoulder-length hair was silky, her mouth was a pillowy pout and she had those big eyes you could swim in; naked if you were lucky. He was beginning to regret that he had made up a girl-friend.

Even her walk had a seductive air to it, a little wiggle that did lovely things to her tight top.

Doug caught his look. 'This is Lisa,' he said.

Mack wondered whether if he put his glasses on he would look like a sexy swot.

Lisa gave him a slow, loaded smile. 'Hello, Matt. You're

the writer, aren't you? Got any pencils you need sharpening?'

'Right,' Doug said abruptly. 'You want to give me a hand at the bar, Matt?'

'Word of warning,' Doug said when they were ordering the drinks, 'you want to watch that Lisa. She's a bit of a man-eater.'

Yesssssssss.

Doug's masking-tape eyebrows met his hairline. 'She's had a go at most of the men in the group and last year some of Finlay's sixth-formers came to help backstage, and it was carnage.' Doug handed the barman some money. 'I mean, divvn't get me wrong, she's a smashing lass. Really good accountant, canny actress, just has a lay 'em and leave 'em attitude, you know?'

What a wasted opportunity.

'I see.' He tried to look Matt Harper's brand of shocked.

'Aye, well, thought I better warn you seeing as Sonia said you had a lass. Been gannin' out long?'

'Couple of years,' Mack said hoping he'd managed to sound happy about it. 'And thanks for the warning, but I don't think Lisa would be interested in me.'

'You've got a pulse and your own teeth,' Doug said, pocketing his change and handing Mack two pints of beer to carry, 'she'll definitely be interested.'

Mack returned to the back room with something of a spring in his step and under Doug's direction got the drinks to the right people before deciding that the pint he'd drunk earlier was now pressing on his bladder.

'Just going to the bathroom,' he said loudly, pleased at how that had come out slightly old-fashioned. Still no sign of Jennifer or this Finlay bloke, but they couldn't be long; it was after half past and there was, as Doug had said, now standing room only. Passing Lisa, he gave her a smile, aiming for something that looked encouraging without being promiscuous. He was spoken for, after all. That made him laugh to himself in the toilets and he had to remind himself to focus.

Remember who you're meant to be. Stop getting distracted by the lovely Lisa. You're here for Jennifer. She's the target.

He arrived back in the bar to find two new people had arrived, and from the knot of people gathered around them, he guessed they must be Finlay and Jennifer. He felt his stomach tighten and his mouth go dry, but in some weird way, he was looking forward to getting started.

Bring it on.

'This is Matt,' Doug said, spotting him. 'Matt, this is Finlay.' The lanky man by Doug's side came towards him, his hand outstretched and beaming as if Mack was his long-lost relative, but Mack wasn't sure later whether he did ever shake Finlay's hand because as he reached forward he saw the woman with the blonde hair turn to look at him and his mind registered the lovely posture and the beautiful high cheekbones before the reason why there had been no picture of her in O'Dowd's briefing file became horribly clear.

He stared at the scar on the right-hand side of her face running in a jagged line from the corner of her eye to the corner of her mouth, branching out at a couple of points mid-cheek to form tributaries that disappeared under her hair at ear level. Where it touched the corner of her eye it made the upper eyelid droop a little.

His first thought was that whatever had happened to her, she was lucky not to have lost that eye.

His second one was crap, crap, crap, crap, crap.

CHAPTER 9

Jennifer saw the look of disgust in the new guy's eyes before he could hide it and turned away immediately, head down. She took a deep breath in and let it out, and by then Finlay had taken charge, pumping the guy's hand up and down and saying how marvellous it was to see him.

'We don't bite, do we?' Finlay said, indicating the group with a sweep of one of his long arms, and Jennifer looked around for somewhere to hide. Neale leaped up as if his piles had just burst into flame. Sitting down, she ducked behind the fuss of getting out her A4 pad and a pen.

Finlay called the meeting to order, and she glanced up to see Doug was watching her, and when he smiled, encouragingly, there was such sweetness in his big face that she wished she felt able to smile back.

She was aware that this new guy, Matt Harper, was sitting off to her left and she guessed he would be staring at Finlay with a glassy expression, and that wild horses wouldn't get him to look her way again. She'd seen it before; he'd be sorry he couldn't have handled it better and now terrified that if he did look at her again it would seem as if he was gawping.

She wrote the date on her pad and forced herself to concentrate on Finlay working his magic, enthusing them all with his eagerness. Keep her mind on that, and the first shockwave of humiliation would go.

'So, another Shakespeare,' Finlay said. 'You did such a fantastic job on the Scottish play it's a pity to let all that experience go to waste.'

'Not to mention the scenery,' Doug added.

People laughed and Jennifer saw that Matt Harper was about a beat too slow to join in, as if he was only doing it because he'd suddenly realised everyone else was. Probably as chewed up as her. She noted how Lisa had managed to bag the stool next to him.

Well, her first impression of him, the one she'd grabbed before scurrying behind her hair, had been right: he was good-looking. The kind of good-looking that made all your nerve endings shift about. Certainly the sexiest guy she'd seen since she'd come back home. Brown hair, quite shaggy, with a slight wave in it, and brown eyes. Bit of stubble. She looked down at her pad of paper. Made her think of a pirate somehow; all he needed was an earring. A pirate in a horrible jumper.

'What do we know about *Twelfth Night* then?' Finlay said when he had their attention again.

Jennifer wrote down 'Twelfth Night' on the pad for no other reason than it made her think about something other than what had just happened. She turned her head slightly so he was just on the edge of her vision. Despite his lumpy jumper, Matt Harper looked quite athletic, not solid. Nice legs. Good hands.

'*Twelfth Night* isn't a tragedy, of course, but it does deal with the big themes – love and its delusions, deception, mistaken identities. A twin brother and sister, Sebastian and Viola, get shipwrecked and each thinks the other is dead. Alone in a strange land, Viola dresses as a man . . .'

'Whoa, it's that kind of play is it?' Doug asked, again to much laughter.

'. . . and gains employment with a duke called Orsino. Now, this duke is in love with a lady called Olivia, and he gives our Viola the task of carrying love messages to her. But Olivia doesn't want the Duke and the poor woman falls for Viola, whom, obviously, she thinks is a man. In the meantime, Viola herself has fallen for the Duke.'

'Just a normal day on *The Jeremy Kyle Show*,' Angus joked.

Jennifer wondered why she had imagined this Matt Harper would be middle-aged.

'Will it be in modern dress again?' someone asked.

Jennifer wrote down 'modern dress' and looked at the words as if they meant nothing to her.

'No, Elizabethan costume this time.'

Jennifer distinctly heard Lisa say, 'Have you ever worn a codpiece, Matt?' and Jocelyn, sitting opposite, looked at Matt Harper as if she wanted to take a bite out of him.

'Jealous Jocelyn,' Jennifer wrote on the pad and then

hurriedly scratched it through and replaced it with 'Elizabethan costume'.

Why do I always have to be on the outside looking in these days?

'The important thing with Shakespeare,' Marjorie announced, 'is speaking the verse properly. So few people can. Clear enunciation, feel the rhythm, don't gabble. Feel, feel, feel.'

There were a few covert smiles around the group, but Finlay practically left the ground. 'Exactly, Marjorie. You've hit the nail on the head again.' The way he clapped his hands together suggested he wanted to start rehearsing right there and then.

Was it envy she was feeling now? She didn't know, hard to tease it out from the other feelings of discontent. It was these moments of meeting someone new that made her feel most cruelly the gap between what things had been like before and what they were like now. She could still remember that delicious feeling of being at the start of something; recognising that the other person found you as attractive as you found them. The teasing and pirouetting of a good flirt. All gone. She wasn't even going to think what a man would do if she came on to him.

'Scripts are on the pool table,' Finlay said. 'Auditions Monday, hall over the road as normal. Isn't that right, Jennifer?'

She started. 'Isn't what right?'

'Village hall,' he said patiently, 'booked for Monday for the auditions?'

'Yes,' she said. 'Six thirty, no, sorry, seven thirty. Um . . . No, it's seven . . . seven . . . Sorry.' Brilliant. Now Matt Harper was going to think it wasn't only her face that had got damaged.

'So, Jen will pass round a pad. Put your name on it and whether you want to act or help backstage.'

Matt Harper put his hand up.

'Can you give me some idea of the timescale involved, for rehearsals and then the play? Sorry, the rest of you probably know all this off by heart.'

'Matt, my dear man,' Finlay said using the heel of his hand to pummel at his forehead, 'I am an idiot. Everyone, this is Matt, here writing a book, comes from –' Finlay raised his eyebrows and Matt said 'Bristol', and a couple of people made 'ooh arrr' noises before Finlay went on – 'In answer to your very sensible question, we only have a six-week rehearsal period, but it's three rehearsals a week – Monday, Wednesday, Thursday, plus some Sunday after-noons as we get nearer to performing. Play dates? Thursday, April fifteenth and Friday, April sixteenth. Just before Easter. All quite intense, I'm afraid.'

Jennifer saw Matt Harper put on some glasses and write something in a notebook. Now he looked like a pirate who probably had A-levels in piracy. She passed the pad to Pamela on her left.

'So, Harper?' Lisa's voice drifted across. 'Probably Viking blood in you. They were always round here pillaging. How's your pillaging?'

She didn't hear Matt Harper's reply because Pamela had

reached out and grabbed her hand. Jennifer braced herself. Poor Pamela, she saw herself as a caring, sympathetic person and would be mortified to know people called her 'the leech' behind her back.

'Are you all right, Jennifer?' she said, her head at an angle and her thick glasses magnifying her eyes so that she seemed like a very caring owl. 'Only I couldn't help noticing that awkward moment with the new man, can I just suggest—'

'Sorry, Pamela,' Jennifer was already getting up, 'I've just remembered I need to help bring the sheep in for the night.'

Pamela blinked. 'The sheep in—'

'It's something new we're trying; keeps them safe from rustlers.'

'But, but—'

Jennifer left Pamela's buts behind and found Doug.

'I think I'll head home,' she said. 'Could you say bye to Finlay for me, tell him I'll call him tomorrow?'

'Aye, will do.' Doug looked across at Pamela. 'And ignore the leech, you're doing canny. Just think, this time last year you couldn't have handled being here at all; now you're back and fighting.'

Funny how Doug's sympathy bolstered you up, not sucked the lifeblood out of you with its mawkishness. Pamela could have learned a thing or two if she'd stopped talking long enough to listen.

'Bet you, this time next year, it'll be you back auditioning for the main parts. That'll wipe the smirk off Jocelyn's face.'

'Language, Doug.'

'Sorry. That *cow* Jocelyn's face.'

'Much better.'

She left the pub after that, not looking in Matt Harper's direction.

Doug was right, this time last year she couldn't have sat in a crowded room; she *was* making huge strides. But, however big they were, she'd never arrive back where she used to be. She'd never be sitting where Lisa was now, chatting unselfconsciously to an attractive man just after meeting him, or believing that if the magic was right, she might find herself alone with him later and discover what lay beneath that horrible jumper.

And she couldn't imagine how that was ever going to make her feel any less miserable than she did right now.

'Do you have any bloody idea what time it is?' O'Dowd's voice stormed out of the phone.

Standing in the absolute blackness of a Northumberland night, perched on Peter Clarke, Mack thundered back, 'It's twenty past eleven, I'm still in the same time zone as you up here . . . and I'm ringing to tell you I'm not doing this. No. Never. No.'

'Ah,' O'Dowd said, 'you've met her then? How bad is it?'

'You bastard. You should have told me, you should have said something.'

'Thought it might have been a deal-breaker. Anyway, think about it. This makes it easier – she's got low self-esteem. Good-looking guy like you giving her a bit of attention bound to make her come on side quicker.'

'What, you couldn't find any blind kittens I could kick to death instead?'

He knew he should be freezing, but all he could feel was red-hot hatred for O'Dowd. 'I'm not doing it. Not to someone already damaged.'

'You're doing it. As agreed. Rory Sylvester has sent Cressida a car; he's never done that before. Can you imagine if her and him get together? The bloody world's going to go apeshit, not to mention his wife. Little South American spitfire, and her dad's that director who wins all the prizes for foreign language films—'

'Not listening.'

There was something that sounded very much like a growl from O'Dowd's end of the phone.

'You'd better listen, my son, or I'll start up with the little drip-feed pieces in the paper to keep the public's anger alive. You know, something about new evidence emerging that Sir Teddy might have had a lover. Yah-de-yah-de-yah.' That raspy laugh got a little outing. 'I knew you'd go all touchy-feely on me. Mack the Knife? More like Mack the Old Wife. Nasty little seam of pity in you, a mewling conscience. You're doing this, or Phyllida gets it, the whole family gets it.'

'We'll cope.'

'Really, how exactly does a four-year-old cope, or a seven-year-old? They're going to have a lovely time in the playground: Granny's a traitor and a dipso. Probably have to leave Bath. Can't see that brother-in-law's business getting many orders after this, can you?'

Mack couldn't think of anything that would draw the sting out of those words.

'Put your bleeding heart away and get the job done. Anyway, you didn't say how bad it is. Looks repulsive in the photos. Want to know what happened?'

'Bugger off,' Mack said, but O'Dowd told him anyway.

'Went through a windscreen one Saturday night after drinking at a party in Manchester. Daft bint didn't have her seat belt on. Her and Cressida were in the car—'

'Wait, what? Cressida was with her, I've never seen that anywhere?' Out of habit Mack looked over his shoulder as he spoke.

'Did a trade-off, dished the dirt on one of her past lovers, anonymously, of course, in return for a total news blackout on the accident. Her management are a fierce bunch. Juicy details she coughed up too, remember? It was about the guy who liked to use—'

'Thanks. I've got the picture.'

He finished the call and then listened to the messages on his own phone, including one from Tess saying she was glad he'd arrived safely. Trudging back to the cottage, he tried to hang on to the comfort of her voice. He sat in the armchair and stared at the depressing pile of grey ash and cinders in the grate.

However much he rammed his head against the problem of Montgomery and Phyllida, he couldn't force a way through. Phyllida, at a pinch, he could sacrifice, but never Tess, Joe and the girls.

He thought of Jennifer again and closed his eyes. Perhaps then that scar wouldn't dance in front of them. But closing his eyes only made the scar appear more livid, and so he opened them again and went upstairs, unlacing his boots, taking off his socks and just sitting there with them in his hand until the cold got too much and he wrapped himself in his duvet and lay down.

This whole thing stunk worse than he imagined. He'd always known that he ran the risk of landing up in court, that O'Dowd would deny having hired him, but he'd reasoned that it was better he got hung out to dry than his whole family. But when he saw that face . . .

Get a grip, get this back into proportion. All you're doing is getting her trust. You're not going to tell her she's beautiful or try to get her into bed.

He turned over, but his doubts and worries followed him into his new position.

How low had he fallen? She already looked pretty fragile to him.

He turned over again.

It's her or the whole family. Make a good job of it and ask for forgiveness later.

If only he'd got a glimpse of her before she'd seen him, though, then he could have had a different expression on his face, not the one of . . . what was it? Disgust?

The lousiest possible start. She'd have erected the barricades against him already. If he imagined the task in front of him as a journey from London to the Rosebys' farm, at this moment he was somewhere off the coast of France. And, if he didn't do something quickly, he was probably in danger of drowning.

CHAPTER 10

Jennifer watched Sheila throwing the books down on to the floor to form two rough piles.

'But just getting community service is good, isn't it?' she asked.

'Yeah, it means he won't get locked up, but knowing bonehead Reece, he won't learn his ruddy lesson.'

Jennifer made some soothing noises, but Sheila was off again: 'And you know what Loopy Lionel downstairs had the nerve to suggest? Massage. Not for me, mind you, but for Reece. Lowers the levels of aggression, evidently. Said the penal system in Sweden has been getting very good results.'

Jennifer had to work very hard not to laugh. Typical Lionel, eager to help and completely misguided. She was amazed Sheila had not decked him. Still, at least Sheila did not have to put up with him smiling wistfully at her when they worked together. For a while now she had suspected that Lionel's feelings towards her were warmer than the usual ones that existed between a library supervisor and a library assistant. It was like being cocooned in a soft, comfortable jumper.

Sheila's bad mood and Lionel's galumphing naivety were welcome distractions from those brown eyes of Matt Harper's and the way they had looked at her. In bed last night, over breakfast this morning, on the drive into work, the sharp pain of that first awkward meeting had kept rising up like silt disturbed in a pond. No doubt the next time they met he would either avoid her like the plague, or overcompensate by being extra friendly and extra jolly.

Why couldn't he have been fat with halitosis?

Jennifer turned her attention back to Sheila's truculent book-sorting.

'I could tell you a snippet about Cress to cheer you up, if you like,' she said and was pleased to see some of the force go out of Sheila's hurling technique. 'She had a paparazzi in her pool.'

'What, as in "had"?' Sheila said, perking up even more.

'No. He dropped in.'

'To visit?'

'No, literally dropped in. Fell out of a tree. They're all buzzing round her, trying to dig up the dirt on her love life.'

Sheila immediately descended back into moroseness. 'Must be nice to have some dirt in your love life for someone to dig up.' She held out a book for Jennifer to see. 'Scrap pile or sell pile?'

'Scrap, I would think, look at the bite marks on it.'

'Well, biography of Margaret Thatcher, what do you expect? Hey up, what's wrong with Li-Li?'

Lionel was standing in the doorway. 'There's a young man downstairs for you,' he said. The set of his mouth suggested he felt put out about that.

Jennifer saw who it was as soon as she started to come down the staircase: Matt Harper, a carrier bag in his hand and a dark-red rucksack over one shoulder. She concentrated on the metal steps. He was smiling cheerily at her; one of those fixed smiles she'd come to loathe.

She could do this, show him she didn't care about yesterday and she really didn't care about him. Only problem was, just at that moment she couldn't raise her chin.

'Hello,' he said and she nodded at his brogues, two shoes that were perhaps among the most horrible ever made. Lionel was watching them under cover of checking out books and was being quite rough with the date stamp.

'I'd like . . .' Matt Harper said, and then stopped.

She waited, and when he didn't start again, she did look up and registered the deep brown of his eyes and that unruliness in his hair which made him look as though he'd had a busy time in bed.

God, you're good-looking.

His attention had obviously been taken by something behind her.

Jennifer saw that Sheila had come downstairs and was hanging around, not very subtly, pretending to tidy the newspaper rack.

'Sorry,' he said, looking confused, 'that woman, I just thought she was somebody else for a second.'

'Sonia at the village shop. In Brindley?'

He nodded, looking more perplexed.

'It's her sister. Sheila.'

'Ah. Small world. Right.' Out came his cheery, irritating smile again. 'Look . . . sorry . . . I'm making a hash of this. Is there anywhere a bit quieter we could go?'

'This is a library,' she said, 'everywhere's quiet,' and saw him look surprised that she had a sense of humour. That figured. Scarred face equalled not quite up to speed. It was a piece of arithmetic she'd met before.

'More private, then,' he said, gently.

Lionel came round the desk.

'Everything all right, Jen?'

Jennifer looked at Lionel and saw the familiar layers of wool waiting to be wrapped around her. She looked at Matt Harper and didn't know what she saw, but something was pushing her to find out.

She led Matt Harper to the modern literature section.

'Bright chairs,' he said in a distracted tone, putting his carrier bag down on one, and irritation that Sheila and the furniture were proving to be more interesting than she was began to outweigh her embarrassment. She concentrated on Matt Harper's jumper, which was another horrible one and the same style as Lionel's. He didn't look like Lionel in it, though. That icky cord jacket was a mistake.

'Sorry, this is a bit tricky, but I knew I had to come and

do this,' he was saying. 'You must be sick of it – people looking put out when they see you, and then pretending they weren't and being over-the-top normal.'

She felt as if he'd shoved her. Or peered into her brain and seen her real feelings.

He was talking again, his hands moving as if smoothing over the words.

'When I saw your face in the pub, I didn't react very well. I fear I looked as if I found it disturbing.'

She had changed her mind: she did want to go and be wrapped in Lionel's jumper. Matt Harper's hand had come up in a kind of 'Stop' gesture as though he sensed that.

'Please listen,' he said, 'my only excuse is that I was knocked back by the contrast with everything else about you.'

Oh God, her throat was going. She felt herself blinking too fast, but somehow her brain was processing that beneath the breath-taking, brutal honesty was something that he probably thought was a compliment.

'Meeting new people must be hard enough for you without them standing there like a wounded goldfish.'

His eyes seemed to be searching her own for clues about how she was feeling. There was a little furrow in his forehead as though he was struggling with a headache.

'I . . . don't . . . you . . .' She dried up.

His hand went to one side of his face and he rubbed it slowly as he spoke, as if he was at some deep level trying to process the subject of faces and skin and scars. 'I'm very afraid I'm making this worse and humiliating you even more.' His hand stopped and he gave her a self-deprecating smile. 'I spend too much time walking or staring at a blank sheet of paper; not enough time with people . . . or so my girlfriend says.'

This time her words came: 'No, it's all right. It's just you're very . . . direct.'

'Tactless is what you mean, but you're too kind to say, I suspect . . . but I'm glad you're taking it like that, such a relief.' Suddenly he had his hand out. 'How about we start again and I promise not to be so in your face?'

All Jennifer could hear was the blip of the barcode reader followed by the thump of the date stamp. A quick look at him confirmed that the words had been a nervous blurt, not intended, but they had felt like little thorns nonetheless.

His hand was still extended towards her, although looking a little limp now. It was a nice hand, attached to a good-looking man, but it was beyond her.

'I have to get back to the desk,' she said and walked quickly past Stephen King and Hilary Mantel and George Orwell. She knew that it must have seemed abrupt and strange, but if she hadn't moved then, she suspected she would have sat down on the floor.

He had followed her back to the desk and she got herself behind it and on to a chair. Sheila appeared like a shot. Lionel was still in a sulk.

'Bye, then,' Matt Harper said, with that cheery smile which looked rigid. He nodded at Sheila and Lionel and was gone.

Sheila didn't even wait for the door to close. 'Right, Jen, who is that, why is he talking to you and just how peachy is that backside?'

'Sheila, not in the library,' Lionel snapped, 'there are children here.'

Jennifer told them who he was and why he was in Northumberland, but not why he had come to the library. Sheila gave her a sly look. 'Well, you kept that quiet, missy. I'm seeing that play of yours in a whole new light now. Sulky Neale squeezed into a pair of big bloomers and tights wouldn't get me away from *Coronation Street*, but he would. Tea break, I want all the gen on him, Jen.' She laughed at her own joke.

'Writing a book on Northumberland from a walker's perspective?' Lionel said, his mouth looking a bit funny again. 'How utterly ground-breaking.'

Jennifer buried herself back up in the office, but she was still focused on Matt Harper. That hand extended in friendship, why hadn't she taken it? Because of that last nervous blurt of his? All that blunt honesty?

Or because she knew that putting her skin against his was going to make her feel all kinds of things she hadn't felt for a long time; things that were pointless for someone who looked like she did now to feel for someone who looked like him?

Mack wondered whether anyone would notice if he stood outside Tyneforth Library and repeatedly hit his head against the wall. 'In your face'. Brilliant. The one thing he shouldn't draw attention to and he'd done it.

He found a coffee shop and mainlined a double espresso and chocolate muffin. Jeez, what a mess. Despite practising his apology on the bus it had been a lot more difficult faced with the flesh-and-blood reality of that face. The way she walked away at the end without shaking his hand, was that a sign that he should just hand Phyllida a shovel and tell her to get digging?

Still, out of the wreckage he'd picked up some things that might be useful. Like the fact the guy on the desk obviously had a thing for Jennifer; that Sonia had a scarier, bigger sister called Sheila and, Jennifer's tone suggested, all was not right between them. Oh, and that he had the same taste in jumpers as the woolly Romeo. He'd almost laughed out loud when he'd seen that.

He looked around. Finding one of these coffee shops up here in the frozen north was a bit like finding a sushi bar in the desert.

That scarring was horrible, though. You couldn't stop staring when you were talking to her. Took your mind right off those high cheekbones and blue eyes. She had a bit of an Eastern European look, or, with that blonde hair, perhaps it was more Scandinavian. The thought of Vikings made him remember Lisa's comment about pillaging and he spent a few, satisfying minutes thinking about her breasts.

Still, Jennifer wasn't the slightly out-of-it, sad soul he'd imagined from the way she'd acted yesterday in the pub.

Genuine sense of humour lurking in there, which he supposed shouldn't surprise him: if she'd been set on being an actress she must have been outgoing, pretty confident.

He got another coffee and the code for the Wi-Fi, found a seat where he couldn't be overlooked and retrieved his laptop from the rucksack. He'd missed being able to dig into the Internet or speak on his mobile whenever he felt like it and spent the first few minutes answering emails, giving the impression to friends he was still in Bath. Then he did a bit of research on the village Tess thought he was living in. Bloody typical, that one had a pub. Trawling through gossip sites he saw that Cressida had rescued a drowning member of the paparazzi. Nice bit of PR. She'd probably been tempted to push him right under.

Back out in Tyneforth, he bought some thick gloves and had a wander to get his bearings. Despite the number of charity shops, the place had a prosperous feel to it, modern supermarkets down by the river and then the older buildings stretching up the hill. The architecture was a jumble of ages and styles, but the overall impression was of old stone and old brick. He poked his head inside the ancient abbey that dominated the market square and made a note of any cafés or sandwich shops where Jennifer might get her lunch and where he could 'accidentally' bump into her.

He could have been in any market town in any shire in England, except for the soundtrack of that accent: 'I had a one of them', 'He went off for to buy a paper', 'That lad needs fed'.

Feeling a long way from home, he walked back round to the library and, crossing the road, entered a park via an arch commemorating old wars, before passing a war memorial commemorating more recent ones. Down the path he went towards an ornate bandstand and huddled inside it to ring Tess. She sounded chirpy, and first Fran, and then Gabi were put on to talk. As he'd suspected Tess had looked up the village on the Internet and he told her the beer and food at the pub were great, the cottage was great, on Monday he was going up to Hadrian's Wall.

'So how are the natives?' she asked with a laugh.

'Incomprehensible, but not unfriendly.'

'They don't burn southerners for entertainment?'

'Warmth maybe, but not for fun.'

He felt Tess thaw him out, although the news that Phyllida seemed to be behaving after her tantrum sent a slight chill through him again: he suspected more deviousness, but how was it helping Tess if he voiced that?

They talked for a while longer before Tess had to go.

'The girls have sent you something,' she said before she went.

He walked out of the park, not relishing having to ask the Third Party to go and retrieve whatever Tess had sent, but at least he could give Mack some more cash when they met up, because right now he was going to spend what he had left on a couple of fan heaters, an electric blanket and speakers for his iPod to get his music chasing away the deathly quiet of that cottage. In fact, he was going to hoover up as many bits of modern life as he could carry back on the bus without it looking suspiciously like he was a softie with too much money.

The prospect of spending O'Dowd's money geed him up a bit as he walked towards the shops, but then the realisation hit him that when he caught the last bus to Brindley he'd be back in the cottage by six, hemmed in by all that green.

Three days, he'd barely been here, three days. He could be here two months, perhaps more. How the Hell was he going to handle that?

CHAPTER 11

Mack opened his front door the next morning to find two pints of milk and an incredibly old man. Looking as though he'd been scrubbed and smelling faintly of soap and toothpaste, he was leaning on a stick, and his face, with its watery blue eyes, was dominated by a long, sharp nose.

'Remove my top for me, would you?' he said in that funny sing-song accent with the rolling 'r's.

'Your top?' Mack looked at the man's jacket and jumper and wondered which one he meant.

'Aye.' A jar of horseradish was thrust towards him.

Mack reached out and took the jar, not sure if this was one of his neighbours, or if the old man had travelled some way to land on his doorstep. Perhaps Mack had moved into a cottage whose occupants had traditionally provided this service, just as there were people you could go to in Swiss towns who would tell you whether the fungi you had picked in the woods was safe to eat.

He loosened the lid easily and handed it back. 'Pleased to meet you, I'm Matt Harper.'

'I know.' The man eyed him suspiciously and then walked back down the path very slowly, obviously finding it difficult to hold the jar, his stick and clutch at the railings with his free hand. He stopped at the top of the steps and then slowly bent down and put the jar through the railings on to the path next door.

Ah, so you're the curtain twitcher. Figures.

He continued his journey down the steps, round the gate post at the bottom, up his own steps and stopped to bend and pick up the jar again, before continuing to his front door.

'Bye, then,' Mack said and was ignored as the man pushed at the door and went inside.

Mack went back to the notes he was making on his laptop, deciding that it wasn't really worth adding: 'Ancient man next door, unfriendly, eats horseradish.' The bell rang again.

'Another top to take off?' he said as he pulled open the door.

Jennifer Roseby looked startled and then lowered her chin.

Mack felt momentarily nonplussed and then decided that was all right, that was a normal reaction. 'Sorry,' he said, 'I thought you were the man next door.' Realising that sounded even weirder, he was glad to be distracted by a carrier bag being held out towards him.

'Oh, goodness, that's where I left it, in the library. I thought I'd left it on the bus. Thank you so much.' He pretended to check that his notebook and pen were still in it and then looked up to see she was now holding out a pile of paper, stapled together in one corner.

'We know you said you only wanted to help backstage, but Finlay would like you to read for the part of Sebastian.'

He felt that saying all that in one go and more or less maintaining eye contact with him had cost her a lot.

'Finlay can be very persuasive,' she added with a smile, pushing the script into his hands. He had to stop himself from looking away. In the daylight those scars looked even worse, obscene somehow, like someone had vandalised a picture. When she smiled it did strange, puckering things to them and he hoped his answering smile didn't look as false as it felt.

She was turning to go, but he knew that he shouldn't waste the gift of the two of them being alone like this.

'I hope you're still not annoyed at me for my stupidity at that first meeting in the pub,' he said, '. . . and in the library.'

'Well you could go for the triple,' she replied, staring at a place on the door frame.

Ouch. Didn't see that coming.

'Ah, yes, well, I'm glad you can joke about it. It's just you still look a bit . . .'

'. . . frosty-faced?' she said, raising her eyebrows.

Hell, he had been going to say that.

What is wrong with you, are you going through the thesaurus for phrases with face in them?

'Upset,' he burbled, 'I was going to say "upset".'

'No, no, I'm not. I didn't mean to give that impression.'

She stopped and frowned. 'It's to do with the scar, near my eye, confuses my facial messages a bit, I think.'

'Of course, of course,' he said hurriedly, 'I understand. So, I'll see you at the auditions, then?'

She gave him a quick nod and turned to go down the path and he noticed how slim she was, how her clothes were fashionable and her shoes, although casual, were an expensive brand.

She turned back as the man next door suddenly reappeared.

'Hello, Mr Armstrong. How are you today?' she said.

'Fair,' he replied and stopped level with her, him on one side of the railings, her on the other.

'Just been meeting your new neighbour.'

'Reading a paper?' Mr Armstrong replied, frowning. 'Why are you telling me that?'

'No, meeting your new neighbour,' she repeated, indicating Mack and he saw her little grin and caught her eye and grinned too. She broke the look first, turning her attention back to Mr Armstrong.

'Going to the shop,' he said. 'Bicarb for my cabbage. Have to shift for myself at the weekend.'

'Here, let me help you.' She lifted one leg over the railings, then the other, and it was done so swiftly and so elegantly that Mack was not sure it had happened, except there she was, next door. She started to walk beside Mr Armstrong, not grabbing at his arm and making a show of helping him, but letting the old man lift his hand on to her arm himself to steady his progress.

At that moment she reminded him of Tess, and he quickly went back inside and shut the door, not even saying goodbye. He stood back from the window watching the slow progress the pair of them made towards the shop, feeling grubby that he'd made her say that about her facial expressions, but knowing there was a lot more grubbiness to come.

'Seems a nice man, your neighbour,' Jennifer said to Mr Armstrong when she was sure that Matt Harper had gone back inside.

Mr Armstrong nodded. 'More decent than her in the shop, I hope.'

'Writes books about walking. That's good, isn't it, healthy exercise, you'll approve of that?'

She heard Mr Armstrong click his tongue in that particularly judgemental way he had.

'Walking's no indication of good character,' he said, 'everyone can walk. Her in the shop, I've seen her out walking. Hitler, Pol Pot, Stalin. They could all walk. Even Judas Iscariot, the great betrayer, he walked.'

Unable to think of anything to say to that, Jennifer took the opportunity of arriving at the shop to gently remove her arm from Mr Armstrong's, open the door for him and then wish him goodbye.

As she walked back out of the village she stopped at the Peter Clarke bench and wondered what had made her say that about her facial expressions. Now he'd think she was looking for sympathy. He'd certainly looked sad after she'd said it. Or it might have been uneasiness: she had, after all, just picked him up on his face-related Tourette's. He had something going on there anyway, under all that bright breeziness.

Those brown eyes, though, they got right inside you, particularly when he grinned.

The embarrassment of what she'd said to him came over her again and she looked at the view for a while and then laughed. Where on earth had he bought those jeans? In a properly cut pair he'd look, well, better even than the hills she was looking at now. His clothes seemed to be wearing him, not the other way round. Didn't they have proper clothes shops in Bristol?

That enthusiastic delivery of his was quite dork-like too. Yet overall the effect he was having on her wasn't of a dork with dreadful fashion sense.

She laughed again, but this time at herself for trying to get to the bottom of what she liked about him. He was just one of those men who had 'it' in bagfuls.

She took her time walking home, allowing herself to dwell on those eyes of his and hoping that his acting was better than his fashion sense.

CHAPTER 12

'Good turnout,' Finlay said, peeking out into the hall. A murmur of conversation drifted into the room. 'I'm always amazed they want to put up with me bossing them around again.'

'Oh come off it, Finlay,' Jennifer said, 'they'd read the phone book if you asked them.'

Finlay's laugh started off low and ended almost as a hoot and he closed the door and came and sat back in his chair, scooping up several biscuits from the plate as he did so. Popping one in his mouth, he chewed rapidly, his face, all planes and bones and twinkling eyes.

'Lot of auditions to get through today.' He flicked some biscuit crumbs off a list in front of him, 'But at least we've got one part sorted already. You get to play Viola.'

'No,' Jennifer said sharply.

'Ah, Jennifer, I remember when you were in my drama class in the Upper Sixth, you made me cry with—'

'It was a long time ago,' she said, as if time alone was the only reason she wasn't going to take the part.

Finlay put his teacher's voice on. 'Jennifer Roseby, there is no one who can do that part like you can. And you played her in that production at Manchester, I remember Ray telling me he'd braved the M6 to go and see it.'

'I think Lisa would make a good Viola, and Jocelyn, though it pains me to say it, should probably be Olivia.'

'Stop trying to distract me, Jennifer. Let's get back to thinking about Viola.'

She said 'No,' again, this time more sharply, feeling swamped by the fear that always took hold of her whenever she thought about standing on a stage again. She put one of the biscuits in her mouth to shut down the conversation, but it felt like a wad of cotton wool and she could barely chew or swallow it down.

'It's just that first step, isn't it?' Finlay said and gave her the gentlest of nudges.

She couldn't answer.

They sat quietly for a while before Finlay suddenly stole the last biscuit and sprang to his feet.

'You know, Viola's not that good a part,' he said briskly. 'I was thinking about *The Merchant of Venice* next year. I think you're more suited to Portia.'

Jennifer felt the fear subside, but there was disappointment lurking under it. She'd been allowed to retreat. Again.

Finlay waved the biscuit around. 'OK, brace yourself: let's wheel the first one in.'

Mack gave the room a quick once-over. Two-bar fire, load of old paperbacks on the windowsill, furniture that had seen better days. The walls were painted an alarming blue colour – hey, that must be why it was imaginatively called the Blue Room – and on one of them a large cork noticeboard showed details of forthcoming events. There was a strong smell of damp and burning dust from the fire.

Out of the window it was possible to see a graveyard that belonged to the church next door, and in the flare of a security light the high, old gravestones looked like people standing round shoulder to shoulder. It made him feel as if he was being watched and judged by something and he turned away.

'So glad you could come, really glad.' Finlay advanced on him with a smile that made Mack feel as if he was fundamental to Finlay's continuing happiness. Behind him, sitting at a large table, Jennifer had her chin down.

'Oh dear,' Finlay said, looking at Mack's feet. 'Hurt your-self?'

Mack realised he must have limped into the room.

Think of an excuse that doesn't involve you not being used to walking.

'Just turned my foot over. Stupid really. Loose stone when I was up on the Wall. It's quite spectacular,' he added enthusiastically.

For a wall.

'Isn't it, though? Which walk did you tackle?'

'Just a gentle stroll from Housesteads to Steel Rigg and back.'

Seven miles. Seven pigging miles.

'Ah, some of the best bits.'

Jennifer lifted her chin and nodded. 'Marvellous views,' she said.

Yeah, marvellous views if my feet hadn't been bleeding. And let's face it, it's good, but it's not the Great Wall of China.

He noticed again how well dressed Jennifer was. Grey cashmere sweater today and grey trousers with a faint pinstripe. They were well-cut trousers too, trendy. He tried not to think about what his jeans must look like. She wasn't wearing jewellery, even though her ears were pierced. So, dark clothes, no jewellery and just lipgloss. Interesting. It was tempting to say she was making the classic attempt to fade into the background, but that trendiness was intriguing. Like she had started to fight back.

Best not to think about that.

They were both looking at him expectantly.

'Now, Matt,' Finlay said, 'we know you don't want to act . . . but the actress we have in mind for Viola is young and, of course, Sebastian is her twin brother. So, as you're here, a gift from the god of drama landed in our laps, as it were,' Finlay's laugh made Mack wonder if he was slightly unhinged, 'well, silly not to try and persuade you. Fancy reading some of Sebastian's lines for us? Got your script?'

Finlay's tone was not wheedling or hectoring, but it made Mack lift up the script and meekly hand it over and then, when Finlay handed it back, scan through what he was being asked to read. He looked towards Jennifer and made sure he wetted his lips a little as if he was really nervous.

'Perhaps if you stood up,' she said encouragingly and so he did.

He was pleased with himself when he'd finished. It wouldn't have been possible to make more of a mess of the speech if he'd cut it up into small pieces and thrown it about the room. He'd run on lines that should have stopped. He'd stopped lines that should have run on. He'd stressed the wrong words, gulped down others. At one point he'd stopped completely.

Throughout, Finlay and Jennifer's faces had been devoid of any expression, and when he finally finished, slowing his whirling arms and bringing his erratic breathing under control, Finlay had said softly, 'That was quite something.'

'Quite, quite something,' Jennifer agreed.

He waited for them to say that perhaps, after all, it might be better for him to stay backstage and he was getting ready to look slightly disappointed when Finlay said, 'It won't work, Matt. We know what you're up to.'

Whaaaaat?

'Yes,' Jennifer said, 'you've been rumbled.'

He was sure that his face was now registering something between panic and shock. He stared at them. Had someone sussed he was a journalist?

No, hang on . . . they don't look angry, in fact Jennifer's face suggests she's amused. What do they mean then? Say something, you ruddy idiot.

'Rumbled?'

Finlay let out a deranged laugh, and he saw that Jennifer had started to laugh quietly too.

'Only someone who is very good at acting could be that bad, Matt,' Finlay said, 'believe me, I've seen enough terrible performers to know, and you're not one of them. I mean, all credit to you, a quite inspired peace of pretence, but the actor in you snuck out every now and then.'

'It did?'

'When you weren't whirling about, your stance was very good, lots of grace,' Jennifer chipped in. 'And although you tended to grab at the lines, every now and then you gave them space, got the rhythm just right, stressed the important words.' She darted a twinkling look at him. 'Marjorie would have been proud of you.'

Marjorie can go stick her head in a bucket.

'We know why you did it, Matt,' Finlay said.

'You do?'

'Of course, you don't want to put the other men's noses out of joint by landing a plum part. We're right, aren't we?'

No, I'm a scum-sucking bastard who wants to remain anonymous.

'There's no fooling you two, is there?' he said, like a little boy who'd been caught out. He fully expected to be zapped by a bolt of lightening from that graveyard.

'Don't you worry about the men, we'll get them sorted.' Finlay stood up and held out his hand. 'The part's yours. Welcome on board.'

Now the relief at not being outed as a journalist crashed up against the realisation that he was going to have to be in this play.

Bugger, bugger, bugger.

He stood up and shook Finlay's hand and got a smile from Jennifer that made him look away sharply, not because of what it did to her scarring, but because of the warmth. It was too . . . shaming. And then he was out the door with the words, 'First rehearsal, Wednesday, at seven thirty,' following him.

He was still wobbly when he got outside and found Doug waiting for him. Out of the jaws of defeat he had snatched a little victory and earned some brownie points. But it had been close.

'How did it go?' Doug asked, and when Mack told him, the slap on the back he delivered reverberated down Mack's spine. 'That's worth a celebration. And you know what? I got the part of Antonio the sea captain, and you and me are best mates in the play aren't we? How about we get in character in the pub? You can hoy a few pints down yer neck and I'll give you a lift home afterwards.'

Mack looked at his watch and thought of all those hours ahead of him in the cottage. 'Why not?' he said.

The next time Mack looked at his watch he was surprised to see it was 11 p.m.

'Call it a night?' Doug asked, finishing off his orange juice and Mack nodded, although a third pint would have been just the thing to take the edge off returning to Chez Rathole.

Despite knowing that he shouldn't, he was warming to Doug. They'd had a good couple of games of pool and Doug's easy way of chatting and his self-deprecating humour had smoothed away any fears Mack had about constantly being on his guard. When the conversation veered his way, it was no problem to steer it back to Doug.

Mack had assumed that Doug, with those rough hands and that rough accent, was some kind of labourer, but not long into the evening he'd said he 'did things with metal' and when Mack had said, 'What, like a blacksmith?' Doug had looked shy and said, 'Nah, like a sculptor. I do commissions mainly. Museums, banks, art galleries, councils. Just done one for the square ootside the Sage Music Centre. Big bugger, that one. "Art Ascending" it's called; flock of larks that changes into a load of minims and crochets. Play on words about that Vaughan Williams piece, of course,' he added matter-of-factly.

My God and I had you down as an idiot.

'Something up?' Doug asked.

'Just in awe. That's some skill.'

'Nah, get away. 'S just titting around with fire and metal. Not like writing, that's a real skill.'

Mack wanted to ask further questions, but as they were putting their empty glasses on the bar a woman came into the pub and everything about Doug suddenly looked folded in on itself, and he did a little spasmy thing with his arm and knocked over one of the glasses.

'Hi, Doug,' the woman called, and Doug made a grunty noise and then coughed and snot came down his nose. He wiped it with the back of his hand and in the process managed to knock over the other glass.

Mack took a good look at the woman. Bit older than

him, he guessed, with long auburn hair. She had a healthy, fresh look about her and was dressed as though she'd just come from some kind of exercise class. There were six or seven plaited cotton bracelets on one wrist. Mack thought her face was kind of familiar. She gave Doug a final wave and went to join a group of people sitting near the door.

'Oh Man,' Doug said, 'oh Man, oh Man, oh Man.' His eyes were closed as if he was in pain and then Mack remembered where he'd seen the woman: delivering the post. He'd watched her take a parcel into Sonia's.

Vibrators probably.

'She's the postwoman, isn't she, drives a van?'

Doug nodded and managed to get out the word, 'Pat.'

It was Mack's turn to blow snot out of his nose and he had to pretend he had something irritating his throat.

'I need to leave,' Doug said. 'Now.' He prised himself away from the bar and on his journey out managed to stumble by Pat's table and then push the door instead of pulling it.

'Is there a problem with you and Pat?' Mack asked when they had driven some way in silence. Doug said nothing and continued to throttle the steering wheel so Mack wittered on about his trip to Hadrian's Wall, lying about how impressed he'd been by the scope and stark beauty. He borrowed phrases from Finlay and the guide books to make his love of the Wall sound more believable and edited out the long bus ride and the way the wind had whipped and sliced at him as he'd walked.

All he got back was a heavy sigh and a 'goodnight', as

Doug dropped him outside Brindley Villas. Mack watched him drive off.

So . . . what have you learned so far? Sonia at the shop may have a young lover and there's something fishy about her relationship with her sister in the library; Doug's in torment over the lady postman; the guy wearing my jumper in the library has the hots for Jennifer; Lisa will give me a good seeing-to if I ask her and possibly organise my finances at the same time; Finlay may be mad and Jennifer used to drink and drive.

Just an everyday story of country folk.

CHAPTER 13

Jennifer woke to the sound of a pig grunting and in her drowsy state took a while to register that there weren't any pigs on the farm. The noise was coming from her handbag.

'Sorry, Cress,' she said when she had retrieved her mobile, 'I didn't realise it was you at first, you sounded like a pig.'

'Charming. Remind me to get some more elocution lessons.'

'Danny's been messing with the ringtone. He's working his way through farmyard animals.'

'Ah, Danny. Doesn't change. How's the Amazon?'

Jennifer glanced towards the bedroom door. 'Cress, stop being bitchy. Bryony is fine. So, eight o'clock here, you're up late. What can I do for you?'

'I'm returning your call, birdbrain. The one you left, when was it, Thursday night your time? Sorry, life's been hectic, couldn't get back to you before now.'

Jennifer paused. After that first meeting she had rung

Cress, desperate to vent about Matt Harper's inability to hide what he thought. Cress was the only person who combined the two things Jennifer had needed right then: the ability to sympathise, plus an inability to do anything about it. Tell anyone closer to home and they'd be up in arms and then up the road to Matt Harper's cottage.

Now she wasn't sure what to say to Cress.

'How was the wrap party?' she asked, playing for time.

'Wonderful. Fabby hotel, "Sunset Tower". Behaved myself beautifully. Schmoozed everyone and did not drink, snort, inhale or inject anything. Was a complete lady, then gave my PR people and the studio's PR people a cheery goodnight, waved graciously at the photographers outside the hotel and my driver took me home.'

'Where you curled up in bed with a milky drink, of course?'

'Ah, how well you know me. I sneaked out to Jo's house, you know, that nice Canadian girl I told you about, where we were joined by several like-minded members of the cast and proceeded to get completely, dance-on-the-tables drunk and re-enact *Toy Story 3*.'

'Re-enact?'

'Had it on the DVD player, sound down.'

'And you were?'

'Barbie, plus Slinky Dog and for a time, Mrs Potato Head.'

'For a time?'

'Something happened to the DVD player and it stopped working. Well, actually someone was sick on it. Well, specifically, me.'

Jennifer leaned back against the pillows and laughed.
'Poor you.'

'Oh, don't feel sorry for me, feel sorry for that DVD
player.' Jennifer heard a yawn. 'Anyway, got to go and pack
for New Mexico when I can be arsed. Flying out tomorrow.
So . . . tell me about Finlay's big plans.'

When Jennifer didn't speak immediately, Cress was on
it like a dog.

'Jen, has something happened?'

'The play's all cast. Lisa is Viola; Jocelyn's Olivia. Neale's
going to have a hissy fit because he's got Malvolio instead
of the Duke. And . . . and a new guy has joined us. He's
here for a few months researching a book on walking in
Northumberland.'

'Sounds a real page-turner. So what's he like: pubic-
hair beard with an unhealthy interest in Lycra and real
ale?'

'Bad clothes, certainly, and get this, brogues, Cressida,
real, old-fashioned brogues.'

'Lovely. And?'

'Well to cut a long story short, he didn't have a very
good reaction to my face when he saw me at the meeting
. . . no, don't interrupt, Cress, I'm not imagining it, he
didn't, and then he apologised. Came to the library to do
it. He was very honest and very direct.'

In the silence that followed, Jennifer could almost hear
Cress's brain working things out. 'Jen,' she said, 'you know
how your voice does that little lilt when you're being
evasive . . .'

'No it doesn't,' Jennifer said and immediately heard it herself.

'You're hesitating to tell me something else, aren't you, sweetie?' Cressida's tone softened further. 'Is it because you think I'll immediately start firing questions at you that you haven't worked out how to answer yet?'

There it was; the reason why Cress, despite the miles between them, was the only person who understood her.

'How about I promise, hand on heart, not to ask you anything and just listen?'

Jennifer looked around her bedroom and wondered why this was so hard. She felt like a secretive schoolgirl about to reveal a crush. Over the years she'd woken up in quite a few different beds with quite a few different men; she knew all the names for all the bits of their bodies and what you could do with them. She was a grown woman. She focused on a point on her wall just above her desk and just below a watercolour of a beach.

'He's called Matt Harper, Cress. He's young. He dresses like he's walked into a nerd's washing line, but he's sex on a stick.'

'Ah, I see.'

'He's got these really expressive brown eyes. And brown hair too that's usually mussed up.' She looked at the wall again. 'Rugged good-looking rather than smoothly hand-some, if that makes sense. Kind of intelligent face.'

'Tall? Muscled? Lean?'

'You said you wouldn't ask questions.'

'Well, it's like listening to paint dry.'

'He's my height and ... lithe ... daft word. From all that walking, I suppose. Good legs, Cress.'

'Good bum too, I'll bet. You always had an eye for those.'

'Oh. Yes. Indeeeeeed.' As they both laughed, Jennifer remembered a strip of photos lying around in a box somewhere of her and Cress in a photo booth in Newcastle when she was about thirteen. They'd been giggling about some boy they both fancied.

'So, pretty hot, then?'

'Lisa was practically sitting on his lap.'

'Lisa's sat on a lot of things.'

'When I first saw him I thought he looked a bit like a pirate—'

'What? Syphilitic and with an eyepatch and a hook?'

'No, idiot. Like he just needed an earring to be a bit, naughty, you know. But then he's also slightly dorkish, not in a trainspotter way, just very enthusiastic about everything. And considerate too – he stuffed up his audition on purpose because he didn't want to put the other men's noises out of joint.'

'Heathen! Doesn't he know the most important rule of acting is to kick the competition to the floor? So ... let me see ... he'll be playing Sebastian, I guess, whether he wants to or not? That's Lisa scuppered: tell her Viola can't shag her own brother.'

The thought of Lisa doing anything to Matt Harper made Jennifer stop before saying, 'He seems a bit detached at times, as if there's something disturbing him and he can't quite hide it.'

There was a groan from Cressida. 'Oh no, not a tortured soul with brown eyes, they're sooooo hard to resist. He sounds almost too good to be true. Where did you say he came from?'

Jennifer didn't miss the change in Cressida's tone. 'I've checked him out already, Cress. Don't worry. He's written two little books on the West Country. Lives in Bristol now.'

'OK . . . OK, as long as you've looked him up, done a bit of digging. So . . . you fancy him and I'm guessing that's disturbing for you as that hasn't happened since the accident.'

Jennifer nodded.

'Jen, if you're nodding you have to tell me.'

'Yes.'

When Cressida spoke again, Jennifer sensed she was going carefully, like a person carrying a large piece of delicate china over a pebbly beach. 'Jen . . . about this Matt Harper . . . will you promise me something?'

Jennifer started to slide under the duvet.

'Will you promise me that you won't decide, right from the start, that he's not going to be interested in you? Don't let the fact that you're unsettled morph into you somehow feeling . . . inadequate.' Jennifer had almost heard the big breath Cress had taken before saying that last word, the word that had got the piece of delicate china safely over the pebbles.

Easier said than done, Cress.

'Promise me, Jen?' Cress repeated.

'I promise . . . but, Cress, it doesn't matter anyway. He's got a girlfriend.'

'They can fall off their perches.'

And then men normally trade up.

'All right, I promise, O Wise One, not to write the script for this beforehand. I will lust after him and see what happens.'

When Cress had rung off because, as she put it 'Beelzebub in a leotard' had just turned up for her fitness-training session, Jen pulled the duvet right up over her head. That conversation had been like having a tooth extracted. And she wasn't sure she'd been entirely truthful about seeing where it led with Matt Harper because she already knew: the exciting, all-singing, all-dancing destination of friendship. Laughy, joky, conversational friendship, when what you really wanted was to put your hand on someone's bare chest and feel what you did to their heart.

CHAPTER 14

The first read-through was always exciting, everyone looking forward a little nervously to what the coming weeks would bring. Over the rehearsal period they would put aside all their usual gripes and disagreements and bond into a family. Well that was the theory. In reality there was usually the odd flurry of backbiting and bitchiness before everyone pulled together.

But looking round the circle of people in the hall tonight, Jennifer couldn't help feeling that 'odd flurry' should read 'prolonged blizzard'. Angus was being particularly tactless about the fact he'd snaffled the part of the Duke, the part Neale wanted, and Neale was sitting straight-backed with his arms crossed, talking to no one. Lisa had failed to get the seat next to Matt Harper and was leaning across a miffed-looking Jocelyn to try to talk to him. Marjorie was looking daggers at Pamela the leech, because she was busy talking, when Marjorie presumably wanted to explain how important it was not to gabble

Shakespeare. And most of the men were impatient to get started as there was a Newcastle match on the telly.

Matt Harper was simply looking like a sensitive pirate.

'OK,' Finlay said, getting to his feet. 'As I explained at the first meeting, there are many things going on in this play – how people are not always what they seem, and how, sometimes, it is our own desires that make it easier to deceive us. That's particularly true for poor old Malvolio, whom Neale will be playing.' Finlay looked at Neale a little uneasily, 'The poor man's fooled into thinking his mistress loves him and that she wants him to do all kinds of weird things to prove his love for her, which gets him locked up as a madman.'

'Not much of a stretch for you then, Neale,' Angus said, and Finlay hurried on, 'There are all kinds of misunderstandings along the way until it's resolved at the end with Viola and Sebastian reunited, the Duke realising it's Viola whom he really loves and Olivia marrying Sebastian.'

Jocelyn, who was delighted she was playing Olivia, smirked at Matt Harper and Jennifer felt as if she were standing at the wrong end of a telescope, miles away from the centre of things.

'Any questions?' Finlay asked.

'Will we get home for the footie?'

'Absolutely not.' Finlay let rip with a big gust of laughter. 'Not even if there's injury time – with the football, not the rehearsal. Right, one more thing before the warm-up. We have the lovely Jennifer with us tonight.' Jennifer gave a weak smile towards no one in particular. 'She'll be our prompt when you've learned your words, but for now she's helping Lydia and Wendy in the Blue Room with costumes. If you haven't already given Jennifer your measurements, pop in this evening when you can. All right, chairs away, let's get those shoulders rolling.'

Jennifer stayed long enough to see Lisa sprint for a place next to Matt Harper for the warm-up exercises before walking unenthusiastically towards the Blue Room. Measuring and sewing came pretty far down her list of ways to spend her time, possibly only just above listening to Mr Armstrong read soft porn out aloud.

Two women, both with similar grey helmets of hair, were perusing the doublets and breeches, bodices and skirts that were piled on the floor. Lydia, the elder of the two, had sharp features to match the cutting nature of her tongue, and while Wendy standing near her was no retiring violet either, her feistiness was tempered by a tendency to kindness that had become more pronounced since she'd been widowed. The two liked to score points off each other whenever possible and Jennifer feared she would be playing the role of referee.

'We're looking to see what costumes we can recycle,' Lydia said, holding up a dark-blue doublet. 'Got that cast list?'

Wendy was examining a red velvet skirt and flexing the waistband. 'This is going to be too tight for most of the women. Although maybe Jocelyn ...' She peered at Jennifer's list and made a mocking noise. 'Size twelve? She's never size twelve.'

'Might be,' Lydia said, 'it's a long time since you were a size twelve, Wendy.'

'That doublet,' Jennifer asked, quickly taking it from Lydia's hands, 'would it do for Lisa?'

Wendy looked at it. 'Maybe, but we'd need some heavy-duty strapping to keep those breasts of hers under control.'

'Shame you can't strap up her nether regions too,' Lydia snapped, and both Jennifer and Wendy decided almost in unison, to bend down and take a much closer look at the clothes. Club gossip suggested that Lisa had once been discovered snogging Lydia's husband in the costume loft at an after-play party.

Jennifer started matching clothes to actors, conscious of the chatter and laughter coming from the hall and then listening out for individual voices as the cast started to read through the play. She could not discern a trace of West Country burr in the one she was really listening out for.

When the cast started to appear in dribs and drabs, they were either handed costumes and sent to try them on, or stood looking uncomfortable while Jennifer measured them. Out came the old, slightly nervous jokes about warming the end of the tape measure when getting anywhere near an inside leg.

Pamela the leech, being laced into a bodice, was flapping her hands around and complaining that it was too tight and she couldn't breathe properly, something Jennifer thought might be a blessing.

Which was when Matt Harper walked in.

'So, jumper off, I guess,' he said, putting his glasses on the table.

Jennifer watched him pull it off over his head and the tape measure became like a piece of unmanageable rope in her hand.

Deep breath in. Deep breath out.

Underneath the jumper he had on a thick black T-shirt which made his eyes and hair look even darker.

'Thermal,' he said, with a rueful grin, pushing his hair out of his eyes. 'So what do you want first?'

What did she want first, or last or ever? What was she doing standing here with this tape measure in her hand? If she reached up and pushed that stray bit of hair out of his eyes would he mind?

'Chest,' she said and he raised his arms obediently. He was like a little boy – in which case she was having completely inappropriate thoughts about a minor. She took a step nearer and leant in towards him and tried to keep her head down and put her arms around him to position the tape measure without her breasts actually coming into contact with his chest. She could feel the heat coming off him, a slight tang of something citrusy and she wondered what his chest looked like under that T-shirt. There was certainly no flab. She straightened up and read the measurement.

'Puny?' he asked, laughing, and she kept her eyes on the tape and wrote down 97 cm next to his name on her notepad.

'And now?' he said, raising his eyebrows.

'Shoulder to wrist.'

She placed the tape on his shoulder and ran her fingers down it to keep it taut, ending up at his wrist. Every inch of the journey down his skin stirred up something in her she didn't want stirred up.

Go away and leave me alone.

She bent over the notepad again.

'Waist,' she said when she came back, thinking of something else, of the river at home and of the warmth of the kitchen, something baking in the oven. She kept her head down as she put her arms around him again and passed the end of the tape measure from one hand to the other and then pulled it tight. That figure got written down, and as she wrote, the spectre of the next set of measurements she would need hung over her.

He was looking embarrassed, as if his mind had also galloped ahead.

'Ah,' he said, 'bit ... um ... all this, isn't it? Do you want me to do the um ... inside leg ... thing.'

Is it worse to say 'yes' or 'no'?

'Hip measurements too,' Lydia shouted across and Jennifer decided now was the perfect time to do some acting.

'Don't worry,' she said lightly, 'it will take no more than a minute.' She bent and fed the tape around his hips, concentrating on a patch of his T-shirt just above the buckle on his belt. Quite a nice belt really, compared with the jeans. Kind of punky.

Do not look at his groin.

'OK,' she said before whisking the tape measure away from his hips and getting down on her knees.

'If you could just open . . . I mean, stand with your legs wider apart?' She remembered other times and other men, kneeling like this. Of bedroom carpet under her knees.

'Of course, of course,' he said and moved his feet apart and she delicately, delicately, as if his whole groin area was radioactive, measured from the centre seam in his jeans to a point just level with his knee.

She was pretty pleased with how well that had gone until she stood up and splashed back into those brown eyes. He was looking down at her intently and she could not understand what his expression meant. It was there for an instant and then gone.

Lassoing him with the tape measure, pulling him towards me and kissing him would be too forward, would it?

'All finished?' He stepped backwards.

She managed to write down 84 cm for his inside leg measurement and then couldn't remember the figure she'd had in her head for his hips.

After he'd told her his shoe size, making some joke about really needing bigger ones for all his walking, he said thank you, picked up his jumper and left. Wendy had to run after him to give him back his glasses.

'Now Jen,' Lisa said, coming into the room next, 'is there any way, even though I've got to wear bloke's stuff, that you could make it, like, a bit sexier? Maybe show off my arse?'

'No,' Lydia said sharply.

'Jen?' Lisa's tone was plaintive.

'We'll see,' Jennifer mouthed at her, happy to lose herself in thinking about Lisa's body rather than the one she had just had under her hands.

In the pub afterwards, she sat at the large, round table listening to the excited chatter about who had messed up the reading and who had not, and wondered if anyone would be interested in how she'd threaded a needle, pinned a pattern. There was no adrenalin rushing round her body after managing to stitch a seam.

She came back into the conversation as Gerry was bemoaning how badly he'd read his part of Andrew Aguecheek. Steve, who was playing Sir Toby Belch, seemed engrossed in checking his ponytail for split ends, but did break off to say, 'Oh come off it, Gerry, you were great. Particularly the way you read out the stage directions as well.'

Jennifer had always enjoyed this gentle bitchery in the pub, the mix of whispered, almost camp asides and full-on ribbing. No harm was meant, none taken. But you had to be careful with Jocelyn and Neale. One could tear your ego to shreds with a barbed, throwaway verdict, and the other was not above having a hissy fit and stalking off.

Right now though, Neale looked as if he was putting aside his earlier disappointment at not getting the part he wanted. 'I think I can make something of this Malvolio chap,' he confided in Jennifer, and she had the waspish thought that Shakespeare had already made something of it – all Neale had to do was not unmake it.

Laughter rippled round the group as Angus, already on his third pint, his neck and cheeks flushed, pronounced that he felt the Duke and he were very much alike because both of them were 'in love with love'. When Steve flicked his ponytail and said dryly, 'in love with sex, you mean', Angus looked delighted.

Jennifer glanced across at Matt Harper talking by the bar, looking relaxed and slightly dishevelled, and felt the desire to go over to him and stand just close enough to be able to see the extraordinary brownness of his eyes. Instead she watched Lisa make an attempt to corner him before Doug appeared to block her.

Lisa retreated to a seat near Jennifer. 'He's nice, that Matt guy, isn't he? Bit dorky, but I'd still give him one.'

Lisa's conquest of men was such a force of nature, like a wave curling to shore or a squall of wind, that Jennifer was always amused when people judged her. It seemed a pointless waste of time. Lisa's heart was in the right place, however far other bits of her body might roam. Jennifer remembered her coming to visit after the accident, picking her way over the farmyard in her high-heeled shoes and just as expertly navigating a route through Jennifer's misery. There was no patronising; no avoidance. 'That scar's minging, Jen,' she had said, before hugging her and adding, 'but not half as minging as thinking of you being dead.' Other times she had just popped in to sit and witter on about work and who she'd been knocking around with: all the gossip and small talk that represented some much-needed normality when everyone else seemed too afraid of saying the wrong thing.

Jennifer saw Jocelyn circling and agreed with Lisa that, 'Yes, Matt Harper did seem nice.'

Jocelyn pulled up a stool. 'Heard you kicked Alex into touch. Not lining Matt up as a replacement, are you?'

Jennifer heard the message under the words: that such an idea was laughable and felt the usual jumble of embarrassment, shame and anxiety. This trip to the pub was shaping up to be as bad as the last one.

'Bugger off, Jocelyn,' Lisa said, eloquently.

After she'd gone, Lisa said she'd really like to ram Jocelyn's broomstick up her backside, and Jennifer put her hand on her arm and said, 'Jocelyn lashes out at all of us, it's just my turn. Don't get yourself worked up, Lisa, I'm really not upset.'

There it was again: the need to make everyone feel better but herself. Why couldn't she lose her temper, fight back?

Lisa was looking over in Matt Harper's direction again. 'I'd be doing everyone a favour ripping his clothes off, wouldn't I? They're minging. If only Doug would get out of the way. Oh, hang on.' Her mobile was ringing and she went out into the porch to answer it. When she came back she grabbed her jacket off the back of the chair.

'Change of plan,' she said with a grin. 'I'm off. Stewie's just finished his shift. Know what they say, "bird in the hand" and all that. Mind you I always think "two in the bush" sounds more fun.'

Jennifer was trying to work out which of Lisa's boyfriends Stewie was when Doug plopped himself down on Lisa's vacated stool. Matt Harper came and stood behind him, looking self-conscious, and Jennifer was torn between wanting to run and wanting to stand up so she could get nearer to him. She fought the urge to lower her chin, even though she felt exposed to those brown eyes.

'Couldn't help me out, could you, Jen?' Doug said. 'I offered Matt a lift back home, but then remembered I'm meant to be nipping and seeing a bloke about a sundial I'm designing for him. Any chance you could give Matt a lift instead?'

Being alone in a car with Matt suddenly seemed frightening, but then she saw him shift his weight and wince as if his foot was still hurting him.

'Of course,' she said, 'I have to go right past your door.'

Mack could tell that Jennifer was tense and wondered if she was always on edge. Or maybe it was a hangover from the measuring session – she'd certainly been uncomfortable when she'd had to measure his inside leg and it had made him uncomfortable too; made it hard to keep up that irritating brand of Matt Harper cheeriness. The way that she had run her fingers down his arm had particularly unsettled him – not because he found it pleasant, but that he hadn't found it as unpleasant as he had expected. Unlike when she put her face too close to his; then he'd found it really hard not to flinch.

He supposed if he was honest, which was rich coming from him, the thing that had spooked him the most had been the urge to raise her gently back to her feet when she had been on her knees. He had no idea what expression had been in his eyes when she'd got back up.

No point in beating himself up about it; he might be a deceiving git right at this moment, but the impulse to save someone from the discomfort of a hard floor was a natural one.

He let her settle into the drive and as she did, it occurred to him that from this side you could see nothing of her scarring so that the picture he was getting was a kind of 'Before' version. It was a version that would have attracted his attention, no doubt about that. In fact, he'd have probably thought she was out of his league. Those cheekbones really did give her a Scandinavian-princess look.

He stopped staring at her and looked back out of the windscreen at the white lines picked out in the headlights. Stretching his leg, he winced, to play up his ankle injury. He had three miles and that stupid extra bit to break the ice and work her round gently to at least mentioning Cressida. That was as far as he'd push it tonight.

'They're a lovely bunch, aren't they?' he started. 'I really enjoyed myself tonight.'

Apart from during that stupid warm-up when I had to pretend I was moving a pip around in my mouth and letting it slowly grow into a gobstopper and then back to a pip before I spat it out and generally wanted to die of friggin' embarrassment.

'And Finlay's a real character, so inspirational. He's a teacher, isn't he?'

She nodded.

'Did he ever teach you?'

'Yes, and he works his magic on everyone. We had hard nuts in my class who wouldn't even pick up a script because they thought it was "gay". By the time he'd finished with them they were in the end-of-year play with everyone else; captain of the rugby team playing a love scene in a dress, the lot.'

OK, so we're getting somewhere now.

'Doug's great too, isn't he? Can't wait to see one of his sculptures.'

A little nod and a smile.

He persevered, talking about a walk along the Tyne Valley he had planned for later in the week; telling her how he had lost one of his notebooks. He only got the odd nod back. What had happened to that lovely smile she'd given him after his audition?

One thing left to try. Perhaps she was just sick of all this tiptoeing round her and people assuming it was her intelligence that was broken and not her face.

'Sorry you got landed with taking me home,' he said, 'you probably wanted a bit of time on your own. It must be hard watching the rest of us rehearsing when you're not acting any more.'

He wasn't sure if he imagined the intake of breath, but he did not imagine the way the car weaved before she corrected it.

'Yes,' she replied after a silence which was so long he had started to wonder if he had completely stuffed it up, 'it's difficult.'

'I hope you don't mind me saying that, it's just I heard you did a drama course and couldn't finish it.'

She turned her head in his direction and then looked back at the road. 'It's all right, you can say the words "had an accident".'

'Of course, of course. Had an accident.'

She didn't speak again for the rest of the journey, but this time he felt the silence between them was not the chilly barrier it had been earlier, and that possibly she was thinking back through his words and judging him favourably.

When they pulled up outside Brindley Villas he wondered if he should say anything else other than 'Thank you for the lift,' but he never even got those words out because when he looked up from undoing his seat belt it was right into those blue eyes of hers, the perfect one and the one that was clipped by the scar. There was a look of such sadness in them that it stopped him shrugging off the belt and getting out of the car.

Was there nothing anyone could do, about that scarring? Nothing to make it less noticeable? He supposed it would fade in time, perhaps it already had. It was never going to be invisible, though: it had permanently changed the contours of her face, as if plates had shifted under the ground.

He knew that her smile, when it came, was a supreme piece of acting. 'Enjoy your walking and ... thanks for being understanding about me, well, not being very talkative tonight,' she said.

He went straight into the cottage without watching her drive away, heading for the remains of a bottle of Merlot in the kitchen. All his years with Phyllida had taught him that drink wasn't the answer, but he needed something to take the edge off that last scene in the car. A little bit of anaesthetic to stop him thinking that if he'd have been a different kind of man, he would have tried to comfort her in some way.

CHAPTER 15

Jennifer manoeuvred the lamb between her Wellingtons to hold it steady, tipped back its head a little and put the teat of the bottle to its mouth. Immediately it tossed its head, knocking the teat away and so Jennifer gently held its mouth, aimed the bottle again, and this time with a bit of holding and wiggling on her part the lamb got its mouth properly on the teat and started to draw down on the milk. Now it had the idea, it was taking a good feed, and Jennifer knew if she looked behind her she would see its tail wagging wildly.

She yawned. It had been a long night, lying there thinking about Matt Harper, and she had a headache that wasn't helped by the constant high bleating of the sheep. How noisy they were contrasted sharply with her recollection of how quiet she'd been in the car; almost struck dumb by the reality of being alone with Matt Harper and his brown hair and his brown eyes and all those lovely measurements. And he'd tried so hard to talk to her. She could tell he was confused by her frostiness. Why wouldn't he be? He thought he was just having a lift home with Jennifer; a nice lift and a nice chat. He'd have been rocked back on his heels to hear her thoughts: *Stop talking, Matt, let me just enjoy sitting here in the dark with you.*

'I'm going to have to tube-feed that black one on the end,' her dad suddenly said from two pens away. 'He's not getting the hang of the bottle at all.'

It was her who'd been rocked back on her heels in the end though, wasn't it? How did he understand what she felt? He was completely on the button, and he'd been so tactful about the accident.

Off to her left Bryony was treating the umbilical cord of a new lamb with antibiotics. The lamb looked like a stuffed toy in her large hands.

It was funny how Matt Harper's level of understanding was so much better than Alex's, someone who had known her for years. Great, he was sensitive and good-looking and no doubt also kind to small furry animals. Jennifer looked down at the one she was feeding and watched it start to slow its gulping. When the teat came out of its mouth this time she reached down and felt its tiny stomach, now rounded and warm, and lifted it up gently and put it back in with its mother, before picking up another lamb and starting the process all over again.

She wasn't going to dwell on the way she'd looked at Matt Harper before he got out of the car; felt flustered even now thinking about it. Like some lovesick cow who had the urge to say, 'I'm in pain here, so just for a second, if you don't find it too off-putting, please wrap your arms round me.'

'You look a bit peaky,' Bryony said, wiping her hands, now free of lamb, down her overalls. 'Not sleep very well?'

'No, no, I'm fine.'

Jennifer did some more smiling and Bryony was either convinced or decided to back off. She looked at her watch.

'Anything you want me to see to before I go, Ray?'

'No, pet,' drifted back over the pens.

'Off for a sleep?' Jennifer asked.

'Yes, just waiting for your mum to come back with Louise.'

'Where's Danny?'

'Putting some lambs back out. Top field.'

Ray ambled to join them. 'You do look a bit pale, Jen. I can carry on with that if you want to go back and have a bit more of a lie-in.'

'I'm fine, Dad, honestly.' She didn't need more solitary time in which to think. 'I'll just go and mix up some more milk. Where did you say Mum's gone?'

'Just to—'

'Buy some bacon,' Bryony cut in.

'Aye, bacon, that's it,' Ray agreed. 'That's it. Bacon.'

Mack emerged from Sonia's shop with a lot more than his groceries. As he'd suspected, Sonia had proved to be a fount of gossip. He'd had a lucky break when he'd found her and her cleavage leaning on the counter reading a magazine in which Cressida was modelling several thousand pounds' worth of jewellery and couture. How flab-bergasted he was at the news that she was Jennifer's cousin and as his reward got a bucketload of information, including some tasty stuff about Alex Lambton, one of Jennifer's old boyfriends from school.

Now he knew how rich Alex was because his family owned, rather than rented, a huge farm further north; that the Lambton sheep had as good a reputation as the Rosebys' and that although Jennifer had kicked Alex into touch when he went off to agricultural college, people suspected he would marry her on the spot if she said yes. Sonia didn't think that was likely as a little bird had told her (tap of the nose) that Jennifer had recently made it clear she saw Alex only as a friend, which would have annoyed Brenda Roseby, who had always looked favourably on him.

As Sonia had worked through Mack's shopping list, she'd also confirmed O'Dowd's version of the accident. Local people, evidently, knew Cressida had been in the car, even if the public at large didn't, and they suspected drink was involved, although Jennifer had been too badly hurt to be breathalysed. Sonia was of the opinion that it didn't matter if it had been Jennifer's fault, she was the one who'd suffered.

Mack had tried not to listen to the next bit about how Jennifer had fallen apart completely after coming out of hospital. How she wouldn't eat properly, couldn't sleep, had to be persuaded to let friends visit. By the end of it the pained expression on his face was genuine.

A phone call had halted Sonia's flow, and Mack had heard her, beyond the beaded curtain, talking and giggling with someone called 'Gregor'. They seemed to be arranging a date in Tyneforth. Mack presumed it was the foreign hunk he'd seen before and the flushed look on Sonia's face when she returned seemed to confirm that.

'Appreciate you coming in here for your stuff,' she'd said as she packed his groceries. 'You could get the supermarket to deliver. A lot do.'

'Oh no,' he'd replied, 'I like to support the local community.'

And the supermarkets are rubbish at providing this standard of gossip.

As he knew she would, she came out of the shop after he'd left to slip his glasses back into the pocket of his fleece.

'You're hopeless. Does your girlfriend normally have to look after you like this? I bet she does. I bet she makes sure your mittens are on an 'ickle string round your neck.'

'Oh dear,' he said, grinning in a boyish way. 'I think my secret's out.'

Back in the cottage, he was cosying a packet of rice up to a tin of tomatoes in one of the crappy cupboards when the doorbell rang.

The woman on the doorstep was Jennifer's mother; he could see that straightaway. She had the same high cheekbones and good posture and a kind of haughtiness that made him think of a duchess. Her eyes were the same blue as Jennifer's too, but whereas Jennifer's were often cast down, these eyes had locked on to his.

'Morning,' she said sharply and he knew that whatever was coming was a test. He had to remember that good old Matt Harper had nothing to hide, so he'd probably be a bit confused by her visit.

'Um, hello,' he said, 'can I help you?'

'I'm Brenda Roseby, Jennifer's mother.'

'Jennifer's mother? Jennifer from the Drama Club? Well, I'm really pleased to meet you.' He smiled and held out his hand, and she grasped hold of it firmly, gave it one shake and then let go.

'Jennifer's been very welcoming,' he said, 'the whole Drama Club has, and it's very nice of you to come and introduce yourself.'

'You're a writer?'

He did some rapid blinking. 'Just a little book on Dorset coastal walks—'

'And one on North Somerset. Yes, I know. Found them a bit dry to be honest.'

Whoa . . . you've actually bought them?

'Dry? You think so?'

Her face was merciless. 'Mind you, I'm not fond of writers. We had some other people calling themselves writers here before – in the village, outside our farm. Journalists.'

'I don't quite understand—'

'Really?' she said, with an unpleasant laugh. 'I've just

seen you come out of the shop. Sonia must have filled you in on who my niece is?'

'Well . . .'

'Likes to chat, does Sonia.' There was a hint of lemon there before she added, 'Although to be fair to her, she's pretty tight-lipped with journalists.'

Mack kept his face absolutely gormless-looking. 'Yes, she did mention it, but to be honest, I don't take much interest in these things.'

'So you're not that kind of writer, then?' Those blue eyes gave him a sharp look to match the tone.

Yuk. Direct question. Calls for a direct lie.

'No, wouldn't know where to start.'

'Actually, the problem is they don't know where to stop.'

He could tell she wasn't finished with him and watched her fold her arms.

'So, you're going to be in the play? Bit strange, isn't it? Only here for a while and want to join in? You don't know anyone.'

'It's because I don't know anyone I like to join in.' He was pleased how neatly he'd turned that around. 'It's a lonely business, writing.'

She studied him and then pointed towards Mr Armstrong's door. 'I deliver lunch here. Meals on Wheels, kind of thing.' The blue eyes seemed harder. 'I'm here twice a week. Every week.'

And you'll be keeping an eye on me. Nice warning.

After a few more questions about where he was planning to walk next she said goodbye and went back down the path to an old green Fiat parked at the kerb. When she opened the door, he could see that there was a baby strapped in the car seat and presumed it was her grandchild. Just then he couldn't remember if Jennifer's brother had a daughter or a son.

Back inside, he sat down on the arm of the chair, misjudging it and nearly ending up on his backside on the carpet. He had no idea if he'd passed the test, not a clue, but he understood perfectly well that she didn't trust him and didn't like him. Was that because of the journalists or some other, more personal reason? She was protective of Jennifer, no mistaking that.

He sat down properly in the chair and stared into the fire. He couldn't imagine Phyllida ever looking after him like that. Whenever he'd been picked on she'd just told him to 'toughen up'.

The bell rang again and his heart went into overdrive. He didn't know if he could withstand another bout of questioning.

It was Mr Armstrong.

'Cup of tea?' he said in a gruff voice.

Mack was about to say that really he was a bit busy, thank you all the same, when Mr Armstrong took a step forward and he understood that the old man was inviting himself in. He stepped aside to let him pass.

'See you've had that Jennifer's mother here,' Mr Armstrong said as he shuffled in. 'Dreadful business with her niece going to America – Sodom and Gomorrah, it is there. And that Sonia over the shop,' there was a sound of air being drawn in rapidly, 'she's bought that latest husband of hers off the Internet, you know, some foreign boy. How her father stands it I don't know, carrying on right under his nose.'

Mack followed Mr Armstrong into the house and shut the door. 'Really, that's fascinating, you must tell me more. Come and have a sit-down. Fancy a bit of toast with that cup of tea?'

CHAPTER 16

A week into rehearsals and Mack knew that, were Shakespeare still around, he would have jabbed him repeatedly with his quill. Instead of developing some kind of on-stage chemistry with Jocelyn, who was meant to be playing the love of his life, he wanted to slap her soundly. The more he saw of her the less he liked her, particularly the way she stuck the knife into Jennifer. Which was pretty rich, seeing what he was planning to do to her, but it irritated the Hell out of him. Jennifer's response was invariably to walk away, but from the set of her shoulders and that chin going down, he could see that each little snide remark hit home.

Shakespeare would also have been discomforted at the amount of on-stage chemistry that *was* present between brother and sister, Sebastian and Viola. Mack was pretty disturbed by it himself – not least because if he didn't make it clear to Lisa that he wasn't interested, she was going to keep on acting like a lovely pneumatic wall stopping Jennifer coming anywhere near him.

Those were just two of the things he hated about the play. Others included: the number of references to people not being what they seemed, the stupid costume he was going to have to wear, the fact he had to be in it at all and the almighty fiasco it looked like becoming. Doug kept crashing into him whenever he tried to read his lines and move at the same time, Neale was playing Malvolio as if he was some kind of international terrorist and Steve and Gerry had taken the message that they were the source of a lot of comedy in the play as an excuse to turn into Ant and Dec.

Right now he was watching Viola wooing Olivia on behalf of the Duke, and it was painful. Lisa was striding around and slapping her thigh like a principal boy in panto and Jocelyn was coming across as a woman on heat rather than a dignified lady. And if Pamela the leech, who was meant to be Olivia's witty maid, didn't stop screeching and flapping her arms around, the audience was going to think she was a hyperventilating seagull.

Little wonder Finlay was doing a lot of placing his hands on the top of his head and swaying. Did this club have to pay the audience to come and see them?

Mack looked across to the Blue Room, where Jennifer was kneeling on the floor cutting a pattern out of some material with a large pair of scissors. Her blonde hair had fallen forward and he was beginning to think of it as a shiny blonde shield. She was wearing a skirt today, which was now spread out around her like pale, powder-blue water, and he wondered idly whether she was in danger of cutting through it when she cut out the pattern. She straightened up suddenly and her hair swung back and as always the sight of the scarring made him feel uneasy. He screwed his eyes up a little and tried to imagine what she had looked like without it.

Doug was giving him a quizzical look when he opened his eyes properly again. That was the trouble: while he was watching Jennifer, there was always someone watching him: her mother, the people in the library, Doug. All those people looking out for her and only him looking out for his entire family.

'Right-ho,' Finlay said, 'Doug and Matt, let's have another go at Act Three, scene three, where Antonio and Sebastian take leave of each other.'

Instead of my senses.

Doug lumbered to his feet and gave him a thumbs-up as the door to the hall opened, and a tall, tanned guy walked in. Doug did something funny with his face and Mack saw Jennifer stand up quickly and smooth down her skirt.

'Hello, Alex,' Neale said, 'looking for Jennifer? She's in the Blue Room.'

Ah, the famous Alex Lambton, the one who's carrying a torch for Jennifer.

Alex said hello to various people as he passed through the hall and seemed to make a big show of talking to Finlay and apologising for disrupting the rehearsal. Mack could see Jennifer through the open door, stooping to pick up the bolt of material and the pieces she had cut from it and then placing it all on the table. Then she moved the bolt of material off the table and leaned it against the wall. She fiddled about with the scissors, first placing them on the pieces of material and then directly on the table.

You're feeling cornered in that little room.

Mack heard Finlay say, 'Matt, if you would . . .' and went and stood on his opening mark and saw the door of the Blue Room close behind Alex. Damn, he'd made spectacularly little progress with Jennifer since that car journey; he got the impression that she was avoiding him. If she did talk it was either with her chin firmly down or turned away, so that the perfect side of her face was all he saw. He could almost feel her embarrassment like a fence around her.

Now this Alex had put the kibosh on getting any further this evening.

Pressed up against the bar in the pub later, Mack's original impression that Jennifer felt cornered hadn't wavered. She was looking marooned at one end of the large table with this Alex, his back to the rest of the group, effectively blocking her off. Which confirmed Mack's other impression: Alex didn't really care much for the Drama Club, and all that bonhomie in the hall earlier had been false. And Mack knew false when he saw it.

All in all, this Alex was a bit of a stuffed shirt . . . although the guy deserved some points – from Sonia's information it seemed as if the accident hadn't changed Jennifer in his eyes.

Mack decided not to think about what he would have done in the same circumstances and worried instead about the more pressing problem of Lisa. Literally pressing – she had him right up against the bar, and although Doug seemed to be giving her his full repertoire of filthy looks, she wasn't taking the hint. He was therefore relieved when he saw Alex get up and come towards him, causing Lisa to back off a little.

Within seconds, the guy's superior attitude had got right up his nose. He was showing off in front of Jennifer, who had come to join him, and Mack understood pretty quickly that it was at his expense. He had to play this straight down the line – to be pleasant and naive. To be Matt Harper.

'Jennifer and I go back a long way,' Alex said when hands had been shaken and Mack saw Jennifer's lips do a little twitch.

Next Alex assumed a cod West-Country accent to say, 'Hear you're from Bristol, down in Yokel Land.'

You prick.

Matt Harper nodded amicably.

'Fancy yourself as a bit of an actor, do you, then?'

'Well, I—'

'Used to do some myself. Too busy now, of course. Leave it to those who've got more time.'

And talent.

'Like to keep up with what's going on, though. In fact, Jennifer and I have just decided to go to a play on the Quayside next week.'

Mack noticed the way Jennifer was holding her glass and wondered if it was Alex who had really decided about the play.

'That's nice for you both,' he said.

There was a patronising smile. 'Yes, it will be. So ... the Derrick family, know them in Brizzel?'

Ooh, comedy rendition of Bristol, there's no end to your talents.

'I don't think I do,' he said, looking as though he was thinking, 'but that's not surprising, it's quite a large city.'

'But they're a big name down there. Important family.'

Thanks for the put-down.

'In farming, Alex,' Jennifer said, pushing forward. 'Remember, Matt Harper isn't a farmer, he's a writer.'

Alex had a supercilious look on his face, 'Of course, a writer, not a farmer. Don't like getting your hands dirty, I suppose?'

Matt Harper merely smiled in an apologetic way, but Mack Stone thought: *You have no bloody idea how dirty my hands are, mate. Even if you spent all day with yours halfway up a cow's backside, they still wouldn't be as dirty as mine.*

This time it was a rooster on the back seat that had almost made Jennifer drive off the road on the way back from the pub. She cursed Danny gently for messing with her ringtones again, before trying to ignore it. When the rooster would not shut up, she bumped back on to the grass verge by the side of the road and turned off the engine. Anyone watching her erratic progress was going to think she was doing some kind of Northumberland kerb-crawl, although as she was on a country lane with fields both sides, the only thing she was likely to pick up was a sheep. Well, that wasn't unheard of.

Soon she was giggling away at Cress's saga about a photo opportunity the studio had set up with Rory Sylvester and his wife prior to the start of filming.

'. . . we pitched up at this hip restaurant in Santa Fe, paps all outside, of course, because they'd been told we were coming, and we had to make it look as though we were completely surprised and really we always go out for pally meals.'

'Food good?'

'I had a yummy selection of salad greens with the tiniest sliver of tuna. Lucky there wasn't a draught or the whole meal would have blown away. Rory had a steak and Anna Maria had something with a lot of chilli peppers in it. She very kindly gave me some to taste. Yup, she wouldn't take no for an answer.'

Jennifer was building up a good picture of Rory Sylvester's wife.

'We all got on like a house on fire. Anna Maria has thoughtfully requested that some of the love scenes between Rory and I are rewritten before we start shooting next week – she feels they may be too "full on" for me.'

Jennifer burst out laughing.

'Rory agreed, of course, in fact when Anna Maria went to the bathroom he said that films these days had become too explicit. His exact words were, "Why splash these things around for everyone to see, we all know what's going to happen when there's chemistry between a man and woman." Don't you think that's nice?'

'Not the splashing bit. And . . . did you let him have a nibble of your pudding?'

'No, but he really wanted some. I, however, kept thinking of that museum in Venice.'

Jennifer remembered the chastity belt she and Cress had gawped at in its glass case. However hot Rory was for her, Cress was not, it appeared, having any of it.

Jennifer looked out at the darkness and wondered when Cress would work around to asking her about Matt Harper and what she would say in reply. Matt Harper? Why couldn't she just call him Matt? She said the name to herself and felt it was too intimate. Had she somehow become a virgin again in the accident?

'Hmm, now, what rhymes with Cat, Hat and Bat?' Cressida said innocently, and Jennifer could only laugh.

'That's dreadful, Cress. Blatant hinting. And really . . . there's nothing to tell.'

'Nothing?'

'Well, I gave him a lift home one evening. He seemed to understand exactly how I felt seeing people acting when I'm not. Sympathetic without being patronising.' She didn't mention that she'd avoided giving him a lift since, had engineered it so she left rehearsals before he did.

'Well that's good, isn't it? Jen? Come on, talk to me. Have you got to the stage where you're imaging him naked yet?'

I haven't even got to the stage where I can call him by his first name.

'Look, Cress,' she said, desperate to make herself understood, 'I know I promised to see where this led, but it's pointless. Remember when I had that counselling and they said that there's sometimes a period where your mind lags behind what's happened to your body? Well this is just an aspect of that – I'm still fancying men like Matt Harper because that's who I used to fancy. But why would he choose to go out with me? All he's going to get is people looking at him and thinking poor—'

'Jennifer Elizabeth Roseby,' Cressida shouted so loudly it actually hurt Jennifer's ear. She stopped talking and swallowed repeatedly to try and get back in control.

As Jennifer struggled she heard Cress say, away from the phone, 'No, I'm not coming. Family crisis. I don't care; I'll be there when I'm ready.'

'You have to go, Cress,' Jen said wiping her eyes with her free hand.

'I do not have to go. I've had to wait around for some people who shall remain nameless to get their lines out properly, now they can wait for me.' There was the sound of a door slamming before the less ballsy Cressida said, 'Jen, you won't believe me when I tell you this, but you're incredibly beautiful.'

'Half of me is,' she said before starting to sob.

'All of you is, Jen. And all that grace you've got . . . it's what made you special on the stage; it's what makes you special in life. All that's still there.'

After that Cress just made little 'there there' noises down the phone until Jennifer had stabilised again. 'Please listen to me, sweetie,' Cress said eventually, 'have I ever given you flannel about people not judging others by the way they look? No. Have I ever denied that when people first meet you they get distracted by that scarring? No again. But this Matt has had time to get to know you. Which means you're way ahead of the pack, should that girlfriend fall by the wayside. If he can't see how great you are, maybe he should take off his sodding pirate's eyepatch.'

Jennifer tried to butt in, but Cress was on a roll. 'What you're doing now is second-guessing how he might feel and being insulting to him and to you, and I won't let you be sad about a rejection you haven't had yet. Tell all those fears I can hear gnawing away at you to bog off.'

Jennifer did laugh at that and then stopped abruptly when Cressida said, sounding a little wavery, 'If you don't, Jen, how do you think that makes me feel? I've had to sit by and watch you hide, Jen; say nothing while you push people away, like those uni friends. I can't let you do this with Matt. Not when I'm the one who—'

'Cressida,' Jennifer said, sharply, and there was silence; just two women either side of the Atlantic clutching at their mobile phones.

'Bloody Hell,' Cress said eventually, 'you're a worse drama queen than me.'

'Crybaby,' Jennifer retaliated.

'Wet blanket.'

'Trollop.'

Hysteria set in not long after that, neither of them sure

if crying or laughing was the thing they were doing. By the time Jennifer ended the call she felt her stomach muscles aching.

All right, Cress. I will focus on the now and not the future.

She drove home with the window down, only guilt at not telling Cress about accepting Alex's invitation to the theatre marring her improving mood. She really wished she could replay that scene in the Blue Room. Alex was so crafty, saying he knew they'd only be going 'as friends'. It had left her no wriggle room: if she'd refused to go, it would have made it sound as if they weren't even friends any more. How could she do that after he'd stood by her from day one?

She reached Brindley and forced herself not to glance towards No. 3 Brindley Villas, but as she got to the end of the village there was Matt Harper standing on Peter Clarke's bench, his mobile to his ear. Seeing him so soon after talking and thinking about him made her fist press on the accelerator and then hit the brake. He looked startled and lowered the phone, and she felt she had to do something, so wound down the window.

'Are you all right? You look frozen,' she called to him.

'Just talking to my girlfriend.'

'Of course, forgot the village is a blind spot for phone reception. They're meant to be sorting it out. It's OK again by the time you get along our track.' She fluffed winding up the window, but apart from that made a clean getaway and refused to look in the rear-view mirror until she knew he was out of sight.

Back at Peter Clarke's bench, she would have been confused to hear the voice on the other end of the phone say, 'Girlfriend, am I now, my son? And there was me thinking you were *my* bitch.'

CHAPTER 17

Mack was beginning to feel that as much as he had always hated the ribbed glass in his mother's front door, having it installed in No. 3 Brindley Villas would be a good idea. At least then every time his doorbell rang his heart wouldn't jump and swoop until he opened the door and found it wasn't Brenda on the other side.

This time it was Doug – a rather embarrassed-looking Doug.

'I've been crap at every rehearsal,' he said, 'and I wondered if you could help me oot a bit. Finlay only has to tell you what to do once and you do it. Me, I canna get me head around it. Don't suppose you're free today?'

'Well, I was thinking of doing a walk over the moors and down into Blanchland.'

Thinking about it, but not intending to rush out and do it. Not after that walk yesterday where I stood in a bog. And that was the best bit. The only reason I'm doing any walking at all is because some stupid bugger in the cast always wants to chat about where I've been.

'I'd be really grateful,' Doug said, his eyebrows jiggling about. 'I'll make you yer tea.'

When Mack agreed, Doug said, 'Gan on then, marra, get your script.' He peered over Mack's shoulder into the cottage and wrinkled his nose. 'We'll go to mine. Does it always smell like this, or is that you?'

'Why did you call me a marrow?' Mack asked when they were driving away.

'Daft shite. Marra . . . friend . . . did they teach ye nae English at school?'

They drove past the end of the track leading to Jennifer's farm and took the narrow, metal bridge over the river at little more than walking pace before climbing steeply and then levelling out on a meandering road flanked by a low dry-stone wall. After about a mile there was a humped-back bridge over a stream, a sharp right turn and then they were heading down a bumpy lane, trees on either side. The trees gave way to grass and the stream to a pond, and Mack could see that what he had first taken to be discarded machinery were various sculptures – here a great bird, wings caught at the moment of lift-off, there a bunch of sunflowers, faces up to the sky. Doug pulled over near a two-storey stone house. Some way behind it was a large outhouse, also in stone, with double doors at the front flung wide open. It could have been a normal barn, but for the chimney up one side. There was a steady thump-thump of heavy-metal music and a different kind of thump, of metal against metal.

'You have staff?' Mack said, looking towards what he took to be the forge.

'I call them "my lads",' Doug replied, his cheeks flushing red, 'come on, come and have a look.'

Mack supposed that one day he'd find out what Hell was like, but Doug's forge was a little foretaste. It seemed to be one hot, noisy, sulphurous-smelling place, and the smallest of Doug's lads, dressed in leather apron and goggles, looked particularly demonic.

'Hoy, turn it down a minute,' Doug shouted and the music died away.

Doug gave him a quick tour. 'Gas forge, coke forge, shearing machine, pillar drill, power hammer, oh, and anvil, of course.' Mack stood and watched one of the lads take a bar of metal, glowing orange at one end, from the coke forge, and tap it to get the crust off. He began beating it with a hammer, moving it around as he did so. For something so judderingly noisy, it was almost hypnotic.

'It's more about rhythm than strength,' Doug shouted.

'I thought there'd be more sparks flying about,' Mack shouted back and the expressions told him he'd said something daft.

'Where you see sparks, it's just been set up for the cameras,' one of the lads said, his face grubby and sweaty. 'If you've got sparks, it's starting to burn.'

'Be all pitted,' Doug agreed.

'OK, I see. And what's that over there?' Mack pointed to what looked like a big tank of water.

'It's a big tank of water,' they said in unison and laughed at him.

Looking around at the heavy machinery, feeling the

heat and the noise, looking at the muscles on the lads, it all seemed like a very macho environment. Yet Doug produced these beautiful sculptures. Mack watched one of the lads take infinite care to create a twisted flower, heating up tiny wires in the forge for stamens.

'We do the heavy stuff too,' Doug explained as they emerged back into the welcome cool air outside, 'but I really like all the experimenting that goes into the complex stuff, trying different ways to get something to work. Right, fancy a beer?'

In Doug's kitchen with its huge flagstones and sparse, solid furniture, they practised a couple of their scenes and Mack did what he could to slow down Doug's delivery and get him to breathe in the right places. He felt a surprising amount of satisfaction when little by little a line that had been incomprehensible suddenly fell clearly from Doug's lips. He would have preferred it if Doug had not been speaking the line 'But come what may, I do adore thee so', just as one of the lads came into the kitchen.

'Don't worry about that,' Doug said when the lad went back out. 'He's into bloody line dancing; he's not got a leg to stand on.'

After another hour spent working on their movements, Doug clapped his hands together. 'Time for a barbecue.'

'Do you do it in the forge, somehow? All that fire and heat?'

Doug stared at him in a way which told Mack that what he had just said was akin to suggesting Doug had sex with his own mother. He suddenly had a sense of how powerful Doug was.

Doug looked away from him as though that was the only way to calm down before saying, 'Nah, we're gannin' up the beach.'

'Up the beach! But it won't be light much longer. And . . . isn't it too cold?' Mack flapped.

'Get away,' Doug said, his good mood returning, 'perfect conditions today.'

Short of clinging on to the table leg and refusing to budge, Mack had no choice but to get in the car. On the journey, he tried not to look as if he was sulking. To get some kind of silver lining out of the situation, he dropped into the conversation that he'd really like to have a look around Jennifer's farm, but felt it was a bit pushy to ask. Doug called him a 'daft shite' again, and Mack knew that at some point Doug would now ask Jennifer for him.

By the time they got to the beach, the light was going and there was a gusting wind, but Doug enthusiastically loaded Mack up with blankets and hefted a great carrier bag and a windbreak into his own arms before leading the way over the massive sand dunes to the beach. It felt like a real trek before they got to the wide, firm sweep of sand, the breakers just visible rolling into the shore and a faint taste of salt in Mack's mouth.

Why should I sit on a frigging cold beach to eat my tea when I could sit in a house in the warm? With a table?

As soon as the windbreak was up, Mack stationed himself

inside it and wrapped himself in most of the blankets. Doug seemed unbothered by the cold, keeping up a running commentary as he set up two barbecue trays and got them alight. 'Over there is Lindisfarne. Now and then people get the tides wrong. Have to be rescued by helicopter.'

Mack made a note of that; just what he needed, to be on the local news dangling from a harness.

'And further round's where Grace Darling rowed out to rescue them sailors from a shipwreck. Her and her dad.' Mack thought about that story and knew he wouldn't have had the guts to do what she did in the face of a storm. No, he'd have been the guy interviewing the survivors, asking them how they felt seeing their fellow sailors smashed against the rocks.

As the darkness and the tide came in, Mack sensed that Doug was getting increasingly jumpy. It was there in the way he kept shifting position, first sitting on his backside and then his knees, and in the many reports he gave on the progress of the charcoal in the barbecues.

'Are you all right, Doug?' he asked at last.

It was as if he had removed a blockage.

Doug shook his head. 'Often come up here when I get really frustrated, you know, about Pat.'

'The postwoman?'

'Aye.' Doug's open clown's face looked misshapenly long in the flames licking at the barbecue charcoal. 'You saw her in the pub that night, after the auditions. I've fancied her for ages, but whenever she comes near me it's like

I've got an allergy: spasms, falling into things, over things; cannna speak properly.'

Mack waited and counted the waves coming in. One, two, three.

'Well, when I say I fancy her, it's more than that,' Doug stumbled on. 'I think I love her.'

'Love her? For how long?' Mack felt more stupid asking that than when he'd been reciting Shakespeare.

'A couple of years. Nae one else knows but Jen.'

Figures. It would be Jen.

'You haven't told Pat?'

'Nah,' Doug shot back, 'divvn't be daft. She's way oot of my league.'

Mack listened to the waves again, choosing his words. 'Why, Doug? I mean no disrespect to postmen . . . women . . . people, but why is she out of your league?'

'Doctor's daughter, went to uni. Was married to a doctor too. She's divorced now, just does this job to get her oot and aboot. What would she want with me? I barely finished school. She'd think I was after her money.'

Mack didn't get the opportunity to tell Doug he was looking at this all wrong, because Doug suddenly sprang to his feet.

'When it all gets a bit much,' he said, 'I come up here and I get myself in the sea and it numbs me a bit, takes me mind off it.'

'Get yourself in the sea?' Mack yelped as Doug started to root about in the large bag. Something was thrown in his lap. It was a light on an elasticated headband, the kind he'd seen potholers wear. 'Get in the sea, in the dark. In the sea. The North Sea. In the winter?'

'Not much difference between summer and winter,' Doug said stripping off his clothes. 'Just gan in as far as you can, stay in as long as you can. When you come out, the barbecues will be ready for the burgers.' Doug was down to his underpants and, as they came off, he fitted the torch round his head and switched the beam on before turning and running towards the sea.

Mack scrabbled for his own torch and switched on the beam and watched this large, chunky, lovesick guy wobble towards the waves.

'He's got to be bloody joking,' he said out loud, but Doug's entry into the sea suggested he wasn't. Mack stood up and saw Doug's wobbling buttocks cresting a wave.

'You don't actually swim?' he shouted after Doug, now only able to pinpoint where he was because of the big guy's torch beam.

A faint 'Canna swim' drifted back.

'Oh, bloody Hell,' Mack said and started tearing his clothes off too.

Mack wasn't sure how long they were in the water, but when he was very much afraid that his penis had shrivelled up and fallen off and he had bitten his tongue with the violence of his teeth chattering, he had to agree with Doug that it was a brilliant way to take your mind off everything. He'd once got his fingers stuck to an ice-cube tray and the sensation he felt in the water had been similar. Except more all-enveloping.

With his clothes back on and wrapped in a blanket, his mouth full of beautifully burned burger, he worried about what was happening to him. He wanted to keep Doug's secret for him, for a friend. Correction, for a marra. He took another bite of his burger and listened to the wave's steady rhythm behind him, wishing he could stay on this beach forever feeling trusted, life and warmth slowly returning to his extremities.

CHAPTER 18

Finlay poked his head round the door of the Blue Room, where Jennifer was trying to mediate in a heated discussion between Lydia and Wendy about whether gold braid for the dark-blue doublet would or would not make Lisa look like a camp majorette.

'I couldn't borrow you for a few minutes, could I?' he asked. 'Wendy, Lydia, could I borrow Jennifer? I need her to work her magic.'

Jennifer hoped the magic she was being asked to perform involved a dorkish pirate, but it was Gerry, Steve and Pamela whom Finlay was steering her towards.

'They're trying their best, but not really pulling together as a team,' Finlay said quietly. 'No one is going to believe they're thick as thieves and plotting to trick Malvolio.'

Jennifer had some sympathy with the three stooges who were now facing her. This period of rehearsal was always difficult, people trying to remember where to move, but still needing the odd check of their scripts. She looked across to where Doug and Matt were working on a scene together, and was surprised to see how well they were moving and speaking. She felt slightly cheated of that rueful smile Matt Harper had worn whenever Doug crashed into him. Never mind, that new smile, almost as if he were proud of Doug, was doing just as good a job of sending little scurries of excitement across her chest. This evening perhaps she should act on Cressida's lecture and talk to him rather than run.

'OK,' she said, 'Steve, do you want to go from that bit about the letters you're going to drop on purpose for Malvolio to pick up? Start with Sir Toby Belch's line.'

Steve stood for a few seconds, obviously building up to it, before saying to no one in particular: 'Excellent! I smell a device.'

There was a long pause, then, 'I have't in my nose too.' Gerry made a big show of touching his nose, but not looking at the others at all.

Another long pause before Steve rushed at, 'He shall think by the letters that thou wilt drop, that they come from my niece and that she's in love with him.'

They all waited and Pamela suddenly screeched, 'Oh, it's me isn't it? Sorry. I was thinking it was Gerry again, but no, it's me. Now . . . ah yes, here we are . . . "My purpose is, indeed, a house of that colour."' Pamela beamed at them.

'Not house, you daft bint,' Steve said, 'it's horse.'

'Well, there's no need to be so rude,' Pamela huffed at him. 'At least I just forgot it was my go, I didn't keep everyone waiting for my line on purpose. And at least my eyes weren't all over the place when I spoke them.' She looked at Gerry.

Jennifer raised her hand to cut off any response and wondered what to do with these two lumps of wood and the speak-your-weight machine.

She set them some exercises. Pamela shrieked her way through the first one, where she had to fall backwards and trust the others were going to catch her. At one point it looked like Steve was contemplating a nasty case of 'butterfingers'. Then they'd taken it in turns to think of an emotion, arrange their body and expressions to convey it and see if the others could guess what it was. Steve had got most of the ones right that Gerry acted out, which was something of a miracle as Gerry's way of conveying everything from sorrow to anger looked as if he was having a particularly difficult poo.

Slowly, slowly they started to tune into each other's body language and pick up on cues. Jennifer felt her shoulders relax, her neck feel less tense. A little victory. She hoped Matt Harper had been watching closely.

Her feeling of elation didn't survive Jocelyn sauntering past and saying, 'Teaching them how to make funny faces, Jen?'

She should have just caught hold of Jocelyn at that point and asked her exactly what her problem was, but she was too busy panicking that Steve had heard and his obvious shock would blossom into anger that would engulf them all in embarrassment. She could see Finlay frowning and moving his head, as if trying, from the other side of the hall, to work out what had happened. More distressing was the knowledge that Matt Harper, wandering past to fetch his script, had heard the comment too.

She retreated to the Blue Room, seeking sanctuary and calmed her breathing enough so that Wendy and Lydia, immersed in a squall about the correct use of Velcro, would not notice her agitation. Uncanny how Jocelyn had the ability to say the things that wounded the most. No consolation that her vitriol was the juice of sour grapes: Jocelyn knew that if Jennifer chose to step on a stage again, she herself would be acted right off it.

Jennifer understood she was not alone in suffering the sharp side of Jocelyn's nature; that Jocelyn's father had been a vile bully and sarcasm had been Jocelyn's only defence. She should feel sorry for a woman who eventually alienated all but the most hardy. She kept telling herself that and was sick of hearing it.

When Wendy and Lydia packed up to go home, Jennifer said she'd stay a while, finding comfort in the steady rhythm of needle through material. It was even more comforting if she imagined the material was Jocelyn's backside.

Another few minutes and she would pack up too. The urge to talk to Matt, or just sit near him in the pub, gone. She was too distracted, fighting away this horrible mix of inky-black shame.

When the door opened and Matt walked in she couldn't look at him and hoped he would be quick and go. She kept on sewing and breathing. Her face felt as if it was burning.

She heard him put his rucksack on the table and something else that crinkled. She glanced up. A Primark carrier bag.

He had wandered over to the rail of costumes and was looking at his brown doublet.

'This is coming along marvellously,' he said, and she said, 'Mmm.'

She heard the sound of the coat hanger and presumed he had taken the doublet down from the rail and was perhaps trying it against his body. She couldn't stop herself from looking.

Oh God, you look gorgeous, all dark and dishevelled. Just go, will you?

'I've come straight from Newcastle today,' he said. 'I really liked it. Very vibrant.'

She caught the forced brightness in his voice and knew he was trying to cheer her up.

I don't want you to feel sorry for me. I want you to feel . . . attraction, lust . . . oh, I don't know, just not bloody sorry.

All Mack could think to do when faced with Jennifer's obvious misery, was to go and try the doublet against his body. He looked down at it. Yup, that was going to make him look exactly like the turd he was.

Well, Plan A was in tatters, thanks to Jocelyn. Getting a lift home, all his pre-rehearsed patter about his family, which was going to lead nicely to Jennifer talking about hers, blown out of the water.

Just the way she was stabbing her needle into that material told him that. It was a shame it was the only place she could think to put all that emotion: Jocelyn's backside would have been better. He'd have helped her.

He probably shouldn't have come into the room at all, he felt as if he was intruding. He'd do better going out again.

Then he thought of Fran in the playground, the other children jeering at her. A bewildered Gabi having to move to another city.

He picked out a suitably hearty tone and told her where he'd been today and how much he'd liked it, he left out the bit about meeting up with the Third Party again and wanting to vomit when he'd pressed some more of Tess's post into his hand.

He chanced sitting down next to her and watched her needlework become less ferocious. Perhaps Plan A wasn't dead.

'I got my nieces some presents in Newcastle,' he said, 'couple of furry animals to add to the pile they've already got.'

'In Primark?' she asked.

'No, that's just a sweatshirt for me.' He was certain he saw her mouth twitch.

Yeah, OK, I know what you're thinking, but I only got the sweatshirt for the bag it came in, because it hides, beautifully, the pair of Paul Smith slim-fit trousers (zip detail) that I also treated myself to. A way of spending O'Dowd's money and remembering who I am.

He steered her away from his sweatshirt and back to

his family. 'I sent the furry animals straightaway, caught the post. Kind of thank-you present for the "Missing You" pictures they drew me.' He wondered whether he should get the little sheets of paper out of his pocket before remembering Fran had written a convoluted riddle on hers about Bath and rain and having to have a Mack with you.

He saw Jennifer hesitate, and then she was looking at him for the first time since he'd come in. 'My niece is only nine months old, she's teething at the moment.'

He made sympathetic noises before asking if the niece lived nearby and soon Jennifer was telling him about her brother and his wife, and he supplied more information about his nieces and about Tess and Joe, and there they were chatting away. It felt easy and unforced until he got too relaxed and mentioned that he'd already met her mother. He saw from her reaction that this was news to her, and not particularly welcome news.

'I miss my sister,' he said quickly, 'I'm very close to her.'

'I miss my cousin; she's in America at the moment. New Mexico.'

It was like laying a little trail of breadcrumbs.

'Ah,' he said, 'I think Sonia mentioned her. Cicely, isn't it?'

'Cressida. Yes, I'm sure Sonia did.'

'Gosh, sorry, Cressida. And are ... are you close?'

'Yes, she's more like a sister than a cousin. I can talk to her about anything.'

Good girl, come on, gently does it.

'That's nice. Hard to chat properly on the phone though, isn't it? I find that with my—'

They both jumped as Finlay opened the door. 'Locking up in a minute, you two.' He went out, giving Mack a 'well done' smile that made him feel even more shoddy than normal.

Somehow the interruption had swept away all the progress he'd made, and the piece of material was getting a real seeing-to again. He swore he could hear the upset and anger thrumming away in her over the sound of the cotton coming through the fabric.

'I'm sorry. Really sorry,' she suddenly said, and before he knew what he was doing he had put his hand over hers and stopped her sewing.

Jesus, Gods, what the Hell are you doing?

'Were you apologising?' he asked, bending his head towards hers.

She nodded and he saw her lips were pressed tightly together as if she was afraid she might cry.

There was something catching in his own throat and he only just got out, 'Oh Jennifer, I don't think it's you who should be apologising.'

He heard her sniff and she turned her head a little to look at him. 'Do you always do that?' he went on, making his voice as gentle as he could, 'take it upon yourself to make other people feel better when someone sours the atmosphere? You think perhaps you have no right to be upset or angry?'

She was looking right into his eyes now. Her hand felt cold under his.

'That's exactly how I do feel,' she said.

The words stayed in the air between them.

Don't answer her; don't speak; get off this bloody chair and go.

He thought how different her eyes were from her mother's, even though they were the same blue. 'Well, that's a shame,' he heard himself say, 'because you had an accident; you didn't lose your right to be treated with respect or get angry if you're not.'

He no longer had his hand over hers, but was holding it.

Whaaat, are you channelling some kind of self-help book? Move your hand . . . now.

She was looking as stunned as he felt.

Take your hand away and move.

He rubbed his thumb over the back of her hand. 'Why put up with things you wouldn't have put up with before your accident? You haven't changed, have you? Your face just looks different.'

That's it, final warning, get up, get out.

Her nod had something of the punch-drunk about it.

He was leaning in closer, those blue eyes inviting him to do it. 'You're so much better than Jocelyn,' he said, 'in every single way. If the tables were turned, I can't imagine you saying any of the things she says.'

Up. Now. Run.

'You need to remember that, Jennifer.'

'I . . . I'll try,' she said and blinked, and suddenly he saw how close his head was to hers, how it looked holding her hand like this. He gave it a final, consoling squeeze, got to his feet and managed a bright 'Better be off'.

Picking up his rucksack, he almost sprinted for the door and felt as if he was tottering out of the hall, just managing to wave at Finlay.

What the Hell had he done? It had been too friendly, too intense. He walked rapidly away, his heart gunning until the panic started to subside. It was all right, no harm done, get a grip. And maybe he'd done the right thing. Some part of his brain must have been telling him that honesty was definitely the best policy with Jennifer. Well, his brand of honesty anyway. That's why he'd blurted, that's why he'd done that hand-holding.

He should stop thinking about how weird it had been and think about what he'd done right. He'd got her talking about Cressida; shown her he wasn't hyper eager to find out about what she was up to. Getting Cressida's name wrong was a touch of his old magic. It was all good stuff. And when he got to the cottage, he'd put on his new trousers, turn up the music and give O'Dowd the finger.

He stopped walking. The carrier bag, where was the carrier bag? With all that emoting he'd genuinely forgotten it. What if she opened it and found the trousers? How would he explain them? He started to race back to the hall. Was he actually turning into forgetful Matt Harper?

As he reached the hall, Jennifer was coming out with the bag. 'Here you are, you left it on the table,' she said, 'and, you know, Matt, don't think I'm being funny, but there's more to Newcastle than Primark. It has some really good clothes shops. Or I could point you in the right direction on the Internet; I buy a lot of mine like that.' She was giving his jacket and jeans and the carrier bag a sympathetic but pained look, and he knew he was safe.

'Sieve for a brain,' he said stowing the bag safely under his arm. 'Better be off.'

'No, let me give you a lift.' There was real warmth in her voice and it was there later in the car when she said, 'Thank you for earlier, Matt. You're really . . . tuned in to how it feels sometimes. You always seem to know the right things to say.'

'Not always.' He felt all at once out of his depth. 'Ha . . . hmmm . . . I think we both know I can really put my foot in it sometimes.'

She gave him a little sideways glance that made him wish he'd insisted on walking home.

'Oh, yes, I know about your foot,' she said. 'In fact, back there I was half-expecting you to tell me to put a brave face on things.' She gave him her lovely wide, warm smile, and he thought what guts it took to laugh after that humiliating incident and how much he liked it when she pulled his leg.

He wobbled along to Peter Clarke after she dropped him off, needing to hear O'Dowd's voice to toughen him up.

'I'm making progress; we've started to talk about Cressida. And she called me Matt for the first time,' he reported like the good little lackey he was.

'Hold the front page,' O'Dowd said tersely, but Mack was looking upwards at the stars, wondering at how much brighter they were here and how behind the main ones you could see great swathes of other, fainter ones. Lack of light pollution, he supposed.

'Hey,' O'Dowd said, 'stop doing whatever you're doing and listen. The old bastard upstairs has started making grumbling noises, he hasn't got my patience. He wants a bit more progress. That girlfriend you made up ...'

Mack stopped looking at the stars. 'Ye-es.'

'Make up some problems you're having with her. Women love all that, you can cry on Jen's shoulder, she can offer you advice. That'll lead nicely on to Cressida's love life.'

'You're joking, that girlfriend is my insurance. I'm not doing ... Aahhh ... whaaat ... no, no.'

There had been a sudden noise in the grass near the legs of the bench, something bashing about, and then Mack saw a rabbit disappearing at speed, followed by something reddish-brown, long and sinuously fast. There was a bout of high squealing in the dark and then nothing.

'What the Hell's going on?' O'Dowd shouted.

Mack got his breath back. 'Something in the grass chasing a rabbit ... think it's just caught it and killed it.'

'Let that be a lesson to you, my son,' O'Dowd said slowly. 'Now do what you're told about that girlfriend and next time you ring ... more progress.'

CHAPTER 19

Jennifer sat in the pub and wondered if that was Matt's knee touching hers or the leg of the table. She didn't dare move to find out. She wasn't going to do anything to mar this little bit of perfection: just the three of them, Doug, Matt and her around a table. No Lisa, no Jocelyn, no one else.

Funny how Doug being there didn't feel wrong, but comforting. Like having stabilisers on your bike before you launched yourself off for the first time unsupported. And she was definitely in pre-launch mode. She remembered that: the way you couldn't get enough of seeing the other person's body. She thought about Matt's knee under the table and watched him talking, moving his hands in that expansive way he had. She looked at his eyelashes; those incredible brown eyes, and the pleasure of it all felt like pain. She wanted him; her body was telling her that. Under that jumper and those jeans there was a body she yearned to feel naked and vulnerable against hers. She wanted to smooth her hands down over his backside and pull him in to her. She looked at his hands again, wondering how many women they'd held and imagining how they would feel on her skin.

Doug said something and laughed and Jennifer was bumped back into the reality of sitting across a table from a good-looking man who a) had a girlfriend and b) probably wouldn't go for someone who looked like a dropped vase.

'Sorry, Doug?' she asked and he repeated what he'd just said about Angus.

'It was like watching some barfly perving your old auntie.'

Jennifer understood they were picking over Angus's performance again. Somehow, since the last rehearsal, Angus had decided to play the Duke as himself: a slightly past-it ladies' man, unaware that his large gut and aged patter had tipped him over into a parody of the fanciable, cheeky lad he used to be. It had been a master class in making a tit of yourself.

Finlay was now making him stay behind to apologise to Lisa and Jocelyn, one of whom was not put out at all, while the other was snarking for Britain.

Jennifer looked towards Matt to see what he thought. He had his mobile in his hand and was frowning down at it.

'Sorry, need to answer this,' he said, getting up and going out. Jennifer felt his knee still against hers and realised it had been the table leg all along.

Doug appeared to be checking who else was in the pub,

and she wondered if he was searching for Pat. There were just the old guys playing dominoes over near the window and a couple doing synchronised crisp-eating in what looked like an excuse not to talk to each other. Someone was playing the slot machine and there was a steady beat of blips and buzzing.

Doug pursed his lips. 'Doesn't look promising,' he said, jerking his head in the direction of the door. 'Told me on the way here, she's giving him a hard time. Sounds like round two's just starting.'

From that whole speech, Jennifer only heard, 'she' and 'hard time'. Picking up her glass, she fumbled it to her lips, hoping the cool orange juice would meet the rising heat in her chest and somehow cancel it out. She wasn't sure what emotion she was feeling: it could be fear.

Don't get ahead of yourself; it's simply a bit of trouble with the girlfriend.

Doug was frowning so hard he looked all nose and eyebrows. 'Mind you, seems a bit of a strange relationship. Together two years, yet he never mentions her. It's like she doesn't really exist. Divvn't even know her name. Do you know what she's called?'

Lucky. 'No, I don't. I get the feeling he's a bit shy about her.'

Jennifer needed the cool orange juice again when Matt returned. It was obviously raining outside, and his hair was wet. She watched a droplet of water run down the side of his face until he brushed it away, and she had a sudden picture of him wet in the shower.

There it was then. She *was* thinking about him naked. She really had to concentrate hard to listen when Matt said to her, 'Sorry, explained to Doug, I'm having a bit of argy-bargy with my girlfriend. I was hoping she could come up at the weekend, but no go.' He made a face and put his phone on the table, and Jennifer felt like a hypocrite when she offered sympathy. She didn't have time to feel it too much because Doug suddenly asked, 'What's she called?'

Matt looked a little taken aback, said 'Sonia' quickly and then shut his mouth.

'Sonia?' Doug repeated uncertainly.

'Uh huh.'

'Sonia what?'

Matt picked up his pint and took a large gulp.

'Sonia what?' Doug repeated. 'What's her surname, your Sonia?'

'Hadrian.'

Doug couldn't hold in his laughter, and Matt gave him a hurt look.

'Sorry, sorry,' Doug said, 'but think about it – Sonia at the shop and Hadrian at the wall, it's a bit funny. And you had the nerve to laugh at Postwoman Pat.'

'I did, didn't I?' Matt said gloomily.

'Perhaps she'll be able to come up another weekend, or for the play?' Jennifer suggested.

'Doubt it.' He looked like a kicked puppy. 'That was her only free weekend for a while. Big case on at the moment. HM Revenue and Customs. Bit hush-hush.'

Doug gave an impressed whistle and Jennifer wondered if Matt's girlfriend had a lovely face to go with her important job.

Matt was on his feet again, pushing away his pint. 'Sorry. I'm terrible company this evening. I'm going to walk home, clear my head.'

'Are you sure? In this rain?' she said. 'It's really no trouble to drop you off.' His defeated expression was getting inside her, making her forget that he was out of her reach. So easily, she could just stand up and put her hand on his face and find out what his skin felt like.

He shook his head; wouldn't hear of having a lift from either her or Doug and just ambled off. They had to call him back to pick up his phone. On his way out, the barman handed him a notebook, telling him he'd left it in the Gents'.

'Poor bugger.' Doug looked thoughtful again. 'You might be right about that shy thing – told me he'd love to have a look round a Northumberland farm, but felt it was too pushy to ask you.'

I'll go and get him, take him there now.

'I'll check with Dad,' she said, and Doug winked at her. 'Good lass. Be even better if you could arrange it for this weekend; take his mind off things.'

'You're a really nice friend to have,' she said and watched Doug blush, and in all honestly she didn't know whether she was talking on Matt's behalf or her own.

When she returned home later, she made two phone calls. The first was to Alex and she told him slowly and very distinctly that she could not go to the theatre with him, she was sorry, but something had come up that made it impossible.

The second call had to wait till early morning and even then she dithered, picking up her phone and putting it back on the bedside table next to the glass of water and the copy of *Twelfth Night*. She was acutely aware of the silence of the house – her mother sleeping, her dad and Danny out in the barn.

When she picked up the phone again, she did dial, and a sleepy Cressida answered.

'Sorry, Jen, I'm completely knackered. We've been doing riding scenes today. Hang on . . .' Jennifer guessed Cress was counting the time difference out on her fingers. 'It's the middle of the night there, what's wrong?'

'Nothing's wrong . . . but could you do that thing where you talk until I'm ready to?'

There was a soft giggle. 'Hey, there's nothing I like better than talking about myself. So . . . let's see. Filming's started, of course, got a horse that likes me, the director a real sweetie, and very patient. Most of the cast and crew not bad, although there seem to be a lot of ponytails and beards around. Very 1980s.'

'How's the temperature?'

'Let's just say, the climate here was cool for the first few days, with not a cloud in the sky. Well, it was for me, but Rory's voice coach was getting very hot and bothered and that's when a nasty storm came up from South America way. Now the poor voice coach has been sent back to LA slightly singed round the edges.'

'She'll not be helping Rory with his diphthongs anymore?'

'Indeed not. Anna Maria felt it was too much for the poor girl, too hands-on. Consequently there now seems to be a real build-up of heat right over my trailer, which I'm trying to cool down, and South America's looking stormy again.'

Jennifer wondered if this sounded like gibberish or whether it was obvious Rory had been pre-occupied with screwing his voice coach until Anna Maria had got her sent home. Now Cress was having to cool Rory's passion and keep on the right side of his wife.

'Also, that nice Canadian girl,' Cress said, 'she's got a part—'

'Matt's having trouble with his girlfriend,' Jennifer got out, all in a rush.

'Ah, I see.' Cress said, carefully, 'I see, and . . . how does that make you feel, sweetie?'

Jennifer looked around her bedroom as if the wardrobe or even the desk could offer an escape route.

'I'm imagining him naked. He was wet with rain earlier, and I kept seeing him in the shower. But I shouldn't, it feels way too much like . . .'

'. . . hoping?'

There it was: Cress was spot on again.

'Much too much like hoping, and I'm not sure I'm ready for that. All I know is that I feel like I've been sleepwalking for months and months and now I'm not. It's wonderful and painful at the same time.'

'Jen, that's good. No, brilliant. And remember what I said. Don't run in the opposite direction if he advances.'

She looked at the wardrobe again. If she just got in and closed the door, could she stay there?

'He'll have to come to me, I can't go to him.'

'Fine, but don't put him off. Promise?'

'Did anyone ever tell you you're really bossy?'

'Only all my boyfriends and fellow actors. And, missy, there's something else you're not telling me, isn't there?'

'Not just bossy, but like a little terrier with a bone. All right, all right. He's coming to the farm. Well, I have to ask Dad, but I know he'll say yes.'

'Am I allowed to say "Whoop de whoop", and "Get in there, Jen"?'

'No, look, he's just coming as a friend, Cress.'

There was a loud raspberry noise from Santa Fe. 'Coming is coming, Jen. Things are moving forward, even if you don't want to admit it. And very soon you're going to have to think about "hope". But we'll leave that for another time, eh? Let's take it easy . . . but, remember I'm here at the end of the phone, sweetie.'

By the time Jennifer wished Cress goodnight, she felt calmer until she started thinking of Matt naked. Naked and glistening with water. She lay down on the bed and moved the fantasy back a few frames, to helping him undress for that shower. She was pulling his black T-shirt up and over his head and bending to press her lips against his chest and run her tongue down his belly. She could almost feel the smoothness of his skin against her mouth.

She remembered the buckle on his belt, saw herself undoing it and then relieving him of those terrible jeans.

Soon she was lying naked with him and in her fantasy she was the old Jen and he was as she imagined him, lithe, sensitive, a little naughty. She ran her hands over that incredible backside of his and pushed herself against him and his brown eyes looked at her with lust; not pity or revulsion, but dirty, unmistakable lust. She rode the fantasy, stringing out her pleasure, stopping when it got too much, starting again and building up the heat; revelling once again, after so long, in how sexy she felt.

Mack squelched into the kitchen. The waterproof outer shell did its job on his top half, but his jeans were soaking, and during most of the walk his torch had kept flickering and he had been waiting for the moment when it would go out entirely and whatever was out there would savage him. A four-legged version of O'Dowd probably.

It had been a nice, sad-lover exit from the pub though, and hopefully that would be the image they would be left with, not the memory of that balls-up with Sonia Hadrian. Sonia ruddy Hadrian! What the Hell had possessed him? He knew the name of his fictitious girlfriend off by heart: the lovely Sara Jeffries, with the slightly scary, suitably mysterious job. But when Doug had put him on the spot like that, his mind had emptied completely. It was only sheer luck he hadn't said Grace bloody Darling.

He struggled out of his wet things and wrapped himself inadequately in the kitchen towel. O'Dowd had been right about the effect girlfriend trouble would have: Jennifer's face had been a picture of sympathetic concern. Doug's too and, if Mack had got the guy sussed, a few minutes after he had left the pub he was certain Doug would have mentioned to Jennifer about visiting the farm.

He shivered and took himself upstairs and under the duvet. So, if he'd successfully manipulated Doug, Jennifer would tell him shyly tomorrow that he was welcome to come to the farm. An invitation to the enemy's camp. He thought back to that long, wet walk home and how the sheep had 'baa-baa-d' at him as he'd passed. In the rain it had sounded like 'baa-stard, baa-stard'. It was a judgement he could only agree with.

CHAPTER 20

Jennifer watched Matt struggling into the dark green boilersuit, her father helping him, and wanted to reverse the film and take it off him. His jumper was in her arms, handed to her along with his fleece, and she was very tempted to hold both to her face and breathe him in.

'All set?' her father asked, patting him on the back and when Matt nodded and looked across at her as if to ask if she was coming too, she said, 'I just need to help Mum with a few things,' and went back into the house. She was buying herself time in which to calm down and not turn into a gibbering, self-deluded wreck.

He was here for the farm, nothing more. Clinging on to that thought, she headed for the kitchen and the straight-backed, full on lemon-drop example of womanhood that was currently her mother. If Ray was pulling out all the stops to be welcoming, Brenda was pushing them back in again, and the way she was relieving the potatoes of their skins suggested just how pleased she was to have this guest.

'Need any help?' Jennifer asked, draping Matt's jumper over the back of a chair and seeing her mother turn and look at it.

'No. It's all under control.' Brenda nodded at the jumper. 'He's all kitted up, is he?'

'Yes. Dad's been really helpful and friendly with him.' Jennifer saw her mother turn abruptly back to the potatoes. She went to stand behind her and looped her arms around her shoulders. The steel backbone relented a little.

'Come on, Mum. I know you think you're protecting me, but it makes me feel like a child. Being like this; visiting Matt ... well I'm guessing you weren't offering him Meals on Wheels?'

Her mother did laugh at that.

'Is it because you dislike him, or because he's not Alex?'

Her mother seemed to consider that before replying. 'I can't help liking Alex, or thinking that life would be simpler if you and he—'

'Simpler for you.' Jennifer let her arms drop, suddenly cross that she'd had to introduce Alex into this shining, exciting day.

Her mother put the potato she was still holding on the draining board, gave her hands a shake over the bowl and turned around.

'You're right, love, I guess I do mean that. But, I'm not stupid. I do appreciate that you and Alex, well, you probably can't reheat what you had.' Her mother put a wet hand on her arm. 'I just want you to be wary, that's all. This Matt's bright and cheerful enough but there's something under all that.' Her mother gave her a querying look. 'You know what I mean, don't you?'

'I'm going out now,' Jennifer said, 'need to make sure Danny hasn't played some awful practical joke on him.'

Mack was glad to be out of the lambing sheds and all that steaming, bleating, ripe-smelling new life. He didn't know how Danny and Ray stood it. At times they'd been working flat out, delivering lambs, moving ewes, trying to get one lamb from a set of triplets accepted by another mother. Mack had helped deliver a couple of lambs himself, trying not to gag at how squelchy the whole experience was, although he had felt a bit wet-eyed as he watched the ewes slowly licking their new arrivals.

His nerves had been on high alert all day, but Danny and Ray couldn't have been friendlier, even if Danny had managed to convince him they gave all the sheep names. He supposed that pulling his leg was a good sign. Better than pummelling him to death for deceit.

Now he was hanging on to the edge of a high-sided trailer, being towed by Ray on the quad bike. As they bounced downhill to go and feed the sheep out in the fields, he had to soften his knees to stay upright, and he felt a bit like Boadicea in her chariot. He watched the sheepdog running out and back, out and back to the trailer.

Somewhere Jennifer was walking down to join them, and no doubt she'd laugh when she saw him splattered with mud that had been thrown up at him from the wheels of the bike. He hoped it was mud.

As they neared the bottom of the valley, they had gathered a long line of sheep behind them, and Ray whistled and the dog instantly fell back, not crowding the sheep and sometimes lying on its stomach, its eyes darting left, right, ahead. Ray stopped and uncoupled the trailer, and Mack helped him split open the bags of brown, yeasty sheep nuts that were balanced across the handlebars of the bike. When Ray started up the bike again, he rode in a straight line, letting the nuts spill out on to the ground and soon there was a struggling, shifting line of sheep, heads down, eating. As Jennifer joined them, slightly out of breath, Mack saw Ray's lips moving.

'Are you counting them?' he asked, amazed.

'Aye,' Ray said, 'but I never get to the end. Always asleep by then.' He had laughed, but Mack could see he was concentrating on the rising land off to their right where the gorse bushes were particularly dense. His face relaxed when a large ewe, with some arrogance, emerged and started to trot towards the food.

The dog made a move and Mack asked what it was called.

'Mack,' Jennifer said and for a second he wondered if he was having his leg pulled before he remembered that was not his name up here.

Just before the ewe reached the rest of the flock, the dog behind it came too close, and the ewe turned right round and, after a stand-off, headbutted it hard.

'My goodness, do sheep often do that?' Mack was

reassessing everything he had ever believed about sheep being stupid and placid.

'When they've got lambs in them they do.' Ray whistled for the dog to come back. 'Mack's still young; bit overeager.'

On the journey back to the farm, clinging on and trying to keep his weight forward this time as they climbed out of the valley, Mack knew that he and the sheepdog had a lot in common. Here he was, answering to O'Dowd's whistle, speeding up or falling to his belly as required. And that sheep, he was very afraid that sheep might be Brenda.

Over supper later, he was certain it was, although he had to admit she knew how to cook. He'd had double helpings of her shepherd's pie (which under the circumstances he thought was an apt menu choice) and piled buttery carrots and leeks, peas and tiny broad beans beside it on his plate. He was ravenous, and he supposed it was the hard work and fresh air.

All had gone well until Jennifer had disappeared to the loo and Ray had ambled back out to the yard.

'Thank you for inviting me,' he said to Brenda with his best smile. 'And providing supper too.'

'I didn't invite you. It was Jennifer.'

He remembered the headbutting sheep and felt the need to fight back. Even Matt Harper would react to that rudeness, wouldn't he?

'I sense you don't like me much, Mrs Roseby,' he said. 'You're very direct.'

Oh no. Really I'm not.

'I try to be,' he said, endeavouring to meet that drilling blue gaze.

'Well, maybe you do . . . but I have to think of Jen. You're here for a while and then gone.'

He thought how clever that was: implying it was the fact he was passing through that she objected to, rather than something about his character.

'I don't see why that should stop me being friends with Jennifer.'

She gave him a long, assessing look. 'So it's just friendship you want then, is it?'

'Of course,' he said and terminated the conversation by feigning interest in the lamb-cam. It showed Danny and Ray and a load of sheep. As an idea for a reality show, it was rubbish.

When Jennifer returned, the rest of the meal passed without any more headbutting, but he knew Brenda was watching his every move. He purposely kept up a stream of chat with Jennifer, not that it was hard, and tried to enjoy the plum crumble. As coffee was put in front of him, he thought of the weird, chaotic meals his mother had used to assemble with bits and pieces that never quite went together: corned beef and peas; tinned tuna and baked beans.

The only time Brenda really smiled was when the door opened and what Mack took to be a passing Valkyrie came in, a large baby in a pink snowsuit on her hip. Brenda's face looked as though it belonged to a sunnier person, and she suddenly had the baby in her arms and Mack was not sure how it had got there.

The Valkyrie almost broke his hand when she shook it and he discovered she was Danny's wife. He wondered how much strengthening their bed needed with those two in it.

'I should really think about getting home,' he said. 'Let me help you with the washing-up before I go.'

Brenda, as he had calculated, would not hear of any delay-making washing-up, and she showed an almost rude haste to say her goodbyes. He got a warmer send-off from the others, Ray telling him to come back any time he wanted – next time they might not be so busy – 'Normally we just stand around leaning on a gate and chewing grass,' he said.

Jennifer walked him up the track to the road, shining a torch ahead of them, and he knew now, in the dark, with the memory of the warm kitchen still in their minds, was the perfect time to move things along.

'Thanks for taking my mind off my Sonia,' he began.

'There's no need for thanks. Happy to help. Are you still . . . I mean, talking?'

'Yes, bit wobbly, but where there's life . . . Do you think I should send her some flowers? I was a bit sharp with her on the phone about not coming up.'

Jennifer's voice came back through the dark. 'Yes. But ring her afterwards to say sorry too. Best not to assume one bunch of flowers will do it.'

'Sensible advice.' He left a little gap to give the impression he was thinking and was acutely aware of the sound of Jennifer breathing, the cool of the dark around them. 'Tricky, isn't it, having to rely on the phone?' he tried. 'I find it hard to say what I want to say, not just to Sonia, but to friends as well . . . if I was at home I could just go to the pub, chat to them. The miles between us all make it difficult.' It was a little hook in the water and if he was in luck, Cressida and how far away she was would come up.

'You can always talk to me,' Jennifer said. 'If you want to.'

Great; wrong fish on the end of the line.

They walked for a while, listening to the sheep bleat in the fields around them, the torch picking out stones and bits of sheep poo.

OK, time for the 'give and take' approach – I'll confide in you about something and maybe you'll offer me some titbits in return.

He stopped walking. 'You know, I would like to talk to you, Jennifer, if that was a serious offer. I . . .' Another pause as if he was dredging up the courage to go on. 'Thing is, my girlfriend isn't staying away because she's busy: she's punishing me. She wants me to give up writing, the walking books, the novel, and get a proper job with a proper wage. I'm not sure she really understands how much I love what I do.'

Oh Hell, my girlfriend doesn't understand me. You can do better than that.

Jennifer made a kind of agreeing noise. 'It's hard when people don't get what makes you tick,' she said slowly, and he noticed how she was keeping the beam of the light from her torch down as if it was easier for her to talk in the dark. 'That's why . . . that's why I think Cress only goes out with other actors or people in the business.' She started walking again, and he was careful to slow the pace.

'Yes, I can see that makes sense,' he said.

'It does, but mixing work and pleasure has its downside, means you can never get away if things get tricky.'

'Do things ever get tricky for Cicely? She seems such a strong person.'

A little laugh. 'Cressida. And yes, she's only human, of course she has problems. At the moment she's doing a film with this guy Rory Sylvester.'

'Sorry, I don't think I've ever—'

'He's big, believe me, and he's taken a shine to her, which is complicated enough, but add in a very jealous wife . . . Cress is working just as hard at keeping her sweet and not slighting him, as she is on acting.'

Is she, now?

'Poor Cressida.'

He was hoping for more, but Jennifer stopped walking again.

'You know what you were saying about your girlfriend wanting you to give up writing?'

'Um . . . yes.'

'Well, you never know when you'll have a breakthrough. One TV show was all it took with Cress to make it happen. Matt, I'd say unless you're absolutely forced to give up something you love, don't do it.'

If her tone at that point had been self-pitying he could have shrugged it off, pressed her a little more on Cressida, but it sounded like hard-won advice to him.

When he said goodbye at the road he turned on his own torch and sprinted up the road, pretending he had bags of energy, what with him being a keen walker and everything, but by the time he got to Peter Clarke he was nearly on his knees. He sat and congratulated himself for surviving and getting that little nugget about Rory. Was it all starting to kick off?

Laboriously clambering into a standing position, intending to ring O'Dowd, an image of Jennifer going home to sleep in the bedroom she'd had as a child and already left behind once swamped his mind.

He tried to push it away by pulling his own mobile out of his pocket. There was a missed call from Tess. Just what he needed, a reminder of why he was doing all this.

'Hi,' he said, forcing himself to sound energised, 'you'll never guess what I've done today. Only delivered a—'

'Mack!' Tess said, and he heard the wobble of fear in the way she said his name. 'Mum's had a fall, sometime this morning, we think. I found her when I went round just after lunch. She's in the Royal United with a broken leg; they're having to pin it.'

CHAPTER 21

As the train reached Doncaster on his way back north, Mack found it hard to believe it had only been three weeks since he'd done this journey for the first time. He felt years older, probably older than Mr Armstrong. The past two days alone had added a good fifty years to his life.

He had arrived at the hospital to be greeted by Tess, who had put her arms around him and cried. If, at that point he could have scooped her and her whole family up and taken them away, he would have done.

When he had soothed her, great clouds of guilt accumulating over his head, he had learned that Phyllida had not been on some paralytic bender when she fell, but had simply stumbled backwards over a bag of shopping she'd just put down on the kitchen floor.

But Mack was in no mood to cut Phyllida any slack. When Joe arrived to join them, Mack was pleased to see that he too seemed to have hardened his attitude.

'It wasn't the drink this time, Tess, but it's going to

happen, isn't it?' Joe said. 'And she'll have you in here too with all the extra work and worry.'

After going in to see Phyllida, who barely acknowledged that he'd travelled the length of the country to see her, Tess and he collared a doctor to discuss their options.

It had been like trying to knit fog. With the spectre of patient confidentiality flapping around him, the doctor had hidden behind general terms and hypothetical cases. The message was that they couldn't ask for help on Phyllida's behalf, unless they could prove she was mentally incapable of asking for it herself. All the doctor could do was point out to Phyllida that her children had concerns, highlight her physical condition and see what happened during her hospital stay.

When Mack told Phyllida what they had done, she went as ballistically ape-shit as it was possible for anyone with a broken leg to go, shouting that he had no right to talk to the doctor behind her back, that it was ridiculous to suggest she had a drink problem. Perhaps he should try getting his own life in order? Had he messed up that book opportunity yet?

Mack was glad when a nurse came and ended the skirmish, as he was having to fight the urge to tip her out of bed and break her other leg. He joined Tess and Joe in the waiting room.

'We'll have to have her live with us when she comes out,' Tess said, looking at Joe for confirmation, 'she won't be able to cope on her own for a while.'

'Just till I get back from Northumberland.' Mack looked

at Joe too. 'Another three, maybe four weeks. I'd come back earlier if I could ...'

Joe grunted and picked up one of the magazines on the table next to him.

After Tess had gone to collect the girls, Joe put down the magazine. 'You and I need a heart-to-heart,' he said and in his straightforward way told Mack that he didn't believe he was writing a travel book, that he thought he was up to his old 'slimy tabloid' tricks, and that if he did anything to hurt Tess or the girls he would never, ever forgive him.

Mack had looked at Joe's scuffed knuckles and the way his wedding ring dug into his finger and had been tempted to tell him the truth and assure him that it was to protect Tess and the girls that he was back in the tabloid swamp, but in the end he couldn't. He lied and blustered and stuck to his story and when Joe got up and said he'd wait for Tess in the car park, Mack couldn't blame him.

The rest of his visit had been more of the same: Phyllida snarling at him, Tess crying on him, Joe looking at him like he was scum. Back in his flat, lying in his own bed, he found himself wanting, actually *wanting* to get back to Northumberland and lose himself in the nicer person he was up there. Well, the nicer person he was pretending to be. Most of all he wanted someone to talk to. Someone gentle and funny and understanding. Doug would have done. Jennifer would have been better.

Jennifer.

He looked out of the train window and then back at

his script. Books down when he got back – at least he'd be word-perfect in the play, even if in real life he was always speaking with a forked tongue.

His last view of Phyllida, after a frosty cheek had been slanted towards him to kiss, had been of her asking Tess to go and get her some tea from the machine. He thought of Tess wearing herself out over the coming weeks, of what that meant for the girls and for Joe, and then he thought of Jennifer again. Jennifer, who was coming to him slowly and surely with her little confidences and big blue eyes. He felt as if he was holding up a set of scales with his family in one bowl and Jennifer in the other, and it was madly tilting first one way and then the other and making him queasy.

Why couldn't Jennifer toughen up like he'd had to? She needed to stop going around like a blue-eyed, injured Bambi and settle down with that Alex bloke and forget about drama.

She was his get-out-of-jail-free card and to think of her in any other way was like naming your lab rat.

By the time he got to Newcastle he felt gritty-eyed with frustration and anger, and he snatched at O'Dowd's phone when it rang as he walked over the station concourse.

'Hear your mum's taken a bit of a tumble, my son.'

'News travels fast,' Mack said tersely, wondering just who O'Dowd had got checking up on his family.

'Poor old Phyllida.'

'She's not that much older than you.'

'I was talking vodka age, not real age.'

Mack switched off the phone, not caring that he'd get a tongue-lashing later and put his bag in Left Luggage before going out into Newcastle. He was looking for something and not sure what it was. He pushed through groups of leery lads in short-sleeved checked shirts and girls dressed in tiny scraps of clothing and high, tip-tapping heels. The whole city seemed alive, and he remembered it was Friday night. It was like walking though twittering birds and suddenly the twittering solidified into someone shouting 'Matt!' and he saw Lisa calling to him from the other side of the road.

He'd never seen her in full warpaint, or with so little on. He dodged through the traffic and was engulfed in a vibrant, cheeky group of girls, and it seemed to him they were as drunk on the night and what it might bring as they were on the trebles for a fiver they'd necked. The smell of perfume coming off them was nearly overpowering.

'Come here, you,' Lisa said grabbing him round the neck and planting a kiss on his cheek. 'How did it go? Get your girlfriend sorted?'

There was an exaggerated 'Oooooh' as Mack wondered what she meant. Had Doug thought it was a crisis of the heart that had sent him scurrying off? He'd better put that right, he needed that girlfriend. He looked at Lisa's face turned up towards his, at her little pillowy lips and the way her breasts were swelling against the material of her vest top and said, 'No, didn't get her sorted. It's all off. Finished. Over.'

Now he knew what he needed tonight: Lisa. The perfect way to forget everything pressing down on his shoulders. She was carefree and alive and up for it.

He could not miss the little smile from her as she said, 'Oh, I'm sorry,' and then they were being swept along to the next bar, Lisa introducing him to the girls who all seemed to work for the council. Lisa explained who he was and what he did, and that 'though he dresses like a tit, he's lush'. They all agreed, and who was he to argue as they screeched past some seriously scary bouncers and into the thumping heat of a bar.

'Don't worry, I'll look after you, Matt,' Lisa said, her hand resting on his thigh, 'only it can get a bit wild. Better take your fleece off, you'll look soft.'

He was tempted to tell her he'd been to parties where people snorted coke off the breasts of glamour models, but he smiled politely and played to the gallery by asking where he could hang his fleece.

'On them chapel hat-pegs,' one of the girls said, thrusting her breasts towards him, and he looked suitably shocked and offered to buy the first round. They liked him even better after that. He watched them knock their drinks back and knew he'd have to pace himself.

After a couple of drinks they were off again, this time to a bigger bar, where they squeezed themselves next to a huge group of blokes who were all wearing T-shirts for someone's stag do. Soon the two groups were mixed up; one girl who Lisa said worked in Housing Benefits was snogging a guy with a neck as wide as his head.

'First strike to Natalie,' someone shouted, and that seemed to call for another round of drinks. Mack poured half of his surreptitiously on to the floor, but when he was lifting what was left to his mouth a lad knocked into him and spilt the rest down his shirt.

'Buyyouanothermate,' the lad slurred.

'It's all right, there's no need.'

'Buyyouanotherfuckin'drinkmate,' the lad repeated, clutching the front of Mack's shirt. 'What'swrongwithyouse?'

Lisa rescued him and after that the evening speeded up as they went to other bars, drank different drinks, lost some of their group and gained new people. He felt himself getting more and more drunk, no matter how much he sloshed down his shirt or tipped on the floor and Lisa was definitely getting more touchy-feely. Her hand was on his thigh, on his bum. He felt himself respond to it.

In the street someone stopped to be sick and next time Mack saw them they were drinking a pint of lager. There was a fight between two groups of lads. He lost his fleece, and then Lisa shouted something that seemed to be the name of another bar and they all started to hurtle towards it, but suddenly, it was just him and Lisa drinking shots near a roped-off area where through the gloom it was possible to see long-legged orange women and champagne bottles and people who, Lisa informed him breathlessly, played for Newcastle.

Lisa made an attempt to get over the rope and was turned back by a bouncer. However much she pursed her lips and pouted she couldn't blag her way in. Mack knew he could if he put his mind to it, but not tonight.

'They're just people,' he said, putting his arm around her. 'Usually vain, selfish and not very bright. Not as nice as you.'

'Don't care,' she said, looking sad and defeated. 'Just want to be on the other side of that rope.'

He used one of his last twenty-pound notes to get her a glass of champagne and felt her good mood return. She snuggled up to him and then they were off out of the bar and careering along a cobbled street that twisted its way down to the Quayside. He was aware of passing smartly dressed, quieter couples, returning from the theatre or dinner, but it wasn't that side of Newcastle he craved tonight. Soon he was standing in a drunken queue of people, most of them shouting or singing and waiting for a kebab.

The kebab tasted sublime to him, that's when he knew he must be really drunk, and he told himself to mind what he said and be careful what he did, but despite that he let Lisa guide him down an alley and push him against the wall. He looked up and there was the Tyne Bridge, green and huge above him, the lights reflected off the river. Tides of people swept past the end of the alley and Lisa said 'Here, hold this' and shoved her kebab into his free hand and got down on her knees and instinct took over and he spread his legs.

'Get in there,' someone shouted as they passed and he flung wide his arms and wondered if he looked like some kind of perverted Angel of the North as Lisa undid the button on his jeans and pulled down the zip.

Leaning back he waited for her warm, wet mouth to take him in and make him forget everything: blonde hair, blue eyes, scars, sadness: the lot.

CHAPTER 22

Jennifer pushed open the door of the hall, trying to ignore all the 'what ifs' and 'maybes' that had been rattling around her brain since Doug had told her he'd taken Matt to the airport to get a flight to Bristol.

Matt had not said why he was gong south, but she'd agreed with Doug's conclusion that it was another acute case of girlfriend-crisis-itis. Shame that Doug, under intense questioning from Jocelyn, had blabbed that to the whole Drama Club.

Never mind, today he was due back – the first Sunday afternoon rehearsal, the first time without scripts. She would no longer be lurking in the Blue Room, but sitting in the prompt chair. Ringside seat for some serious Matt-watching.

Her eyes went straight to the group of people gathered in a little semicircle and was surprised to see Jocelyn already there: she usually liked to turn up late and make an entrance. The way the others had their chairs angled towards hers suggested she was holding court. Neale, bizarrely, was dressed in his Malvolio costume.

Doug was on his feet, moving quickly towards her and offering to take the skirt and bodice she had draped over her arm. 'I'll come through and help you hang them up,' he said and made a grab for the skirt, fumbled and dropped it.

'Don't worry, Doug,' she said quietly, as he picked it up, 'first time without scripts is tricky for everyone. You'll be fine.'

'Oh, calm down, Doug,' Jocelyn drawled behind him, 'Jennifer's a woman of the world, and she's not going to be shocked that Matt was out with Lisa on Friday night. Not just out with her, hanging off her. They were so wrapped up in each other they didn't even notice me.'

'Guess that answers our questions about how it went with the girlfriend,' Steve said.

'Yes, I guess it does,' Jennifer said. 'Well . . . must put that fire on in the Blue Room for Wendy and Lydia.' She walked, not too quickly, not too slowly, towards the door, opened it carefully and closed it behind her softly.

Before it closed she heard someone say 'Ah, here he is' and knew Matt must have arrived. She flicked the switch on the fire and watched the bars go from grey to orange. She hung the skirt and bodice on a coat hanger and added it to the rack of clothes. She ran her hands over the materials and looked at each costume, but she did not touch the brown velvet costume at the end, the one that matched his eyes.

This had always been a script she knew could only be acted a certain way, despite what Cressida had tried to make her believe. Despite that lovely, shining day on the farm.

She hauled the club's sewing box up on to the table and lifted the lid. The tears were there, she could feel them, just ready to slide.

How had she imagined Matt was different? He had turned out to be just another offering for Lisa. The last few days without him had felt flat and dry, an arid time. Was that what it would be like when he went?

Perhaps she needed to do something about that – ask Cress if she could visit her and sit in the sun, she was always begging her to. Going to a place that prized perfection had scared her before, now it felt like running away. She could do running away.

And today? How could she cope with today? Finlay would have to find someone else to prompt. She could handle Wendy or Lydia, their fighting might be a distraction, but the rest? She selected the largest pair of scissors and went to fetch Jocelyn's costume from the rail.

Mack pushed open the door to the hall and saw there were already a few in. Neale was wearing his Malvolio costume, unless he'd taken to dressing like a depressed crow.

Mack still felt rough, but at least today he wasn't praying for death and vomiting on the hour. He was ruddy freezing, though. With his fleece still in some bar in Newcastle, he'd had to walk the hundred-and-fifty-thousand miles to the hall wearing his cord jacket.

'I went into town with her once, you know,' Angus said, giving him a conspiratorial nudge as he joined them. 'Ended up in a police cell.'

Mack heard Jocelyn and Steve laugh. Doug was staring at him in a disconcerting way.

'Her?' Mack asked.

Angus clicked his tongue. 'Nice try, "Her?" Anyway, as I said, ended up in a police cell. Arrested for trying to have sex with a statue. Naked.'

'You or the statue?' Steve asked.

'Bet Matt lost more than his notebook this time,' Jocelyn said, turning to him.

The 'her' they were talking about suddenly made sense.

'What's Lisa been saying?' he asked.

Jocelyn opened her eyes wide. 'Lisa hasn't said anything. It was me that saw you both. Very pally you were, I must say.'

Must you really? What a nasty, nosy piece of work you are. O'Dowd would hire you like a shot.

'So,' Steve said with a slap to Mack's back, 'did she eat you up and spit you out?'

Angus laughed. 'No, she doesn't spit. I remember that.'

'Now, now,' Doug said and got up and walked away.

Jennifer loosened the stitches holding the Velcro on the waistband of Jocelyn's skirt. If she did it subtly, the witch wouldn't notice as she was fastening it up and it would hold together for a few minutes before plummeting floor-wards.

She looked at what she was doing, really looked, and put the scissors down. Did she honestly want to disrupt everything, however satisfying the prospect of embarrassing Jocelyn might be? Undo Finlay's hard work along with those stitches?

She jumped as the door opened and wondered if she'd conjured Finlay up.

'Jennifer, my love,' he said, 'I'm going to go over some of the verse speaking with Neale and Pam; the others are practising their lines with each other. I won't need you to prompt for about an hour.'

'I may not be able to prompt at all today,' Jennifer said, but Finlay had already bounded away. Threading her needle, she began repairing the damage she'd done. She was going to rise above this. She jumped again as Lisa came in.

Please, please do not rub my nose in it. Have him, but spare me the details.

'I've come to try on my outfit. Mam helped me make myself flat-chested before I came out.' Lisa looked down at a chest that was definitely less perky than usual.

Jennifer nodded and went to fetch the dark-blue doublet and breeches from the clothes rail and the tights from the windowsill and when she came back, wondered whether there wasn't something less perky about the whole of Lisa today. She watched as Lisa took off her own clothes and slipped on the outfit, helping her to do up the fastenings. As she'd suspected, in her costume, Lisa looked like a sexy page-boy.

'I think just a bit of tweaking on the shoulders,' Jennifer said, happy to fuss over such distracting details. 'Do you want to stand properly, you're all hunched up?'

Lisa gave a heavy sigh and pulled back her shoulders, but there was still a droop to her stance.

'Lisa, is there something you're not happy with about the costume? It doesn't make you look butch if that's what you're thinking. I know Jocelyn said it would. Quite the reverse: I'm more worried you still look like a sexy woman.'

'Really? Tell that to Mr Writer Man.' Lisa's shoulders sagged some more. 'No bloody ink in his pen, that's all I can say.'

Jennifer sat down. 'I'm sorry?'

Lisa was picking at the material of her sleeve. 'Bumped into him Friday night by the station, me and a whole group of mates. Seemed a bit down, said it was over with his girlfriend so I thought, "Go for it, Lisa." Then, well, sorry, Jen, but I was down on my knees—'

'I don't want to hear this.' Jennifer stood up again. 'Look, come here, let me pin the shoulder seams.' She reached for the pincushion and roughly pulled out a couple of pins.

'Nothing to hear. I was about to get started and he was up for it, if you know what I mean, when he suddenly pushed me away. Not nasty like, but it was a definite push, I nearly fell over backwards.'

Jennifer felt a pain in her finger and realised she had stuck one of the pins in it.

'He apologised really nicely and put me in a taxi and

buggered off. Thought he might ring yesterday but he didn't.'

It felt natural to put her arm around Lisa. How quickly life could turn. Ten minutes ago, it was her feeling like the miserable, rejected one. Cress had been right, she had a habit of allowing her brain to leap ahead and decide something was going to play out badly. He had turned down Lisa. Why had he turned down Lisa?

When the door opened this time, Lisa's aggrieved sniff told Jennifer that Matt was standing there.

He was pale and slightly more untidy than usual, his hair looking as though he hadn't brushed it for a while. The dark sweep of stubble down his chin made Jennifer want to discover what it felt like under her palm. His gaze travelled first over her and then Lisa. He frowned.

'Jennifer,' he asked, 'would you mind if I had a quick word with Lisa?'

'Of course not,' she said and got herself out of the room as quickly as she could.

Mack was slightly taken aback to see Jennifer's arm around Lisa's shoulders and the vision that was Lisa in her doublet and breeches was another surprise, but he couldn't afford to be distracted. He had to get this right if he was going to undo the damage he'd done on Friday night: one slighted woman, one woman who was looking at him as if she'd never trust him again, a big guy with huge eyebrows who was avoiding him like the plague and one kaput girlfriend who could no longer keep him safe. He couldn't do much about the last thing, but he had one shot at placating the others.

He began by telling Lisa he was sorry if she felt he'd humiliated her, but letting her carry on would have been wrong.

She looked at him as though he was speaking Martian. 'Why?' she said. 'I wanted it, you wanted it.'

'I didn't know what I wanted, Lisa. I'd just split up with my girlfriend and I was confused and drunk. I got carried away.'

'It was just a blow job, Matt. I give those all—'

Please do not say that, it is well over four months since I had any kind of sex and my groin may burst into flames.

'Well ... um ... that's great if you're happy with that,' he blustered, 'but for me, I like these things to be more private, to mean something more than just a ... well, what you said.'

That got a smile out of her. 'You're a bit old-fashioned, aren't you? Makes me fancy you even more.'

A page-boy, that's what you look like, a particularly sexy page-boy. Oh my God, I'm fancying page-boys.

He shook his head at her. 'Sorry, Lisa. I like you, but that's as far as it goes. I'm not in the market for anything else at the moment.'

'And when you are I expect you'll be back in Bristol.'

'Probably.'

'Soft southern Jessie,' she said, still twinkling at him. 'Well, it's your loss. Getting wankered and having mad sex might be just what you need. Clear the cobwebs away.'

'I quite like the cobwebs. Sorry.'

He judged that was the moment to leave the room, and went back into the hall. People were looking at him, even if they were pretending not to, and probably wondering what he had been saying to Lisa and whether they'd sent Jennifer out so that they could carry on from where Jocelyn had suggested they'd left off on Friday night.

So, stage two. He caught up with Doug in the kitchen. 'Look, Doug,' he said, 'I'm not about to talk behind Lisa's back and tell you what actually happened in Newcastle, but trust me, I'm not Angus.'

He didn't wait to see what Doug's reaction was, he had to get to Jennifer now, and hope he'd timed it right. Ah yes, Lisa had just come out of the room and Jennifer had gone back in.

She was hanging up Lisa's costume.

'Hi,' she said and he could tell that Lisa had filled her in on the details. Knowing Lisa, she'd have been fairly anatomically correct in her description of how far things had gone. He wished he'd come to his senses before she'd unzipped his flies.

'Jennifer,' he said hesitantly, 'you and Doug are my closest friends up here, and I can't bear you to think badly of me.' He paused to make it look as though he was struggling and was then confused to discover that when Jennifer raised her chin and looked at him, he was actually feeling tongue-tied. 'Uh ... what I'm trying to say is that I got a bit carried away with all the drink on Friday after just splitting up with Sonia, and when Lisa seemed a bit hungry and I realised it was for me, I was slow to nip it in the bud and something nearly . . . nearly happened. The only thing she polished off in the end was her kebab. And mine. But I'm not really making a joke of it. I was an idiot and I feel bad.'

His heart was kicking around in his chest and it seemed supremely important that she say something to show there was not going to be any nasty atmosphere between them over this.

'There's no need to feel bad,' Jennifer said matter-of-factly, 'you're a grown-up, you don't have to explain anything to me. But I am sorry about your girlfriend, it's a long time to be with anyone and then have it end.'

He made a brave face and retreated back to the hall feeling cheated. Why was that? Because he'd wanted her to be more emotional? No, it was good she was so straight-forward about it, wasn't it? If she'd been frosty or cross it would have suggested she'd been jealous and that was the last thing he wanted to make her.

He should be thankful he'd saved a tricky situation and he wasn't going to have to explain to O'Dowd how he'd cocked it up.

Nice if Jennifer had looked a bit happier about it though.

He couldn't stop thinking about that when he was running through his lines: and when Finlay called a halt and they got ready to start acting, he waited for Jennifer to come and prompt, realising he was impatient to see her.

The sweet smile she gave him as she sat down on her

chair told him they were still friends, but he wanted that warm, wide smile she was capable of, never mind what it did to that scarring.

He sat and watched the afternoon's rehearsal as people struggled for words without their scripts, talked over each other and generally kept Finlay and Jennifer busy. They were going straight through, just to see how it went. Badly, Mack felt was going to be the answer to that. While he and Doug were nearly spot-on with their words, the rest hadn't come on very far in the few rehearsals he'd missed. Angus was the worst and Jennifer more or less read his part for him while he pranced about striking poses.

There were some bright spots: Neale seemed to be hitting his stride with his portrayal of the snobbish Malvolio, although perhaps he'd taken the instruction to look down his nose at Gerry and Steve a little too literally: the audience were going to have a great view of the contents of his nostrils.

Mack knew he kept looking at Jennifer, at her tight-fitting top and skirt with black boots. Graceful even sitting down.

Lisa was on her feet now, still a little sulky, and she started up with the speech where she professes her love for the Duke without him being aware of the true meaning of the words. To Mack it sounded as if she was making a hash of it, and he saw the look that passed between Jennifer and Finlay.

Later, when they broke off for tea and flapjacks, he tracked Jennifer down to the kitchen and stood just out of view, not because he thought he'd pick up something about Cressida but because he didn't want to interrupt what he was hearing. Jennifer was obviously helping Lisa with her speech, and in Jennifer's mouth the thing that Lisa had just murdered was raised into something intensely affecting. He imagined Jennifer's body moving in response to the words, adding a trace of lightness here, some weight there.

He heard Lisa have a go and it sounded like someone reading a shopping list in comparison.

'Thanks, Jen,' Lisa said when she'd finished, 'didn't realise you knew the whole play off by heart.'

'Oh, come on, Lisa, I'm not that sad.' There was that soft laugh. 'But I've played Viola so often, she's kind of in my head.'

They took another hour and a half to limp to the end of the play, the fight scene between Mack and Gerry being a particularly low point, when Gerry, unused to any physical exertion, managed to smack Neale in the eye. Neale wasn't even in the scene, just standing off to one side learning his lines.

Mack didn't want to think what the fight would be like with swords, even if they were blunt. On second thoughts, maybe he could impale himself on one, and put an end to the whole stinking charade.

CHAPTER 23

Jennifer thought it was probably time to call a halt to what had started off as a bit of light-hearted ribaldry between her and Sheila. Now Lionel was climbing right up on his PC high horse, which was a tricky manoeuvre as he was also trying to order some books online. The woman he was doing it for was not looking amused.

'It's complete objectification, that's all I'm saying.' Lionel used the mouse from the computer to jab his point into the air.

'Is it, rot,' Sheila retorted. 'It's simply an appreciation of the finer things in life.'

'Really?' The heavy weight on that first syllable indicated Lionel was not convinced.

'Furthermore,' Sheila said, 'you're suggesting women shouldn't voice their attraction for men. And I thought you were a champion of equality?'

Jennifer had to turn away at that, feeling her loyalties were becoming divided. On the one hand, Sheila was having a hard time with Reece again (who wanted to go to Ibiza to join his elder brother). On the other, Lionel was a sweetheart and looked genuinely put out. She suspected that it was *who* was being discussed rather than the words being used that was really annoying him.

'I *am* a champion of equality,' Lionel objected. 'I'm the last person who wants a return to the Victorian age, when women weren't even meant to look at their own . . .' He glanced up at the woman he was helping. Too late. She snatched her ticket out of his hand and walked away.

'Watch it, potty-mouth,' Sheila said with a cackle. 'That's much worse than me saying I thought Matt's backside looked like a couple of ripe peaches. Oh, hey up, here he comes. Ssh now.'

Jennifer turned to see Matt making his way down the spiral staircase and wondered why the metal treads were not melting under his feet. The way he moved, that slightly worried expression that was always lurking, they were making her feel like she wanted to break a lot of library rules.

'Yes, definitely ripe peaches,' Sheila said as Matt came up to the desk and Jennifer heard Lionel 'Tsk' and walk away.

'Peaches?' Matt asked, looking wonderfully puzzled.

'Oh, don't mind me, pet. Just making my shopping list.' Sheila picked up a pencil and waved it about. 'Cat food, beans, broccoli, fresh peaches.'

'This time of year?'

'Oh, it can get quite hot here in Northumberland, end of March.'

'Hot flushes anyway,' Jennifer said quietly.

Matt looked completely confused before saying, 'I'm a bit peckish. How do you feel about lunch, Jennifer, can you go yet?'

'Lionel's meant to be going for lunch first.' Sheila was grinning. 'But don't mind that, you trot along instead. I need to have more of a chat with him about soft, downy fruit and hard, ripe—'

'I'll get my coat,' Jennifer said.

Matt was still looking bewildered when Jennifer met him outside, and as they were waiting for a table in the café, he said, 'Why is Sheila so interested in fruit?'

Jennifer didn't reply, choosing instead to enjoy the intimacy of being shoved up against him as they queued, his shoulder against hers. He repeated the question and she still didn't answer, knowing that he would turn to her to see if she'd heard. When he did, faced with those eyes and his slightly parted lips, she dropped her gaze and said, 'Scurvy, her family are prone to it.'

The sound of a donkey braying saved her from further explanation and she scrabbled for her phone.

'I will kill Danny. Um . . . do you mind if I just go outside and answer this, it's . . . I won't be long.'

Mack watched her go out and stand in the courtyard of the café. Today she had on a beautiful pale mauve suede coat and sexy little ankle boots. Her chin was up and her face animated and he guessed it was Cressida on the phone. There was something telling about the way she was laughing and how her free hand was relaxed, but picking little bits of moss off one of the walls. Cress was up early, what was happening?

Did I just think 'sexy boots'?

He looked at Jennifer again and particularly the scarring. It was the bit near her eye that was most off-putting, probably because her eyes were so beautiful. She turned her back, and he filled in the time wondering how sad he should pretend to be about his late girlfriend.

Tiring quickly of that, he watched Jennifer turn slightly with the phone still to her ear and thought of the call he'd had from Tess earlier. Phyllida was due out of hospital at the weekend and Tess seemed upbeat about how she was – a bit irritable and disorientated, but not bad. That had put Mack on alert and he had asked whether Stephen Fry, Stephen Hawking or Professor Brian Cox had been visiting her. They were the nicknames he had given the motley crew Phyllida drank with and when Tess said they had, Mack knew that one of them must be bringing her in drink. Stephen Hawking was his bet. He didn't say anything to Tess; let her think the best and he'd try and sort it out when he was finished here.

He saw Jennifer put the phone back in her pocket as the waitress waved him towards a free table and, just out of interest, he watched what happened when Jennifer came back in. The waitress, who obviously knew her, simply said 'Hello there, love', a couple of other people smiled sympathetically, some looked and then looked away; one man couldn't take his eyes off her and a small child had to be pulled back round in his seat and whispered at quite fiercely. How the Hell did she get used to that? Always under scrutiny. Bit like Cress.

'Sorry about that,' she said, bright-cheeked from the cold and went and hung her coat up. The blouse under it looked like silk.

'Here,' she said, getting his notebook out of her bag, 'found this upstairs when I went for my coat. We're thinking of stapling all your possessions to your jacket.'

He did a quick assessment of whether she was flirting with him now he was minus girlfriend and did the surprised look he used when anyone handed him something he'd mislaid. Or in this case, had dropped on the floor earlier and kicked under a large bookcase so that just enough was left poking out to be spotted.

The man who had been staring at Jennifer earlier was still staring, and Mack caught his eye and stared back at him. The man looked away.

'Important phone call?' he asked as Jennifer studied the menu.

She mouthed the word, 'Cress.'

'OK, don't say any more.' He put his hand up. 'You must get tired of people wanting to hear about her.'

'No, I'm proud of her. I never begrudge anyone asking about her.'

Hurrah.

'Unless they're just digging for dirt.'

Not so hurrah.

Mack saw that the nosy man was having another sneaky

look. Very slowly he let his hand drop and, checking it was out of Jennifer's sight, gave him the finger. Not long after, the man got up, paid his bill and left.

'She's all right though . . . your cousin?' he asked.

The waitress came to the table and they ordered.

'You said something about a jealous wife . . .' he prompted when the waitress had gone.

There was a nervous check on the people sitting nearby. 'Do you mind if we don't talk about it here? I have to be careful.'

Great, at this rate, you're not only going to be here for the play, you'll be here for the ruddy Christmas pantomime too.

The place was packed. He needed to get her away somewhere quiet if he was going to make any headway. This morning he'd been 'researching and writing up the notes' from his latest walk up to Kielder Forest. It was definitely quiet up there.

Hang on, why's she looking at you like that?

His guilty conscience, never far below the surface, gave his heart rate a bit of a kick.

'Matt,' Jennifer said, her blue eyes brimming with sympathy, 'you don't have to pretend to be all bright and breezy. How are you really feeling . . . about Sonia?'

It took him a second to remember that Sonia was his ex and not the lusty version in the shop.

'I'm fine, really fine.' He did a bit of sighing and tried not to think about how that soft, concerned look from Jennifer was making him feel.

She shook her head, sadly. 'Don't be silly. How can you

be fine, finishing a long-term relationship and being so far from all your friends and family? You told me I should show what I felt more; well, the same applies to you. If you want to sit quiet, I'll understand.'

'No, honestly, Jennifer, I'm actually feeling all right. It hadn't been going well for a long time, me and Sonia, and in a way it's a bit of a relief to get it all sorted.' There was a hiatus while Jennifer's soup and his sandwich were brought to the table, and he watched her shepherd some soup on to her spoon.

'Besides,' he continued, 'I had a lovely walk up at Kielder yesterday that lifted my spirits. Do you like it up there?'

'It's OK,' she answered without much enthusiasm, and before she said anything else he knew that she was going to take another step forward, trusting him with something that was precious to her.

'Actually,' she said, looking down at her soup spoon, 'my favourite place in all Northumberland is Low Newton. It's a beach, but more than a beach.' She looked up then, and her eyes were full of life. 'You should go there, Matt, you'd love it.'

'Oh?' he said softly, 'you think so?'

'Yes.'

'Why?'

'It's hard to explain . . . the light, the colours, the atmosphere . . . they're all magical.'

'That's a pretty big claim, Jennifer.'

'It's a pretty wonderful place, Matt.'

'Prove it,' he said and felt the conversation whisk out of his control.

Prove it? What happened to 'I don't suppose you'd consider showing me, would you?'

She was still looking at him and his mouth had gone dry.

'All right,' she said, slowly as if picking up the gauntlet he had thrown down, 'I will.'

He took several large bites out of his sandwich so that neither of them needed to talk again for a while. She ate her soup. She even did that gracefully.

She put down her spoon again. 'If you don't like Low Newton, you won't do that brutal-honesty thing will you? It's really special to me, I don't want it trashed.'

'Jennifer, if it's special to you, I'll treat it with kid gloves,' he said and did not understand why he had put his hand over hers to say it. He always seemed to be putting his hand over hers.

He saw her blush. It was the only time the scar seemed paler than her skin.

'Would they be kid gloves you haven't lost yet?' she asked, and he felt her turn her hand under his so their palms were together.

'Ah! Here you are,' a voice said and Jennifer's hand was suddenly not under his any more.

It was Alex, walking towards the table, pulling up a chair to join them, making a big palaver of taking off his waxed jacket and rolling up his sleeves.

Nice subliminal message about being ready for a fight there, Alex.

Had he seen Mack touching Jennifer's hand and the way she had withdrawn it?

'I'm just on my lunch,' Jennifer said nervously and then looked at Mack as if realising she'd stated the obvious.

'Yes, I saw you walking this way. Oh, waitress –' Alex stuck his hand up in the air and did something with his fingers that was nearly a click, and Mack caught Jennifer's eye and saw the embarrassment there – 'latte and a toasted teacake.'

No 'please'? No 'hello, Matt'?

'So,' he said looking at Mack, finally, 'only a couple of weeks till your big moment – how are rehearsals going?'

Like you care.

'Really quite well,' Mack said in his jumpy-dog voice. 'People seem to be getting into their stride. The scenes with Pamela, Gerry and Steve are so funny. Tremendous. Most of that's down to Jennifer here.' He saw her colour again and hoped Alex noticed it. He could almost hear the guy working out how to slap him down.

Here it comes.

'Saw Danny yesterday,' Alex said, 'told me you'd been to the farm. What did you think? As a complete outsider.'

Thanks for that . . . Now, what would good old Matt Harper say?

'Fascinating. Never knew there was so much science involved. You know, scanning the sheep to see how many lambs they're carrying.'

Alex shook his head, 'That's the easy part; it's coping with all the bloody regulations and restrictions that's tricky.'

'I don't think Matt wants to know about those,' Jennifer said.

'No, that's the trouble,' Alex replied grouchily, 'the public doesn't want to know anything about the reality of farming, just wants to pick up their cheap chickens in the supermarket.'

'Do you do chickens then?' Mack asked innocently and saw Jennifer's flick of a smile.

'No, of course I don't do chickens. Whatever "do" means. I *do* sheep. I was just quoting an example.'

'Well, I always buy organic anyway.' Mack got up quickly. 'I should go. I'll get the bill.'

Alex did a little flap of his hand. 'It's all right, we'll add it to ours.'

Ours? Jennifer's face is suggesting there is no 'ours'.

'And I'm sorry if I interrupted anything earlier.' Mack saw the little sideways glance that went with Alex's words.

'Matt's been having girlfriend trouble,' Jennifer said very quickly. 'I was just trying to cheer him up.'

Girlfriend trouble? You're avoiding telling him she's history. Keeping everything sweet as usual.

'Oh dear, really? Never mind, you'll soon be back in Bristol. I'm sure it'll sort itself out then.' Alex's satisfied smile made Mack feel as if he'd been dismissed.

Get out of here before you rise to the bait and say something stupid.

'Actually we've split up,' Mack shot back.

The momentary satisfaction of seeing Alex's expression fracture was replaced by the knowledge that he had quite unnecessarily made him suspicious and, worst of all, probably made Jennifer wonder why he was winding him up.

'Bus to catch,' he said before he could do any more damage and left Jennifer to deal with any fallout.

CHAPTER 24

Crossing over the dual carriageway, they headed off down a side road that narrowed and meandered between high hedges, adding to the impression that they were alone on some secret path. Jen wound down the window and took a deep breath.

'That smell,' she said, 'always gets me.'

'Sorry,' Matt replied, 'is it my feet?' Jennifer laughed, remembering as she set off up that rising scale, to show some restraint: she might feel like whooping and hollering, but she had to keep a lid on this happiness. Matt was simply being shown a beach. She didn't know what she was being shown, but it felt pretty wonderful.

'It's the sea,' she said, curtailing the laugh. 'Go on, smell it.'

He put his window down and theatrically took in huge lungfuls of air and just as theatrically coughed it all up again. Her hair started to blow around in the cross-draught.

'Not enough pollution for me,' he said, but she noticed

he left his window down. She gave her full attention to the road again, but the smell of salt lurking in the air was setting off all kind of residual memories of long days on the beach, brushing sand off her skin, trying to get a comb through her hair after the wind and sea had been at it. There had been rare, hot days, but mainly ones like this: blue sky, a sharp zing to the air and the feeling you were on the edge of the world. Anything was possible.

She had worried away at the weather forecasts since he had thrown down that challenge to show him the beach and had been rewarded with this, a day so bright she had to put her sunglasses on to drive. She watched the hedgerows pass, the forsythia in bloom in gardens and was struck again by the sharpness of the light. There were one, two, three clouds away to the east, strung out as if they were too lazy to bother to really be clouds.

'Still don't know how you get the sky so big up here,' he said.

'Special rollers, camouflaged so you can't see them.'

It was him laughing now and she knew that if she looked his hair would be blowing around as hers was, and he'd be doing that thing with his hand where he pushed it back any old how and scrunched up his eyes to look through it when it blew down again.

'Much further?' he asked.

'Just through here and round the bend a bit,' she said, driving past low houses and a school. When the road headed upwards she felt suddenly bold, 'Close your eyes. If you want the full experience, you have to close your eyes.'

'Now, Jennifer,' he said, 'I've seen pictures already. I do my homework, you know.'

She slowed the car to a stop and gave him a look, glad he couldn't see her eyes properly behind her sunglasses.

'OK, OK,' he said, shaking his head, 'I'll go for the full experience.' When he closed his eyes she forced herself to look forward again.

That's what he looks like asleep. Ready for kissing awake.

He made a noise and she turned to look at him again.

'Sorry?'

'Nothing. Just a bit of non-polluted air stuck in my throat.'

'Sure?'

He nodded and she set off again, waiting until the car had come over the hump of the hill and was on the other side before slowing to a halt again and turning to look at him. She wanted to see that moment when he opened his eyes.

'OK, here you go.' She watched his face and there it was: genuine surprise and then a kind of incredulity. A little boy with his bucket and spade.

'Tell me this is a film set?' he said, looking at the view and then at her and back at the view, but she was too happy to want to answer and probably would have sat there for much longer if a car had not suddenly come up behind them.

'Let's go and park,' she said.

*

They walked down the road that ended at the beach and Mack let his face do whatever it wanted in reaction to the sight in front of him. Spread out before them was a bay of almost apricot-white sand. Two lines of low rocks ran out to sea at either end of it, creating an impression that the sea here was enclosed. That impression of shelter and cosiness was echoed by the way the beach was backed by high dunes covered with long, pale green grass. Dotted amongst the grass were huts and larger cabins and the whole feeling was of a little community hunkered down, nestling right on the edge of the sea. That alone would have made it a beautiful place, but what propelled it into the magical league, the kind of place that got into your brain like a siren song, was the feature that dominated the skyline – a ruined castle lying like a mauled and shattered crown on its massive sill of rock. It was impossible to look at it without imagining skeleton knights and ghostly ladies, storms and dungeons, bloody deeds. The juxtaposition of such ruined grandeur next to the tranquillity of the beach did strange things to the viewer's sense of perspective, and Mack felt that in mist or driving rain it would have cast a sinister, haunting air over the place. Today, in full sun, it was simply stunning.

'So let me get this right. You've got the perfect beach, the sea, little houses, a great wreck of a castle.'

'And one of the best pubs you'll ever go in—'

'I've been in a few.' He wasn't sure Matt Harper would have said that, he was going to have to be careful. Mind you it wasn't as big a clanger as the one he'd nearly dropped when she'd told him to close his eyes in the car and he'd almost said, 'I hope you don't do the same.' That would have reminded her nicely of her accident.

They passed hikers and families, people in wetsuits and he was so intent on the view he didn't watch the people watching Jennifer.

'So you've been coming here since you were a little girl?'

She was smiling, had taken off her sunglasses. 'Yes. Dad's not one for the beach, but Mum is. She grew up in Wallsend by the river – her dad worked in the shipyards – she came here on the odd day trip with her mum. She loves it and so do I.' There was a shy little glance his way.

'She's not a farmer's daughter then?'

'Mum? No. Met Dad when she was a teacher, she'd brought her class on a farm visit. That was when Granddad was still running the farm.'

The knowledge that Brenda was from what he suspected was a tough background took his mind off the view for a while and they walked on side by side, Jennifer shading her eyes to look out to sea and then towards the beach huts.

'I've always wanted one of those,' she said. 'I mean, I love the countryside, but imagine waking up to the sound of the sea, the whole day stretching away to the horizon.'

'Couldn't you save up for one?'

She bent and picked up a piece of driftwood, unwinding skeins of seaweed from it. 'It's not as easy as that. They hardly ever come up for sale. They're usually passed down and kept in the family.' She threw the stick into the sea. 'It's a nice dream.'

Another one you've shelved and put away.

'How's the novel going?' she suddenly asked.

He thought of it lying unloved on his laptop. 'Great, wrote another chapter last night.'

'Good. I'm so glad you didn't give it up. Aren't you?'

'Yes, very. Look, do you fancy a sit-down?'

They walked up the beach and found a sheltered spot, and the sun sparkling on the sea was so bright that it made his eyes water.

She was sitting right next to him and when the wind blew her hair it flicked his face. He should move. Put some distance between them. He should work the conversation round to Cressida.

He watched her watching the sea and felt he didn't know how to do this any more.

'They get seals coming in here sometimes,' she said.

'I might meet them later; I'm going to have a paddle.'

'It'll be freezing.' She scooped up a handful of sand and looked as if she was feeling the weight of it, her hand bouncing slightly, and he told her about going in the sea with Doug.

She tipped the sand out. 'I hope he's careful in the water. The current there is treacherous.'

'I wonder if the beaches in California are like this?' He waited a few seconds. 'How's your cousin getting on with that lady married to that man Ralph?'

'Rory,' she said, giving him a playful push. 'You really don't take much interest in films, do you?'

He pushed her back. 'I remembered it began with an R

and that you were going to tell me how she was getting on when we were in the café.' He grinned and wished he hadn't because he wondered if she would think he was remembering how he'd put his hand on hers.

Clearing away some dry sand near where he was sitting to reveal the wetter layer beneath, he began to trace a pattern with his little finger.

Jennifer wondered what that grin had meant. Was he remembering putting his hand over hers?

Don't run ahead. You promised Cress you wouldn't run away, but don't run ahead.

'Well Rory is a bit of a naughty boy,' she said, knowing he wasn't really interested and was just being polite. 'I told you his wife is jealous and it's hardly surprising. He's pursuing Cress right under her nose. A low spot came the day before yesterday when he turned up in her trailer. It was only the runner knocking on the door that stopped her having to slap him right down. As Cress said, "He was trying to get his hand round my U-bend." Oh, sorry, that won't make much sense. Cress and I tend to talk in a kind of code, you see, when there's anything sensitive being discussed. We call Rory the plumber, hence the joke. But it's not funny. Hard to say no to someone who's as big a player as Rory.'

'Poor Cressida.' His brown eyes looked so regretful that she wanted to put her arm around him.

'Don't worry. Cress, clever clogs, worked out a little strategy.' She scooped up some more sand and watched the little rivulets run through her fingers. 'She waited for the next inevitable incident and had a full-on panic attack. She's really good at those ... got us out of a couple of dreadful parties when we were younger. She's told him that she does fancy him like mad, but the pressure of the filming and his wife glowering at her is just too much and she's teetering on the brink of nervous exhaustion.' She laughed. 'Said that she'd give him an IOU on the sex thing, for when the film was over, otherwise she just knew she'd have to have a break from filming.'

'That would be bad, wouldn't it?'

'Disastrous. I think Rory could see the dollars actually going down the drain. Since then he's been treating her like a piece of porcelain, even leaving little presents in her trailer. And she's had a breakthrough with the wife too; she's showing Cress how to knit. Does these amazing cobwebby wall hangings, evidently.'

'You have a very clever cousin,' he said, and she saw him rub out the pattern he had made and begin again. 'I'm presuming she'll never honour that IOU?'

'She'll run as fast as her Manolo Blahniks will let her.'

'Manolo?'

'Shoes, stylish and expensive ones.' She purposely did not look at his horrible brogues. She looked at him instead, wondering how she could have become so attracted to this slightly naive guy, so different from the ones she'd gravitated towards at uni. In a strange way, she felt protective of him, sitting there looking first puzzled and then with that sweet sadness about him. Was he still thinking about Sonia?

'OK,' he said, standing up, 'time for a paddle,' and he was running down to the sea. She watched him take off his shoes and socks and looked at his bare feet and felt a spasm of lust. How pathetic, she was turned on by his feet. She got up and followed him down to the water's edge as he rolled up his horrible jeans, and laughed at the faces he was making while he waded in up to his calves.

'Bet you can't stay in for a minute,' she called, starting to time him on her watch, and then on the spur of the moment as he was coming out, gasping and teeth chattering, gathered up his shoes and socks and ran away from him.

She ran on before she was brought to a halt by a sharp tug on her coat and then she felt Matt's arms come around her and he was trying to get her to drop the shoes. Her heart was pounding more from having him so close than from the exertion and she knew she would look hot and flustered. He was breathing heavily too, fumbling to try to get a grip on one shoe. She let him have it and peeled away from him with the other, running backwards as he came after her. Suddenly anxious about the way he was piling towards her, she threw the shoe she was holding up the beach towards the sand dunes, and balled the socks and threw them too. She thought he would stop and gather everything up, but he didn't, he kept on running and then suddenly she was upside-down over his shoulder and screeching and he was heading for the sea.

'No, Matt, I'm sorry. Stop!' she yelled.

'Too late for that,' he said, and people were looking and smiling and she felt dizzy and exhilarated and faintly afraid.

'In you go,' he shouted and made a movement to tip her right over his shoulder. She screamed really loudly and felt his chest vibrate under her thighs as if he was laughing. When he lowered her back on to the sand they stood face to face and for a wild moment she wondered if he would bend his head and place his lips on hers – there was something in his eyes that told her it was going to happen. Neither of them moved, and then there it was again, that look of regret, sadness.

It was her cue to step backwards and say something about going to get his stuff for him and for him to cough and say, yes, his feet were getting cold and perhaps it was time for some lunch?

They walked back to the pub commenting on the light and the flock of wading birds and the number of walkers streaming along the coastal path by the coastguard station, and he joked that he should be doing that and not going to the pub.

He stopped just before they left the beach, said he wanted to get some shells for his nieces, and she helped him gather them up. She sensed he was as nervous as her about what had just happened.

'I should have known you would like beaches,' she said,

trying to get back that sense of ease between them. 'After you wrote about all those ones in Dorset. What's the nearest one to where you live now?'

'To Bath?' he said, putting the shells in his pocket. 'Not sure if it's Clevedon or Weston-super-Mare.'

'Bath?'

'What?'

She bent down and retrieved a shell he had let slip from his hand.

'You said Bath.'

'Did I?' She heard him laugh as she straightened back up. 'Must be all this water making me think of baths. Meant Bristol. What an idiot.'

Sitting side by side in the pub at a bleached-pine table, he had beer and she had tonic water and they ate their crab sandwiches and agreed there was nothing like fresh crab to give you a taste of the sea. She didn't feel as disappointed as she thought she might about him not having kissed her; she wasn't sure she was ready for that yet. And he obviously wasn't either. She was just happy that for a split second it looked as though he had wanted to kiss her. Actually wanted to.

She knew, as always, that people were looking at her, one woman was really staring and she stared back and raised an eyebrow as if to say, 'What? It's scarred skin, not an extra head.' Today it didn't feel bitter; luxuriating in the heat coming off the man sitting by her side, everything seemed sweet.

CHAPTER 25

Mack sat in the chair in the cottage, the one in the front room where he did all his thinking and which he'd come to think of as the 'torture chair', and took off his brogues and socks. Upending the shoes, one after the other, he tipped sand on the carpet.

Of all the stupid things to do, he had done it. He should have been staying behind that line he'd drawn in the sand, not cavorting about on it. Not getting his Baths mixed up with his Bristols.

It was the exhilaration of getting that little nugget about Rory and Cressida that had made him lose the plot. It might not seem much at the minute, but a wooing superstar plus expensive presents might add up to something other than the ending Jennifer envisaged. Cressida had a habit of choosing good-looking men or powerful ones and Rory was both. Add in Rory's willingness to wait for her and it was a heady aphrodisiac. Would it matter that he sounded like a right knob-head?

He rubbed the sand into the carpet with one of his feet,

watching it settle among the other stains and dirt and remembered what Jennifer had felt like when he'd lifted her up. There was nothing on her, but what there was had felt extremely . . .

He struggled up from the chair and went into the kitchen to get a drink of water.

At least the journey back from the beach had been uneventful, both of them making an effort to hide behind small talk. When he hadn't been talking, he had looked out at the fields, imagining them come spring and early summer, yellow with rape or white-gold with barley and wheat.

White-gold like Jennifer's hair.

Standing at the sink with the cup to his lips, his mind travelled from her hair to her willowy body and soon he was remembering the way the dress she'd had on at yesterday's rehearsals had gently skimmed over her breasts, her belly, her hips.

Get a grip, man.

The doorbell rang and he jarred the cup against his teeth. He hoped whoever it was would go away. When the bell rang again, he opened the door slowly to see Sonia. She handed him his glasses and leaned against the door frame to show herself to best advantage. 'You left them on the counter. Again.' There was a little flicker of mischief in her eyes. 'And what's this I've heard about you turning Lisa down?'

'Um . . . well, I wouldn't say . . . um . . . you know . . . I've never been one to, well, hop from one romance to the next.'

'Really? I have. Though I suppose as you've been having him in for little chats,' she jerked her head towards Mr Armstrong's door, 'you'll know all about that, eh?'

He just wanted to get in the house and close his eyes for a while and think about what had happened on the beach. He couldn't be bothered with all that 'Gosh, no' rubbish; was suddenly sick of being a nervy dork.

'Mr Armstrong thinks you bought your husband off the Internet,' he said, brutally.

She let out a great whoop of laughter. 'Daft bugger. I *met* him on an Internet dating site. Suppose he told you too that Gregor only married me for a British passport? That it's bad enough, the eastern Europeans coming over here for our jobs, let alone our women?' She crossed her arms, looked suddenly aggressive. 'Well, let's put the record straight. Gregor is half British anyway; his mum's from Didcot, though he's lived in the Czech Republic since he was about five. He's a scientist, works for the Forestry Commission up at Kielder Forest. Very brainy. Likes older women, that's why he was on that site. It's not a crime. He's twenty-seven and I'm forty-two and if he doesn't care about the age gap, then neither do I. Dad's slowly coming round to me having a toy-boy husband, as he calls it, but I'm careful I don't rub his nose in it. So, if old Armstrong's said I've been fornicating on the chest freezer, he's lying.' She screwed up her eyes. 'What else? Oh yes, Gregor's my third husband. First one dropped dead in his twenties, six months we'd been married; second one left me for a woman up in Edinburgh. Oh and in between, I've slept with quite a few men, and yes, it's probably me that's done the leading on.' She uncrossed her arms. 'There, straight from the horse's mouth.'

This time Mack did say, 'Gosh.'

'Gosh indeed,' she mimicked and then her expression became knowing. 'And don't think you're fooling me with that butter-wouldn't-melt act. You're sniffing around . . . got your eye on someone. You're all of a jitter and strung out like a young fox on a scent.'

After she'd gone, he felt shaken and wondered how many editions of O'Dowd's paper he could fill with her life history alone. The woman was a walking soap opera and far too nosy for her own good.

Mr Armstrong's door opened and he poked his head out.

'Told you, didn't I?' he said, 'Whore of Babylon.'

Mack went back inside and sat in the torture chair again, the feel of the sand in the carpet taking him back to the beach and listening to that soft laugh and looking into those blue eyes and trying not to feel like the lowest form of human life.

'Say that again slowly, Jen.'

Jennifer shut the kitchen door and stood looking at the table, her mind still thinking about hanging upside down over Matt's shoulder.

'I had the best time, Cress, and . . . at one point, I thought he was going to kiss me.'

'Not that bit, Jen, although that's lovely. Say that other

thing again. The thing you said as soon as I answered the phone. It's wonderful to hear it.'

'OK,' she said, with a laugh she didn't know was coming. 'Hope, Cress. I have hope.'

CHAPTER 26

The trip to the beach had jumbled Mack's brain and now he felt that the two men he was trying to be were at war with each other. Mack Stone; Matt Harper – one was calculating, watching and listening; the other seemed to be living in the moment and doing things he hadn't told him to do. He found himself putting on his walking boots one morning and enjoying, actually enjoying, the thought of getting up on to the moors. He sat down in a chair and took his boots off again pretty sharpish, but then he just spent the whole day hanging around the cottage. When the sun came out, he sat on the front doorstep and got a wave from a woman and child who lived in the cottage next to Mr Armstrong's. Sonia had introduced them to him in the shop. He went inside to fetch a book, came back out and sat reading it. Just after lunch he saw Sonia and Gregor snogging beside Gregor's car. When they came up for air, they waved at him too.

In the evening a car drew up just as he was setting out to walk to rehearsal. It was Lisa offering him a lift.

He got into the car warily. They'd fallen into a joky but strained friendship following the 'kebab incident', but he worried that this lift might be the start of a new campaign to 'bag him'. When she handed him some brochures about personal finances and, on the journey to the hall, asked him various questions about his savings and current account and his pension arrangements, he realised she was after his business, not his body. He hoped he would be able to remember all the made-up answers to her questions. 'Just let me know if there's anything I can do to help,' she said as she parked the car. 'I do Gerry's and Pamela's accounts for them. I'm good, Matt, could save you a few pounds.' She gave him a big wink at that, but it had 'friend' stamped on it, not 'hottie'.

Everyone seemed to love Matt Harper. And Matt Harper had a worrying tendency to love everyone back.

At rehearsal he had wrapped his arms around Doug and given him a spontaneous hug when Finlay had congratulated them on how well their scenes had gone. In fact, he found himself smiling like an idiot as the rehearsal had progressed and the cast had worked through the last act. There were still fluffs and pauses, but for the first time there was continuity; more cues picked up, pace injected; some real character development. Ten days before they were due on stage and they were starting to pull this play together.

As the days passed, he became more and more aware that he was a person pretending to be another person pretending to be an Elizabethan young man. He feared he was going to unravel.

He was in danger of unravelling with Jennifer as well, he knew that. Watching her sitting with the prompt book he couldn't keep his mind from the beach and the way her body had felt against his. He sensed she was thinking of it too. There was none of the chin-down avoidance of the early days, but a certain sweet shyness, as though she did not trust herself not to nick his socks and shoes again.

He told himself he could handle it and he did. They bumped along, going for coffee, sitting by each other in the pub. He even accepted the odd lift home, and she had fed him little snippets of news from America: Rory was still wooing; Cress prevaricating and knitting.

At the rehearsal exactly one week before the first performance, things got more disorientating. Finlay was taking him and Jocelyn through their scenes again and Mack could only sympathise with Finlay's worried look. They made for a chilling couple: Mack found it impossible to hide his animosity and Jocelyn had obviously tuned in to his true feelings. In retaliation she had begun calling him 'Brogue Male' (which he found funny), or 'Mr Jumble-Sale-Wurzle Head' (which he didn't). She also liked to point out loudly that there was only one letter dividing wankers from walkers. Matt Harper smiled placidly.

When they had played their scenes together before, Mack had got into the habit of thinking about Lisa to get some warmth going. This time when he went to conjure her up, remembering her on her knees in front of him in that alleyway, he felt a sharp stab of panic: the head he was now looking down on was blonde.

He needed Cressida to do something soon – fall for Rory, have wild sex with the director, run off with one of the lighting crew, anything, but make it soon.

He tried to put Mack Stone firmly back in control, and when Doug knocked on his door that Saturday and asked if he'd help get the set ready, his mind told him not to get involved; his body shrugged on his fleece and went and sat in Doug's car. He determined that he would only stay a couple of hours but, seduced by the sense of community and warmth in the hall, he was there until the end of the day, putting up flats and steadying the long ladders while members of the backstage crew hung lights.

When Jennifer appeared he tried to be hearty and dorky and not notice what she was wearing and how she moved and that soft laugh of hers. The strain gave him a thumping headache.

Next day he lay low in Newcastle, only speaking to O'Dowd, who, when Mack gave him the latest updates, told him he'd soon be out of there. He said it was just a matter of time before Cress gave in to Rory and then all Hell was going to break loose. Married man, American icon – Mack could almost hear O'Dowd salivating into the phone.

When Mack arrived for rehearsal on the Monday he told himself he didn't care whether the set was half finished and looked like a dog's breakfast. He didn't care about these people, or the play. Except when his eyes saw the set, finished and a credible approximation of an Italian palace courtyard, complete with two box hedges in long stone pots, a genuine 'Wow' escaped from his lips.

'It is pretty good,' Gerry said, screwing up his eyes. 'Not as good as for the Scottish play, mind you. We had a thrust stage for that and a smoke machine.'

'Doesn't matter what it looks like,' Doug said morosely, 'everything will go tits up when we get on it.'

Four hours later Mack understood what Doug had meant and suddenly he was caring about the play and the people again. They were all in it together, and 'it' was a shambles.

Faced with the finished set, the cast had gone into a collective nervous spasm: actors had come on too early in some scenes and failed to come on at all in others. Angus had dried up repeatedly and stood blinking into the lights; Neale only had two volumes: whisper or bellow; and Doug and Mack had morphed into back-slapping dunderheads. Even Jocelyn appeared rattled and delivered most of her lines upstage. Best comedy moment had been when Gerry had got himself entangled in one of the box hedges, but by that point no one was laughing. Just before the end the whole hall had been plunged into darkness.

'Sorry,' a tremulous voice had said from the lighting desk.

'Don't be,' Jennifer said, 'it's something of a blessing.'

Marjorie, who had come along, as always, simply to offer her opinion, was slumped down in her seat, either asleep or in a coma. Finlay leaped to his feet, a big wedge of notes in his hand.

'Not bad, not bad at all,' he said with real enthusiasm, and the cast looked at each other as if Finlay had been watching a different play. 'I love the way you're pacing yourselves, holding back on those big performances I know you're all capable of. Just remember there isn't one scene in this play that we haven't done brilliantly at some time. All we have to do is knit them all together into a continuous whole. Wait until the dress rehearsal tomorrow . . . whoosh.' Finlay did some big sweeping motions with his hands.

Mack saw backs begin to straighten and smiles return.

Finlay was still roaming around. 'So, onwards and upwards, and don't forget, in costume tomorrow by six thirty ready for the photographer from the *Courant*. OK, I have notes for you all. Read them and come back to me tonight if you don't understand anything.' He waved the bundle of papers. 'Form an orderly queue.'

Jennifer did not know how Finlay kept a straight face. At some points they were all over the place with the script and she had felt as if she were watching a piece of wood being turned over and over by the current and not knowing if she should leap in and set it straight. Poor Matt, he had been one of the worst – leaden in his scenes with Jocelyn and then playing Stan Laurel to Doug's Oliver Hardy. She looked across at him and caught his eye and looked away. Every time she saw him she remembered being held upside down, the way his body had felt against hers. She knew he was remembering it too. It was just a question of waiting for that spark to happen again. She was sure it would. She felt something knot low down in her belly at the prospect.

'The thing is, with Shakespeare . . .' she heard Marjorie say, advancing groggily towards her, and Jennifer hurriedly picked up her phone.

'Sorry, Marjorie, I've got to do something backstage. Will you excuse me?' She slipped through the door at the side of the stage and walked down the corridor towards the large room that for the duration of the play would be where the cast changed and sat quietly until they were 'on'. Clothes rails had already been moved into it and two large screens erected to create separate dressing areas for the men and women. In a few days' time it would be a jumble of costumes and people and nerves. Now there were only a few costumes hanging up, some hats in a box and a tangled ball of tights on a table.

She moved to the women's side, put her phone on a table and started sorting through the make-up box and arranging its contents along the windowsill, surreptitiously sniffing one of the tubes of make-up and feeling the memories of past performances rise and drift.

When the sound of a goat broke into her thoughts, she snatched up the phone again and waited for Cressida to speak. Cressida's voice sounded fevered. Wrong.

'OK, Jen,' she said, 'something weird has happened. There have been developments.'

'Developments?'

'Yes.'

'This sounds ominous, Cress, are you all right?'

'It's not ominous, sweetie, sorry, didn't mean to scare you. It's more . . . unforeseen.' Cress went quiet and then said, stumbling, 'I'm a little shell-shocked.'

'Take it slowly.'

'Right. You know that red Hermès bag I had?'

'Y-e-s.'

'I lost it.'

Jennifer took a moment to absorb the news. 'Lost it?'

'Yes. Totally. I mean there have been plenty of times I thought I'd lost it, but I'd only mislaid it for a while. This time I've really lost it.'

'Just like that?'

Weeks before Cressida had gone to America, she and Jennifer had worked out a number of code words for things that must not be discussed openly. Cressida's blood-red Hermès bag was her heart.

'One minute it was there and then the next it wasn't.'

'God, Cress. It's a big thing to have . . . stolen. Didn't you notice it . . . going?'

'No. I didn't in a million years think the person responsible would . . . well, I wouldn't have expected it. I'd arranged to meet them, just for coffee and a chat. Then POW! Bag gone.'

'So he—'

'Please Jen; I need to think this through . . . I'm sitting tight and doing nothing at the moment. I've made that clear to the person who . . . who took the bag. They're not going to shout it from the rooftops either – the fallout for them will be much worse than for me. I know, I know, this won't make sense, but just give me a few days, just to sort it out in my mind.'

'Cress, hang on a minute,' Jennifer said suddenly aware of a noise from the men's section of the room. She got up and peered around the screen. The ball of tights which had been on the table was now on the floor.

'Sorry, Cress, carry on, just something falling down. Look . . .' She chose her words carefully. 'This person who took the bag, did you know them already? Why will it be tricky?'

There was no response, and then, 'Jen, just tell me whatever happens, you'll still love me.' A thick vein of pleading ran through the words, and Jennifer felt her curiosity shift into something more anxious.

'What? Of course I'll still love you, what on earth are you talking about?'

'Whoever this person is?'

Jennifer floundered around until she could think how to fit what she wanted to say into this blasted code. 'Cress, if you're happy, I'll be happy. Just . . . make sure it's not a temporary loss that you're getting out of proportion. Just promise me that. God, listen to me, I sound ancient.'

'Jen. I have to go . . . I'm sorry; I haven't asked anything about the play, about Matt . . . all right, all right, I'm coming. Talk later, Jen. Bye. Love you.'

Jennifer looked at the phone in her hand as if she wasn't sure she'd really had that conversation or whether it had been in her head. She had learned to weather the ups and downs of Cressida's love life, her tendency to be besotted one minute and ripping up love letters the next, but this sounded different. Cressida had always seemed to be in control, perhaps a little more enamoured of the idea of being madly in love than actually feeling it. The way she had just been talking sounded as if she was in the grip of something monumental.

Mack got back out into the hall, just as Finlay had finished with Doug and now only had one set of notes left in his hand.

'Ah, there you are, Matt,' he said, 'well done, well done.'

Mack listened to his heart thumping and pretended to scan his notes, glad that he did not have to talk to anyone right at that moment. When he had calmed down enough to be able to read what Finlay had written he was amazed that there was nothing about being 'a wooden-tongued, numb-faced, passionless dolt'. The comments were upbeat, only touching lightly on the negatives.

You are a cunning bugger, Finlay. Now there's part of me that wants to please you even more, though that other part of me is hoping I'm not even here for your damn play. You're as skilled a manipulator as O'Dowd, in your way.

And talking of O'Dowd ... from Jennifer's overheard replies it was obvious Cressida had been in a right old flap. What had Jennifer said? 'It's a big thing to have stolen.' If only those bloody tights hadn't hit the deck. Did Jennifer mean 'big' as in 'large' or 'big' as in 'important'? Mack felt suddenly panicky. What if some journalist had nicked her diary or something else personal and was just about to splash it over the papers?

No, hang about. You're getting ahead of yourself. Jennifer's the one Cress is confiding in, not some diary. Whatever someone's nicked, it's not the story. Jennifer's the keeper of that.

He let everyone else go to the pub, saying he was waiting for Jennifer. Perhaps he should ask her to go to a different pub? No. After the beach, that would be sending out the wrong message.

When she emerged from backstage, what message he might be sending out was immaterial: she looked completely distracted. He guessed he was on a hiding to nothing, attempting to talk to her.

'I almost lost the will to live in a few places back there,' he said.

'You lose most things,' she replied, nearly at the door, buttoning up her coat.

He tried again. 'I know I didn't exactly cover myself in glory this evening, but—'

'No, you didn't.' She looked irritated. 'Jocelyn and you are still like a couple of plaster dummies. Your feet are wrong too, all nervous, like you're scared if you position them correctly, your bodies will touch.'

It was only when he said, genuinely hurt, 'Gosh, I thought *I* was the brutally honest one,' that she seemed to realise what she'd said. She rubbed her fingers back and forth across her forehead. 'Sorry, Matt, I didn't mean to be so harsh . . . look, I'm a bit tired tonight, I'm going to head home.'

There was no point in asking for a lift, she was already walking quickly along the path to the car park. Whatever Cressida had told her, she needed time to mull it over alone, that much was obvious.

Doug took him home in the end, chatting about Pat and wondering if she'd come to the play. Mack did enough to pretend he was listening. This was all getting serious now; this was what he had come here for. He had to remember that: harden his heart for the last push.

CHAPTER 27

The man in the baggy suit who had turned up from the council to give them a 'little chat' about cost-cutting initiatives was getting only a tiny part of Jennifer's attention – the part that wasn't being expended on Cressida's weird phone call and the man sitting up in the gallery wearing what looked like a new fleece.

However Jennifer twisted and turned over what Cress had said, everything seemed to point towards Rory Sinclair being her new love. How could she have fallen so deeply for him after the way she'd talked about him before? And what was all that about the repercussions for him being worse than for Cress? Rory had affairs all over the place; they were like water off a duck's back. Unless . . . unless he'd actually fallen for Cress as much as she'd fallen for him?

Could a man who seemed so in love with himself, fall that deeply, that quickly? Stranger things had happened in love. She glanced up at Matt, but he seemed lost in his thoughts. Or maybe he was still smarting from all those tactless things she'd said yesterday evening.

Lionel gave her a nudge. Poor Lionel, he looked unsettled, but she did not know if it was in anticipation of what was about to be said or Sheila's probable reaction to it.

Jennifer felt her body yearn to turn and stare up at Matt again, and so she did. This time he grinned down at her, and she not only felt relief, but lust. Would today be the day he'd kiss her? Right now she was going to have to settle for that grin, but who knew, it was nearly lunchtime and he might ask her out. She smiled up at him and felt light-headed with possibilities. Could he really see beyond this scarring?

Stop with the questions, Jen, you'll wear yourself out.

'We're looking at all kinds of initiatives to give the public ownership of our services,' the man from the council was saying. 'We'll be taking self-service checking out and return of books a step further—'

'To self-service putting the books back on the shelves?' Sheila asked tartly.

'Or we might even have to look at staffing levels.'

'With a view to making staff cuts?' Lionel asked, his frown indicating that this was news to him.

'Cuts . . . and possibly closures of smaller libraries.'

Lionel looked as if someone had just stripped his guts out, but Sheila said sweetly, 'Do you know, I think you have a point about giving the public more ownership of our services.' They all looked at her as if she were a leopard who had just turned up in a striped bodysuit. 'No really, we *should* listen to our users more.'

Jennifer's confusion evaporated when she spotted Mr Armstrong tottering his way towards the desk, carrier bag in front of him like a shield of righteousness.

'This is one of our oldest users,' Sheila said, niftily getting round the counter to stand by him. 'He'd love to have more involvement. Has loads of great ideas.' Sheila raised her voice. 'This man is from the county council, Mr Armstrong, come specially to talk to you.'

'County, eh?' Mr Armstrong said. 'About time. Been trying to get through to you lot for years. Nobody listens.'

'You see,' the man from the council said, practically falling on Mr Armstrong in his eagerness to shake his hand, 'this is exactly what I was talking about.'

'Off you go then.' Sheila gave both men a little push in the direction of some seats in the large-print section.

They watched the full Mr Armstrong treatment unfold, particularly enjoying the selection of books he extracted from his carrier bag. Ten minutes ticked into twenty, twenty minutes to half an hour.

'I think the man from the council is signalling for one of us to come over,' Jennifer said.

Lionel squinted. 'I don't see anything.'

Mack saw Lionel emerge at the top of the staircase, sniff and then walk past without even glancing his way. Mack had never been hated by a librarian before. Soon he'd be hated by people from a lot more professions – farmers, teachers, local council employees, sculptors . . .

He guessed that the man in the baggy suit had been

dumped on and watched Mr Armstrong reading to him. Jennifer was walking to the children's section and was soon sitting in one of the small plastic chairs, talking animatedly to a woman and a small boy. She obviously knew them, her chin was up, and she was smiling and laughing. When the little boy jumped up and took her hand to lead her to the DVD stand, Mack stopped looking. He didn't want to see that willowy body stretching. He put his glasses back on and tried to read some of the history of lead mining he'd picked up, but was soon looking down at Jennifer again. She was helping an older child search for something on the computer. He took his glasses off again, and twirled them to and fro as he wondered what Jennifer's hair would look like if she put it up.

'You've been on that same page for a while now,' Sheila said behind him, making him drop his glasses on the table.

'It's quite a complex subject.'

'I'll bet, especially if your attention keeps wandering.' Sheila looked down into the library towards the children's section. 'Anyway, shouldn't you be down there and Jennifer up here?'

'Sorry?'

'Shouldn't you be down there and her up here on this balcony? Oh no, I forgot, it's *Twelfth Night* you're doing, not *Romeo and Juliet.*'

Sheila and Sonia, two great bloodhounds, sniffing you sniffing Jennifer out.

He kept his head down when Sheila had gone, but

couldn't be bothered even to pretend he was reading and just closed his eyes. Please God let Cress loosen her knicker elastic soon, he couldn't take much more of this.

He opened his eyes and watched a teenager in the graphic novels section popping crisps in her mouth under cover of a well-timed cough, and sought out Jennifer again, hoping to pull up some of that revulsion he had felt when he'd first seen that scarring. Nothing came up. It was just what Jennifer's face looked like.

She was walking back to the desk when he came down the staircase, and she gave him that smile. He tried to remember what it did to her scarring, but he was too busy looking at her eyes.

'I'm glad you popped in,' she said, 'I wanted to apologise for being so offhand and critical last night.'

'Then make it up to me. Come for a drink *now*. That pub down by the swimming pool.'

It seemed to him that the very quiet library had suddenly gone even quieter.

Jeez, this feels like flirting. Is this flirting?

'I could be there in ten minutes,' she said, 'would that be "now" enough?'

Oh crap, it is flirting.

As he left the library he swore he heard Sheila humming the theme song from *Doctor Zhivago*.

On the way to the pub he rang Tess, hoping it would focus his mind on why he was doing this. Phyllida was behaving and the only bad news was that Joe was getting a bit fed up with all the visitors she was getting. Some he'd banned.

Good old Joe. He knows what I know. You know it too, Tess, you just won't face up to it.

He ended the call and went into the pub, choosing to go through the door that led to the public bar. The only other occupants were one old guy off in the far corner with a half-pint stagnating on the table in front of him and a couple of women through in the lounge bar eating. Sleepy Hollow. Perfect for what he needed.

And then there was Jennifer. He shot to his feet.

'What will you have?'

'Small white wine.'

At the bar, he caught the way the barman was pretending not to look at either of them.

Sticks and stones, mate.

Back at the table he got his timing wrong, and his opening line sounded like a blurt. 'I was a bit concerned about you last night,' he said. He took his own phone out of his pocket and laid it on the table in what he hoped was a good bit of subliminal product placement.

Phone. Phone call. Phone call from Cressida.

'I'm feeling much better, thanks.' She took a little sip of her drink.

'Are you sure you're all right?' he pressed. 'Not worried about the play?'

'No, it's always all right on the night. It wasn't the play worrying me . . . I had a weird call from my cousin—'

The door swung open and two men walked in. They

were types Mack hadn't seen much of since he'd been in Northumberland: young, loud and in suits. One plonked his posh car keys ostentatiously on the bar and Mack distinctly heard the word 'scarface'.

Jennifer heard it too, he could tell by the way her chin went down and her hair fell forward. Within seconds her hands were in her lap and he felt if she could roll herself completely into a ball she might. The sexy, flirty woman from the library had disappeared.

When the word 'freak' reached him, he was surprised by the speed and ferocity of his anger. He picked up his beer and took a long gulp of it. The smaller of the two guys, the one with the hair that he should have washed yesterday, Mack reckoned he could easily take, but the one with the beige loafers was a lot bigger. He looked at their smug, callous faces. Sod it, he was going to fight dirty and punch them both in their—

'Please,' Jennifer said with urgency, and he thought at first that she wanted to escape, but as he felt the panic coming off her, he realised she wanted him to calm down. 'Alex used to lose it all the time,' she explained. 'He always ended up thumping people. I hate it. Hate it. It's so humiliating, so embarrassing.'

He could see she was desperate for him to behave so he held on to his glass and wondered what he could do to redeem this situation. He needed to get her out of here, calm her down, but somehow her wish to smooth things over was making him even angrier. He was almost shaking.

The door opened again and he looked over to see a

petite, vividly made-up young woman walk in, her skirt only just peeking out from under her short, tightly belted coat.

'Don't think much of yours,' the smaller of the two men said, jerking his thumb in Jennifer's direction, 'but mine's just turned up.' Their laughter alone made Mack want to glass them and see how they felt about scars then.

The young woman looked flustered and went out again, and Mack saw her reappear in the lounge bar. He pushed his pint away, righteous indignation piling on top of his rage.

'Please, Matt,' Jennifer said and her blue eyes echoed the begging tone in her voice. 'Please promise me you won't hit anyone?'

Do not get involved. This is not your life and not your problem. If you get into a fight, the police might come and then your cover could get blown. Pick the pint back up and ignore them. Drink it down slowly and then take her out of here.

'All right, I promise,' he said, dragging his pint back towards him. He concentrated on its colour before draining it and getting to his feet. 'Let's go.'

'Aye, back to the home,' said the bigger guy and laughed directly at Jennifer.

Mack saw Jennifer crumple even further and felt himself freeze. He wanted to kill these men, but she'd made it clear how much she would hate that. So who was he doing it for? It took all his self-control to turn towards her and say in a soothing tone, 'Right, got your bag? Good. So . . . on your feet. Mind the door. Let's go for chips. I fancy some chips and you haven't had any lunch. Can't go back to work without lunch.'

He got her out of the pub and they walked in the direction of the chip shop, but he could see she was in no state to face anyone and diverted to a seat inside the park. He watched her struggling to get herself under control and berated himself for having taken her to the pub in the first place.

'I'm really sorry,' he said, but the words sounded tinny and false. This was only a tiny preview of how she would be when he'd finished with her. Those men in the pub were angels compared with him.

'You have nothing to be sorry for,' she said in a watery voice. 'You were great.'

He didn't know if he wanted to shake her for being too damn nice or just put his arms around her. She was looking at him with that soft blue gaze of hers, but he wouldn't allow himself to meet it. He looked resolutely towards the bandstand.

'I know you wanted to thump them,' she said, 'but you didn't. You listened to me. Not like Alex.'

'You can't blame Alex or other people for trying to protect you,' he said gruffly.

'I know, but when people wade in on my behalf, without even asking me, it makes me feel as if I'm some kind of damaged child that doesn't get a say in what happens – that the grown-ups know best.'

'It's still not right. No one should sit in judgement on

you,' he said, still looking at the bandstand. 'One of those twats was wearing beige loafers, for God's sake.'

He heard a watery laugh. 'You're wearing conker-coloured brogues.'

He had to push himself up and off the seat to stop himself from wrapping his arms around her. When he came back with the chips, she barely ate any, distributing them among the pigeons gathered near their feet.

'Daffodils are pretty,' he said, hardly knowing what he was saying. He saw her look at the great drifts of them running like a nodding carpet down to the bandstand.

'Yes. I always think they seem kind of stupidly optimistic.'

'Yes, kind of hopeful,' he added and made the mistake of looking at her. She gave him a beautiful, brave smile.

'Hopeful. Hope. Lovely words.'

It made him feel shabby again, just as it had when she'd smiled at him after his stupid audition. Whenever she smiled at him. He took her chip paper from her and saw her over the road to the library. They didn't talk much, just said they'd see each other at the dress rehearsal and Jennifer seemed relieved to get inside.

The hatred he felt for himself at that moment seemed all-encompassing, the knowledge that he still hadn't got that information he needed taking second place to his desire to do something for her – even if it was something she didn't want done. He hared back to the pub. He didn't know what he had planned, he was making it up as he went along. A hunch made him look into the lounge bar first. The petite woman was still in there, now cosied up to a man whose ruddy face suggested he worked outside a lot – doing something strenuous, judging by the size of his forearms.

Perhaps he could sub-contract all this anger to keep his promise to Jennifer. 'Excuse me,' he said and was happy to see the aggressive way the guy rounded on him. 'See those men through in the public bar? Me and my girl-friend . . .' He stopped because the word 'girlfriend' had made him feel sad. No, not sad, wistful. He cast around for the dropped thread of what he'd been saying. 'Me and my girlfriend had to leave. They were really nasty about her. And when your girlfriend just popped in there, they were rude about her too. I'm sorry to say that behind her back they called her a slag. Thought you ought to know.'

The guy looked down at the woman as if seeking confirmation.

'I did hear them laughing as I went out,' she said, all big eyes and hurt feelings. This was a woman who obviously *did* like her man to make a scene.

He stayed around just long enough to see loafer-wearing guy being picked up by his lapels and thrown against the slot machine.

Jennifer knew it was official now. She had fallen for Matt, for his stupid clothes and his overeager attitude; for that intriguing sadness and that hint of something a bit naugh-tier lurking in the background. Especially that.

He'd actually listened to her about those men, listened

to her and reined himself in. He'd put her feelings before his own need to show everyone what a man he was. Yes, the incident still caused her pain, but his behaviour had taken some of the sting out of it.

What was it she was feeling? Protected? No. Cherished.

Poor Alex – all those battles he had fought for her, and Matt had simply shown some self-control and got her out of there, and here she was wanting to throw herself into his bed. Would he want her in it, though? She still couldn't believe it.

Or perhaps . . . perhaps she could. A barrier had shifted in her brain in that pub. There was something happening between them. Give him time, just give him time. Making a move on someone like her wasn't easy for a bloke. That incident in the pub was bound to make him think twice about what he was getting into.

She thought of him getting her out of that pub and needed him there among the piles of books and papers, where she could grab him by the hair and bring his mouth down on to hers. The old Jen, the Jen that didn't hide in corners, imagined lying on the table under him. Or out in the fields at home, her back pressed into the grass.

Thaw me out, Matt, come on, stop wasting precious time. Put your mouth on mine and thaw me out.

CHAPTER 28

Mack timed his entry to the dress rehearsal for a few minutes after the departure of the photographer from the paper and was greeted with a barrage of catcalls from the cast.

'Oh, goodness,' he said, 'I'm too late for the photo, aren't I? Really sorry, fell asleep in the chair, only just woke up.'

'I knew I should have come and got you,' Doug said, 'I was starting to worry about you, daft sod.'

He went backstage and Wendy and Lydia helped him change, telling him how dashing he looked. He didn't want to hear that and barely looked at himself in his costume because he was getting to the point where he couldn't stand to look at himself at all. The other costumes were impressive, though: suddenly everyone was carrying themselves differently. Lisa still looked nothing like a man and certainly bore no familial resemblance to him, but she was an arresting sight and she obviously thought he was too. She pulled him to one side.

'You missed the warm-up, but I could do a personal one

for you. Fancy a quickie in the costume loft?' He declined with regret. 'Ah well,' she said, 'worth an ask. You had a chance to read those brochures yet?'

Jocelyn looked every inch a lady in her black velvet, but still sounded like someone from the gutter, making little sniping comments about Lisa's wig and the size of her backside. The most startling transformation was of beery, uncouth Angus into the dignified Duke.

Mack felt his stomach start to churn and didn't know if it was the prospect of standing up on the stage or the thought of Jennifer watching him act.

Neither, it's because you're a lying, deceiving scum bag.

Susan the stage manager put her head around the door. 'OK, beginners. And keep the noise down, the rest of you. Break a leg.'

Mack couldn't remember much about the performance afterwards. Doug and he cocked up in one scene, but dug their way out of it. He managed to give Gerry a real thump with his sword when he drew it; Jocelyn and he still had about as much warmth in their on-stage relationship as a polar bear's arse, but all in all it wasn't bad. Jennifer had only had to leap in a couple of times to nudge the play along. The other hiccup had been Neale coming in with his yellow stockings at half mast which had caused most of the cast already on stage to corpse. Finlay exploded into the changing rooms afterwards to distribute notes and praise.

'You wait till tomorrow,' Doug said, giving Mack a huge hug. 'Having an audience will give you a bigger buzz.'

'That's true,' Angus agreed, 'I've had some of my best sex after opening nights.'

Lydia was picking up pieces of discarded costumes. 'Only with yourself, I should think,' she said.

Once dressed, Mack went to the kitchen, just to have an excuse to wait for Jennifer, and found a piece of flapjack in a biscuit tin on the side. By the time he had taken a bite, Jennifer was there and he had to surreptitiously take it back out of his mouth, knowing he would not be able to swallow it down.

'You were good,' she said, coming and standing by him and touching his arm lightly, and he wanted to shout, *No, I haven't been good for a long time, can't you see that? Can't you see how I'm playing you? Stop being so bloody nice to me!*

Instead he rolled his eyes. 'What, even the bit with Jocelyn?'

'Yes, even that bit.' She gave him a shy grin and he felt disconnected from everything around him, only aware of how close she was and the smell of her. He forced himself back to the surface and said the first thing that came into his head: something about her being a dreadful liar, and part of him wished she would look right into his eyes and say, 'Not like you, then.' This was all getting too intimate, tripping over into something else.

He wasn't sure if he'd leaned towards her, he seemed to be closer, and then she gave a start and her hand was off his arm and she was reaching into her pocket. Out came her phone, and she was frowning down at it.

'Not another weird call from your cousin?' he asked, trying to focus. 'Although you never did tell me if it was weird-upsetting, or weird-funny.'

'It was weird-weird,' she said, and then she was closing the kitchen door and he knew he was close, soooo close, to the reason why he'd come here.

'Look,' she said, 'you mustn't breathe a word of this ... but Cress has fallen in love. She's so shocked she's not doing anything about it for a few days. I mean, not, you know ... acting on it.' He sensed she was embarrassed that he'd know she was talking about sex. He kept his face blank, and she went on, 'The other person ... well ... it's going to mess their life up, evidently. Wouldn't even tell me who it was.' She shook her head. 'And now I've had this text.' The phone was tilted towards him and he read:

Brenda, brick.

'Why's she telling you your mother's a brick? Not that she isn't, of course,' he added, a little too quickly.

'It's code. She's telling me to get Brenda's old phone, it's huge. Cress is a bit paranoid about the press; probably worried someone's twigged it would be worth trying to listen in to my phone.'

'That wouldn't happen, would it?' he said, having to unclench his teeth to get the words out.

'After what the tabloids have been up to recently?'

'Yes, I see. Suppose I'm a bit naive ... but you shouldn't

worry about Cressida.' He waved his hand, hoping it looked light-hearted. 'She sounds as though she's a sensible woman. She's not going to do anything silly. She's not going to tell you she's fallen for the Rodney chap, is she?'

He was trying to read her face, but although she corrected him with a hurried, 'You mean Rory', there was no indication of what she did or did not expect Cressida to tell her. What he did see was a general softening of her look again.

'Do you mind if we don't talk about Cressida right now?' she said and there was a warmth to her eyes and mouth that made him feel it would be so easy to reach out and pull her into him and say, 'You're right, let's not talk at all.'

'Of course, of course,' he said, understanding that he had to leave right that minute, get back on track, stop looking at that mouth and those eyes. 'I know how tired you must be . . . I'm going to peel off home, give you some peace.' She made as if to speak, but he started to move away. 'I won't have a lift tonight, if you don't mind. Feel a bit like I want to be on my own, you know. Clear my head. See you tomorrow. Bye.'

He wasn't sure he hadn't broken the record for sharp exits from difficult situations, and he didn't slow down until he reached his old friend, Peter Clarke. He waited for O'Dowd to answer the phone, feeling as if any kind of thinking was going to rip him apart.

When O'Dowd answered, he simply spilled the whole story.

'What did I tell you,' O'Dowd crowed, '. . . and it's the

real thing, eh? Mind you, surprised Cress has got a heart, always seemed a toughie to me.'

Not like her cousin.

'Still . . .' O'Dowd said, thoughtfully, 'need to be hundred per cent certain it's Randy Rory. You sure Cressida wasn't spinning a line about not doing anything about it for a while? We've got a couple of days to play with? Not going to read about it in some other paper?'

'Told you, she's not doing anything before she talks to Jen again. There will be nothing for anyone to know before Saturday – after the play is done and dusted.'

'Let's hope it's early Saturday, we can hit this Sunday's edition.' There was a laugh. 'Mind you, I bet she doesn't hold out till then. Don't know how she's managed to go this long without sex. Must be getting through the batteries.'

Mack apologised yet again to Peter Clarke for having to listen to O'Dowd's repulsiveness.

'Yeah, this is going to be really messy,' O'Dowd said with glee, 'nasty divorce: he'll be in the sin bin as far as Middle America is concerned, and South America will hate him for dumping Anna Maria. Could lose him a large slice of movie-goers. On the other hand, it'll be great publicity for his and Cress's first film together. Just don't spook Scarface and we're home and dry.'

'Don't bloody call her that,' Mack shouted and felt the shock of what he'd just said ripple out around him.

There was an almost reptilian hiss. 'Now then, what's this? Going soft?'

Mack stayed quiet and looked at the countryside spread out in the gloom before him. If he launched himself into it and kept running, would 'they' ever find him?

'Time for a reality check,' O'Dowd said. 'I have the diaries, I have that photograph, I have you by the short and curlies.'

Mack stomped back to the cottage and sat in the torture chair and desperately wished that he and Jennifer could just be a normal man and woman without all those things lurking behind them: her scarring, his lying, the timer ticking on this story. He desperately wanted to be the knight hacking through the briars, rescuing her, setting her free. Instead he was the villain. He might as well have a moustache that he could twirl.

Jennifer stayed in the kitchen till Finlay came and shooed her out to lock up. She had been so sure it was going to happen then, that kiss. How many inches had separated them? All he'd had to do was half a step, lower his head. Had he felt that same marvellous awkwardness as she had?

She wondered whether she had, unconsciously, been leaning towards him? She knew she'd given him her best loving look.

Then he'd run away.

Had she put him off with that look? Or was he simply not ready for the first step?

What if it kept on being 'nearly, nearly' until he went home?

That thought was too horrible; she wouldn't even let

it back in her head. There had been real tenderness in the way he had been looking at her; she had to cling on to that knowledge. If only Cress's text hadn't landed when it did; it seemed to cool all that promising heat that had been building between them.

She stepped out into the cool night and smiled at how far she'd come. Only a few days ago she'd told Cress that Matt would have to make the first move. Now she wasn't so sure. Maybe it was her who had to break the spell; do the kissing. Perhaps she had to dig down into the old Jen and see what she came up with.

CHAPTER 29

It was like skiing very fast, or how he imagined flying without a plane would be. He was coasting on emotions he was creating in the audience, lifted high on the laughter, steadied by the rapt silence. They were out there in the dark, listening to the story being woven for them.

Doug had been right; the audience had made the difference. From the moment they'd come into the hall and he'd heard the footsteps and the buzz of talk, he'd felt part of some magic that was about to start. It had compensated for his lack of sleep and made him forget what a nasty piece of humanity he had become – on that stage he was Sebastian, loyal friend to Antonio, brother of Viola, lover and husband of Olivia. A man to look up to.

He hadn't even minded the warm-up, and once they'd had a last pep talk from Finlay, he'd wanted to rush on stage straight away. How come nobody had told him about this high?

Sure, there were sticky moments, but the whole play bowled along. The audience laughed when they should and listened intently when they needed to. Ten minutes in he forgot the spectre of somebody 'outing' him.

Even when he wasn't on the stage he enjoyed the camaraderie, standing silently in the wings with the others.

The applause at the end of the play was hearty and fully meant, and they did three sets of bows before the curtains finally closed and he was suddenly part of a back-slapping, hugging mêlée. He wasn't listening to what was being said though, he was thinking back to what had happened ten minutes before the end of the play, when he had turned his head and seen Jen sitting on her stool. With the prompt light shining on her blonde hair and her face turned to the hole in the flats that gave her a tiny view of the play, he watched her lips moving along with the actor speaking on the stage. It seemed a beautiful, tender thing to him, her keeping them on track, and he saw her loveliness shining from her as strongly as the light from that lamp. Even when he forced himself to seek out the scarred side of her face, his vision of her remained the same.

That's when he knew what he had probably known since that day she knelt before him to take his measurements and he had wanted to raise her to her feet.

When he'd been given this job, he'd thought the worst that could happen would be that he would fail and O'Dowd would destroy his family. Then he'd thought it would be getting unmasked as an impostor and O'Dowd still destroying them.

Now he knew that the worst result was falling for the woman he was meant to betray.

So how come just at this very moment it felt so bloody marvellous?'

Jennifer closed the script, turned off the light and sat gathering her thoughts before she plunged into all that back-slapping and hugging backstage.

She didn't begrudge them their happiness; they'd all raised their game tonight. A few minor wobbles, a bit of performing rather than acting, but a decent show – they had a right to be pleased. Especially Matt. She thought back to his audition and laughed. She and Finlay had been right, he was a good actor. A very good actor, the kind you couldn't take your eyes off.

Or maybe that was just the effect he had on her.

She heard a sound behind her and stood up, her smile on her face ready to receive him.

'Well, that was wonderful,' Alex said, clasping her in a Barbour-clad embrace. 'Well done. Well done. Really enjoyed it.'

She wanted to push him away, but he seemed disinclined to let her out of his arms until Doug came by and led them both into the changing room. Her need to be with Matt felt like hunger, but Alex stuck to her so closely that the only time she saw him was when he was shrugging his way back into his black, thermal T-shirt. A few seconds of bare stomach before her view was blocked, but enough to remind her of when she had fantasised about undressing him. Alex gave her a look as though he understood just what she was thinking and by the time the general move was towards the pub he was still attached to her side. She had lost sight of Matt, and Alex kept stopping to talk to people with a great show of enthusiasm for all things Shakespearean that was news to her. She could have screamed, and whenever she looked like straying he pulled her into the conversation, asking her opinion, picking out little bits about the play he wanted to discuss and could Jen help him?

She kept looking towards the pub as if it was some kind of Holy Grail. Matt would be in there by now. Why was she standing here wasting time? What was stopping her just walking on ahead?

It was Gerry now whom Alex had pigeonholed, telling him how marvellous he had been and Gerry was lapping it up. Jennifer guessed from the way his bald head was as flushed as his face that he had already drained the hip flask he kept in the wings during a performance. When she saw him grasp Alex's arm, she took her chance.

'I'll see you two in the pub,' she said, speeding away before Alex could protest, buoyed up on her hope. She could have skipped and, who knew, she might later. Doug came out of the pub doors just as she got to them. He looked beyond her to Alex.

'You're going in the wrong direction,' she said, smiling at him and knowing it was a wide smile, powered by the anticipation of walking into that pub and seeing the way Matt stood, the way he held his beer glass, that first look he was going to give her. She suspected Doug was exiting from the pub because Pat was in there. Well, tonight she might engineer a way to bring Pat and Doug together too.

'Matt's not here,' Doug said quietly, looking beyond her again to where Alex was now freeing himself from Gerry's clutches.

She didn't really understand what he was saying. How could that be possible?

'Said he had a blinding headache, took off home before I could even offer him a lift. He did look like crap, mind.'

She didn't even bother to hide what she was feeling from Doug, knew her face must look as if someone had deflated it. And now the pub faded as the object of her attention and she wondered how she could double back past Alex and . . . and what? She had no car, had got Brenda to drop her at the hall tonight in anticipation of being able to drink later . . . to drink and make that first step towards Matt.

She looked at Doug for help and heard Alex coming up behind her.

'What's the problem here?' Alex said, standing too close.

'I was just going to take Jen home.' Doug kept a straight face. 'She's not feeling too good.'

'I knew it, I knew it.' Alex shook his head as though the whole world were stupid but him. 'I knew it would be too much for you. You're feeling overwhelmed, aren't you?' He was peering at her as if she was a failed experiment.

Jennifer did a quick moral calculation. Telling someone you were feeling wobbly when you weren't was wrong.

Agreeing with Alex that she was overwhelmed and letting him take her home would only make him more clingy and convinced that she couldn't cope without him. On the other hand, it would get her home quickly, and once he'd dropped her off she could get in her own car and set out to find Matt. That shouldn't be too hard, they'd probably pass him on the road.

'Well, I am a bit tired, Alex,' she agreed, 'not overwhelmed, exactly . . .'

Just as Alex led her away, she caught the look Doug gave her. It seemed to say 'Do you think this is one of your better ideas, Jen?'

How bad an idea it was became apparent when they were in the car heading towards Brindley and Alex pulled over to the side of the road and turned off the engine.

His earlier solicitous tone had gone.

'You must think I'm an idiot, Jennifer,' he said. 'First you race to the pub, then after your little tête-à-tête with Doug you're suddenly desperate to go home. And now I can't get a word out of you, you're so busy peering out of the window. Who are you looking for, hmm?' He slammed his hands on the steering wheel. 'What's going on between you and Harper?'

She reached up and flicked on the light hoping it would steady her. 'I'm sorry?' she said, now a stewing mass of guilt about lying to Alex and irritation that he was delaying her journey. There was anger there too at his assumption that he had a right to ask the question in the first place.

'I'll ask you again, what's going on with that writer?' Alex's tone was more aggressive this time.

'That's really none of your business, Alex.'

'I think it is.' The way he was looking at her made her acutely aware how alone they were. 'You don't know the first thing about him and he'll be gone soon. He's just someone messing about with you, filling up his time whilst he's here—'

'Right,' she said, undoing her seat belt. 'I'm not listening to this. I appreciate you don't like Matt, but I do. And why do you think he's just filling up his time? What are you saying, Alex? That he couldn't possibly, genuinely, like me back?'

'No,' he said quickly, 'of course not. But he's going to hurt you, Jennifer. When he goes.' Suddenly he had undone his seat belt and had reached across and grabbed her wrist.

'Listen to me,' he said forcefully, 'there's something not straightforward about him. He comes across all nicey-nicey, but—'

'Stop it, Alex. Stop smothering me.' Although he still held her wrist tightly, she felt a retreat.

'I'm not trying to smother you. I'm trying to protect you.'

'Really?' She shook her wrist free. 'It doesn't feel like it to me.'

He sat back in his seat, and she knew him well enough to understand he was trying not to lose his temper.

'Look,' she said, when he showed no signs of starting the car again, 'I was wrong to lie to you back there—'

'Yes you were. And you have no idea how much that hurts. I've done all the right things; cared for you and helped you and now you're shoving me to one side.'

'Alex, please, we've been through this. Before Matt even arrived we had that chat about us just being friends. I cannot feel about you the way you feel about me. I'm sorry.' She paused. 'You're twisting this in your mind—'

'Have you slept with him?' The words thundered out into the car.

No, I haven't slept with him, but I desperately, desperately want to.

Could she walk to Brindley if she got out now? The silence between them filled the car until there seemed little air left for her to breathe. She wound the window down, surprised at her own composure.

'You have no right to ask that question, Alex,' she said, thankful for the cold air on her face, 'and I am certainly not going to answer it.'

Alex still wasn't moving and she wondered if it was a question of who would weaken first. She went to open the door and Alex turned on her.

'Don't be ridiculous.' He started the car, his truculence evident even in the way he turned the key in the ignition. 'And put your seat belt back on. I know I'm good for nothing else, but at least I can stop you messing up everyone's life even further by making that stupid, drunken mistake again.'

The shock of what he'd said to her felt like a blow. She expected to see him looking taken aback too, as if his anger had run away with him, but he was staring ahead, his chin up, his mouth a downward curve.

She genuinely wanted to run for home now; too strung out to handle anything but being safe.

'Drive me home, please,' she said, and they were the only words she spoke until she got out of the car and said, 'Goodbye.'

Mack came out of the ditch once Alex had driven off again. Why had they stopped? It looked like some kind of quarrel, and at one point it seemed as if Jennifer was trying to fight him off. If things had not calmed down Mack had determined to wrench open the car door and pull the bastard out.

Poor Jennifer.

Lovely Jennifer.

He was glad she was fighting with Alex and then he realised how selfish that was. When he was gone, she'd need Alex. That thought made him stop walking and stand with his head down until suddenly he was running to the bench. Stupid, really, he could get a signal here, he was certain, but it seemed natural to seek out Peter Clarke.

'Any news?' O'Dowd snapped.

'Thanks for asking me how Opening Night went. Listen, need you to do something for me.'

'Money?'

'No. A footballer. Newcastle one preferably, other Premier League team if needs be.' He paused. 'Definitely not Sunderland.'

CHAPTER 30

Jennifer knew Matt wouldn't come into the library today. She remembered how it used to be, the high of the performance followed by the overwhelming need to sleep far into the next morning. She would have welcomed a few hours longer in bed herself. After Alex had dropped her off, she'd taken to the red wine as if it could wash away that horrible scene in the car. Brenda had scooped her up and put her to bed in the end.

'I know it's hard for you, seeing them all acting,' she'd said as she'd turned out the bedroom light.

No, Mum, what's really hard is seeing the man you love strip off his shirt and knowing that you are no nearer to discovering what the skin underneath feels like on your lips.

There were some children messing about near the computers and she watched Sheila give them a sour look but say nothing. Jennifer suspected another Reece-related incident was occupying her thoughts. Yesterday he'd rung from Ibiza to tell her he'd got there safely, but already lost his passport. It was not looking like a promising career move.

The phone on the desk rang.

Matt, it could be Matt.

It was Lisa – Lisa gabbling so fast Jennifer had to tell her to slow down.

'OK, OK, but listen, Jen. I'm wafting about in my dressing gown early on when I look outside and there's only Robbie Trentham.'

'Robbie?'

'Get a life, Jen. Striker for Newcastle. Lush beyond lush. Just standing there in my street, not even eight o'clock, looking under the bonnet of his car. Next thing he's coming up the front steps. Bloody Dad gets to the door before me, but I'm not far behind, sucking in me belly, pushing my puppies out ... I mean, I haven't got a trace of slap on. Says he's got some strange knocking under his bonnet, managed to get the car to Dad's garage, found it shut, asked around, got sent here. Could Dad have a look? Bless him, he sounded really nervous.'

Jennifer heard Lisa breathe in and then she was off again.

'Dad's like, "Wow, can I have a look at a Ferrari? Yes, I can." Anyway, while he's doing that I ask Robbie does he want some coffee? And get this, Jen, we chatted on like anything. When Dad came back, said he couldn't find anything wrong. Robbie suggested we took it for a longer drive, so I ran upstairs, just chucked something on ...'

Jennifer doubted that.

'... twenty minutes later we're haring down the A1.'

'That's incredible. So where did he take you?'

'Leeds. Yeah, just booking into this hotel. Lots of smoked glass, there's this big piano—'

'No, wait, what? Lisa, you have to be back for six-thirty this evening, seven at the latest. Lisa? Lisa? Don't do this.'

Lisa's voice was surprisingly firm. 'Listen to yourself. I'm booking into a hotel with Robbie Trentham. Come on, when am I ever going to get another chance like this? It's fate: he'd normally be training, but he's got a groin strain.' There was an earthy laugh. 'Tell Finlay for me, will you, Jen? And remember, keep your chin up and don't take any crap from Jocelyn about that costume hanging off you.'

With a sudden jolt, Jennifer realised what Lisa meant. 'No, Lisa, come back ...'

Jennifer felt Sheila remove the phone from her hand and replace it on the desk.

'I ... I,' Jennifer said, starting to feel paralysed by the dawning realisation of what was likely to happen now.

Sheila nodded, 'Aye, aye indeed. Do I gather Lisa's not going to make the performance tonight?'

Jennifer nodded.

'Well, I've bought tickets. Lucky you're the understudy.'

'No, no, I'm not.' Had she shouted that?

'Why not? You're the prompt, aren't you, must know it by heart. And didn't you say you'd done it at school? Done it at Manchester? I bet you more or less know all the words.' Sheila was warming to the idea. 'Yeah, you'll have to do it, like in those films ... the show must go on and the understudy saves the day.'

'This isn't a film, it's real life!' Jennifer knew this time she had shouted, the hysteria rising in her throat.

A man in the World War Two history section turned round and shushed her.

'Oh shush your ruddy self,' Sheila yelled back.

Mack waited for the doorbell to ring and knew he ought to go and pack his bags: whether this worked or whether it didn't, he'd be out of here tonight. Although what was there to pack? Not his walking stuff, not his terrible jeans. Let them all stay here and rot. He didn't want anything to remind him of this job when it was over.

He was going to shed Matt Harper like a skin. Trouble was, he wasn't certain there was anything underneath that skin any more.

The ring on the bell finally came at ten minutes past twelve and he wondered which person in a panic it would be.

It was Doug, barely comprehensible, and Mack had to act amazed at his news. Everyone felt Jennifer was the obvious choice to take over, but she was adamant she wasn't doing it. Would Matt come and talk to her?

Mack had suspected that, offered the part on a plate, Jennifer would initially push it away.

'Finlay will persuade her,' he said, getting his fleece off the back of the chair.

Doug didn't look particularly optimistic.

The changing room was crowded when they arrived and somebody had moved the screens against the wall to make more space. The only person missing was Jennifer. The empty seat between Neale and Finlay was, he presumed, where she had been sitting.

'Here comes the cavalry,' Angus said.

'We were just discussing our options,' Finlay explained. 'Jennifer feels she cannot take over from Lisa and we must respect that decision. I might be able to persuade one of my sixth-form drama students to read the part, or we bite the bullet and cancel.'

You are not cancelling this. She has to do this. If I don't give her this, what else am I going to leave her with?

The room was noisy now, people talking across each other, and Mack could tell opinion was roughly divided into two camps: those who felt Jennifer shouldn't have been put in this position, and those who thought that, really, why couldn't she have a go?

Had anyone voiced that last opinion? Was that why Jennifer's chair was empty?

'I hope no one has upset Jennifer?' He looked directly at Jocelyn for that last bit.

'No, no,' Finlay said. 'We've all been very gentle with her, Matt. She's outside taking a phone call.'

He pushed his way from the room and went outside as quickly as he could without running. He listened. She was round the back of the hall.

Jennifer had been thankful Brenda's mobile had rung when it did and gave her an excuse to get away from all those eyes. People were being kind, but she was sure that would change if they voted to cancel the last performance. Everyone would forget then that this was all down to Lisa, not her. She thought again about the possibility of actually getting on that stage. No, she still wanted to throw up and run away, or even run away and then throw up. This was one thing on which she had to stand firm, not try to please anyone but herself.

She leaned against the back wall of the hall and rang the number showing on the register of missed calls. It would be Cress, who else? She imagined her sitting up in bed in the dark of a New Mexico night.

'Jen, listen,' Cress said as soon as she answered, 'I know I said I wouldn't be in touch again till tomorrow . . . your tomorrow . . . but Brenda's just rung to tell me Lisa's on heat . . .'

'Ah.' Jennifer waited for yet another person to try to persuade her to get up on that stage. But Cressida wasn't saying anything.

'Are you still there?' Jennifer asked.

'I am, just thinking what to say to you . . .'

'Forget about me,' Jennifer said quickly, 'you don't sound right. Is it just because you've been woken up . . . or has something else happened?'

There was another long period of silence before Cressida said wearily, 'Jen, I told you . . . I'll explain it all tomorrow when I see you—'

'When you see me? Cress—'

'Just listen, Jen. This is serious. My life is about to go down the tubes and America's going to chew me up and spit me out; I don't know if I'll even be allowed to finish this film. But sod it. I've given into temptation and it's only a matter of days before somebody twigs what's going on. Oh Jen, I'm as scared as hell, but absolutely, absolutely walking on air.'

'Cress, sweetheart, please calm down—'

'And the sex, Jen, it makes everything that I've got up to before seem clod-hopping.' There was a high, hysterical giggle. 'Sorry, I've turned into this romantic fool. That's what happens when you meet someone like this, your brain scrambles. I feel like I've been walking around with my eyes closed. It's ... it's complex, though, Jen, that's why I need to talk to you face to face, and Auntie Bren and Uncle Ray. I can't talk about it on the phone, you must understand that?'

'No, I thought ... Cress, hang on, what about the film?'

'Not needed for a few days.'

'Look, Cress, you don't need to trail over here, nothing can be that bad. I mean, I know Mum will be a bit lemon-drop about ... the plumber ... you know, having a wife—'

Again she thought Cressida had gone, she was so silent. 'Cress?'

'I'm here, I'm here. So ... you've worked out it's *him*?'

'Cress, how long have we known each other? Come on.' This time the laugh from Cress was a wry one.

'I'll talk to Mum for you,' Jennifer said. 'There must be something special about him if you love him.'

'You never judge, Jen, do you?' Cressida said softly, 'never

ever, not once. Look, I'm coming over, don't try to stop me. Gotta go now. Love you, Jen . . . and Jen? I've worked out what I wanted to say to you. One life, that's your lot. You've got to grab it with both hands. I know you think yours has slipped away from you, but things happen, Jen, unexpected things, your life can go in new directions. Be Viola, Jen, do it for yourself.'

'Cress, Cress,' Jennifer said urgently down the phone, even though she knew Cress had gone.

She turned to see Matt.

'Cress?' he asked. 'Trying to persuade you to do the part?'

She wasn't really taking in that it was him, or what he was asking. She was still trying to process how Cress could have fallen for a man like Rory.

'No, no,' she said, 'well, only a bit. She's . . . she's coming over to England to explain it all to Mum and Dad. To me.'

'Explain it all?'

Jennifer was so thankful to be able to talk to him it all came running out. 'It's Rory Sylvester she's fallen for; I suspected it was and she's just confirmed it. Unbelievable, a three-hundred-and-sixty-degree turn-around. I can only think it's a mistake, she's lonely and hounded by the press – he's shown all this interest in her—'

'Jennifer, stop talking for a minute,' Matt said, and she was struck by how uncomfortable he looked, as though he'd rather be anywhere else than standing in front of her. She felt him lift the phone from her hands, and then he bent down, picked up her handbag and shoved the phone into it.

'Forget about Cress,' he said. 'I hear you've refused to take over from Lisa? Do you want to tell me why?'

CHAPTER 31

Mack wondered if he could have stopped time if he'd clamped his hand over Jennifer's mouth before she got out the words 'Rory Sylvester'. But there it was, finally, the confirmation of what he and O'Dowd had suspected for weeks.

Now there was only one thing he could do to sweeten what was going to happen next and he was damned if he'd let her run away from it. He ignored the way her eyes were asking him to give her an easy time, and her heartfelt, 'You know why I can't do it, Matt. Please . . . don't make me spell it out.'

'Jennifer,' he said, 'just take a deep breath and listen, and don't worry, I'm not going to wade in with all that blunt honesty you've come to expect. I want to start by saying what I should have said that day when I was trying to apologise in the library, remember? Which is . . . I can't imagine how you came to terms with having your face scarred; seeing your dream of acting professionally disappear.' As he'd expected, her chin went right down at that, and he was looking at her centre parting and her wonderful blonde hair.

'I don't know how you cope every time you catch your reflection, or every time someone stares – being reminded that you don't look like you used to, yet inside you're exactly the same. It's hard for anyone, but particularly for a woman, particularly when you wanted to be an actress – you got a kind of double whammy. Suddenly your talent counts for nothing.

'You've shown more courage than I think I could – picking yourself up, getting back out and about; and when incidents like that one in the pub happen, I can under-stand why you just put your head down and withdraw. The only thing is, Jennifer, if you can't work out another way of dealing with that kind of thing, if you just go on feeling all this shame and embarrassment, little by little you'll think all those nosy, rude bastards out there have a point. You'll believe you shouldn't try to do anything that draws attention to yourself. You'll keep on doing the safe thing which probably won't be the same as doing what you really want.'

He saw her chin come up sharply at that and then she was bending for her bag and he knew she was intending to run. He got hold of her wrists and coaxed her back into a standing position, kicking her bag to one side as he did so and pushing her gently against the wall. He really had to fight the urge to press his body right against hers and feel her against his chest.

'Which brings us neatly to acting,' he said, staring

directly into her eyes, daring her to lower her chin. God she really did have beautiful eyes, like the sky in summer.

'Now if, hand on heart, you tell me that you can't stand in for Lisa because the words are too rusty, or you don't know the moves, or the costume won't fit, that's fine.' He tried not to look at the way her chest was rising and falling as if she was panicking. 'But if none of those things is true, you've got to ask yourself: what's the worst that can happen tonight? You're on home ground here. People will be rooting for you and yes, they'll look at you, but I'm betting that after ten minutes they'll just be thinking about Viola.'

She didn't say anything, didn't look like she was going to and that was when he let go of her wrists and put his hands gently on her shoulders. It would have been so easy to have kept on going and wrapped his arms right around her, if she'd have let him.

'So that's a "no", about the acting?'

She did something that looked like a nod.

'OK, then I lied about the blunt honesty: here it comes. If you don't do this tonight, that bloody windscreen has won.' Her eyes flared at that, and he felt her start to struggle. He continued to hold her. 'It's won, Jennifer, and all those people who believe we ought to be airbrushed into looking the same, they've won too; and everyone who really believes that people who are a different shape or size or even colour from them are somehow inferior. And those who don't like to see people with disabilities out and about. Oh, and those men in the pub, they've won too. In the end, you're living the life those kinds of idiots want you to live – apologetic, not making waves, buying into their narrow view of what people should look like. Whereas don't you think you should be living the kind of life you want? And really, Jennifer, why are you paying those wankers more attention than the people willing you on? Your mum and dad, Bryony, Danny, Cress? Everyone who really wants to see you being you?'

A little part of him wanted her to register he hadn't included Alex in that list.

She was now looking like he had slapped her repeatedly.

'It's not fair, Jennifer. None of this is fair. People can have the blackest hearts and look like angels, and yet you're kind and true and lovely and you have to put up with all this crap. You've got scars on your face, but they're just a part of you, Jen. They don't define you and if you let them do that, they're always going to dictate what you do with your life.'

This time he didn't hold on to her when she tried to struggle free.

'I can't, really I can't,' she wailed at him, her voice coming in gasps. 'Don't talk to me like this, you have no idea what it's like, how sick I feel just thinking about going on that stage.' He saw tears start to well in her eyes and it made him want to smudge them away with his thumbs. 'I would love to do it, just love to do it . . . but it terrifies me.'

'Of course it does. But just think beyond that first step

. . . you might get to fly again. That's what I felt yesterday, like I was right there in that moment, flying.'

Whatever happened, he would always remember that look she gave him, as if he had jabbed his finger in the most sensitive nerve he could find. She stooped for her bag and barged past him so hard she almost knocked him backwards.

Had he made it worse? Should he have even tried to make her brave when he was about to sabotage her recovery so spectacularly? He had a nerve . . . but maybe he was the only one that did. Or perhaps he was trying to give her this one night of doing what she loved to make himself feel better. He was too strung out to think about it any further.

He walked round to the front of the hall and looked at all that green. Soon it would be a memory and he'd be back in the streets of Bath, a richer and an infinitely poorer man.

He had no idea how he would go back to his old life. This place he'd started by hating now seemed the only logical home for him. With Jennifer. The thought of leaving it and leaving her twisted something inside him, but whether it was his heart or his guts he didn't know.

He looked back at the hall. If he'd got it wrong she wouldn't do the play and he would leave her with nothing but the bitterness of all his deceit and lies. He looked at his watch. Three p.m. already. He'd give it a few more minutes and if nothing happened, he'd go back to the cottage, pack his bags and call for a taxi. That would be it. He could barely breathe with the thought that he might just have seen Jennifer for the last time.

'Hoy!' It was Doug, running out of the hall with that huge brick of a mobile. 'Someone wants to speak to you.' His masking-tape eyebrows all but disappeared under his hair.

The voice on the other end of the phone was clipped, cultured.

'Cressida here,' she said, 'Cressida Chartwell,' as if the surname was at all necessary. 'Jen's just told me you've given her a real dressing-down.'

'Uh, yes. I have.' He was sure she must know he was a lying, cheating scumbag just from the sound of his voice.

There was a softening of her tone. 'Well, I don't know what you said to her, Matt Harper, but she's just rung me back to tell me she's going to try and do it. She sounds a bit wobbly, but I'm sure if you hold her hand she'll get through it. And, Matt . . .'

'Yes?'

'This isn't Hollywood speak, this is me. I will love you forever for doing this. I can't wait to meet you when I come over.'

She finished the call, and he walked towards Doug, waiting in the lobby.

No, you won't love me forever, Cressida. In fact, come Sunday, I'm going to be right up there at the top of your hate list.

CHAPTER 32

Jennifer knew there was a time when she would have to let go of Matt's hand, and when it came he pushed her towards the steps leading up to the wings.

'Go on,' he said, 'show them how it should be done.'

She lifted her head and breathed from her diaphragm. She pulled her mouth wide and then made it as narrow as possible, ignoring how one side of her face felt stiff and as if it was lagging behind the other. She focused on Viola.

She remembered climbing the steps and heard her cue, but she couldn't recall walking out on to the stage. She was waiting for a gasp from the audience, but there was nothing, just the front two rows of faces visible in the lights, turned towards her expectantly – Ray and Brenda, Danny and Bryony, Marjorie, Sheila and just on the edge of her vision, Sonia and Gregor.

'What country, friends, is this?' she said, and then it happened. She was flying … flying … flying …

*

Mack let go of her hand and knew that at least he'd done something right. He hadn't rung O'Dowd with that final confirmation and he hadn't told him Cressida was on her way to the UK. For now, at least, he could pretend he was innocent.

He watched Jennifer from the wings. Even in a costume that did not fit her properly, she looked vibrant and alive and the way she moved was sublime. She was a woman pretending to be a man and she had it perfectly, every little nuance, even down to the way she set her hips. After the first few minutes he stopped worrying that she was going to forget her words or freeze under all that attention, and he felt the play change in her hands to become something bigger, more affecting. Now the audience didn't simply understand the poignancy of Viola having to woo Olivia with words she yearned to use on the man she loved, they felt it too. Jennifer's passion wrapped itself around Jocelyn, and she responded, looking almost drunk with it. Angus, watching from beside Mack, went 'Ohh' in a way that suggested he would be thinking about that scene in all kinds of inappropriate ways later.

Mack clung on to the part of Sebastian like a raft, unable to comprehend how his life after this play would unfold. He could not take his eyes from this woman on the stage, revelled in the confident side of her soaring and swooping over the audience, yet knowing he was about to whisk all of this new-won happiness away from her. He did his scenes as if dreaming, amazed that nobody could see him disintegrating and the only lines he heard were those that seemed to be calling out to everyone that Matt Harper was the only impostor here, the rest of them were merely acting. 'I am not what I am,' Jennifer said and each word thumped into his head.

Near the end of the play, when he and Viola were reunited, he felt Jennifer run her hand down his arm as she had done when she measured him. It was the only time he heard her stumble on her words and he had to think of the cold North Sea to prevent the audience wondering whether Sebastian's relationship with his sister was entirely wholesome.

And finally, finally he got his scenes with Jocelyn right, allowing himself to think of Jennifer as he did them. When he said, 'If it be thus to dream, still let me sleep,' he could not remember anything he had ever said in his life before that he had meant so much.

At the end people were on their feet, clapping and cheering, and Mack saw Jennifer struggling to retain her composure. Most of the cast had given up trying – they knew the bigger drama that had been played out on the stage tonight.

As the curtains closed Finlay strode forward and with infinite care took Jennifer's face between his hands. He dropped a kiss on her forehead.

'Welcome back,' he said, 'to where you belong.'

It was then that Mack saw his own vision blur and he backed away. He would go now, quietly leave the hall and call a taxi. He was all packed, the stuff he was leaving behind stowed in the bottom of the wardrobe, his cord jacket over the chair in the bedroom, his passport safe in the inside pocket.

He looked back at Jennifer and just glimpsed Jocelyn pushing through the throng to get to her. Without considering what he was doing, he rushed across, got hold of her around the waist and pulled her away.

She rounded on him, her mouth open. 'What the friggin' Hell do you think you're doing?'

'First, I wanted to say congratulations on our scenes tonight. I think we nailed them, finally. And then I wanted to tell you that unless the very next thing you say to Jennifer is a compliment, don't say anything at all. I heard you before the play wondering aloud if she'd used all the concealer. Luckily, she didn't. If it's something along those lines, think again.'

'Or?'

'I'll do something to you that's public and unpleasant, and you'll see a side of me you haven't seen before.'

She surprised him by laughing. 'All right, lover boy, no need to prove you've got teeth. I was actually going to tell her that she was incredible, because she was.'

He managed to get off the stage then, but not before a severe hugging from Wendy and Lydia, and by the time he got to the changing room it was a scrum. He felt himself pitch forward under a hearty back slap from Doug, who then got hold of his arm and held it aloft as if he were a victorious prize fighter.

'Round of applause for the new guy,' he said. 'Looks like a right wuss, but he's got balls of steel. I couldn't have done it without him.' There were shouts and laughter, and people were shaking his hand and saying they forgave him for being so young, and had he thought about abandoning the south and coming and living with them?

Mack pulled off his costume and made a hash of getting into his clothes, all the while keeping an eye out for Jennifer. If he played it right he could leave before she even made it off the stage. He heard her in the corridor, being emoted at by Pamela and just caught a glimpse of her as she walked past the door. She mouthed 'Thank you' at him, her eyes still bright and her face a little flushed. He grabbed at his socks and stuffed his feet into them and swore as he tangled the laces on his brogues. As he removed his fleece from the clothes rail, a coat hanger fell to the floor with a clatter.

'Going somewhere, marra?' Doug asked.

'No, just feeling a bit chilled.'

'I'll get you working up a sweat. Come on, help me get the booze oot the costume loft.'

Mack looked at his watch. Ten forty-five. Last plane gone; last train going in about half an hour. He'd get a taxi to the airport anyway, stay in a hotel there, and be on the first flight out on Saturday.

In the hall, the chairs were already stacked to one side and plates of food were being put on long trestle tables. Music was playing. 'Here he is,' Danny's voice boomed and Mack turned to see him and Bryony.

'Wasn't she wonderful?' Bryony said, and Danny just

put his arm round Mack's shoulders. 'Thanks, mate, she listened to you. We always give her too easy a time.'

Mack didn't know if he could bear it, the catch in Danny's voice, the brightness of his eyes that suggested he was close to tears. He heard himself speak, not sure what he was saying and then Brenda and Ray were there too. Brenda took both of his hands in hers. 'I'm sorry,' she said, 'I've been unfair to you. Rude even. You've been a good friend to Jen. Thank you.' Ray simply shook his hand, his lips pressed together in a way that suggested he did not trust himself to talk.

Please, stop being so nice to me.

The hall was rapidly filling with the cast and their friends and relations, and Mack saw Jennifer over near the stage talking to Sheila. He moved slowly towards the main door and the outside world. He would have made it too, if Finlay had not suddenly jumped up on to the stage and clapped his hands and started to make a speech thanking just about everyone and their dog.

'And finally,' he said, 'on a quite amazing night for all kinds of reasons –' everyone saw him look towards Jennifer – 'there's one person to whom we owe a huge vote of thanks, and to show our appreciation, we've got him a little gift. Matt ... where are you, Matt?'

Mack stuck his hand up and was pushed towards the stage.

'Matt, for being a sweet talker and for putting up with a lot of ribbing about your age, we'd like to give you this.' Finlay held aloft a large sugar dummy. There was a roar of laughter and Mack had to climb up on the stage and smile and say thank you.

He looked down at Jennifer looking up at him and felt the happiness radiating from her. This was how he would remember her. He was going to go backstage now and push open the fire-exit door and go. He could ring O'Dowd from the airport hotel.

He found himself standing next to her.

'Hello, you,' she said. 'Was I all right?'

He could have just nodded. He could have just nodded and gone.

'You were brilliant,' he said, 'a different kind of acting. Not like anything I've seen before.' He moved closer. 'Much better than your cousin. Less showy.'

Perhaps she could hang on to this when everything else he'd done to her was going to push her right back into her shell.

She laughed up at him again, and he felt this wasn't fair. Why couldn't he have met her somewhere else?

'Tell me,' he said, looking at her hair, trying to memorise the exact shades of blonde within it, 'now you've done it once, will you do it again?'

'I don't know. It felt . . . it felt . . .' There was that gorgeous smile. 'Fantastic.'

He drifted towards the main door again, but then Sheila collared him and told him that the sight of him in tights had made the cost of the ticket worthwhile, and soon he was back standing next to Jennifer, and Ray and Brenda were waving goodbye from the door.

'They going already?' he asked.

'Yes,' Jennifer said and he felt her hand connect with his and he did not move it away until Angus came and hugged her. He and Jocelyn left together, and Mack wondered if those two were going to have sex tonight.

No, don't think of the S word. Go to the loo and then slip away.

'Time to lock up,' Doug said, jangling the keys at them and Mack was confused. Where had everyone gone? He looked at his watch again. Midnight. He might as well just get a taxi straight to the airport and sit and wait for a plane.

'I'll give you both a lift home,' Doug said, and Mack stumbled out to the car and sat in the back with Jennifer, his thigh resting against her thigh. He felt as if he was and was not there.

When Doug stopped the car outside Brindley Villas and Mack opened the door, the rush of fresh air brought him to his senses. He needed to get away, but as he climbed out of the car he saw Doug turn and say to Jennifer, 'This is as far as I'm going. You need to get out too.'

Soon she was standing by his side and they were watching Doug drive away. There was just the two of them and all that silence.

'Well then,' Jennifer said. 'I'd better head off.' She looked as if she were dreaming too.

'I'll walk you home. We'll need a torch.'

'Maybe not. Look at the moonlight.'

No, I am not looking at the moonlight, or the stars, or at you. He felt her hand touch his again and this time she knotted her little finger around his little finger as they walked.

He would just see her to within sight of the farm and then run back and call a taxi.

They had not even reached Peter Clarke when he felt her let go of his hand and turn to face him and he swore he heard hundreds of things out there in the dark lift their furry heads and look at them.

He knew what she was going to do before she even started to lean forward. He saw her close her eyes and then her lips were on his and although every part of his body was telling him to wrap his arms around her, he put his hands on her shoulders and pushed her away.

'Jennifer, I can't,' he said.

If he kissed her once how would he stop? How much worse would that make his betrayal? Cressida Chartwell was going to throw the book at him for the deception he'd already carried out; go any further and it would be the whole library hurtling his way.

He saw the face that had looked so alive shut down again, and there was that shame back in her eyes. She was stumbling away.

'Don't say anything,' she cried out. 'All your fine words earlier, they meant nothing. You didn't believe any of them.'

He was careering after her. 'Jen, Jen.' He caught her by the arm. 'I know you think I pushed you away because of your face. But it wasn't that.'

She rounded on him and he could see the tears.

'What was it then?'

'I'll have to go away soon.' He tried to catch her other arm. 'I don't want to lead you on and then leave you ... I don't want to hurt you like that.' One last lie: a white one to make her feel better.

She shook herself free of him, made a fierce little sobbing noise. 'Don't treat me like a child; everyone treats me like a child. Shouldn't I decide whether I'm prepared to get hurt or not?'

But you have no idea how badly I'm going to hurt you.

He looked at her with the moonlight shining on her hair, her eyes blazing at him and didn't want to think or talk any more. He reached forward and, pulling her to him, kissed her right on the mouth. It was an angry kiss to start with and she was still trying to pull away from him, but as he tasted her and felt her lips under his it became a falling-in-and-drowning kiss that reached down into his chest and to his groin. Right there under the huge Northumberland sky with the stars spread out above them and the dark countryside wrapped around them, he held her and kissed her remorselessly to show her how beautiful she was to him, and he felt her kiss him back and very soon the only thing he was thinking about was taking her inside and stripping her naked. Tomorrow could go to Hell; O'Dowd could go to Hell and when it came down to it, the entire world could go to Hell too.

CHAPTER 33

I will pinch myself.

She had woken with him wrapped around her, scared to move in case she broke the spell. Perhaps he'd had too much to drink last night: he would look at her in the bright light of morning and all this warmth and happiness would disappear.

'Are you awake?' she heard him say, but did not turn.

She felt him move and then she was being rolled on to her back. She didn't resist even though she wanted to curl into a ball. He looked down at her, his brown eyes bleary, mouth sounding dry.

'Stop trying to bury your face in the pillow,' he said and then bent to kiss her on the lips. She opened up for him straightaway, felt the swirl and heat of desire in her breasts and between her legs. Moving her hands over him she reacquainted herself with what she had uncovered last night – muscled but not muscly, toned, long-limbed, flat-stomached. Skin that tasted faintly of citrus.

'I had the loveliest time last night,' she said, pulling away a little.

'Me too.' He kissed her on the cheek, and she could not stop her smile. He was not making a big thing of proving to her that her scarring made no difference to him. That would have set her teeth on edge. Instead he had treated that part of her like every other part of her. Actually that wasn't true. Other parts of her he had given much more attention.

She felt him kiss a spot at the base of her neck, and then he looked up, his brown eyes no longer bleary but filled with mischief.

'You showed me your favourite place in Northumberland,' he said softly, 'shall I show you mine?'

'Uh . . .?'

He sat up and pulled the duvet completely away and she was so intent on looking at him she forgot to try and hide.

'This is my favourite view,' he said, lying back down by her side and running one hand over her breast. He caressed it gently before letting his hand travel down the sweep of her stomach. 'These hills and plains.' He moved his hand to her thigh and nudged her legs apart. 'This valley. These are my favourite places. You're beautiful, Jen, so beautiful . . . whatever anyone else tells you in your life, you make me want you so much just by looking at you. You're the best view in the world.'

She felt his hand burrow between her legs.

'What are you doing?' she asked, wanting to hear it given a name.

'Exploring. Exploring the beautiful countryside. How you feel. What turns you on. How we fit together.'

She gave a cry and arched her back and soon he had moved his hand and rolled on top of her and was inside her, and she concentrated on welcoming him in, and how it felt to have her arms around him in reality and not in a fantasy.

Sometime in the night Mack had woken up and panic had launched him out of bed before, just as quickly as it had come, it had gone. He had looked down at Jen asleep, her knees drawn up to her chest and suddenly found himself believing that everything was going to be all right. He sat down gently on the bed and knew that his biggest desire was to protect her – not from the world, but from O'Dowd, and now he had her safe in his bed, there must be a way.

He smiled at her sleeping. He knew now that there were other scars: a nasty, jagged one on the crest of her shoulder, a thinner one running up the inside of her arm from just above the elbow to her armpit. He imagined how she had got them, her face and body turning in the impact to break and then snag upon the glass. He saw her hanging half in and half out of the windscreen. It made him sick to think of it.

It didn't make him sick to look at it, though, and when she woke up he was going to prove that to her again. He could see in her eyes last night that she didn't quite believe what was happening, that perhaps he was drunk or it was a pity fuck.

He went round to his side of the bed and got under the duvet and lay down carefully on his side, putting one arm over her and bending his knees so that his legs tucked in behind hers.

Listening to her breathing, feeling her warmth against his chest, he wondered if maybe they all had a chance: his family, her family. Tomorrow, in this bed, in his arms, he could tell her the truth and hope that she would understand and help him get out of this mess. He'd tell her everything: about Teddy Montgomery and Phyllida; his real name; all his lies. He breathed in the smell of her hair. If he could keep her here, get her over the initial shock, maybe they could talk to Cressida, persuade her to give the story to O'Dowd without Jen being mentioned. He had a few hours' grace until Cressida arrived; until O'Dowd started chasing him for news.

It was a long shot. He could imagine Jen trying to get away from him when he told her how he'd cheated his way into her confidence. All he could do was show her and tell her that he loved her. He tightened his arm around her and felt her stir. It all seemed hopeless, but she was worth whatever he had to go through to make this right.

He had to try, but not now. Now he wanted to enjoy lying here holding her until she woke up.

They had been awake just over an hour when Jennifer said, into his shoulder, 'I ought to ring Mum and Dad, tell them where I am.'

'I think they'll have worked it out, Jen.' He cupped his

hand around one of her buttocks and started caressing it and felt her start to move against him, setting up all kinds of friction in his groin. She had such beautiful skin, as silky as her hair, and he could not get enough of feeling it against his tongue, his hands, his thighs. Everywhere. Seeking out her mouth with his, he kissed her and her hands smoothing their way over him, worked down, down, then around and held him. He closed his eyes and then she was leaving him, pulling away and standing up.

'Come back, come back,' he said, reaching out for her, 'Ray and Brenda can wait.' The sight of her standing there, all blue eyed and blonde haired and naked was making him ache.

'I know they can,' she said, 'but you can't. Stand up, Matt. I owe you something. Something you didn't get that Friday.' He squinted up at her, not sure what she meant. 'On your feet, Matt,' she said slowly, dangerously. 'Spread your legs.'

The thought of what she was about to do to him, for him, made him unsteady as he stood and as she sunk to her knees he placed the palm of his hand lovingly on the top of her head.

'Oh God,' he said a little later, 'this is just . . . oh, God, Jen . . .'

He felt her let him go just for a moment. 'I had a life before the accident, Matt,' she said softly. 'I wasn't an invalid and I wasn't always a good girl and –' she took him in her hand and laughed – 'I will expect tea and toast after this, but you can forget the kebab.'

If he hadn't been so busy trying to stay on his feet, he would have laughed too.

Later he fed her toast and watched her sip her tea. When would be the best time to start explaining? How to begin? He decided there were some other things he wanted to say first, just in case he never got the chance to say them again.

'You know the acting thing?'

He saw her guarded look, so fed her more toast. 'Don't look like that, I was just going to say, had you thought of going back, finishing your course?'

He noticed she wasn't chewing.

'Come on, eat your toast. Sweetheart, I'm not hassling you, putting a pitchfork at your back about acting, but it seems a shame to have got so near and then to drop out. And . . . well, even if you think acting isn't going to work for you, aren't there other things you could be involved with? Teaching? Directing? I watched you during rehearsals, those times you helped the others. You have a gift for it, I'd say—'

'All those people looking at me.'

'Looking at you and what, Jen? Thinking that you've got a scarred face and then just getting on with it? You need to build your confidence.'

He could see she was listening, even if she wasn't eager to answer.

'I . . . could think about it, certainly,' she said after a while. 'It would be good to try and finish my degree, but as for acting . . .'

'I told you I think you're better than Cressida.'

She smiled shyly. 'I agree with you. I am a better actress than Cress; I've always known that really. But even before the accident I didn't have her thick skin, her drive.'

'Her ego?' he chanced.

'Oh, I've got a certain amount, pal.' She lifted her chin and looked down her nose at him and the change was remarkable. He felt a little intimidated until she smiled again. 'I've always been a show-off, comes with the territory. No, what I meant was all that PR stuff, the schmoozing, the vacuous interviews, seeing yourself splashed over the paper. Yuk! Cress loves all that really, I mean not the going-through-her-bins stuff, but being the centre of attention.'

'But you like stage work,' he said, eager to change the subject.

'Yup. That was what I wanted. I mean there's still the need to sell yourself, but it's not as intense.'

'You must try with the acting again, Jen. Even if it's only with the Drama Club. You need it.'

He felt he'd got as far as he could for now and wrapped himself and the duvet around her.

She laughed. 'Sometimes I think you're nothing like you were when you first arrived. You're quite tough really, a terrier when you get your teeth into something. Like Cress.' He felt her reach a hand back and rest it on his hip. 'I'll think about what you've said, I promise. I can't guarantee I'll do anything about it, but ... then again, two months ago I couldn't imagine anyone ever seeing me and wanting me again. Who knows what might happen in another two months?'

'I don't just want you, Jennifer,' he said urgently, 'I can't imagine being without you. You do believe that, don't you?'

She turned in his arms. 'Of course I do. You've been so brutally honest with me all along, why would you change now?'

'No reason, no reason.' He kissed her on the nose and even though the prospect of it made him feel sick, he knew that it was time to begin.

Jen, I came up here two months ago not knowing you, and in that time I've fallen for you – but why I came up here was not to write a walking book . . .

'Jen,' he started, 'I came up here two months ago—'

The front door bell rang and he was immediately strung out and on his guard. This was what happened in films when the hero tried to come clean, someone interrupted and spilled the beans to the heroine and everything went to Hell.

'Let's ignore it,' he said, but whoever was outside wasn't giving up.

'I hope it's not Mr Armstrong.' Jennifer looked uncomfortable.

'Bound to be,' he said kissing her again as if that would make the noise go away. 'He wants to make a formal complaint about this librarian who peddles filth and conducts riotous love-making.'

'I'm not a librarian, I'm a library assistant. And we weren't riotous.'

'In my head *I* was,' he said, slowly disentangling himself from her and standing up. 'In my head *I* was whooping and shouting.'

'Oh Matt,' she said tenderly, and he resented having to turn away from her towards the window. He moved the curtain aside a sliver so that he could see who was on the doorstep.

'It's Gregor, Sonia's Gregor,' he reported, looking back round at Jennifer as if she could throw any light on why he was there.

'Better go and see what he wants then.' She snuggled down further in the duvet. 'I'll be here when you get back. Put the kettle on again while you're down there, will you?'

He did a mock salute, pulled on his jeans and fleece and bounded down the stairs, blinking in the light as he opened the door.

'Good morning.' Gregor was grinning and holding out his hand and Mack automatically reached out and shook it. 'We have only met in passing before. The odd wave. But now I have come to give you this.' In his other hand he was holding a brown paper bag and he offered it to Mack. 'My wife, Sonia, she likes a little joke, you know. She wondered if you needed these. Please, no offence.'

Mack took the bag and opened it to see two packets of condoms.

Did everyone know that Jennifer was upstairs in his bed?

'So,' Gregor said giving a little stretch and showing off

his firm abs as his T-shirt rose, 'you have fun.' His shoulders were shaking as he turned and walked down the path.

'How did she know?' Mack called after him.

'My wife, she hears even the lightest kiss in the dark,' Gregor called back.

Mack closed the door and burst out laughing, despite the weight on his shoulders.

'What did he want?' Jennifer shouted down.

'To give us extra condoms,' he called back and was delighted to hear her little scream.

He went through to the kitchen and put the bag on the table. Getting this right, saying it all in the correct order was vital. He filled the kettle and lit the gas under it. Once it had boiled, he'd start his story again. He opened the back door, even though it was chilly out. He just needed to look at the view. It was beautiful out there, you could see for miles.

'I'm just going to the loo,' he heard Jennifer call from upstairs.

Jennifer got out of bed and hopped around shivering until her gaze fell on Matt's cord jacket on the back of the chair. She picked it up and pulled it on, wrapped it around herself and ran to the bathroom. At the sink she nicked some of his toothpaste, putting it on her finger and making a rough pass over her teeth. There was a wonderful man downstairs, a wonderful, funny, kind man and he'd not only wanted to have sex with her, he'd wanted to have sex with her a lot. Or even lots of sex with her. She stuck her tongue out at her reflection.

Who knew life could be as sweet again?

As she went to sit on the loo, she heard someone ringing the bell again. What now, surely not more condoms? She pictured the look on Sheila's face when she heard what her sister had done.

Mack opened the door to Mr Armstrong. He had a magazine of some kind in his hand and looked quite put out.

'I want a word with you,' he said.

Mack sighed. 'Look, Mr Armstrong, we're adults. We have a right to do what we want.'

'Eh?' Mr Armstrong's eyebrows were lowered so far they seemed to make his eyes disappear. 'What are you talking about?'

Mack thought of Jennifer upstairs. 'I'm a bit busy, is there something I can help you with?'

'Take a look at this.' The magazine was pushed into Mack's hands and he opened it up. It was a copy of the *Methodist News*. He stared first at it and then at Mr Armstrong.

'There.' Mr Armstrong jabbed the page with his finger and Mack started to read.

' "The Reverend David Nickalls, minister in the Bridport and Dorchester circuit, is delighted to announce that his daughter Mathilda is now the proud mother of twins, delivered by Caesarean section on the 24th March at St Michael's University Hospital, Bristol. The twins, a boy and girl named Tim and Daisy, are thriving and keeping Mathilda and her husband, Jonathan Harper, fully occupied. The lucky grandparents thank the Almighty for this exhausting but longed-for gift. Mathilda, who has published two walking books – *A Guide to Dorset Coastal Walks* and *A Walk Around North Somerset* – under her pen name of Matt Harper, says her writing career will have to be put on hold for a while ... 'I can't imagine clocking up many walking miles with the twins strapped to my back,' she says. I'm sure all our readers wish her and her family strength during the coming months."'

As he reached the end of the article Mack stepped out on to the doorstep and pulled the door almost closed behind him. He couldn't see properly and his heartbeat seemed to be one over-long surge.

Matt Harper is a woman? A woman? Mathilda?

He was reading the article again.

Calm down, calm down. This will be all right. Jennifer won't have heard, she's still in the loo. This is mendable. Soon it won't matter, not when you've told her everything.

Jennifer sat on the loo. Cressida was right; loving someone turned you into a romantic fool. She had no idea where this would lead, or what would happen when Matt had finished that walking book. Cress was right again: you really should grab life by both hands; it could take you in amazing directions. Having him on her side, fighting battles with her, rather than for her – well, she could almost feel the old her unfolding and stretching.

She felt something digging into her and put her hand to the inside pocket of Matt's jacket. Another of his notebooks, one he hadn't lost yet. She pulled it out to have a sneaky read and frowned. Not a notebook, it was his passport. She opened it to see if his photograph was as dreadful as most people's usually were. No, it wasn't bad, and then she was up off the loo and staring at the words by the photograph. Mack Stone, they said. It was Matt's photo, but the words said Mack Stone.

Oh my God, oh my God. Why is he called something else? Is this his writing name? No, no . . . the name in the passport must be his real one . . . Matt Harper must be the made-up one, but why would he have a made-up name?

She clung on to the sink until she could make her legs move, and then she was running back to the bedroom, tearing at her clothes, trying to get them the right way out and pulling them on. She went to the window and twitched the curtain aside as she had seen him do earlier. It was Mr Armstrong. She could barely breathe for the fear that was rising inside her. She looked at the bed and felt dizzy. Who had she slept with, whose name had she been calling out in the dark? This was all wrong. She pulled her boots on, leaving her socks behind, and stood at the top of the stairs. She couldn't make out what they were talking about. Slowly, stealthily she made her way downwards.

'But she's got the same name as you,' Mr Armstrong said indignantly, 'how can that be?'

'It's a coincidence.'

'Can't be.' Mr Armstrong took back the magazine. 'Look, it gives the titles of the books. They're yours, aren't they? You want to complain, someone claiming to have written your books.'

'Can we talk about this some other time?' Short of pushing Mr Armstrong over, Mack couldn't think how to get rid of him.

They both heard the kettle whistle.

'You got the kettle on?' Mr Armstrong asked, his tone hopeful.

'No.' Mack tried to back into the house.

'All right, all right,' Mr Armstrong grumbled, 'I'm going. Don't understand this though.' He was looking at the magazine again. 'Have to ask someone else how this can happen.' Mack saw him look towards the shop.

Nooooo. Think, think, before Sonia the bloodhound arrives.

He moved closer to Mr Armstrong. That bloody kettle was still whistling. 'Listen, it's a long story. Can I trust you?'

Jennifer reached the bottom of the stairs. They were still talking. Slowly, slowly, she moved into the sitting room. That man out there with Mr Armstrong, the one who'd held her in his arms, all those lovely things he'd said to get her on to that stage, his caresses ... who was he? She felt sick as she rushed for the kitchen, aware there was a breeze coming from somewhere. The kettle started to whistle. She stopped moving.

What will you do if he comes back in to turn it off?

There was a noise as if the front door was being opened and she held her breath, but he did not appear and she heard the talking resume. She forced herself to go into the kitchen, her heart leaping at the sight of the open door and then she was running along the back lane, the passport clutched in her hand.

'Of course you can trust me,' Mr Armstrong said, his eyes suddenly alert.

'OK then, well . . . it's police work. The woman in that magazine is the real Matt Harper. I've taken her name. I'm working undercover.'

'Undercover? Why?'

Mack let his gaze drift to the shop. 'Illegal immigrants,' was all he said. It was enough. Mr Armstrong was almost jubilant. 'I knew it, I knew it,' he said, 'I knew he was an illegal.'

'Shhush, shush,' Mack looked up at the bedroom window. 'Not a word, Mr Armstrong, or you'll blow open the whole case. I have to go now, there's some . . . some surveillance to do.'

'Got you,' Mr Armstrong said, and he was back down the path in a positively sprightly way.

Mack went inside and rushed through to the kitchen to turn the kettle off. Good job the back door was open or the place would be like a Turkish bath. That was close. He needed to get upstairs now and tell Jen everything, sod the tea. Couldn't afford any more neighbours lumbering by. He bit his lip and was amazed that he could laugh. What were the freakin' odds on Matt Harper being a woman? Or fate dropping the news in Mr Armstrong's hot little hands? Life was stranger than fiction, sure enough.

He bounded up the stairs, practising again what he was going to say and saw Jennifer was still in the bathroom. He sat on the bed and waited for her, grinning at the memories of what they'd done under that duvet. And on top of it. He was still feeling ill at the thought of what she would do when he told her, but it would come good, he could sense it.

She was taking a long time in that bathroom. 'Jen,' he called. No reply. He went and gave the door a tentative push. Empty. He looked in the spare room, not sure if she was messing about, playing some kind of hide-and-seek. He went back to his room and opened the wardrobe. That was when he noticed her socks on his bedroom floor. Only her socks.

He spun around and saw that his jacket wasn't on the back of the chair any more, but flung behind the door. He rushed to it and picked it up.

No, please, not that, please, not now.

He knew before he put his hand in the pocket that his passport would not be there.

Jennifer was running and stumbling out of the village and as she reached Peter Clarke's bench, she looked behind her. Climbing on to it, she took her phone from her bag and tried to ring home, but her fingers were trembling so much it took her a few attempts. She looked behind her again.

It was Brenda who answered. 'Hello, love,' she said, 'it's all right, we didn't expect—'

'Stop talking, Mum,' she shrieked into the phone, 'listen, just listen, I need you to go to the computer and look up a name.' She ignored the way her mother was trying to butt back in. 'Mack Stone, look it up for me.'

She could hear Bryony in the background and then her mother again.

'Mack what?' her mother said, sounding out of breath.

'Stone, please hurry, Mum.'

'I'm looking, I'm looking, and Bry's on her way. What's happened, love, has he hurt you? Has he—'

'What, Mum, what have you found?'

Her mother's voice was panicky. 'He's a journalist. Freelance down in Bath, but before that on one of the tabloids.'

Jennifer felt the phone drop from her hand and clatter off the bench and the world tilted around her and she was on the ground on her knees. She slammed the bench with her hands, registering on some level that she was hurting herself, but still doing it. She was shrieking something, and then the thought that he might be coming after her got her back on her feet. She ran for home, all those scenes in bed playing in her head; that time on the beach, the way he always put his hand over hers. None of it real. She had been nothing to him, just a way to get to Cress.

What had she told him, what had she blabbed?

She turned on her ankle and fell, and then she was aware of nothing until Bryony was lifting her under the arms and half-carrying, half-dragging her towards the car.

CHAPTER 34

Mack told the taxi to wait where the track divided and, as he walked towards the farm, saw Ray coming towards him. There was no trace of the usual ambling, relaxed attitude.

When Ray lifted his head it looked as if, since yesterday evening, the muscles under his skin had sagged.

He halted a few feet from Mack.

'You're unwelcome here,' he said in a voice devoid of any emotion. 'Get gone.' Mack felt his passport hit him on the arm as Ray threw it. Down it went on the path, and he did not bend to pick it up.

'Ray, please. I need to know how Jen is. I need to talk to her.'

'Don't you . . .' Ray said it with such force it made Mack flinch. 'Don't you talk about her.' His hands, down by his sides, were working away at themselves, clenching and unclenching.

'Please, Ray, I can explain. I know what it looks like—'

'It looks like what it is.' Ray laughed bitterly. 'You used

her. You used all of us. Coming into our lives. Coming into my home. Lying.'

'No, it wasn't like that.'

Ray turned his head away, the look of disgust unmistakable and Mack rushed on, the words tumbling out. 'I mean that's what it was at the start and, Ray, I'm so, so sorry about that ... but it changed, I changed. I fell in love with Jen. I know you won't believe me. But I was going to tell her the truth, just before she found that passport; I was going to tell her the truth.'

Ray started to walk away.

'No,' Mack shouted, running and getting in front of him. He put his hand out to try and make contact, and Ray looked down at it and then up at him from under his brows.

'Don't touch me.'

'I just need to know how she is.'

'How she is? How do you think she is?' Ray looked out over the fields, but Mack felt he was seeing some other place. 'What have you done to us? I thought the worst day of my life was sitting in that hospital knowing that people would look at my lovely Jen and only see that scarring. That her life was going to be so different from what she had planned. But Bren said we had to pull ourselves together, be positive, we could have been putting her in a box.' Ray shook his head as if dislodging that image. 'So how do we get her back on her feet now, Mr Stone? She's just lying there asking why someone would treat her like this. That's how she bloody is.'

Mack pictured that and could not bear it. 'Please, Ray, let me go to her, talk to her, explain everything. I really love her. Last night was real. Tell her it wasn't all about fooling her ... I never meant to do this ... I mean; I did before I knew her. No, I mean—'

'You can't even get your story straight for yourself. You used my daughter to get to Cressida. For money.'

'No,' Mack said trying again to reach out and touch Ray, 'not for money, there was another reason. My mother—'

'You must have been laughing up your sleeve at us. Thick northerners, so easy to win over. We're not even real people to you are we, so far from London?'

'Ray, I had to do this job to get my mother—'

'Stop lying to me,' Ray shouted and the ferocity of the words from a man who had always seemed so gentle made Mack dumb. 'Look me in the bloody eye,' Ray said, 'and tell me this wasn't about making money for somebody who's already rich. Go on.'

Mack hung his head.

'What, suddenly lost that famous gift of the gab?' Ray stooped, picked up Mack's passport and came and shoved it in his pocket. 'Callous enough lying to her, but making her believe you were attracted to her? That's evil. Now get gone. Danny's away off taking Louise to visit her other granny; he's no idea what's happened, but he'll be back soon. I don't want him put away for what he might do to you.'

Ray started walking again and Mack knew there was nothing else he could do, not now. He returned to the taxi, stopping and looking down at the farm before he got in to try and commit the fields and the trees and the river to his memory. On the drive to the airport he imagined Jennifer lying dry-eyed on her bed, believing that all he'd done was use her and that she meant nothing to him, and it seared through him like a burn.

When O'Dowd's phone rang, he ignored it. Probably angling to see if Mack had heard anything yet. He would get a flight to Bristol and a taxi to Bath and think what to do next. But what was there to do other than confirm Rory Sylvester was Cressida's lover? He wound down the window, hoping the fresh air would make him feel less queasy.

At the airport he stood in the queue to buy a ticket and suddenly felt an arm come around his neck and pull him backwards.

'You shit,' Doug said, hauling him round and then smacking him right across the face, 'you conniving little shit.' He no longer looked like a clown – his face flushed with colour, his eyes stormy.

People were looking, moving away hurriedly, and Mack tried to open his mouth to speak, but Doug hit him again. There was blood on his tongue and suddenly a security guard was piling towards them.

'Break it up, break it up,' he was shouting, 'I'm going to . . .' He stared at Doug. 'Hey, is that you? Doug Bythorn?'

Doug stared back. 'Why, Len, yeah, yeah it is. Long time no see.' Doug held out a hand for shaking, still keeping a firm hold on Mack with the other one. 'How's it gannin'?'

'Champion, Doug. You're doing great too, seen some of your stuff.' The guard was smiling, but he looked at the gathering crowd and then at Mack. 'What's the problem?'

'Tabloid journalist,' Doug said, giving Mack a shake. 'I won't tell you what he's done to a good friend of mine, lovely lass, but beating's too good for him.'

The guard tutted. 'I'm sorry about that, Doug . . . but I can't let you fight in here. You'll have to go outside.' He lowered his voice. 'Place up the side of the building, where I go for a sly tab: it's a CCTV blind spot.'

Mack felt himself being dragged towards the exit, the crowd parting before them. He didn't struggle; he deserved what was coming.

Doug pushed him up against the wall, his feet scuffing aside the cigarette stubs, and Mack waited for the pain to start.

'I liked you, I bloody liked you,' Doug said putting his hands round Mack's neck, and Mack remembered that night when he'd seen Doug squeezing the life out of the steering wheel.

'I liked you too,' he rasped back and felt Doug's grip tighten.

'Bloody liar, you were laughing at me, but it's Jen I'm doing this for.' Mack couldn't breathe properly. He had spots in front of his eyes.

'Kill me, Doug,' he croaked, 'you'd be doing me a favour.'

Doug gave him a shake and then, confusingly, his grip started to loosen.

'You bastard,' Doug said, removing one hand from Mack's neck to wipe over his own eyes. 'I threw you two together all the time. It's my fault, all my fault.'

'No Doug, listen—'

Doug removed his other hand from Mack's neck. 'I'm not going to touch you any more, you're dirty, a virus. Get on your plane.' He gave Mack a final shove and strode away.

Mack got himself back in the queue for the tickets, the security guard shadowing him, and he was nearly at the desk when he felt himself being pulled backwards again.

'Say your prayers, scumbag,' Danny shouted.

When he finally made it on to the plane, the stewardess came up the aisle to hand him a paper towel with bits of ice in it. He sat and held it to the cut on his forehead and just let the blood from his nose dribble on to his shirt. He wasn't sure that one of his ribs wasn't broken, but he had escaped lightly. If Bryony hadn't pulled Danny away he was under no illusions about what would have happened. The fury coming off the guy was like another fist.

He leaned forward and got the sick bag out of the pocket in front of him and retched into it. People were staring, and he was in real pain, but he knew it was nothing compared to what Jennifer was feeling. He retched again.

'Rough stag night?' the woman next to him asked.

CHAPTER 35

Jen sat on the side of the bath, her legs shaking, and remembered being in Matt's bathroom before she'd found that passport.

No, not Matt. Mack.

All those lies, all that acting. Those wonderful things he'd said to her. Had he been acting in bed too? She couldn't think about that.

There was a knock on the door.

'Jen, are you in there?' her mother said.

Her mother had been right all along, and she hadn't wanted to hear it. She was too busy grabbing at that shiny strand of hope he'd dangled in front of her. How could she have thought he would find her attractive? She imagined him laughing on the phone to his friends in ... in where, where did he come from?

'Jen,' her mother shouted, 'answer me.'

She looked at the toothbrushes in the mug on the shelf above the sink and at her father's razor. Creature of habit, Ray, he'd never used the electric one Danny had bought him. She got up and put her hand on it. Only once before she'd thought about this, a couple of months after coming out of hospital when something had clicked in her mind and she'd realised that how her face looked was permanent.

Would it hurt as much as this hurt now? Oh Matt, Matt, you were so lovely and I was so gullible. If she could only go to sleep and not wake up again.

She heard other voices outside the door.

'Open the door, Jen, love. Now, Jen!'

She took her hand off the razor and drifted back towards the door, unable to work the bolt, but then managing it.

'You were right, Mum,' she said when she opened the door. 'All the time you were right about him.'

Her mother put her arm around her and steered her back to the bedroom. 'Let's not talk about that now, love. That's not important. Come on; have a little lie-down before Cress gets here.'

Jennifer let Brenda put her into bed and felt tiredness start to pull her down. 'Cress is going to be so angry with me,' she said.

'Don't be daft, nobody blames you, darling. It's him we're all angry with. So angry.'

'How can you be?' she said. 'He doesn't exist.'

CHAPTER 36

It was muggy in the room. Mack tried to open one of the sash windows, but his ribs hurt too much. Outside, grey houses faced him, uniform and dull, the Bath stone looking depressing under the clouds. He wished he was looking out on all those different shades of green.

Picking O'Dowd's mobile out of his pocket took some effort and when he had, he went over yet again what his options were. Ignore O'Dowd and he'd print what he already had and throw him and his family to the wolves. Result: he'd have still lost Jennifer and shafted his family. Or, ring O'Dowd and confirm it was Rory. Result: he'd still have lost Jennifer, but his family would be off the hook.

He wasn't even going to think about what Cressida Chartwell would to do to him when she found out. Correction, what her lawyers would do.

He got out his own mobile and tried Jennifer's number again and the number of the farm. No reply. Had he really been expecting one?

He'd have to ring O'Dowd soon. What if someone spotted

Cressida flying into the country and O'Dowd rang, full of fury about why he was the last to know she was here?

He plonked both phones on the bookcase and limped over to the sofa. Lowering himself on to it, he worried away at what he should do, trying to tune out the throbbing in his ribs until it filtered through to his brain that someone down in the street was ringing the front doorbell.

That's how it started this morning.

Nobody knew he was back. He waited for the ringing to stop, but it seemed to intensify and now he was sure he could hear banging too.

It's Danny, he's followed me here.

That thought should have scared him, but maybe if he was beaten senseless he couldn't think about Jen. He moved tentatively out of his flat, catching sight of his puffed-up eye and massive lip in the mirror on the landing and clutched at the banisters as he went downstairs. Just before opening the front door he had the insane idea that it might be Jen herself out there. His heart bucked in his chest.

It was not Jen, or Danny, or anyone else from Northumberland. It was a man who appeared to be totally square and his delicately braided hair looked incongruous on top of all that bulk. Seconds later, Mack found himself lifted off his feet and was being hauled back up the stairs. The pain was so intense that he swore he could hear the front doorbell still ringing in his ears.

He must have looked like a cartoon, his legs a blur as

he struggled to keep up. In the flat he was deposited on the sofa and closed his eyes to cope with the pain. When he opened them again Cressida Chartwell was standing in front of him. She took off her sunglasses.

'Pull the curtains and turn on the light please, Chuck,' she said in that cut-glass, but somehow classless accent of hers. When Chuck had done as he was asked, she indicated the ladder-back chair, and it was placed a few feet from the sofa. Cressida sat in it and very politely told Chuck to make himself comfortable in the kitchen. She would call him if she needed him.

'I want to start,' she said, looking Mack straight in the face, 'by telling you why Chuck is called Chuck when his real name isn't even Charles. It is because when he finishes with people they look like chuck steak. This is no exaggeration. I hope you believe that?'

He nodded, although he was finding it hard to believe anything, particularly that this was not all some kind of hallucination brought on by his injuries. Cressida Chartwell was here in his living room. Hollywood had worked its magic on every inch of her – she smelt headily exotic; the suit she was wearing was pale and obviously expensive; her nails were buffed; her hair glossy; her shoes so delicate they would only just get her from red carpet to limo. An aura of languorous glamour hung about her as if she was some rare orchid. Except today she looked red-eyed and drawn, and Mack knew that this was probably down to him. Why was she here? Why hadn't she gone straight to the farm?

'I see that someone has already started teaching you a lesson, ratboy,' she was saying, her calm delivery very, very disturbing. 'You'll have to forgive me if I seem a little slow to wade in myself. Jet lag, getting this news just as we landed: I'm making up my response to it as I go along, on the hoof as it were. But whatever I decide it will involve letting Chuck back in this room.'

He tried to disappear into the sofa, unable to think of anything other than how much he deserved this. He was pathetic. Scum of the earth. A lying, deceitful bastard.

'You are pathetic, scum of the earth. A lying, deceitful bastard,' Cressida said.

It sounded worse coming out of her mouth, each vowel and consonant given its proper weight. He wanted to shout 'I know, I know'. What he tried to do was tell her why he'd even set out on this job in the first place.

'Save it, not interested,' she cut across him. 'My concern is Jen and how to sort out this current mess. Of course I'd also like to crucify you afterwards, bring a case against you for, oh, I don't know, obtaining pecuniary advantage by deception, breach of privacy . . . anything my lawyers can think of. I would go for you as much as someone who's willing to pay anything can go for someone. I'd go for that bastard O'Dowd too and the bigger bastard who owns the paper – the lot.'

'Luckily for you,' her mouth did a little twisting motion, 'that's not going to happen. I have talked to Brenda and Ray on the way here. They're adamant that it ends now. Can't bear having Jennifer's life paraded through the

courts for everyone to gawp at. So . . . regretfully, I have
to concur with their wishes. Which just leaves me with
damage limitation. I am going to keep Jennifer's name
out of this if it kills me. I'm presuming that although
O'Dowd hasn't rung me yet to gloat, this is going in
tomorrow's papers?'

She was on her feet, moving around the room, stopping now and again and then pacing on, and he was
waiting for her to mention the words 'injunction' or even
'super injunction', but she suddenly stopped by the bookcase and snatched up one of the phones.

'This the one you call O'Dowd on?' When he nodded,
she chucked it at him.

'Ring him back. Tell him I'll flesh out his story if he—'

'He hasn't got the story yet, well not the confirmed
one,' he said quickly. 'I never rang him back after you
talked to Jen yesterday.'

She shook her head as if she despaired of how stupid
he must believe her to be. 'You really think that's going
to save you, that dumb lie? You hit the jackpot yesterday
afternoon and you're still sitting on the news? I think not.
Ring him back—'

'Please believe me. I haven't talked to him – I can show
you the call register if you like.' He fumbled with the
phone. 'O'Dowd wasn't expecting any news till today. He
doesn't even know you're in the UK, not unless someone
else has—'

'Liar,' she screamed at him. 'Coward. You're just trying
to save your skin.' She came and stood in front of him

and he looked at her skirt because he was too ashamed to look at her face. He waited for her to hit him or push him, although her words were violent enough.

'I should have checked you out,' she stormed, jabbing her finger towards him. 'I should have looked after Jen like she's always looked after me. Too tied up in myself to do it ... And to think I was grateful to you. Stupidly grateful because I loved the fact Jen had found someone who made her sound as if she was ... back. I thought you were making her brave again, when all you've done is teach her if she *is* brave, she'll get punished.'

He would not have been surprised if she'd spat at him, such was her anger.

'Who could blame Jen if she finally decides the world's too cruel to cope with on her own? And guess who'll be waiting to carry her off on his bloody white charger?'

His face must have registered shock.

'Oh, don't give me that mock concern.' Cressida clicked her fingers. 'Safe life, safe man, safe marriage. All down to you. In a few years' time she won't even remember what she was capable of.'

As Cressida had been speaking he had struggled to keep control, but that sent him over the edge and he let go, his body bringing up great convulsive sobs that made his ribs ache even more. He should have felt embarrassed, but he felt nothing but hatred for himself and sorrow for Jen.

'No, no,' he spluttered, 'you can't let that happen. Not with Alex. Please, please believe me. I love her.' He wiped his nose with his hand. 'I didn't want to do this job. Cross my heart, O'Dowd had me right over a barrel—'

'Shut up,' Cressida snapped, 'I don't give a toss about you.'

'I don't give a toss about me either.' He was almost wailing, rocking himself back and forth on the sofa. 'I didn't set out to do this damage. I thought I could just be her friend . . . I tried not to fall for her, make her fall for me . . . but . . .'

Cressida looked down her nose at him as he continued to cry.

'You're quite the actor,' she said at one point, 'I can see how you pulled this off.' Without warning she swept down and gave him a mighty slap across the cheek. The shock made him close his eyes, and when he opened them she was running her fingers carefully over the palm of the hand she'd used to slap him.

'Real tears,' she said, 'my, you are good.' She continued watching him as he sniffed and snivelled before moving to open the door and call for Chuck. He feared she had lost patience and was going to have him beaten up, but she calmly asked Chuck to see if there were any paper towels in the kitchen. When he brought a roll, she threw it into Mack's lap.

Next time he looked up she was at the window, tweaking the curtain back. Seemingly satisfied with what she saw, she resumed watching him.

As he blew his nose, he just caught her saying, 'If you don't stop crying, I will personally rip your tear ducts out myself. I have no idea exactly where they are located, but

I was thinking of going in via the groin . . .' She moved towards him, and he flinched, but she was heading for the ladder-back chair again.

'Before I ask you, yet again, to ring O'Dowd back, and yet again you lie and say you haven't already coughed up your juicy little snippet, I'd like you to tell me one thing.' Her eyes were as steady and probing as Brenda's had been that day she had interrogated him on his doorstep. 'When Jen told you about Rory, you'd got what you wanted. Why still get her up on that stage? You could just have slipped away without being missed.'

'It was the only thing I could give her. I wanted her to feel like she was flying again. I . . . I just hoped she'd be able to remember that after everything else I'd had to do to her—'

'There was no "had to" about it. Don't try being mealy-mouthed with me, ratboy. You probably tore O'Dowd's arm off to get this job.'

'No, he made me do it, I tried to tell you—'

'Ah yes, and up to now I've not been interested, but hey, guess what . . . take the floor, Mack Stone, let's hear your explanation.' She waved her arm at him as if introducing him to an audience.

'It was my mother . . . he had some . . . some dirt on her . . . I had to do the job or he'd have published it.' He had addressed the words to the carpet rather than her, knowing what reaction she would have. Sure enough she said sarcastically, 'And no doubt, you're going to tell me you can't divulge what that dirt was? Conveniently.'

'It's a horrible secret,' he said miserably. 'If I tell you, I wouldn't blame you for getting your own back and selling it the highest bidder. In the end I had to decide between destroying my family or . . .'

He knew Cressida would supply the missing words and waited for the vitriol, and possibly another slap.

Confusingly, she said, 'Interesting body language there, ratboy.' Before he could think what she meant, she went on, in a weird conversational tone, 'So, you saw Jennifer act? She's a good little actress, isn't she? Not top-flight, but I think she'd have found regular work.'

He heard himself make a strange noise and then he was struggling up from the sofa, not caring about tear ducts or Chuck or cracked ribs. 'Who are you kidding?' he shouted at her. 'She's a bloody good actress, better than you. She was wonderful on that stage. She was Viola; hundreds of years after she was created, there she was.'

'Well, you've got balls, at least,' she said frowning, 'or did you work out that you shouldn't just agree with me because it would sound better if you defended Jen? I can't make you out – those things you were doing with your body when you were talking about O'Dowd and your mother . . . fair bit of anguish there. Hard to fake, even if you were as good an actor as me . . .' She pursed her lips and studied him. 'So . . . what exactly do we have here?'

Bending forward, she placed both elbows on her knees and rested her chin in her hands. Now she was really scrutinising him and she reminded him of a clothed version of *The Thinker*. What she was thinking about, though, he didn't have a clue.

'Films are so much easier than real life,' she said, when she slowly unwound herself and sat up straight again. 'You find someone has wronged you and your family; you hunt them down; do a little speech about retribution, and then –' she made a little gun shape with her fingers and pointed at him – 'you blow them away. Real life, however, is more complex.' The gun was a hand again. 'I could make some kind of deal with O'Dowd, get Chuck to give you a beating you won't ever forget. But where does that leave Jen?'

She seemed now to be talking more to herself than him and he got a sense of how quick her brain was and how mercurial her nature, because the next moment she was on her feet, walking round the room again, arms crossed, saying forcefully, 'But if I could put this right? If *this* time I could do that?' When she stopped walking he didn't like the way she was looking at him.

'Right, hesitate over the answer to this next question, ratboy, and it's Chuck time. Tell me exactly what you'd like to happen next?'

'What?'

'I told you not to bloody hesitate . . . Look, if you could make anything in the world happen now, what would it be? Come on, snap to it.'

He eyed her warily, not sure where the Hell this was going. 'I'd . . . I'd like to tell Jen why I did it and that I genuinely love her. I'd like to take away all that pain she's feeling, and then I'd like to get O'Dowd off my back.'

Cress nodded slowly. 'Good answer. Right order.' She turned and went and looked out of the curtains again and remained there for so long he didn't know whether he should prompt her to speak.

'OK,' she said, turning round and, with a defiant flick of her hair, a smoothing-down of her clothes, Cressida the star was back in the room. She sat opposite him again. 'We need to get this done quickly. I've another private plane waiting to take me north, and if I'm quick, I'll get there before your friends, not to mention my management team, the studio, Uncle Tom Cobley and all, twig I'm in the UK.' She gave a ladylike snort. 'You have no idea how many favours I've had to call in for this ... Right, I am going to do two incredibly stupid things. I'm doing them for Jen ... because I believe, God help me, that underneath all that crap I'm looking at right now ...'

She reached across and flicked his nose, using her thumb and middle finger, and it made his eyes water up again.

'. . . underneath all that crap is someone who understands that Jen needs to get back to where she was ... well, if not back exactly, at least somewhere near. She does not need some monumental bore to lock her in a high tower and throw away the key. I am taking a chance on you, ratboy, and you will not let me down.'

Mack nodded, although what it was in response to, or anticipation of, he didn't know.

'All those other things you want to happen,' she said, 'they're up to you ... but I wouldn't hold your breath about Jen ever listening to you again, let alone forgiving you. But. You. Will. Try. And . . . getting O'Dowd off your back, well, that I can do.' She laughed. 'God, that's the trouble with being in love, you think you can solve everything, make everyone as happy as you are. I may be mad.'

Mack gave no sign that he feared she might be too.

'So,' she said, reaching down to her red handbag, 'despite being very tempted to hand this to a rival paper just to spite you . . .' She pulled out a pad and then a pen and chucked them both into his lap in quick succession. 'Despite that . . . here we go. Ready?' She lifted her chin and breathed in the way he had seen Jennifer do just before she walked on the stage.

'Rumours have been swirling around Cressida Chartwell that she has fallen deeply for Rory Sylvester, her co-star in her new film *The Unfeeling*. But we can reveal exclusively that the rumours are only partly true. It *is* a Sylvester who is warming the English rose's bed, but it's not Rory, it is his wife Anna Maria. Yes, our Cressida is head over heels in love with the Latin spitfire and Anna Maria has already determined to leave her megastar husband to set up home with her new lover.'

She paused and raised her eyebrows.

'That enough of an exclusive for you, ratboy?'

Mack did not know what expression he had on his face, but he did know he had stopped writing at the words 'Anna Maria'.

He closed his mouth and then opened it to ask, 'How the Hell did you manage to keep that a secret?'

'Well it was a secret to me and to Anna Maria until a few days ago and, really, who would think I would be looking at another woman with my track record? People see what they want to see.'

Like Jennifer did.

Mack understood now why Cressida hadn't rushed for an injunction to stop the Rory story. As long as she could keep Jen out of it, she was probably looking forward to seeing O'Dowd get hold of the wrong end of the stick.

'But you told Jen—'

Cressida momentarily closed her eyes as if some of her ribs were also hurting. 'Yes, and it's the first time I've ever lied to her, but when she came up with Rory's name it seemed easier not to put her right over the phone; I could just sort it out when I got here.' A look of disdain hardened her expression. 'And, of course, I didn't know there was some little shit listening in.'

He sat very quietly, looking at his knees, not wanting to stoke that disdain into anger again. Which meant he was not aware that the little coughing noise and the two laboured intakes of breath signalled the moment when she started to cry. He raised his head and saw her reach out for the roll of paper towel.

It was real-life crying, not Hollywood-film crying: the tip of her nose reddened and her beautifully made-up face started to look crumpled and blotchy. When she wiped her eyes, her eyeliner smudged.

'People will understand,' he said, moved by her distress, 'about Anna Maria. They'll forgive you.'

'Don't be a fool,' she said, sniffing aggressively. 'Why would I cry about that; about meeting my soulmate? That's perfect.' She screwed up the paper towel and blotted one eye and then the other. 'I'm crying about what I've done to Jen. Yet again, I've hurt her. Pure accident this time, not stupidity like last time.'

Last time?

He went back to sitting very still and felt the tension in the room thicken.

There was more blotting and sniffing before Cressida said, sounding weary, 'So, the second most incredibly stupid thing I'm going to do today: another exclusive. And this one, you mustn't tell to a soul ... if you do, you're going to Hell in a handcart. If you don't, well, it might just make Jen trust you again.'

Mack threw the pad and paper on to the sofa, hoping she'd see it as a sign of how sincere he was, but she wasn't looking at him. He had no idea what her eyes were focusing on, but her body language looked cramped and self-conscious now. She was running one of her hands back and forth along the arm of the chair in what seemed to him to be a fretting motion.

'You know, I suppose, that I was in the car with Jen when we had the accident?' she began. 'I'd been visiting her for the weekend, dodging the press, messing about with disguises. Anyway, the night before the accident I'd misbehaved as usual and ended up in bed with one of Jen's drama professors. Handsome sod, bit left-wing and scruffy and ... the next night he invited us to this party.

He and I had a bit too much to drink, I said something stupid and he announces to the whole room that he'd only slept with me so he could say he'd "bagged a star".' Mack saw the little hike of her shoulders. 'I had hysterics, as you can imagine, and Jen got me out of there and into the car. We started to drive to her flat, but as we came off the motorway on to the slip road and Jen slowed the car to take the bend, I decided I wanted to go back and give that bastard a piece of my mind.' Her hand stilled on the arm of the chair. 'I undid my seat belt and tried to get the car door open. And . . . and Jen stopped the car, pulled the door closed and put my belt on again. Which is when we got hit from behind. Rammed into a sign.'

Cressida Chartwell didn't look like a Hollywood star any more, but a frightened young woman. 'I caused the accident and it was my fault she went through the windscreen. I remember her undoing her belt to get right across me and close that door.'

Mack was not assessing how huge a story this was; he was imagining Jen again, half in and half out of the car, the glass broken all around her.

'I wanted to come clean after the accident,' Cressida said, sounding absolutely wretched, 'but Jen was adamant she hadn't done her belt up properly in the first place. She won't even discuss it. She's had to put up with all that rubbish about her being drunk.' Cressida started to gulp again. 'Pass me another bit of bloody kitchen paper, will you?'

'I promise on my life, I won't ever talk about this to

anyone,' he said when he thought she was listening properly. 'And if I don't . . . you'll . . . tell Jen?'

She let the screwed-up pieces of paper towel fall to the floor. 'I will, although whether she'll want to listen is another thing. But yes, when I think she's ready to hear it, I'll tell her.'

He should have shut up then, but the journalist in him was still after answers. 'Why have you really come clean to me about this? It's a bloody risky thing to do. At the very least you should have got my secret out of me first – made sure I couldn't tell yours without you dumping on me in return?'

She made an irritated little swipe with her hand. 'Maybe I'm hoping you *will* tell everyone and I can finally stop carrying the weight of what I did around with me. Perhaps it's that touchy-feely, trite crap: I can't forgive myself and feel I should be punished.' Her bottom lip started to waver. 'All I know is I put Jen where she is now. My self-indulgence and vanity put her there. I'm as bad as you are.'

'No. You hurt Jen by accident. I set out to do it on purpose.'

'Same end result though,' she said and started to cry again.

CHAPTER 37

Expecting a phone call to confirm that Rory Sinclair was their man, O'Dowd had at first reacted with stunned silence when Mack had revealed that Anna Maria was their woman. Next he had asked if it was some kind of joke, until finally Mack had told him about Cressida's visit and he had become increasingly incoherent with excitement before announcing that Mack was a genius and he'd always known he would come good.

Mack had waited for the inevitable question about whether there were any photos of the two women together – you know, *those* kinds of photos. He now had a pain in his chest to go with the one in his ribs, and it had been there ever since Cressida's revelation about the accident. Jen's refusal to let Cress reveal the truth was humbling. Nothing as good as her was ever going to come his way again, he knew that.

'This is better than some third-hand gossip,' O'Dowd crowed, 'a lesbo, eh? Cunning little witch, fooled the lot of us. We'll be shifting papers by the boatload. Then there's the syndication rights.'

'So. I come into the office: you shred the diaries and photo in front of me. I want a written assurance that no photocopies or digital records remain and that you won't use this information to elicit further work from me.'

'Won't need to, old son, we'll all be rolling in clover after this. The money will be in your account by the end of the week.'

'Not soon enough,' Mack said, drawing on all his anger to make his voice hard and unyielding. 'I want it all in cash, half couriered over to me tomorrow, the rest by mid-week, that's Wednesday, not Thursday. And don't give me any crap about not being able to get that kind of cash at short notice. You know you struck a good deal.'

O'Dowd was laughing. 'You're right there. Sold yourself a bit short, my son, but don't worry, you're made for life. The job offers will be pouring in.'

'I don't want my name on this.'

'You're joking.'

'You can put your name on it in return for a promise that Jennifer Roseby doesn't get mentioned.'

'Her? She's out of the loop, a sprat to catch a mackerel.'

It was all Mack could do not to hurl the phone at the wall. In the end he just chucked it in the bin, then he used his own to ring for a taxi.

At Tess's house, he didn't even make it over the threshold before he was in tears again, clutching Gabi and Fran, fending off Joe's questions and Tess's concern about who he'd been fighting with. He wouldn't tell them anything until the girls were settled upstairs with a DVD.

As he explained about Phyllida and Sir Teddy, he saw the way their faces mirrored his own when he'd heard the news from O'Dowd – all those subtle changes to and fro between disbelief and fear. The momentary satisfaction that they understood what it meant for the family if Phyllida's past had been revealed was whisked away by the knowledge that he now had to tell them what he'd done. He talked on, and Tess's face looked more and more waxy. When he reached the part where he'd fallen for Jen and she'd fallen for him, Tess lowered her chin, and the movement reminded him of Jen so much he had to halt for a while.

Mack knew that if Tess got up and walked out of the room he was finished. Losing Tess, losing Jen, what was the point of anything then?

Joe was looking at his wife.

'I knew he was up to something,' he said, 'he's always been a shifty sod.' He turned on Mack. 'Ever thought you should have treated us all like grown-ups and told us everything from the start? Four heads are better than one, even when you count Phyllida. We could have come up with something better than the mess you've got yourself into now, the damage you've done to that poor girl.' Joe gave Mack a particularly penetrating stare. 'Mind you, what you're telling us now could be a pack of lies too.'

'I wish it was, but it's not, Joe ... and whatever you think you could have done, let me tell you it wouldn't have worked. O'Dowd wanted that story; he would never have let go.'

Please say something, Tess.

There was a noise outside the door before it opened and Phyllida walked in. She had filled out a little and was smartly dressed, with a string of pearls at her neck, but she was limping badly and leaning heavily on a grey, metal crutch.

'The girls woke me up,' she said sulkily, 'some cartoon they're watching in your bedroom. Why couldn't they watch it down here?' She did an almost comical double take when she saw Mack.

'Fighting at your age?' She nodded at his face and tutted, before laboriously lowering herself on to a chair.

Tess still had her chin down.

'Great, Phyllida, hello to you too,' he said, getting up. 'Thank God it wasn't just you I was trying to protect, or I'd feel a fool on top of everything else.'

Phyllida looked from Joe to Tess as if she could pick up a clue to what Mack might be talking about.

It was then Tess started to speak.

'Mack's just been telling us what he was really doing in Northumberland,' she said. 'He wasn't writing a walking book, he was getting friendly with a cousin of Cressida Chartwell's so he could get the inside story on her love life for O'Dowd. He managed to do it, and it'll be in the paper tomorrow, but he fell in love with the cousin, Jennifer, her name is, and she fell for him and they had sex and now he's probably broken her heart.'

The whole speech had been delivered in a monotone and not once had Tess looked at him. He wanted to shrivel up and die, hearing it all from her lips.

Phyllida looked aghast. 'You've done what? What? You disgusting, filthy wretch. How could you? I am deeply, deeply ashamed of you.'

'Stop it. Don't you dare talk to him like that!' Tess suddenly shouted.

Joe looked at her uneasily. 'Love – take it easy.'

'No, I won't.' Tess's face was screwed up and hardly recognisable. She was on her feet, standing over Phyllida. 'Go on, Mum, ask him why he did it.'

'Money, I would think,' Phyllida said, drawing back from her daughter.

'That's where you're so wrong. He did it for you. He's told us why and I believe him. I know he's lied to me about everything else: I know that he's always made up stories and if he could tell a lie for an easy life, he would. But I believe him about this. He lied to protect you and protect us and you're not even grateful.' Tess seemed to be towering over Phyllida. 'But why does that surprise me? You're never grateful, not even to me. Always at your beck and call, putting the girls and Joe to one side *and* you're still drinking on the sly. You did it in hospital, you're doing it now. Oh, that's a good face, Mum . . . is that your surprised one? Little Tess, sunshiny Tess, knowing that?' She bent down until her face was level with Phyllida's. 'If there's anyone in this room that disgusts me, it's not him.'

'Tess, love,' Joe said, standing up.

'What? Go easy on her? Mind what I say? I'm sick of that. So listen to this, Mum, Mack did it because O'Dowd was going to splash all over the papers that you were Sir Teddy Montgomery's lover.' Tess had crossed her arms, but was still looking at her mother with fury. 'Mack's been a good son to you and look where it's got him.'

'O'Dowd told you I was Sir Teddy Montgomery's lover?' Phyllida said, touching the pearls round her neck.

Mack nodded. 'He had diaries, a photograph.'

'You saw them?'

'I didn't need to; he gave me enough details to know it was you. That wavy scar by your backbone, that noise you make when . . .' He looked at Tess and hesitated.

'. . . When you have sex,' Tess finished for him.

Phyllida's eyebrows shot up.

'Besides, you confirmed it yourself that day on the patio before I headed north. I asked you if you knew anyone called Teddy and you fell apart, said something like "It was madness, a stupid passion."'

What had he expected? A big hug? A thank you for all he'd done?

'You stupid bloody imbecile,' Phyllida shouted.

CHAPTER 38

'I'm thinking about going back into work today,' Jennifer said and waited for them to try to stop her. If she could only keep talking, keep the momentum going, she could find her way through this. The thing was to keep her mind occupied, and work was the place for that, not here with everyone back to treating her as if she was an invalid. They couldn't help themselves – she'd seen Brenda whisk the *Courant* off the table as she'd walked in.

How easy would going back to work be, though? She thought about all those times Matt had sat up in the local history section and looked down at her. No not looked, spied. And it wasn't Matt, it was Mack.

'You've had more phone calls,' her mother said. 'Lisa, Finlay again, Angus, Lydia, oh, and that drippy Pamela woman. I have to say, she means well, but what a drain she is.'

Bryony placed a mug of coffee in front of her. 'Have a drink of this before you go.'

Yes, she was fine. People would think she was an idiot, but then they were right, she was . . .

She noticed the chrysanthemums in the big blue jug. 'These are nice.'

She saw the look that flitted from Bryony to her mother.

'They're from Alex, love. Delivered yesterday. Remember?'

'Oh, yes,' she said, but did not. Alex with his big white charger. Or Land Rover. It was all the same.

'Cress rang again, of course,' Bryony said. 'She couldn't stay long. Said things were mad, Rory's walked off the film, no one knows if he'll be back.'

Jennifer saw her mother making signals to Bryony to stop talking, and she wished Bryony would. She was giving herself a break from Cress for a while. Too mixed in with Matt.

Not Matt. Mack.

She got up and retrieved the newspaper from down the side of the dresser, turning the pages until she saw the photograph that had been taken of the cast. No picture of him, of course, that's why he'd been late for the dress rehearsal. And only a review of Lisa as Viola, not her. The invisible woman meets the man who never was.

'I'd better be off,' she said, and there was that little flitting look again.

'What?' she shouted. 'Just say it – stop doing those looks!'

Her mother came over to her softly, as if approaching a nervous cat. 'Jen, it's already half past two. Go into work if you want, love, Bryony will drive you. But it's the afternoon, Jen.'

She looked at her watch and couldn't make sense of it.

'Well, I'll just have a walk round the farm then. Get some fresh air.'

'Let Bryony come with you.' Her mother was now also employing a nervous-cat-calming voice. 'Just in case any of those journalists aren't keeping to the road.'

At the word 'journalists', Jennifer felt everything give that familiar tilt. She sat down and curled her fingers around the seat of the chair, certain that if she didn't she might pitch forward.

'They're not here for you, Jen,' Bryony said quickly, 'it's because of Cress and Anna Maria. Remember?'

Like he'd only been here for Cress and Anna Maria.

'Jen, are you all right?' her mother asked.

'Of course. I was just trying to think about Bryony protecting me from the journalists and I had a joke in my head, you know, something about that being like shutting a door after a horse has galloped off, but I can't think how it goes.'

This time she couldn't muster the energy to tell them to stop those looks and took herself back up to her bedroom.

CHAPTER 39

People streamed past, eyes down, talking on mobiles, some knocking into him and not saying a word. Everything seemed speeded up, for no reason at all, and the different accents coming his way sounded flat. No sharp freshness in the air, either.

He went in through the revolving door, across the marble floor and was ushered into the lift as if he himself was some kind of celebrity.

He wasn't surprised, when the door opened, to see Serena standing there in what she probably hoped was a nonchalant stance. His stock had risen, after all, and suddenly he must look a lot more attractive.

'Don't even bother,' he said when she looked as though she was going to speak, but there was no satisfaction in the exchange: tit-for-tat seemed a petty little game when he had something much more important to get through.

He moved towards O'Dowd's office and saw how they were all trying to pretend they weren't looking at him. Once he'd viewed this place with such excitement; where he'd felt part of an inner circle, getting to know what was happening in the world before anyone else.

It's just a big open-plan office with a lot of wise-ass cynics hunched over computers.

'Mack,' O'Dowd said, coming to greet him, and Mack had to force himself to look at him. It stirred up everything black and treacly that lay slicked down on the underside of his own character. He wanted to turn away, there was every possibility he might bottle this.

'Come in, come in,' O'Dowd said. 'Here, look at these.'

On O'Dowd's desk was a pile of newspapers; titles from the UK, the continent and the US, all with a tearful but brave-looking Cressida on the front. Beside her stood a woman with long dark hair and a mouth that even in black and white you knew was a voluptuous bright red. 'Out and About', shouted one headline, 'The Rose and the Spitfire', another.

No such thing as bad publicity. For some.

'The old bastard is very, very happy,' O'Dowd said. 'You happy too? Money OK? Good to feel flush? So, what can I do for you? Thought it was tomorrow we were doing the great diary-and-photo shredding, but we can do it now if you like. Only have to call the legal guys to bring the stuff along.'

'No need. Change of plan. I've got another scoop.'

'I knew it,' O'Dowd crowed, 'it's in your blood.'

'How true.'

'So come on, sit down. Is it about Cressida again?'

Mack thought about that big shiny secret he had been

given and wrapped it deeper inside himself. The blood was thundering round his body, he could almost hear it pumping and surging and he tried to calm it by thinking of the beach and counting those waves. One. Two. Three.

'No, not about Cressida. It's about a guy called Gordon O'Dowd. You heard of him?'

'Don't get your drift, my son.' O'Dowd's look was suddenly guarded.

'There were no diaries, were there?' Mack said, as evenly as he could. 'No photograph either? In fact, no affair between Phyllida and Sir Teddy Montgomery?'

O'Dowd looked away, and Mack could tell he was trying not to laugh. He felt nausea scurry up from his stomach and then retreat.

'You worked that out finally then?' O'Dowd said, looking back at him, and then he did laugh, a short bark of a thing. 'But don't blame me, you wanted to believe it of old Phyllida. You were so scared I could smell it.' He spread his arms wide. 'Come on, no hard feelings. I did you a favour. Look at the money you've made.'

'Oh don't worry; I'll never, ever forget what I owe you.' Mack managed a smile. 'So, where was I? Oh yeah. You played a blinder, especially with those little personal details about Mum. Reeled me in nicely. 'Course Phyllida didn't help by going into a tailspin when I asked her about Teddy. It all seemed to be true.' He shook his head. 'Stupid Mack didn't realise there was another Teddy lurking in this story. Remind me again of your full name, will you?'

O'Dowd didn't answer.

'OK, I'll remind you. Gordon Edward O'Dowd. I knew that, of course; knew you didn't like the "Edward" as it was too posh. Just didn't twig that some people, select people, get to call you "Teddy".' He folded his hands in his lap. 'You were Mum's lover, not old Montgomery. That's how you knew those details about her.'

'Well done, my son.' There was not a trace of remorse on O'Dowd's face.

'Crafty old Phyllida ... she was seeing you and Dad at the same time. You were her nasty little secret, "madness, a stupid passion" as she so rightly said—'

'He was a tosser, your dad,' O'Dowd stated, as if it was a fact, and Mack thought of all the things that 'Tosser' had done for him.

'Tosser or not,' Mack said, 'Phyllida chose him in the end. Must have hurt, top-flight woman like Phyllida picking you up and then dropping you. Niggled at you all these years, hasn't it? Then, stroke of luck, I turn up all bright-eyed and eager to work for you.' He laughed. 'God, you were poisonous to me. Never understood why. And then you saw your chance with Sir Teddy. Phyllida was so befuddled and I was so down on my luck and desperate to protect her and the family, you could have made me do just about anything.'

O'Dowd looked about as bothered as if someone had been reading him the shipping forecast.

Mack took the brown A4 envelope from his pocket, unfolded it and placed it on O'Dowd's knees. Then he studied that face, looking at the angle of the nose, the brow line, fitting it all together. That nausea was back.

O'Dowd pretended more disinterest, but was soon tearing the envelope open with his stubby thumbnail. He pulled out a piece of paper.

'Your birth certificate,' he said warily.

'Well done. Mother: Phyllida Grayfield, Father: Graham Stone. Nice and neat.' On purpose, Mack leaned back in his chair and put his hands behind his head. 'Pile of lies, like most of your paper. The name under Father should be Gordon Edward O'Dowd.'

He was never going to get used to saying that – it felt dirty in his mouth, like an obscenity.

'Yeah, right,' O'Dowd said, but his eyes were shifting around, as if trying to latch on to some certainty. 'I was always careful.'

'Sure? Phyllida told me to remind you about a party in Clapham. You were drunk and wouldn't listen to "No". Gave her a black eye. You being violent wasn't unusual, evidently, being too drunk to put a condom on was.'

O'Dowd's face clouded. 'I never doled out anything to your mother she didn't ask for.' Mack took his hands from behind his head and sat on them. This man opposite him was his father, and that was a monstrous fact to carry round in his brain. Far worse, though, was the suspicion that he might be taking after him. Like father, like son. What he'd done to Jen; what O'Dowd had done to Phyllida – was it that different?

'Besides,' O'Dowd said, all defiance again, 'how come

you're suddenly mine when she was sleeping with Saint Graham too?'

'Because Graham wasn't a saint. Returned from one of his trips with a nasty dose of "not being particularly choosy about who you have intercourse with". Treatable, but sex wasn't on the menu for a few months. Guess when that was?'

O'Dowd looked as though he was trying to laugh that information off, but his mouth was not set in quite the right shape.

That thundering was back in Mack's ears. 'Funny, isn't it? You calling me "my son" all the time? Turns out I am.' He grabbed one of the newspapers, rolling it up and shoving it microphone-like under O'Dowd's chin. 'How do you feel, Mr O'Dowd? Could you cry a bit for us?'

The paper was slapped away. 'What are you after?'

'Nothing. I'm pretty disgusted by the things you've already given me. I like to think that all the bad things in my character are down to you and all the good things are down to Graham. Knew I wasn't his and still did his best. More than his best, I suspect . . . he was that kind of guy. Whereas you, Daddy dearest, got your own son to betray a wonderful, brave, beautiful woman who was probably the love of his life.'

'Yeah, well.' O'Dowd's gaze strayed to his watch.

'Thought that would be your caring reaction,' Mack said, getting to his feet, 'which is why you're about to understand that old expression: "Don't care was made to care". Phyllida and I have drawn up a list of all the women you've cheated on your wife with and put it in a letter.' He looked at his own watch, glad to know O'Dowd would get the echo of his own action just seconds before. 'What time does your post arrive at home?'

O'Dowd got to his feet and Mack saw him pull back his arm and got his own punch in first. It made his hand jar and sent a horrible pain up through his wrist and arm and then across to his still grumbling ribs. O'Dowd stumbled back into his chair.

'I'll have you and your mother,' he bellowed.

'Don't think so. The list's not complete: the juiciest ones we left off, like that MP who fiddled her expenses. Tut tut, there's your sister paper bleating on about political corruption and there's you getting your leg over in that big old pricy flat of hers. And it all goes on the internet if you try anything funny.' He winked at O'Dowd. 'We've found your Achilles' heel, my son.'

Which was when the phone started to ring.

'That'll be your wife wanting to discuss the post.' Mack stepped swiftly towards the door. Serena was standing outside. Probably listening.

'God, you're hard-faced,' he said, and down in the lobby he punched the air and picked up the neat display of newspapers and scattered them over the floor.

Back in the café, Phyllida and Tess both stood up as he came in and Phyllida got the waiter to bring a large espresso while Tess held his hand tightly. It was the one he'd used to punch O'Dowd, but he didn't mind.

'You needn't think I'll stop looking out for you just

because you've been demoted to half-brother,' she said and then clicked her tongue. 'Stupid expression, you're a complete brother to me ... complete pain sometimes too ... but that's why I love you. Makes me feel superior.'

Jen would have loved you. You'd have loved Jen.

Across the table Phyllida was watching him as he tried, with his free hand, to lift his coffee cup to his lips.

'You're shaking as badly as me,' she said, before giving him what looked suspiciously like a kind smile.

CHAPTER 40

Jennifer had made it into work, lying on the back seat of Bryony's car as they went past the journalists still hanging around near the road. There were fewer now – the real story was over in Hollywood – but Bryony accompanied her into the library through the back entrance just in case any were loitering there. Jennifer had pulled the hood on her sweatshirt around her face, and when a thin, bored-looking chap had stepped in front of them and said he was from one of the papers in Newcastle, Bryony had advanced on him executing a full-on Haka taught to her by Danny on their wedding night and taught to him on a rugby tour of New Zealand. The thin man had retreated so fast he had backed into a bollard and was last seen clutching his knee.

Once inside, Jennifer had gone straight to the upstairs office, where she had done very little all day except get used to being there. She would have found it hard to say which emotion, shame or humiliation, had gained ascendancy over her; both had combined to create a dark fug of misery which seemed to close her off from everyone else. How desperate she must have seemed to him. How easy to fool. He had smelled out the need in her and fed off it. There was no consolation in the fact that few people would know she had slept with Mack; that she was attracted to him had been obvious to a lot more.

She had been hunted down and cheated.

But all this was surface pain compared to finding the bliss of loving someone and being loved back was a mirage. There was anger and bitterness mixed in with that broken bliss, and maybe they'd come to the fore later, but right now it was her heart that was aching so badly that her hand kept straying to where her bra met the skin of her chest as if she could soothe it.

Lionel was studiously kind and thankfully did not make any suggestions regarding massage or other remedies and Sheila distracted her with stories of Reece's latest exploits. She only mentioned the whole Matt/Mack thing twice; once to say, 'Stop beating yourself up. I got sidetracked by that bum too,' and 'Funny, though, the way he looked at you from up in the gallery . . .'

Jennifer ate her sandwiches at her desk, not caring if they were ferret meat or rhinoceros and Bryony came to take her home. This time there was no thin, bored-looking man outside the library and fewer journalists near the farm. There was, however, a Land Rover in the yard.

'Do you want to see him? Shall I put him off?' Bryony asked.

Another person who had looked at Mack without lust-coloured spectacles and not been fooled. Anything Alex might say she deserved.

They sat together in the sitting room, Brenda maintaining a diplomatic distance down the hall and Alex told her he was very sorry she had been hurt and that as far as he was concerned Matt Harper was history.

She wished she could erase it all so easily from her heart, but she appreciated the sentiment and when he reached out and held her hand she let him. It felt safe and familiar and solid. Nothing like a mirage.

CHAPTER 41

Four weeks after running south, Mack came up past the Angel of the North and tried to convince himself that today its wings were spread in welcome and it was not living up to its nickname of being the rusty flasher. Although that would have been the greeting he deserved.

Past the block-like sprawl of the MetroCentre, with the sun shining off hundreds of windscreens in the car park, and then he was leaving the city and the suburbs, and the countryside opened out around him, absolutely at its blossoming, sumptuous May best under a wide blue sky smeared with wispy cloud. The beauty of the place tore at him and he could barely wait to get off the dual carriageway. Soon he was slowing to take the dips and crests of the lanes and then tearing along the Military Road, which lay like a straight spine along a great green back. He was high up here, the view unbroken off to either side, and now and then he passed walkers on Hadrian's Wall. He remembered his first visit, when he had skulked about like a truculent schoolboy on a history trip, and added it to the pile of things he regretted.

His first sight of the road sign to Brindley made him slow to a halt and turn off the engine. He felt himself pulled by the desire to be there, like the wind was pulling those clouds, but turning up out of the blue was not the right first step.

He restarted the car and drove on, trying to concentrate on being positive, and for a few miles he distracted himself by thinking about Phyllida. Relations between them had been far less glacial since the O'Dowd revelation, and a couple of weeks before he headed north she had told Tess and him quite calmly that she thought a large chunk of O'Dowd's cash, if they didn't mind, should be spent on something that would really irritate him – there was a clinic on the outskirts of Bath that had a good rehabilitation programme for alcoholics, and although she didn't think she was one of those (cue some serious shoe examination by Mack and Tess), perhaps a residential spell there might be in order.

Tess and he had waited for her to change her mind, or to dig her heels in once she was there, but neither of these things had happened. On his last visit to the clinic she had looked pale and exhausted, but had managed to smile wryly at the large glass of orange juice in front of her on the table.

Tess and he had decided to take each day without incident as a good sign.

Mack came to the familiar hump-backed bridge and the

sharp bend in the road, and turned up the lane. The trees were in full leaf now, and he drove through light and shade to park near the pond. As he got out of the car, he repeated to himself the promise that he had made to Joe before he left Bath: no more lying, no more sweet-talking; no flannel, no flattery, no avoiding, no skulking round corners. He was going to keep that promise and do the things he had told Cressida he wanted to do. He would accept his punishment like a man. Maybe after punishment would come forgiveness.

Trouble was, now he was here, Joe's mantra sounded even scarier. He hesitated and looked towards the forge, a place with fire that burned and large, heavy tools that could cut and grind and beat. He thought of Jennifer and walked on towards the house.

'Wasn't sure you were going to get oot of the car,' Doug said, opening the door. He had on a brown leather apron, and behind his ear there was a pencil. His face was expressionless, those big eyebrows still.

'I was plucking up courage.'

'Well now you've plucked it, fuck off. If you've come here for more dirt, I'm not selling.'

'That's not why I'm here.' He knew it was important not to come across as cocky or assured. 'I've come to apologise to people, particularly to Jen, explain why I did what I did and—'

'Good acting, tosser.'

Mack remembered when he had been 'marra' not 'tosser' and felt his throat constrict.

Doug leaned against the door frame, folded his arms. 'Good leather jacket as well. That new? Along with the car? You must have made a canny pile.'

Here we go, Joe, wish me luck.

'I did. But the jacket's old, the car's hired. I've still got my debts. I did use some of the money for my mother's, um, medical care. No . . . I'll call it what it is, her rehab. The rest is in an account. For Jen, if she'll ever take it from me.'

Doug gave a great whoop of laughter. 'Regular saint, aren't you?'

Mack pressed on, explaining about Phyllida and what he thought had happened with Sir Teddy Montgomery, but as soon as he got to the bit about it all turning out to be a lie, Doug snapped, 'Very neat. One minute you have a canny reason for being a callous swine and then, vavoom, it's gone.'

'Maybe, but it's true . . . and Doug? How is Jen?'

Doug was suddenly in front of him. 'Want another bit for your paper about her, do you? What'll it be? Something about her being gutted by her cousin's choice of lover, maybe? Whereas we all know she's gutted because of you.'

'I love her, Doug, genuinely love her. It happened slowly, but I fell for her. I need to get her to understand that.'

'Are you cracked?' Doug thundered at him. 'Can you imagine how painful it would be for her to see you again after what you did? It's taken her this long to pick herself up and get back to work. She barely returns any calls.

There's a lot of anger around here about you. Go home before Danny knows you're here. Or Alex.'

'Alex?'

Doug grimaced. 'Yeah, stepped right in to look after her. Now get lost.'

Mack felt his arm being gripped and suddenly he was facing away from the house and being marched towards his car. A push had him bumping off the paintwork. He turned round, expecting Doug to be right there, but he was striding back to the house.

'Doug,' Mack shouted, 'I'm sorry, I did such a wrong thing here, but I want to put it right. I love Jen, hand on heart.'

'Oh you've got one then?' Doug called back and, without waiting for a reply, crossed the threshold of his house, turned and very precisely shut the door. That precision seemed to suggest, 'You do not warrant my anger. I view you only with disgust.'

'That could have gone better,' Mack said to himself as he drove back down the track, his hands trembling on the steering wheel.

Two hours later he was standing in the park, looking at the main door of the library, willing it to open, and for Jen to walk out. And then he'd do what, exactly? He sat down on one of the seats but got up again quickly when he remembered it was the one he and Jen had sat on together after those men in the pub had insulted her.

No daffodils this time. The blossom was just going and

there was some kind of flower he didn't know the name of in the flowerbeds.

The thought of how exposed he was standing in the park made him look around to see if anyone was watching him. Pointless worrying really. News would get out that he was back, and then he was going to really have to honour that promise to Joe and take it all like a man. He calmed himself by concentrating on the war memorial and remembering that people had been through worse.

The abbey clock chimed four. A whole hour till she came out, if she *was* back at work. He'd go and see if he could spot her car around the back, perhaps wait round there.

He was suddenly face-to-face with those unnamed flowers in the flowerbed, something heavy and squirmy on top of him. He struggled and squirmed too until he managed to turn enough to see who it was.

Lionel? Lionel without his glasses?

'Lionel, let me explain,' he panted, trying to get out from underneath him, but Lionel's method of fighting appeared to be to cling on like a bushbaby. All Mack managed to do was get on to his back with Lionel still grasping him, and the situation struck Mack as farcical until he felt Lionel's knee in his stomach and let out a cry that had Lionel springing to his feet.

Mack stayed on the ground, on his side, his knees pulled up to his chest and waited for the blunt pain to subside. He tried to squint up at Lionel, who was bouncing around on his feet like a prize fighter.

'I do not agree with physical violence, no, no, the last resort of the failed negotiator,' Lionel wagged his finger in time to the delivery of the words, 'but you asked for it, you . . . you cur.'

Cur?

Mack staggered to his feet and, in retrospect, decided his first words were a mistake, for he had no sooner got out, 'How is Jen? I love her, Lionel,' when he was sitting among the flowers again.

'Don't you mention her name,' Lionel screamed. 'You've just come back to gloat.'

'No. I've come to apologise. To everyone.' He flung his arms wide and Lionel, without glasses, must have mistaken it for a threatening gesture because he took a few steps back, shouted 'Callous swine!' and ran from the park.

Mack had soil down the neck of his shirt, his stomach and ribs ached and his leather jacket was scuffed all down one arm, but he didn't think there had been any real damage done. He crawled over to the seat and pulled himself up on to it. Round One to the peace-loving librarian.

Jennifer ignored her mobile phone ringing and tried not to feel irritation at her mother. She'd already rung to see if she'd arrived safely this morning and again after lunch to check she'd eaten something. It was like being stalked. No, actually it wasn't. That had been quite different.

If it wasn't her mother ringing, it was Cressida. They were tortuous, stilted conversations these days. Cressida was always trying to dampen down her obvious happiness so that she would not appear tactless, and Jennifer underplayed her own misery. That deep connection between them seemed to have fractured. The last phone conversation had ended with Cressida in tears. 'Jen me having Anna Maria doesn't mean I don't need you any more, you mustn't think that. You never call me any more, it's always me calling you.'

Jennifer had assured Cressida that she didn't feel supplanted by Anna Maria; she was happy for both of them; glad that Rory had agreed to finish the film; delighted that Cressida was heading for a long break in Argentina after the end of filming. She would try to ring more often. She was fine, absolutely fine. Really.

Jennifer opened the office door and walked quickly to the top of the stairs. Every day was getting easier. Well, the working and walking and talking bit. Not the thinking bit. She still found herself teasing out every conversation she had ever had with Mack, seeing where he had fooled her, how he had wormed his way into her confidence.

She would not allow herself to think of that last day and night. His actions then were bewildering and she could not think of any motive for them beside pity or guilt. Who wanted to think that someone had slept with you because of either of those?

She should be voicing all of this to Cressida, but she couldn't bear to bring him up, and her cousin never pressed her. She knew Cressida was being kind, but somehow it made her feel worse – as if what she had done was so incredibly stupid and naive that Cressida couldn't stand to go back over it.

She arrived downstairs to see Sheila on the phone. She was looking extremely serious, and Jennifer concluded it must be Reece calling once more. He had managed to break his arm falling off the roof of a car – the details were hazy – and was contemplating coming home, as the owner of the bar he was working in was unimpressed with his behaviour. It had been his car.

Sheila was still offering the odd monosyllabic reply when the door opened and Lionel walked in looking as if he'd been rolling around in a flowerbed. There was mud on the knees of his trousers, and his shirt, which was hanging out, had a tear in one sleeve.

'Bloody Hell,' Sheila said, putting the phone down quickly. 'What happened to you?'

'I had an altercation.'

Sheila frowned. 'Is that a fight to the rest of us?'

'Who with, Lionel?' Jennifer was unable to grasp the idea of Lionel having a fight.

'Someone I bumped into,' he said, reaching under the counter for his glasses. 'I know it's not right, fighting, but sometimes a man's got to stand up and be counted. Defend those who can't defend themselves. Be brave.'

'How do you feel?' Sheila asked.

'Quite shaky actually.'

'Run and get him some camomile tea, will you, Jen?'

'Of course, but who have you been fighting, Lionel?'

Lionel looked as if he was about to answer, but Sheila

plonked him down in a chair and rammed his head between his legs. 'Camomile tea now, Jen,' she said firmly.

Jennifer went off to the kitchen, not really sure what to make of any of it, and when she came back with the tea Lionel was still hunched over on his seat.

'I'm an animal,' he said, 'a complete animal.' He looked so guilt-ridden that what with giving him his tea and sympathy, while also checking out books and answering queries, it was a few minutes before she realised Sheila had disappeared.

Mack was walking over the road with the intention of going to check on Jennifer's car when he saw Sheila tanking out of the library towards him. Her language was indescribable and so was the pain when she grabbed him by the hair.

'You and your lovely locks,' she said, getting a real hiss into that last 's'. 'Let's see what you look like bald.'

'Sheila, Sheila,' he screamed, trying to disentangle her fingers from his hair, 'please stop, just listen.'

Amazingly she did, but when he straightened up he could see it was not because of him. Sonia was standing a few feet away in a too-short, too-tight dress.

'What are you doing here?' Sheila said, her tone aggressive.

'I've come—' Mack began.

'I'm not talking to you –' Sheila nodded towards Sonia – 'I'm talking to her.'

'That'll be a first.' Sonia folded her arms, making her

dress ride up higher. 'Been to the dentist, spotted this little creep in the park.' She pointed at Mack. 'You owe me money, took off without paying your bills.'

'Sonia, it's all right: you were on my list of people to visit.' Mack reached for his wallet.

'Typical, Sonia,' Sheila said, ignoring him. 'Typical. Not concerned about Jen, just your bottom line –' there was a perfect pause – 'which, in that dress, everyone can see.'

'Well, at least Oxfam hasn't given me a loyalty card.' Sonia laughed at Sheila's rather snug skirt and top. 'And I do care about Jen.'

Sheila moved nearer. 'No you don't, all you care about is money and men. The younger the better. How's that husband of yours, weaned yet?'

Sonia took one large, furious step towards Sheila. 'How are those boys of yours, still running wild?'

'No,' Sheila blasted back, 'they're sitting around waiting for you to come and seduce them like you did their dad. You can say you've got the matching set then, you cow.'

Now understanding what had caused the rift between Sheila and Sonia, Mack decided it might be fortuitous to take a step to one side. Slowly, as the women continued to square up to each other, he backed away. They didn't appear to notice he had gone.

Joe's mantra stopped his withdrawal. 'Hey,' he shouted, 'you were meant to be having a go at me, not each other. Sonia, here's some of your money. Sheila, come on, get what you want to say to me off your chest.'

He wished he hadn't phrased it like that, not with the size of Sheila's chest.

The women barely looked his way. 'We'll get to you in a minute,' Sonia said.

'Yeah, later,' Sheila agreed before they started shouting at each other again. As he walked round the back of the library, they were nose to nose.

Jennifer left Lionel contemplating what an animal he was and nipped out of the library to find Sheila and Sonia at what looked like boiling point.

'Hey, hey, hey,' she said loudly and managed to get both of the women's attention. 'Come on, Sonia, come on, Sheila. Fighting in the street, you're better than that.'

Sheila suddenly looked as if she had woken up.

'Jen, love, you shouldn't be out here.' She caught hold of Jennifer's arm, 'Let's get you inside.'

Sonia was looking around, confused. 'Where's—'

'Shut up, you,' Sheila screamed, 'not another word. We'll finish this later. I'll ring you.' Jennifer had no time to find that last bit funny before Sheila was almost lifting her in through the library door.

'What an earth is going on with you two today?' Jennifer said, smoothing her clothes back down when they were inside the library. 'Have you been taking testosterone supplements?'

'Might have done.' Sheila was looking at the desk.

'Possibly,' Lionel agreed and would not meet her gaze either.'

*

Jennifer's car was parked around the back of the library and Mack patted it warily. After the events of the last half hour he would not have been surprised if it had turned and bitten him. Should he stand by the car or back off a little? Jennifer would know he was here by now, and he didn't want to look as if he was stalking her.

Not again.

He loitered by the wheelie bins.

'Waiting for them to take the rubbish away?' Doug was walking towards him. 'See you've had a run-in with someone already.'

'Lionel.'

Doug whistled. 'Lionel, eh? The crowd of people wanting to kill you must be bigger than I thought.' He was looking over Mack's shoulder, 'And you know what? I think your day is about to get worse.'

Mack turned to see Alex rushing towards him and then he was down on his knees again, but this time it was on concrete and he had not been pushed, but punched. He just had time to feel the pain bloom across his back before he was hauled to his feet.

'You bastard.' Mack could feel Alex's spittle landing on his face. 'What you did to her was unforgivable and you've come back for more?' Mack was being shaken vigorously. 'No one wants you up here – especially Jennifer.'

His promise, to take whatever was thrown at him and not fight back, shattered when faced with Alex. Mack pushed him away and was pleased to see him stumble on the kerb.

'Well Jen doesn't bloody want you either,' he shouted

and then ducked as Alex threw another punch at him. 'You were history before I came along.'

This time Alex's fist did connect with his face and Mack stumbled back against the wall.

'Shut up, you little prick,' Alex said, grabbing him by his jacket and twisting him round so that his face was flattened against the stone. Mack felt his arm being pushed up his back and Alex's mouth was right by his ear.

'The people who love her are looking after her, putting right the damage you've done. I won't have you upsetting her again. Take this as a warning and go.'

'So you can move in on her. Smother her? Get her up on that farm of yours and bury her?'

'I'm protecting her,' Alex snarled and Mack felt his hair being tugged. His head was pulled backwards before it was smacked forward into the stone. He was so stunned he didn't feel the pain until he started to slide down the wall.

'Hey, now,' he heard Doug say, 'not his head, not on the wall, that's too much.'

'Oh, you think so,' Alex replied and Mack felt a sharp pain as he was kicked in the thigh.

'Hey,' Doug shouted, 'enough. He's on the ground. He's bleeding. Leave it.'

Mack was being lifted to his feet again, but this time it was by Doug.

'Careful, Doug,' he muttered, 'I'm dripping on you.'

Mack saw Alex's hand was on Doug's shoulder. 'Move aside, Doug. Don't you dare get in my way or I'll—'

'Or you'll what?' Doug asked sharply, 'Have me horse-whipped, run me off your land? I'm not your serf, and I say this stops.'

There was some other shouting which Mack didn't catch as Doug had let him go and he was too busy crumpling on to the pavement and trying to stop the blood from dripping into his mouth. He was aware of Alex stalking away still shouting before Doug returned to lift him back to his feet.

'Make it easy on yourself,' he said peering at the cut on Mack's head, 'gan and get yourself patched up and then leave.'

Mack tried to shake his head, but it hurt too much. 'Can't, Doug. I have to tell Jen how much I love her, make her believe all those good things I told her and forgive me for all the bad things.'

'It'll never work. They won't let you near her. And what you did really was unforgivable.'

'Got to try.' Doug's head appeared to be lengthening and then shortening. 'Stand still, Doug. I want to know: Postwoman Pat, you asked her out?'

'You're gibbering, you soft git, I'm not moving at all. And it's none of your business if I've asked her oot.'

'That means "no", doesn't it? Ooh that's bad, Doug, very bad, and I'd tell you why if you stopped swaying about. It's not good Doug, it's making me feel sick and dizzy. I've already bled on your jeans. I think I might vomit now.'

'Oh, bugger,' Doug said, 'why do I get landed with this? Howay. Let's get you to A&E. Can you walk?'

'Learned when I was a toddler.' He felt himself start to disconnect with everything around him except Doug manhandling him along the road.

'Not a good start to your campaign, is it?' Doug was saying. 'You might want to consider some kind of private health insurance if you're serious about staying up here.'

Jennifer had only just got herself back up into the office when her mother and father appeared in the doorway, with Sheila behind them. Her immediate thought was that something had happened to Danny or Bryony, or even Louise.

'It's all right, love,' her father said quickly, 'it's not bad news. Well . . .'

She saw him look towards her mother.

'Jen, love,' her mother said, 'Doug rang to say he'd had a visit from . . . from that . . . that Mack. Earlier. And since then he's been spotted in Tyneforth. He's back.'

Jennifer heard the words but there was no meaning underneath them, it was too incredible, too unlikely. But then she thought of all the things that had happened this afternoon. That one scrap of comfort she had dressed herself in over the last four weeks, that it couldn't get any worse, was suddenly whisked away. She was naked and raw again. He was back? For what? To laugh at her, rub her face in it? Her scarred face? She felt her father's arm around her shoulders.

'I'm really sorry,' Sheila said, 'your mum couldn't get you on your mobile, so she rang me and, what with Lionel and then Sonia, I—'

'Where is he now?' she asked, feeling the panic start to swirl in her.

'I don't know, not outside.' Her dad had his hand under her elbow. 'Come on, love, we'll get you home. Stay there for a bit. Lionel said take as long as you want.'

Jennifer let herself be led out to the car, jumping at every noise and every man who had even a hint of soft brown hair, and on the way out of Tyneforth she could not bear to look out of the car window.

Why was he back?

CHAPTER 42

Mack woke up to hammering in his head and after lying on his back for a while, not daring to move, realised the hammering wasn't just in his head. He was at Doug's.

Getting dressed took a long time and he stared at the dried blood on his T-shirt and the front of his jeans, not certain of exactly how it had got there. Standing up straight for any length of time made him feel dizzy, so he leaned and crouched and sidled his way downstairs to find the kitchen door open and the sun already warming the large flagstones in the kitchen. It was all a bit too bright really, and those pigeons, they had to keep on with that noise, did they? He screwed up his eyes as he tottered over to the forge, the noise getting louder and louder and braced himself for the moment when he actually had to stick his head around the doors. Doug was holding a piece of metal under the power hammer, gently manoeuvring it into a new position each time the hammer lifted. His two assistants were, bizarrely, building a curved wall with bricks and cement.

'Didn't die in your sleep then?' Doug said, turning off the hammer and coming to the doors.

Mack couldn't shake his head. 'Why the wall?' he asked, screwing his eyes up against the heat.

'Building a replica of the one them little buggers will be fixed to in the Diving Centre.' Doug held up what looked like a splodge of flat metal. 'They'll be shells and seahorses when I've finished with them and I need to get the curve on them exactly right.' He went over to speak to the lads and Mack meandered back to the house.

Finding Doug waiting outside A&E when he'd emerged yesterday had been a huge surprise. Being offered a bed for the night had been an even bigger one. As he'd driven him home Doug had said he didn't want Mack's death on his conscience.

'Breakfast,' Doug said behind him and set about making toast and coffee while Mack carefully felt his head and slowly tested which parts of him hurt and which did not.

'Was it just coincidence you turned up at the library?' he asked when Doug sat down.

'Nah, I came to warn Jen. I'd rung the farm too. Divvn't know how Alex knew you were back, Danny, I guess. Now shut up and eat your breakfast.'

Mack did as he was told, wondering what his next move should be. Another trip to the library, or should he bite the bullet and go to the farm now they knew he was back? First of all, he supposed, he needed to get back into Tyneforth and find a bed and breakfast.

Doug chewed his toast and said nothing, and Mack didn't

feel like talking either. The enormity of the task that faced him had been brought home to him yesterday. Forgiveness seemed like a sheer cliff-face, dotted with people waiting to swipe him off. Even if he got past them and reached Jen, that was when it really got hard.

He was close to her here, though, and there was comfort in that. The most comfort he'd felt in the last month. He had been thinking about her in bed last night as he'd drifted off. Thinking of how her skin had felt against his, the beautiful yielding sounds she'd made underneath him.

Lovely, funny, graceful Jen.

'If you're set on staying, you might as well bunk up here,' Doug said, putting his knife down abruptly.

Perhaps Mack's hearing had been impaired when he'd been hit. 'Here? Doug, that's . . . but I can't. It would make you really unpopular, with the Rosebys, with Alex, with every—'

'Divvn't care. What you said yesterday about Alex burying Jen away . . . touched a nerve.' Doug scraped the crumbs on the table into his hand and went to the door and chucked them out. 'He's been paying visits to the farm again; he'll be looking to get his feet back under the table.'

Doug wandered out of the door and Mack got up and slowly, clutching his coffee cup for support, followed him. They ended up sitting by the pond in the sun, Mack lowering himself, over several minutes, into a sitting position.

'Still think you're a first-class shit,' Doug said when

Mack's backside had finally made contact with the grass, 'but Alex's a bigger one ... on the sly. Never liked the wanker.'

'Any particular reason? I mean, you don't need one ...'

'Was up at their place, the Lambtons', few years ago. Making a gate for them. Yeah, a big "Sod off, plebs" gate. They were having a drainage trench dug at the same time and suddenly up came this piece of stone; carved it was, a young boy, holding a cup. Obviously Roman. I went over to have a look and, it was lovely. Such workmanship. I wondered whether it had been carved here or brought over from Rome. Couldn't get over that the last eyes that had seen it before ours, well, who knows who they belonged to?' Doug broke off a piece of grass and started to tie it in a knot. 'Old Lambton was there, and Alex, and it was obvious there was a load more stuff uncovered down in the trench.' He shook his head. 'Know what they did? Smashed it up into tiny shards and chucked it back in the trench and then covered it all up again. They put the drainage pipe further over.'

'But—'

'Didn't want the authorities there digging up their land, you see, documenting it, perhaps ordering more digging. I couldn't stop them and I knew if I told anyone that would be me buggered on the work front. People like the Lambtons can do what they like. Or they think they can.' Doug chucked the knotted grass into the pond. 'Felt bad about it ever since. So ... I'm not saying I believe your reasons for doing what you did, but coming back, having the shit beaten out of you, well, you didn't have to do that. I'd say the jury's oot in this house.'

Mack fought the urge to wrap his arms round Doug, afraid that might be pushing the truce a little too far. 'I'm really, really grateful', he settled for instead.

'Aye, you should be. And remember, if I think you're taking the piss, we'll be gannin' up the coast and one of us won't be coming back.'

'Understood.'

'That's sorted then,' Doug said in a kind of drawing-a-line-under-it voice. 'Do what you can to really piss Alex off, and in return I'll protect you when everyone you've upset marches up this drive with pitchforks and blazing torches.'

The sound of a car turning up the lane stopped any more discussion. It was Ray and Danny, and Mack felt clotted shame settle on him at the thought of facing them again.

'Talking of people who hate you . . .' Doug said, walking towards the car.

CHAPTER 43

Sitting in the kitchen, Jennifer felt she was part of a Victorian tableau of suffering. Brenda was standing behind her chair, Ray was sitting next to her, holding her hand, and Danny was leaning against the dresser, arms folded, head down. Louise, asleep in her car seat, added an extra little dash of pathos. Only Bryony, standing near the sink, seemed out of place: she looked more like a giant sheepdog, primed to round up anything that moved.

Danny and Ray had returned from Doug's with the news that they didn't know why Mack was here but he had refused to go away again. That didn't make any sense to Jennifer, and she understood from the looks that were passing between her mother and father that they were hiding something. The gut-clenching panic she had been experiencing ever since her parents had appeared in the library was slowly being tinged by something that might be impatience. She still wanted to run, but now she wanted some answers before she went.

'He agreed not to try to see her in the library, or come to the farm?' Brenda repeated.

Ray nodded. 'Said he wouldn't actually come into the library, but that's all he'd promise. Said if he bumped into her that was just fate.'

'Brass neck of the man. Did you tell him about the police?'

'Yes, Mum.' Danny peeled himself away from the dresser. 'But until he actually hassles her all they can do is warn him off. We could go through the courts, try for a—'

'I am sitting in the room, you know,' Jennifer said, standing up and breaking up the little poignant scene. 'And I have a name.'

'What is Doug playing at?' Brenda said bitterly.

'Are you sure he didn't say why he's here?' Jennifer tried. 'He must have said something?'

A Land Rover drew into the yard.

Perfect timing.

Jennifer looked at Danny. 'Why is Alex here?'

The door opened and Alex rushed in as though he had run all the way, rather than driven.

'Everyone all right?' he asked, looking from face to face, and Jennifer wanted to snap, 'We are not under siege from marauding Visigoths.'

Guilt and gratitude as ever, stopped her. 'We're fine,' she said. 'I'm fine.'

'You can't be, Jennifer.' He came over and looked as though he might put his arm around her. 'It's been a terrible shock. You just leave it to us.' He was addressing them all, 'I've had a word with him – warned him off. Brenda, Ray, I suggest we keep Jennifer here until we get this sorted.'

We? Keep?

Her irritation was back, she couldn't fight it. She looked at the way he was holding his hand. 'Did you hit him?' she asked. 'You did, didn't you?'

'I thought Danny and I could take a trip over to Doug's too,' he raced on, 'ask the idiot what he thinks he's playing it. Just when we should all stick together, he does this. Always a loose cannon, that man. Townie, you see,' he added.

Jennifer saw her father frown and Brenda, ex-townie herself, was short with Alex as she explained that Ray and Danny had already been to Doug's.

'Well, I might still go over anyway,' Alex said, unfazed, 'ask him how he can treat her like this, taking in that man when he's meant to be her friend.'

'Can I remind everyone again that I am still in the room,' Jennifer said, getting very close to losing her temper. They were all hiding something, she could sense it.

'Why is he here, Dad?' she tried once more, but Ray just pressed his lips together and did that look towards her mother. 'I mean, is there a minuscule detail I didn't tell him about Cress and he's come back for it? Like what toilet paper she uses or what colour knickers she favours? He must have given some reason for coming back, even if it was a whopping great big lie like everything else that comes out of his mouth.'

She registered the way Bryony was looking at Alex. It was as if she wanted to slap him.

'Bryony, was there something you wanted to tell me?' she asked gently.

'Yes.' Bryony moved over to Louise and lifted her out of the car seat, holding her into her chest as if she were a shield. Louise gave a hiccupy wriggle.

'He says he loves you, Jen.' Bryony was being careful not to look anywhere but at the soft hair on the top of her daughter's head. 'He told Ray he loved you on the day he left and he's saying it again now. Says he fell in love with you and wants to put it all right.'

'Bryony,' Alex snapped.

'She should know,' Bryony said so loudly that Louise opened her eyes wide. 'She's a grown-up, not a baby. I can't bear seeing you all keeping her in the dark. It's not doing her any favours hiding it from her – let's face it, there's only one person in this room *that's* helping.' She repositioned Louise in her arms. 'Right, I'm going upstairs to change this one.'

The door closing was the only noise as Jennifer tried to process Bryony's piece of news.

'It *is* another huge lie from him, then,' she said, feeling hot and smothered by the way the others were looking at her. 'I'm . . . just going upstairs too.' She left the room, not even looking at what their faces were doing, and over-took Bryony on the stairs, getting out a quick 'Thanks, Bry', before making the sanctuary of her room.

He loved her? How could you love someone when over

weeks and weeks you had deceived them? Set out to deceive them and achieved it? What an insult to her intelligence. Love? He must think she was completely stupid to fall for that story twice.

A memory of lying with him wrapped around her in bed sifted treacherously in and out of her brain, followed by little snippets of the things he'd said to get her on the stage. She chased it all away by forcing herself to think of the way he had eavesdropped on her phone conversation backstage, actually tiptoeing into the room on the other side of that screen. She could just about cope with knowing the whole thing was an illusion, but to imagine bits of it were real? No. Best to concentrate instead on all those lies, on the knowledge that at some time before he had come into her life he had sat in a room and discussed her as if she was some cracked stepping stone he had to tread on to get to Cress.

She grabbed her mobile phone and dialled Cress's number, forcing her fingers to hit the right numbers, but lost courage just before the call connected.

Bloody Mack Stone, he'd taken so much from her, even Cress.

CHAPTER 44

They probably looked like matching bookends – Doug on his mobile by the pond, Mack on his, just inside the kitchen. From the expression on Doug's face, the conversation he was having was nowhere near as heartening as the one Mack was having.

'She still looks very tired,' Tess was saying, 'but she's doing everything they say. Made a few jokes about feeling like a pincushion what with the vitamin injections and everything. She's made a friend – another writer. Writes children's books, addicted to cocaine apparently.'

'I want to laugh at that, but I know it's wrong,' Mack said and was pleased to hear Tess giggle.

When Tess rang off Mack waited for Doug to tell him which particular person had rung him this time to shout at him.

'Pamela,' Doug explained as he came back into the kitchen. 'Bit like having your life slowly sucked oot of you by a knitted jellyfish. And before that, Jocelyn. Gave her short shrift after the way she's always treated Jen.' He glanced back out into the garden. 'That shut her ... Oh, no ... bugger ... bugger ...'

Doug's eyebrows seemed to be all over his face, his mouth working silently as he stepped backwards, knocking the table and making the salt and pepper pots wobble. Mack didn't need to look to see the post office van was coming up the lane. By the time Pat was walking to the house, her auburn hair swinging in a ponytail, Doug had morphed into a man who was incapable of recognisable speech or movement.

'She looks good in shorts,' Mack commented and heard Doug ricochet off a chair.

'Parcel for you, Doug,' Pat called into the kitchen. She started as she saw Mack come forward to collect it. 'Ah, heard you were holed up here,' she said. 'Why did you come back? Not do enough damage first time?'

Mack gave her his explanation, careful not to sound glib or rehearsed and watched how she took it. There was something of Bryony's brand of clear-skinned heartiness about her.

'Don't know what to think about that,' she said when he'd finished, 'but if Doug's given you house room, well, must be something in it. Good judge of people, Doug.'

'I've ... left something ... a thing ... somewhere,' Doug gasped before barging out of the room.

When Mack tracked Doug down he was sitting on his bed, staring at the carpet.

'I'm not sure what kind of sign you're waiting for from

Pat, but from where I was standing she was giving out a fair few. Paid you a compliment. Smiled at you. Looked disappointed when you left.' He tentatively placed his hand on Doug's shoulder. 'She's lovely, Doug. Ask her out.'

'Perhaps you ought to sort your own love life before you start on mine?' Doug said irritably, casting Mack's hand away. 'She's oot of my league. I blew it again. Bugger off to Tyneforth and see if Jen's at the library, or get yourself lynched. One or the other.'

By lunchtime Mack had discovered that Jen was not in the library and that not only did a lot of people hate him, most of them seemed to have come into Tyneforth on market day to tell him. In quick succession he saw Angus, who gave him the finger and crossed over the road; Neale, who crossed over the road specifically to give him the finger; and Gerry, who turned around and walked back the way he had just come. Lydia cornered him near the abbey and gave him a tongue-lashing that he was certain raised welts on his skin. Wendy did likewise, just by the cheese stall. All he could do with both of them was wait for them to finish and go slowly, honestly, through his explanation. They both made a point of showing him they didn't believe any of it.

He bumped into Lisa down by the old swimming pool, and she immediately put away the phone jammed to her ear and gave him two hearty slaps round the face. 'One for Jen and one for me,' she said, all traces of her previous warmth towards him gone. That second slap told him that she'd worked out her date with the footballer was a set-up and it hadn't gone well.

'Boring, self-centred, spent most of the time looking in the mirror. Tightwad too, and when I did make it into the VIP room, the other women were all cows, trying to nick him and sneering at my clothes and shoes. He went off with one of them and then pitched back up at the hotel as if nothing had happened. Took me on another couple of dates, but I've told him to sling his hook.' Her smile was grim. 'Did get some accountancy work from it, mind. His brother, one of his friends. More money than sense, the lot of them.'

He began his explanation, but she walked away before he'd finished.

He had to go and sit in his car for a long time after that, but then thought of Joe's mantra and drove up to Brindley, careful not to choose the route past the farm. Sonia and Gregor were both in the shop and Mack stood and listened to himself described as the lowest form of human life in English and Czech. Sonia presented him with a bill that he knew bore no relation to what he had actually bought, not unless he'd been scarfing down sides of beef and champagne in his sleep. He paid it without protest. He had barely started on his explanation before they chucked him out of the shop, Gregor actually taking hold of the back of his collar and placing his boot on his backside and pushing. It would have hurt less if the door had been opened first.

Mack knew that Sonia's anger at him was particularly

fierce because he had ruined her reputation for always knowing what was going on.

When he limped up Mr Armstrong's path, hoping it was not Brenda's day for delivering meals, he could not imagine how the old guy would react. Mr Armstrong was still under the illusion that Mack was from the immigration service and when Mack tried to explain that he was a journalist and the whole thing had been a lie, Mr Armstrong just looked crafty. 'I'll give you this,' he said with a chuckle, 'you're good.'

For old times sake he went and sat on Peter Clarke and looked at the view. The best one in the world if only it had Jennifer in it, walking towards him, smiling. He counted up the people he hadn't apologised to yet and knew there was one he was particularly dreading seeing. Best get it over with.

Sitting in the reception area at the high school, the jouncing, jittery feeling in his bowels reminded him of how he used to feel before getting a detention.

He distracted himself by looking at the trophies in the glass cabinet: the pictures of boys and girls in cricket whites; the netball team, the rugby fifteen. He remembered Graham standing on touchlines watching him play, showing him how to clean his boots properly afterwards. Graham would always be his dad, alive in a whole slew of childhood memories. O'Dowd was the one who was dead to him, only existing in that newspaper office.

A reflection of Finlay bounded towards him and he turned and saw the real one.

'Oh Mack, Mack,' Finlay said sadly. 'There was I thinking Viola was the one in disguise and it was you all along. I'm very, very disappointed in you.'

Mack mumbled that he was very disappointed in himself.

'I should think you were. It was a monstrous act ... monstrous and I see someone has been pointing that out to you. I should think there's a lot more of that to come.' Finlay did one of his little detours across the floor and back. 'I trust you're as beaten up inside.'

'I hate everything about myself, if that's what you mean.'

'Well, that's a start.' Another detour. 'So, as I'm one of those people who like to talk rather than hit, start at the beginning. Tell me everything ... I mean, I've heard it via the bush telegraph ... how you love Jennifer, etc., etc.' There was a Finlay-esque flourish of the fingers. 'But do you want to give it to me first hand?'

With the schoolkids streaming past him to go home, Mack told Finlay everything and, as he spoke, haltingly and having to go back over certain bits to get the order right, he heard the echoes of that day when he had done his terrible audition. When he had finished, Finlay screwed up his eyes for a few seconds, and then Mack was being wrapped in a hug. It was incomprehensible, and he was struggling not to cry.

'How can you be so nice to me, Finlay? I don't bloody deserve it.'

'Ah well now, Matt, Mack, whatever you call yourself, I don't really go in for all that "deserving/undeserving" stuff

... not sure I have the qualifications to judge. What I do know is you pulled that up from your heart, not a bit of acting in sight. You've done something terrible, truly dreadful, and I'm not certain you can put it right, but all in all I am very, very glad to see you.'

'You're one of the few people in the whole of Northumberland who thinks that,' Mack said, sniffing.

'Rubbish.' Finlay stepped back. 'It won't be easy, but keep being sincere and more will follow. Now, tickets for *The Pirates of Penzance*, a hundred and twenty children, a piano and half the costumes still being made. Can I interest you in tickets?'

Mack bought a couple and then wended his way to the supermarket, hoping that he could just get in, buy what was on Doug's list and escape without being seen. He did well for the first two aisles and then stopped walking or thinking. Probably even breathing. She was there. His lovely Jen.

He had imagined that first meeting with her would be somewhere beautiful; perhaps beside a wide, clear stream, green hills mounded behind them.

She was looking at the label on some frozen cod.

It didn't matter though, she still looked wonderful to him; a little thinner, and the sweatshirt and jeans she was wearing had seen better days, but he stood and watched her, waiting for that moment when she would notice him. He wanted it badly and dreaded it at the same time.

He saw her reading falter and the shock as she registered that he was there. She was clenching the packet of fish so tightly that he imagined it must be burning her hands and her expression suggested she wanted to run, but did not know how to do it. The fish fell back into the freezer and he so much wanted to go and kiss her hands warm again.

'Jen, Jen,' he said taking a few steps forward, 'please don't run away. I know what a terrible thing I did to you, it was unforgivable.'

'Leave me alone,' she said, and hearing her distress for the first time was terrible. He'd done this to her.

'Jen—'

'Go away; there's nothing that comes out of your mouth that I want to listen to. How could you do this to me? And how could you come back?'

'I had to come back. I love you. Whatever else was a lie, that wasn't.'

Her laugh was sardonic before she said, almost to herself, 'You've got a leather jacket on. I just knew your clothes were all wrong.'

'Jen—'

'Stop it. Stop it,' she said more loudly, and he saw people turn to look. 'Stop telling everyone in Northumberland that rubbish about loving me. You're just trying to make yourself look better. You must think I'm an idiot as well as being needy.'

She was breathing so fast he was worried about her. He took another couple of small steps forward, but she moved away from the freezer and he could see she was poised to go.

He held up his hands as a man does to show he is not armed. 'I'm not going to come any closer, Jen. I just need to talk to you. To tell you how desperately sorry I am that I hurt you. Just let me do that, and explain how much I didn't want to do what I did, how much I've missed you. How much I want you.'

'Shut up,' she screamed, 'shut up, shut up, shut up!' More people were stopping and looking. 'Is this your idea of fun, coming back, seeing what else you can prise out of me—'

'Jen, sweetheart, I love you, and you loved me . . . we know that, the night we had—'

'I loved Matt Harper, I don't know you,' she said, with a cry.

'I'm him, Jen, all the main bits, I'm him.'

'Liar,' she screamed. 'You made him up out of bits and pieces of lies and acting. Cobbled him together into the kind of person you knew I'd fall for.'

He expected her to run at him, scream and shout, pummel him with her fists, but the way she was standing, legs locked, suggested she was still holding back from letting her feelings rip out. She was still reining in her emotions as she always did. He looked around – more people and only a matter of time before security was called. He walked over to the shelf containing the pillows of pasta and picked one up.

'Remember how I said you had a right to show if you were angry or upset because of the way someone had looked at you or treated you? Well, no one has ever hurt you more than me, or made you more wretched, so show me, Jen. I understand that there's no way you want to get any closer to me than you are, and I don't blame you. But . . .' He dropped the pasta on the floor and kicked it towards her.

Please, please pick it up and throw it at me.

He felt tears prick his eyes when the packet of pasta landed in his chest and had to blink them back as he saw her rush to the display and grab two packets of rice. They were heavier, but he didn't mind. They split when they bounced off him and landed on the floor, making those watching take a few steps back. It was couscous next, thrown with greater accuracy and hitting him on the cheek. He placed a protective hand over the cut on his head, but did nothing else, and soon she was screaming at him as she threw, random words, swear words, and then the litany of all the ways he'd lied and deceived her.

He could see the extent of her hatred for him and knew that if at that moment someone had handed her a rock she would have thrown that too.

Something heavy and sharp did hit him in the back and he stumbled forward, not sure how Jen had managed to loop something round behind him.

He turned to see Brenda. She was holding a tin of rata-touille in one hand and another tin was rolling among the spilt rice and packets of pasta. Her face was stern, immobile, her eyes gleaming under the strip lighting. 'They do a family size,' she said dropping the tin in her hand on to his foot. 'Get away from my daughter.' She gave him a hearty shove against the shelves. 'Leave her alone. You're a cruel liar. A manipulator of people's feelings. She doesn't want to see you. Nobody wants to see you. Go home.'

Mack had expected to be terrified at his first meeting with Brenda, but he was too busy watching Jennifer. She was staring at the packet of mung beans in her hand. She put them neatly back on the shelf and looked disorientated. His heart was racing just looking at her, his breath coming as fast as hers had.

'Sorry, Brenda,' he said, 'but I'm staying. I love Jen and I regret every single thing I did except loving her and getting her on that stage.'

Brenda looked as if she'd like to club him with something heavier than tinned ratatouille. 'You're twisted. There's not one part of you thinking about how much pain this is putting her through, is there? It's all about what you want. When are you going to stop hurting her?'

She walked past him, took hold of Jennifer's hand and started leading her away.

'I'm sorry for making a scene,' he called after them, and then, 'Did you get my letters, Jen?' He saw hesitation in Jennifer's progress before she disappeared round the end of the aisle to be replaced by a large man in a blazer bearing the supermarket's logo.

'Come with me, please,' he said. 'You're going to have to pay for all this and then I'm afraid I'll have to escort you from the store.'

'Fine,' Mack said, high on the adrenalin of what had just happened, his heart still hammering, 'but if I'm paying for all of it, I'm taking it home.' He got down on his knees and started to gather up the individual grains of rice, thinking that even if he was here all night, he *had* made contact with Jen, and revelling in how beautiful she'd looked, her hair swinging back from her face as she lobbed things at him in anger.

Jennifer got up in the early hours of the morning, put on her clothes and let herself out of the house. She wasn't going to look at the moon, hadn't really been too keen on looking at it since *that* night. She set off down to the river, sheep skittering away from her, a fox away in the woods, barking. Sitting by the water, she did up her jacket.

Lying in bed or sitting out here she was still seeing Mack standing in the supermarket. Throwing those packets at him had been some substitute for what she really wanted to do: tear at his flesh and hurt him as much as he'd hurt her. He was such a liar, those brown eyes packed with all that sincerity again. Even his clothes had been a lie before. Now he looked ...

Sexy and beaten-up.

She tried to let the river carry that thought away, but when it went, questions came in behind it. He'd been writing letters – Brenda admitted they had gone straight in the bin. Ten or eleven of them, she'd said. What kind of letters? And Doug, why was Doug giving him house room? Doug was no fool, well no bigger than everyone else had been. How had he managed to worm his way back in with Doug?

Why was he doing this? He must be after something, but what? If he wasn't Sebastian and he wasn't Matt Harper, who was he? Who was this Mack Stone?

She took the phone out of her pocket and rang Cress's number. It went straight through to voicemail and she was glad. An easy first step back. 'Hi, Cress ... it's me. Look, I'm sorry, I've been distant with you. I know you think that I'm uncomfortable about you being in love just at the time when I've been ... or maybe that I blame you for that ... that journalist hunting me out. Anyway, neither of those things is true ... Damn.' The voicemail cut her off. She rang back. 'It's more that I've felt so embarrassed and so stupid for being taken in and telling him everything that you were telling me. I betrayed you, in a way. And you haven't wanted to talk about him, which has made me feel that you kind of agreed. It's been like this big, horrible thing between us. All I wanted to say was, ring me. I need you, Cress. He's back.'

CHAPTER 45

By the time Jennifer got into the library the next day she understood that it was biologically possible to have both PMT and menopausal mood swings. She had woken up expecting to want to turn over and stay in bed, but anger had got her up and downstairs. How dare he think he could come back, did he have no understanding of what he'd done to her? Did he expect that anything he ever said or did could wipe that out? She would show him he was severely mistaken about that.

Her resolve had faltered a little over breakfast as Brenda had tried to persuade her to stay home. When Jen had reasoned that she would be safe in the library with Sheila and Lionel on guard, Ray had taken her side, his only stipulation being that she didn't drive herself. She agreed, sensing that Bryony would enjoy a chance to escape from Danny for a while. Since she had blabbed that day in the kitchen, Danny had been uncharacteristically terse with her.

When Jen returned from having a shower and getting

dressed, she saw Alex pulling into the yard, and his opening words 'Now, what's all this about going back today?' told her that someone had rung him. Her money was on Danny, although Brenda, currently looking evasive near the kettle, was her second bet.

'It's important to me to go in,' she said. 'I need to show him he doesn't matter.'

'You don't need to show him anything.' Alex smiled. 'Now come on, let's stop all this nonsense. How about we go for a drive, have a pub lunch and you think about going back tomorrow . . . or maybe next week?'

All this nonsense? Is that what my determination means to you?

'No, Alex. Bryony's going to take me.' She picked up her bag, walked from the kitchen and along the hall. She heard him behind her. She went out through the porch into the yard and looked around for Bryony.

'OK, OK,' Alex said, 'you need to go in, I get it. But let me take you.'

She might have got into the Land Rover if Danny had not appeared.

'Good man,' she heard him say, and she felt like some Victorian woman being passed from family to betrothed.

Ten minutes later she was driving up the track in her own car, watching Danny and Alex get smaller and smaller in the rear-view mirror. Her driving was erratic, but she felt as if she had offloaded some things she'd been meaning to offload for a while. Poor Danny, he had looked genuinely scared when she'd shouted at him. She couldn't remember everything she'd said but it had gone along the lines of reminding him he was her brother, not Alex's stooge and he'd better start being nice to his wife again. Alex she had told to back right off.

She was still fizzing with outrage when she got to work, and rang Alex again from the upstairs office. Before he could start in on anything else, she asked him not to fight her battles for her, especially if that involved actual fighting. She was sick of it and, really, she needed to fight them for herself. Also, could he just have a think about how it made her feel to see people with any kind of injury, particularly ones about the head and face?

Then she tried to hunker down in the simple cataloguing job Lionel had given her, but her mind merely flitted around it before heading back to that leather jacket and the guy inside it and the question of when he would try to see her again. She knew it was 'when', not 'if'.

'Heard Northumberland County Cricket have signed you up,' Sheila said when she came in to the office, 'spin bowler, especially effective with pasta and pulses.'

'News travels fast.'

'Like that pasta. Girl from the wine section told Sonia.'

'Told Sonia . . . so you and Sonia?'

Sheila did a kind of shrug that suggested yes, they were talking after ten years, and it was no big deal. 'Anyway.' Sheila lowered herself into a chair. 'Do you want the good news or the bad news?'

'Neither,' she said, knowing whom it would concern.

'Sorry, that's not a choice. The good news is he's not

in the library. The bad news is he's sitting in the park. Lionel's just taken him a cup of tea—'

'Hang on, Lionel's what?'

Sheila rolled her eyes. 'Long story. Heard the Peachmeister had ended up in A&E, so was eaten up with even more remorse, terrified he'd hurt him that badly. Was so overcome with relief when he found out it wasn't his fault, took him over tea and came back with a message.'

'I don't want to hear it, Sheila. Talk to me about anything else. Talk to me about Reece.'

Sheila screwed up her face. 'Reece is back. Last night. Unlikely he will be allowed entry to anything Spain owns ever again. There was an incident involving a Spanish taxi and some chickens.' Sheila rubbed the back of her head slowly and looked at the floor, defeat evident in the set of her mouth. 'Anyway, he'll be in the park every morning, rain or shine.' She paused. 'Not Reece, obviously, the world spins off its axis if he's ever out of bed before noon.'

'I hope it does rain then,' Jen said. 'Or hails: stones the size of teacups.'

Sheila nodded. 'That's the spirit.'

Mack drove out of Tyneforth after lunch thinking it hadn't been a totally wasted day. Just after eleven, Susan the woman who had been stage manager, had come and sworn at him and Sheila had detoured through the park to tell him to 'bog off'. He guessed one of the sandwiches in her hands was for Jen. The highlight, though, had been Jocelyn, who suddenly appeared to have rewritten history so that she was Jennifer's best friend. When he had told her his story she had said terrible things about his mother and suggested that he was the reason she was an alcoholic. That had touched a bit of a nerve.

Up in the hills above the town, he walked till his muscles started to complain, and was able to laugh at his new-found affection for his walking boots. They were becoming two of his best friends, although given his current popularity, they didn't have much competition.

Having walked off the top layer of despair that had settled on him, he rang Tess and got Joe. Somewhere during the conversation, Mack let slip that his honesty had already resulted in a few fights. Joe's cheery 'Just keep telling the truth, it'll come right' sounded hollow. The flaw in Joe's argument was that nobody believed he was capable of telling the truth now, even when he was.

He told himself that he was only in the foothills of his campaign for forgiveness. How easy had he expected it to be? And really, this wasn't about him, it was about healing Jen.

Back at his car, he took off his walking boots and thought about the other positive thing he'd set his mind to achieving. Soon he was heading towards the MetroCentre with a shopping list that included industrial quantities of brown paper, large, not too heavy items and rolls and rolls of sellotape.

CHAPTER 46

Jennifer was determined not to look in the direction of the park, but when she did, she saw him, and he raised his hand and waved at her, but did not get up. She scuttled into the library, pulse all over the place, feeling outrage. This was where she lived, not him. He had done something wrong, not her.

She fretted and stewed, the images of him kissing and holding her invading her head if she didn't cram it with cataloguing and reading lists and stock transfers. If only Cress had rung back.

Just before lunch she took a deep breath, assumed the mantle of Lady Macbeth and went over to the park. It felt strange to walk towards him when she should have been retreating. She clung on to her anger.

He leaped to his feet, the magazine he'd been reading dropping to the ground.

'Given up on newspapers?' she said, not looking at him. 'Well, give up on this farce too. You have a bloody nerve, and I don't want you here. This is cruel of you, crueller even than last time.'

'It's not meant to be cruel, Jen. There's no other way to convince you that I bitterly, bitterly regret what I did and that I love you. Please let me explain what happened.'

'Don't bother. I've heard the tale you're spinning from everyone else. You deceived me all the way through.'

'No, not near the end, all those things I said to you then, I meant. And even at the beginning, I was really trying to do what I had to do without hurting you ... I couldn't help trying to comfort you—'

'Don't patronise me.' She looked at him when she said that, confident that her anger would protect her. 'Everything you did was calculated to fool the poor sap. God, I bet your face was a picture when they showed you mine.'

She saw his eyes widen, and he took a step forward before obviously realising he shouldn't. 'No, Jen, please don't think that. Listen to me; I didn't know you'd been in an accident, not until I saw you that first night. Please believe me.'

She gave him marks for 'doing' distress really well; he was all over the place.

'I didn't know,' he repeated sadly, 'but it wouldn't have made any difference if I did. There was no way I could get out of doing the job.'

'Am I meant to be impressed by your brutal honesty when you tell me that? Because forgive me, it sounds like the same kind of brutal honesty you showed me last time.

No, sorry, it's not honesty, is it? It's just brutal. Well take it and shove it and then get in your car and drive home – wherever you've decided to tell people that is this week.'

'Jen, please, I never set out to get you into bed, I tried to keep it friendly; I made up a girlfriend—'

'So sad little me wouldn't get the wrong message?'

'No ... I mean, yes, but I didn't think you were sad when I met you ... oh shit.'

'Lie after lie after lie, they just keep coming,' she screamed at him. 'Making people up, killing them off, leading Lisa on, pushing her away, getting my sympathy, reeling me in. Go on, tell me more, because that's what you've come back for, isn't it? To point out more humiliations I hadn't even considered?' Her anger took her over the road again, but once inside the library she couldn't settle. She retreated to the toilets to try to clear the wad of emotion stuck in her throat; she went back into the library, but couldn't think of anything that would distract her enough.

She was walking over the road again, shakier this time, but more determined.

He leaped up again, the magazine fell to the ground again.

'I'm telling you to go. I don't want you here, and if you loved me, you'd stop causing me pain and leave.'

'I can't.'

His expression didn't change; it was still intense, apologetic. She had an urge to slap him, but fought it, imagining the *Courant* headline: 'Library Assistant Attacks Man in Park'.

'Jen, I can only keep on repeating that I love you and ask you please to listen to how it happened from the start. How it unfolded. Please, I want to be completely honest with you. I know you want me to go, and yes, in the short term that would be easier for you and easier for me, but where does that leave us eventually? Living the wrong lives with the wrong people.'

She laughed out loud at the cheek of that and walked back over the road before he could say anything else, her legs trembling.

'I'll be here again tomorrow,' she heard him shout. She made a big show of putting her fingers in her ears.

Sitting on the floor in the staff toilet Jennifer closed her eyes and tried to think herself somewhere calm. It wasn't working: she kept finding herself back by that seat in the park. The gall, talking about living the wrong lives with the wrong people – if she did something mad like end up with Alex it would be all Mack Stone's fault. He was the one who told her anything was possible and then revealed it wasn't.

Ending up with Alex. Accent on 'End' there. Better to be a mad old lady with a house smelling of cats. Or sheep.

Her phone rang and she held it in the palm of her hand as if weighing up if she had the nerve to answer it.

Cress only got out 'Hi, Jen,' before the pair of them were crying – huge gulps and sobs.

'We sound as if we're underwater,' Jennifer spluttered.

'Underwater heavy-breathers,' Cressida agreed, and then she was off, 'Jen, I am so sorry; so, so sorry that you think

I feel you betrayed me. I don't think that at all. And I'm so sorry too that when you needed me, I've been side-stepping talking about . . . him.' There was another bout of gulping and sniffing. 'It's not for any of the reasons you said on that message. It's . . . it's . . . oh . . . Auntie Bren's going to kill me, but I have to tell you this: I didn't talk about him because she asked me not to.'

'Mum?'

'When I came to see you after . . . on that terrible Saturday, I asked Auntie Bren if I should tell you that I'd paid Mack a call . . . and that he seemed upset, genuinely upset. You see, I thought it might give you some comfort that not everything he'd done had been a lie. Auntie Bren almost tore my head off, said the best way for you to get over it was to stop talking about him.'

Genuinely upset?

'I don't want to hear it, Cress. Sorry, I can't . . . I . . .'

'OK, sweetie, OK . . . let's leave it, let's . . . how can I help you now? What can I say?' There was a little hiccup from America. 'Oh God, Jen, I've missed you so much.'

The underwater heavy-breathers were back.

'I'll have to go in a minute,' Jennifer said, reaching up and tearing off some toilet paper to wipe her eyes. 'I'm sitting on the toilet floor, I've been missing for a while. If Sheila comes to find me and knows you're on the phone she'll prise it from my hands and want to know all the ins and outs of you and Anna Maria.'

'Not the "Shake it all abouts"? People seem very interested in those.'

'What?'

'The hokey cokey: you put your left leg in, your left leg ... oh, come on, sweetie, you need to get that brain back firing on all cylinders. You've been spending too much time with Anaesthetic Alex.'

'Cress ... he's been really—'

'Smothering. But enough of that twat ... the toilet floor, Jen? You're not ill, are you?'

Jennifer thought about that. 'No, not ill, just ... wobbly. I've just seen ... something horrible in the park.'

'It's not that bloody flasher again, is it? For goodness' sake, he must be about eighty by now, I'm surprised his arthritic arms can still pull open his mac.'

Jennifer started to laugh, and then it slid into more hearty sobbing. She could hear that she'd set Cress off again too.

She helped herself to more toilet roll and blew her nose this time. 'Oh, Cress, you don't know how good it is to hear that stupid humour of yours again. But no, it's not the flasher, it's ... him.'

Please say the right thing, Cress. Please come back to me.

'And you want to kill him?' Cress said slowly.

'Exactly, Cress. I do. I'm so angry with him for all the lies – for him treating me like some little chess piece he could just move where he wanted and outraged he's got the nerve to think that he can come back, look sad and say the right thing and I'll forgive him.'

'Scary, isn't it, feeling like that?'

'Yes. I ... I don't know what I might do to him.'

'But anger's great, Jen. I mean I know it's not an easy fix, but I'm so used to hearing that heart-twisting sadness that to know you're angry is brilliant.'

'It is and it's not. I should get Dad, Danny, anyone to have a word with the police, get him kept away, but my anger makes me want to crush him myself. And that means seeing him to do it. Oh look, I can't talk about this here, on the toilet floor. I'm sorry, Cress. Ring me back tonight. My tonight, not yours?'

'Of course, of course. Dry your eyes, go back to work. I'll ring . . . about eight, promise.'

'There's so much I want to tell you, Cress.'

'Yeah . . . there are a few things I want to tell you too. But perhaps that's not for tonight eh? Tonight's just you and me back in the photo booth.'

'Giggling and being stupid.'

'It's what we do best.'

As Jennifer walked back into the library an image of Mack sitting on the bed, his hair mussed up by her hands, crept into her mind. She felt the painful pull of yearning, but quashed it immediately. She would not let her body betray her like this. She forced herself to remember how he had appeared so dorkish and naive; the sympathy he had got from her over his fictitious girlfriend; the way he'd purposely got Cressida's name wrong, and soon her anger felt like a piece of strong armour again.

CHAPTER 47

'It makes nae sense.' Doug was staring at the three books about fly fishing. 'I can't stand fishing. And why would I want a cat blanket; I divvn't have a cat?'

'No invoice or anything?' Mack asked.

Doug went back over to the torn wrappings and just shook his head. 'Postmarked Newcastle, that's nae help.'

Mack left him shaking his head and passed Pat's van coming up the drive as he headed out. He slowed down and watched in the rear-view mirror as Pat emerged with two parcels and Doug came to meet her. That was a start: Doug's lips were moving and he hadn't fallen in the pond.

Mack had settled into a daily routine of misery. First stop was the newsagent's for a bar of chocolate, then the coffee shop for a latte. He'd decided to concentrate on books from now on, safer than papers and magazines, and the woman in the bookshop had started talking to him, recommending what else he might like to read. If it was fine he sat on the seat; if it rained he sheltered in the bandstand. At about 1 p.m. he had his lunch, always a sandwich also eaten in the park, and was working his way around the different sandwich shops. He was not going back to the one round the back of the hospital. He'd bought something called 'rustic chicken' in a wrap and if the aftertaste had been strange, the effect on his bowels was even worse.

After lunch, just as the abbey clock struck 2 p.m., he left the park, drove into the countryside and walked.

Sitting in the sun, he wondered what today would bring. The number of people still to catch up with him had dwindled, and he got the impression Jennifer's family had decided that if he didn't hassle her, he was best left alone. They all expected him to get disheartened with his lack of progress. He took a large bite from the chocolate bar. Well, they were out of luck there. He had no idea how this was going to unfold, he might still be here when he was a very old man, but he wasn't giving up.

Lack of funds was becoming a bit of a problem, though. He'd been telling the truth to Doug when he'd said that apart from paying Phyllida's rehab bills, the money from O'Dowd was still intact. Tess and Joe had lent him the money to come north and Doug wasn't charging him rent, but Mack contributed to food, had to pay his own petrol. He wondered if anyone up here was hiring silver pirates, afternoons only.

He finished his coffee and tried to read his book, but today Alex kept intruding into his thoughts. He was suspiciously quiet. Was he too busy working his way back into Jen's affections to bother paying him any more visits? Mack had a gut-churning vision of Jen in an apron hanging out washing, little versions of Alex clinging on to her skirt. It disappeared when the real Jennifer walked under the arch into the park.

'What's the book?' she asked. 'Lying and cheating at advanced level or how to upset the scarred and vulnerable?'

He couldn't stop himself saying, 'You look lovely,' and was rewarded with a brittle laugh as she looked down at her clothes.

'Still lying,' she said.

'I didn't mean the clothes,' he replied, and she pursed her lips and sat down on the arm of the seat, her expression telling him she thought he was not only a liar, but a smarmy one.

There was something different about her today, and he didn't know if it was different in a good or a bad way. When she said, 'I've been chatting to Cressida the last few evenings. Better get out your notebook,' he knew it was a bad way.

'Let's see,' she said, playing the part of a gabby gossip to perfection, 'Anna Maria and Cress are hunkered down in a hotel, short break before it's back to filming the scenes they had to reschedule, the ones with Rory. Then they're off to Argentina for a holiday. Rory is milking the situation all he can. He's granting Diane Sawyer an exclusive next week on the heartache of coping with his wife's changed sexuality.' She gave him a horrible fake smile. 'Fascinating, eh? What else? Oh yes, Cress just listened while I told her how much I disliked and distrusted you. How you're starting to make me hate this park. Cress says it's good to get it all out. Take every opportunity to tell you what I think of you. Hey, wait a minute . . . you're not writing any of this down.'

He could feel his throat getting lumpy and dry. 'Jen, please. I know you're bitter, but today, please give me the chance to tell you about my mother. I know the others have given you some of—'

'No,' she said forcefully. 'Not interested. Tell you what; *you* listen to *me*, about my broken heart. You made me believe you wanted me, Mack.'

'Sweetheart, I did,' he said, and she was on her feet.

'Don't call me that. It just trips off your tongue so easily.'

'Jen, I never set out to break your heart—'

'Oh, don't worry,' she said, and he saw the blue of her eyes suddenly bloom as the tears welled up in them, 'broken heart, broken face. Nice to have matching accessories.'

He watched her run back over the road and knew that being beaten up every day by Alex would be preferable to this – to knowing you had caused someone you loved such pain.

He cried then, discreetly, and turned away from the library, feeling today that there was no way back from what he'd done. How could words, however truthful, heal the wounds he'd caused?

But she'd sat on the seat, did that mean something? It was the closest he'd got to her since he'd been back.

That evening Doug took one look at him and drove

him up the coast. Doug had chatted about Pat for most of the way, ecstatic that she was also into heavy metal and when he plunged into the sea, Mack knew that Doug wasn't numbing himself; he was revelling in being alive. It was Mack who now welcomed this opportunity not to feel.

He turned in as soon as they got back.

'Not going to chance the day getting any worse,' he said, trying to make light of it, but Doug wasn't paying attention anyway.

He was examining the football and umbrella that had arrived that morning, his lips in a little smile.

Mack had only been in bed a matter of minutes when his mobile rang.

'Mack, it's Tess. Mum's disappeared.'

He sat up, all his hopes for Phyllida crashing down yet again. 'What? How did that happen? Don't they keep an eye on her?'

'They do, up to a point, but it's not a prison, Mack, she's there voluntarily. She just slipped away: seems she'd planned it with this new chum of hers. She covered for her.'

'I'll drive down,' he said, getting out of bed.

'No, not overnight. Leave it till tomorrow, we've talked to the police. We'll let you know if we hear anything.' The rest of the phone call was Tess crying.

Next morning, Doug chatted animatedly to Pat as she watched him open a parcel containing a pair of tartan wellington boots, but the pleasure Mack should have taken in watching them was severely diluted by the news that Phyllida was still missing.

He went out into the garden and bellowed with rage and frustration. He had been so sure that Phyllida meant to get better this time. Now she could be lying anywhere that served alcohol.

Bloody perfect timing, Phyllida, as usual.

It was hard to know whether he hated his father or his mother more right then, and he set off for the kitchen again, sorry that Pat's giggling and Doug's answering low laugh were about to be silenced by his piece of news. He stopped on the threshold and turned as the sound of a car nosing into the lane reached him.

No, not people with pitchforks now. Not Ray. Not Alex.

A taxi came to a halt by the door and Phyllida got out.

'Ah, delightful,' she said, looking at the house as if she was a visiting member of the royal family.

'Please, Phyllida,' he said, 'tell me you didn't get that taxi all the way from Bath?'

CHAPTER 48

Danny glowered at Mack as if he would be quite prepared, right now, to go off and buy a pig and let it eat him. Mack was careful to do nothing to provoke him, staying exactly where he had been told to sit, on an old tractor tyre right in the corner of the yard with Danny just a few feet away.

He heard his name being called and turned to see Bryony coming down the track with the sheepdog.

'That Mack's an idiot too,' Danny said, looking at the dog.

'Still in there?' Bryony shouted and when Danny shouted 'Yes!' she turned around and went back up the track, peeling off at the top into one of the fields.

Danny resumed his glowering; Mack went back to thinking about how much gumption his mother had shown in coming north. He had left it to Tess to scold her over the phone; he was too touched by the fact that for the first time in his life she appeared to be wading in on his side. Whether she had been drinking during her stopover in London or on the journey north he could not say and did not ask.

When the farmhouse door opened he looked up, but it was Ray, his face almost comical, eyebrows up, cheeks puffed out. He looked across at Mack and blew out his breath.

'My, your mother's a formidable woman.'

Mack had to agree: in a straight fight between her and Brenda he was not sure who would win. He wondered what Jen was making of it all, the fact Phyllida was in rehab and her confirmation of Mack's story about being blackmailed. In an ideal world Jennifer would emerge from the farmhouse soon, her arms flung wide and shouting, 'I understand it all now, Mack, you are forgiven.' In reality he wasn't counting on anything. He felt as if he was waiting for some life-or-death medical results and he could have done with walking about to distract himself, but he knew Danny would be off after that pig if he did.

When the door opened next it was Phyllida and Brenda who came out. No sign of Jennifer. Mack got to his feet and watched the women advance on him. Despite the flowery walking stick that Phyllida was now using, they brought to mind two politicians who had been locked in talks and were emerging to broadcast the outcome.

Brenda gave a little cough. 'Your mother –' she nodded delicately at Phyllida – 'has explained the whole Montgomery thing – your mistake, her . . . inability at the time to give you a clear idea of whether O'Dowd's story was the truth or not.'

Tactfully put.

'Brenda and her family –' Phyllida halted and tilted her

head graciously towards Brenda – 'now have a better idea
of why you became involved in this –' his mother struggled before settling on – 'fiasco. And I have agreed that
you were an absolute idiot not to have double and treble-
checked O'Dowd's flimsy "evidence", and a conniving,
deceitful wretch to have carried this scheme through to
the end.'

'I'm glad you're on my side, Phyllida,' he said and saw
Ray hide what might have been a smile.

'I have also told them that you've been like a poisoned
cat in Bath, overcome with remorse and quite lovesick as
far as I can remember what lovesick looked like. Oh, and
perhaps they could cut you some slack because you have
only recently discovered that the man who is actually your
father is a complete and utter bastard.'

Ray was having trouble with that smile again.

'How did Jen take it all?' He almost couldn't bear to
hear the answer.

'She didn't say much, just listened and then went
upstairs.' Brenda looked uneasily towards Phyllida as she
added, 'Knowing why you did it is one thing. Forgiving
how you went about it is another. We'll ... see how it
goes. We can't say more than that.'

'Well, that seems like progress to me.' Phyllida beamed
around at everyone, quite the gracious dignitary. 'We'll
leave you in peace and again, Mrs Roseby, I am so sorry
for the pain and upset inflicted upon your daughter. She's
very lovely. So graceful.' Phyllida came and linked her arm
though Mack's, and he would have been taken aback if

he had not been struggling to stay composed in the face of hearing her description of Jen.

The Rosebys could have retained their impression that Phyllida was a cultured, slightly eccentric soul, if she had not then stopped, turned back around and said, 'Just one more thing – Douglas the blacksmith said Mack got a nasty head injury from somebody who calls himself Alex. Some gentleman farmer, evidently.' Phyllida did a very elaborate bit of eyebrow-raising. 'Perhaps if you see him, um, Daniel –' her gaze homed in on Danny and he nodded like a man who had only a rudimentary understanding of how to move his own head – 'perhaps, my dear, you could tell him that I know people in Bath who, for a very small amount of money, will twist his testicles off and ram them, one after the other, down his throat.' She gave a jolly wave. 'So lovely to have met you.'

Jennifer watched them talking in the yard and saw Mack help his mother into the car. Now that was an interesting woman. A glacier mint to Brenda's lemon drop.

So here she was sitting in her bedroom again, pulling apart Mack's behaviour and adding this new information and then trying to fit it all back together again. Blackmailed into taking on the job in the first place, terrified of his family being thrown to the baying public. What would she have done if she had been in his . . . brogues?

She lay down and allowed herself for the first time to really think about how he'd got her to be Viola. All those things he'd said to her in bed. All those things he'd done to her in bed.

Could she accept he had been a man struggling with himself? That he had fallen for her somewhere along the line? Did that cancel everything else out?

But he'd been such a plausible fake. So good, it suggested that lying was second nature to him.

She looked around the bedroom. It was beginning to feel like a prison and so she took herself outside and sat on the fence as Ray fussed about selecting the sheep he intended to enter into the County Show. She knew he wouldn't talk to her about Mack; it wasn't his way to force any issue, and she was glad of that. She watched his gentle movements and the assurance with which he looked at hooves and peered into ears, and felt soothed. He had steadily gained a tan over the last week and she remembered how, as a little girl, she had been fascinated at the way it always stopped at the base of his neck and just above his elbows so that he looked as though he was wearing a short sleeved white T-shirt when he took her swimming.

Not a leather jacket.

'All right?' her dad asked as she jumped down from the fence.

'Just going to find a quiet spot. Ring Cress,' she called back.

It was some way into the conversation before Jen told Cress about Phyllida's visit.

'Teddy bloody Montgomery?' Cress said, no longer

sounding sleepy, and Jennifer heard her repeat the words, but this time away from the phone. Jennifer imagined Anna Maria lying next to Cress and speculated on who was the dominant partner in that particular relationship. It seemed to be working though, this partnership. It was impossible to miss the happiness in Cress's voice whenever she rang now. All that pretending to be tougher than she was, cooler than she felt, it all seemed to have been shelved with Anna Maria.

There was a huge gust of laughter and Cress was back. 'Anna Maria asked me if this Montgomery was the one who fought in the desert. But, all joking aside, Jen ... Montgomery, that's huge. I thought it was some rubbish little secret he was protecting, like his mother had some kind of habit.'

'She has.'

'True, but, wow, that was a really big anvil to have over his head. So ... how does this make you feel about what he did?'

'It doesn't change anything.' Jennifer sat forward and then back against the tree trunk, trying to get more comfortable. 'He still lied and cheated. He still wound me round his little finger. All that calculating just what to say, how to look—'

'Ye-es. But sometimes people do bad things for good reasons, Jen.'

Jennifer looked up through the leaves and branches of the tree and frowned. 'Are you trying to defend him, Cress?'

There was a pause.

'Cress?'

'I think ... I think it does change a lot of things, Jen, and before you leap down my throat, just listen.' Jennifer could hear Anna Maria talking in the background and Cress saying, 'Yes, yes, I'm telling her. Shush.'

'Recently, when we've been talking, you know, talking properly again, I've just enjoyed hearing that you were angry with him. It was better than all that sorrow you were lugging around. So I've held back from saying some things I wanted to say, and before I say them now, please understand that I am always completely, utterly on your side. If you decide not to forgive him and not to believe he has genuine feelings for you, then fine. But I think he does love you, Jen. I told you what he was like in Bath, but if anything I underplayed it – he was completely, utterly gutted.'

'I'm surprised he managed to fool you too,' she said, knowing Cress would have picked up on the snitty tone.

'Don't think he did, sweetie. He wasn't acting.'

'I don't want to hear this.'

'I'm sure you don't, but please, just cut me some slack here. We've never discussed why I gave him the story of Anna Maria when I could have fobbed him off with the Rory one. Did you think it was part of some deal I cut to keep you out of the paper?'

'Look, I don't know how these things work ...'

'I gave him the story, even when he wouldn't tell me what his mother's secret was, because something about him made me believe what he felt for you was genuine.'

'That's enough, Cress.'

'No it's not. You'd better brace yourself, because there's something else. You're going to think I'm mad, but I set him a kind of test – told him something that I half-expected him to blab straightaway, but he hasn't.'

Jen stood up and almost knocked herself out on the bottom branch of the tree. 'Tell me you're not talking about what I think you're talking about,' she said, suddenly frantic. 'Tell me, Cress.'

'I can't.'

'Oh God, oh God, what have you done? You can't trust him. He'll just be holding out for a higher price now you're even hotter news.' She put her hand out and felt the bark of the tree under her palm. 'I'll deny everything. It wasn't your fault.'

'Oh, come on Jen, time to grow up. Sorry to be so harsh, but we both know the truth. And if you can forgive me, haven't you got it in you to forgive Mack? Look, tell him to get lost if you like, refuse to forgive him, but if there is the slightest smidgen of doubt in your mind about him being a bastard, swallow your hurt, give him a chance.'

'I have to go,' Jennifer said quickly and ended the call before throwing the phone as far away as she could.

CHAPTER 49

When Mack returned from Bath he found Pat's post-office van parked near Doug's car, which he took to be a good sign as it was ten o'clock at night. In the kitchen Mack saw the two ukuleles, one red, one blue, that had arrived during the time he had been away.

He listened. There was the dull thump of heavy metal from upstairs and so it wasn't really necessary for him to tiptoe to his own room, but he did it anyway. At least he'd finally done something right. Unless in the morning he discovered Doug with teeth marks in his neck, drained of blood.

The Doug who appeared at his bedroom door in his underpants next morning was robustly full of life and kept striding around repeating 'Bloody Hell!' until Mack said, 'Finally got it together then?'

'Yesterday,' Doug said, with a grin. 'It was that ukulele that did it. She's canny, Mack. She'll be back after she's done her rounds. Thinks the sun shines out of my arse, can you believe that?'

'No. I've seen your arse, remember.'

Doug threw himself on the bed and lay beside Mack, his hands behind his head. 'Me and her. Unbelievable. She's first class and I'm just a rough old package with not enough postage.'

'Are you going to talk in postal metaphors all the time now?'

Down in the kitchen, as a massive fry-up spat and sizzled in the pan, Doug asked Mack how much it had cost him to bring him and Pat together.

'You knew all along?' Mack asked.

Doug gave a huge, from-the-bottom-of-his-stomach laugh which Mack took to mean 'Yes'.

'I have to tell you something though, Doug, in the interests of honesty . . . I used some of O'Dowd's money to pay for the things. Sorry . . . don't know how you're going to feel about that.'

There were a couple of seconds when it could have gone either way, but then Doug was laughing again. 'You tight git,' he said, 'you'd think with so much money to dip into you could have got some better presents.'

It was only after they'd eaten, gravitating again to the sun and the pond to drink their cups of thick, brown tea, that Doug told him Jen had called round while he had been away. It had been an emotional meeting as the two of them had barely talked since the after-play party. She had stayed for a couple of hours and, from the look on Doug's face, she had forgiven him for taking Mack in.

'Did she mention me?' Mack asked, trying not to hope.

'She says she understands why you did it, but I couldn't draw her oot any further. Sorry.'

'That's OK, it's hard for you, I know that. But Alex, please tell me she's not getting together with him again?'

Doug chuckled. 'Sorry, should have told you this first off, but I wanted to savour the moment – Alex's not welcome at the farm any more. Aye, you may well look like that. He turned up when Jen was there on her own. She was in the lambing sheds, clearing up some bits and pieces for Ray, and he starts trying to pressurise her into going back oot with him, ranting on about how grateful she should be to him, how she obviously couldn't cope on her own, but she's having none of it and he loses that temper of his. Starts backing her into a corner, literally, telling her she owes him—'

'I'm going to bloody kill him,' Mack said, standing up.

Doug reached up and yanked him back down. 'Hang on, bonny lad. Turns out Jen wasn't on her own. Bryony was in the house with Louise. She'd seen Alex arrive, thought she'd just turn the lamb-cam on, keep an eye on him. Result: end of Alex's visiting rights.'

Mack watched the water boatmen skimming over the surface of the pond and thought of Jennifer being cornered in that barn and not being there to help her.

'Something else on your mind?' Doug asked after a while.

'I was wondering if you'd make a gift for me to give to Jen. I mean, I don't think it'll make any difference, but I've been thinking about it for a while. I've done a sketch; I'll go and find it.'

Doug screwed up his eyes when Mack gave him the piece of paper. 'Should be alreet,' he said, turning the drawing round and looking at it from every angle. 'Thin plate steel, use a gas torch, high-quality lacquer. Aye. Canny.'

Mack asked how much it would cost.

'Nothing. I owe you after those ukuleles,' Doug replied.

Jennifer did not appear in the park for a full week after that, although Mack saw her go in and out of the library. He ate his chocolate and drank his lattes and read his books. He worked his way through the menus of the sandwich shops. In the afternoons he walked around all those places he'd curled his lip at before and had often lied about visiting. He tramped over high moorland and down into the valleys. He got himself lost in the great, cathedral-like conifer forests and he walked along the coast. If he didn't get his daily fix of that huge sky and those endless views he felt cramped and hemmed in, and often he would not get back till ten or eleven at night, enjoying the longer, light evenings this far north.

One place he did not go was Low Newton – too many ghosts on the beach.

During that week he veered between optimism and despair, but on the day she came to him he watched how she moved and knew she had made a decision.

'I've been thinking around everything that happened,' she said, perching on the arm of the seat, 'I know the bind you were in – and I really appreciate that what Cress told you about the accident has remained secret. But . . . no matter how I try, I can't imagine how I could ever trust you again.'

'You could, Jen,' he said, desperately trying to get her to look him in the eye, 'just give me time, I'll prove to you that Matt Harper changed me. I'm not in a hurry. I'll just keep coming back here every morning—'

'No,' she said firmly. 'I made that mistake with Alex, giving him hope, and in the end it's just cowardice dressed up as charity. Go home, Mack, I hope your mum keeps on with the treatment, I hope you start writing that novel of yours again.' She gave him something between a grimace and a smile. 'I'll always be grateful to you for making me believe, really believe, that I shouldn't be crucifyingly self-conscious or apologetic or embarrassed about what has happened to my face. In some weird way, what you did has made me braver. Who knows, I might go out to see Cress soon, travel further afield, take some acting classes. And the next play, well, Finlay was talking about Portia. I just might do it.'

He tried to grab hold of one of her hands, but she pulled away.

'Jen, tell me what to do to make you believe that I love you and that I'll never, ever give you any reason to distrust me again.'

'There's nothing,' she said brutally. 'I can't love you. I loved the other you. I'm sorry.'

She was so calm and so cold it chilled him. He'd done

this to her, toughened her up, and now it was coming back to haunt him. He went to speak again and she cut him off.

'It's pointless arguing. Your mother hasn't swayed me; Cress hasn't swayed me. You were so cunning, employed so much guile, I can only believe it's part of your character. Who knows when it will come out again?' She got up. 'This is it. End of the road.' He felt the lightest of touches on his shoulder before she was gone.

He remained on the seat until the sound of the abbey clock striking the hour roused him. Standing up slowly, he looked around and then walked out of the park and drove back to Doug's. The house was empty and the forge cold, but the thing Doug had made for him was lying on the table, a note on top of it:

Here you go. Not very happy with the colour of the barley – what do you think? Can have another go tomorrow if you like. Staying at Pat's tonight.

Mack still had some brown paper left in his room, and when he'd finished using it, he packed his bag and wrote Doug a few words on the reverse of the note and a stupidly large cheque. He looked at his watch. He had a few hours while Jen was still at the library and so he piled everything into the car and drove to Brindley. Sonia looked surprised, but not angry to see him.

'Just the card, is it?' she asked. He didn't answer as he

gave her the money and knew she was still watching him as he sat in the car and got out a pen.

The package was heavy, but he parked at the fork in the track and carried it all the way to the farmhouse, not wanting to alert anyone that he was there. It was warm today, the light on the fields seeming harsh and so different to when he had first come here.

Laying the parcel down gently on the doorstep, he placed the card on top and then drove away, looking only at the track and nowhere else.

'Jen, I can't stop long, atmosphere on set is manic after all the time we've already lost, but I need you to ring me back. I'm concerned about you. I've been trying to get you all week, Jen. You're doing it again . . . avoiding me. Leaving messages on my voicemail doesn't count as talking to me. I know you're pissed off with me about all those things I said, but this isn't fair, Jen. I had to say them. I had to be honest with you about Mack. We've always been honest with each other. Jen. Talk. To. Me. Oh, bugger.'

'OK, Jen. Part Two, I'll talk quickly or the bloody thing will cut me off again. That message you left yesterday and the one you left the day before – they didn't sound like you. You sound, well, like you're on medication or something. Jen, sweetie, please, this is torture. Look, don't get cross but I've had a talk with Auntie Bren. She's worried too. Jen? Are you there? I'm in Make-up. Please ring back. Pretty please.'

Jen looked at the phone, ran her finger over the dent in it where it had hit the fence, and then returned it to the glove compartment and drove home.

'You're all bloody worried about me. All the time. Poor broken Jen.'

It was all right for Cress, her life was like a film, full of living-happily-ever-after. Real life was a little tougher than that.

Nobody had given her a second chance, asked her if she'd like her face back, so why should she give him one?

Cress had said she would understand if she decided not to forgive Mack, so let her prove it. She'd ring her later, ask if she could go and stay for a while. Perhaps Anna Maria would show her a little of Argentina too. She wound down the window and breathed in deeply.

It had been a mistake to touch him on the shoulder just as she left, she had felt his hair brush the skin on her arm. But looking good and being good were poles apart. What use was a man who you couldn't believe was telling you the truth, even if he was? She laughed and it felt comfortingly bitter.

Alex, who wasn't on her wavelength; Mack, who wasn't on her side. Perhaps the men in America would be better.

She glanced in the rear-view mirror and felt nothing when she saw her face. So, he'd been of some use, then.

In the kitchen there was a reception committee waiting, the whole family. They looked as if someone had died and she wondered whether they'd already wrapped whoever it was in the large brown-paper package on the table.

'Sonia rang,' Brenda said.

'Really. What did the nosy cow want?'

She saw the shock on her father's face and really couldn't give a stuff.

'Love,' he said, 'that's not like you.'

'It might be,' she snapped, wishing he'd get off her back. 'From now on it might be. Oh, here we go, those looks are flying back and forth again.'

She felt Danny's arm round her shoulder. 'Jen, Sonia rang to say she thinks Mack's gone. He bought a card; saw him writing it in his car. And Mum found this on the doorstep.' He nodded towards the package.

She shrugged his arm away. 'I hope he has gone. I told him to go. He's wasting his time up here.'

'Jen,' her mother said, moving towards her, 'has something else happened today? What's wrong?'

'What's wrong? What's wrong? I've got a great scar on my face; I can't be an actress, which is the only thing I've ever really, really wanted to be; I have to take all kinds of crap from people I don't even know; and the person I loved, who made me feel so glad I'd survived that crash, guess what? Turns out he was a lie. Beginning to end, a great big fucking lie.'

'Do you think we should call Dr Crawford?' Ray said to Brenda.

Jennifer was going to make some smart-arse comment when Bryony came swiftly round the table, grabbed hold of her and shook her. 'Open the package, open the card on top of it and stop being a ruddy drama queen. One's enough in this family.'

'Cress calls you the Amazon, do you know that?' Jennifer said, right in her face.

'Good,' Bryony retorted, 'that means you won't be able to stop me if I open this for you, will you?' Bryony let go of her, pinched the brown paper on the package and then pulled, and a huge strip of paper came away. They could all clearly see it was something Doug had made, but what it was did not become obvious until Jennifer moved Bryony aside and tore off the rest of the paper.

Brenda made a little 'Oh' noise when she saw the mirror but there was no sound from anyone else as they looked at Doug's craftsmanship. Here was a twist of metal, with a delicate green gleam, looking like the tendril of a plant; there a clump of ferns fanning out across a corner. Sheaves of barley lay beside a tiny kingfisher worked into a mesh of reeds, before the countryside gave way to the delicate metallic blues and greys of the coast – to fronds of seaweed, pebbles and shells. Ray put his hand out and touched the mirrored glass near the ferns and it looked as if his fingers were about to drop into a stream. When he moved his hand to the glass next to a razor clam, it seemed as if he was dabbling in a rock pool.

Brenda handed Jennifer the envelope and she opened it, still looking at the mirror.

'"For Jen, an ugly mirror until you look into it. Chin up, sweetheart, and break a leg"' she read.

'Oh God,' Jennifer said feeling her lungs struggling to fill with air, 'he always knew exactly what to say.'

CHAPTER 50

Mack watched the lads on the beach playing football, shouting and throwing themselves in great lunging bellyflops after the ball. Slowly, feeling his breath catch as the cold slapped at him, he walked into the sea.

He paused as he got used to the numbing sensation and then took a few more steps, aware that the water had nearly reached the bulky turn-ups he had made when he rolled up his jeans. A few more steps and the water was up to his thighs, the weight of the waterlogged material now making it harder to move his legs. The numbness was dying away, to be replaced by a sensation of intense burning, and after a few more steps he felt his whole body start to tremble. A sharper lick of pain engulfed his groin as the water reached it.

'Offside,' the lads were shouting, 'off bloody side.'

He wondered how hard it would be to just keep walking, and whether the pain at the end would be greater than the pain he felt in his chest. He'd been so hopeful after Phyllida's visit, so stupidly hopeful.

Whatever else happened in his life Jen would always be there, just offstage, as she had been that time he'd seen her sitting in the prompt light and knew he loved her.

He looked towards the skeleton of the castle. Was he saying goodbye to Northumberland forever too? He guessed he was. Ghosts everywhere now, not just on this beach.

He made a move forward, intending to turn, but stumbled as his instep connected with a sharp piece of rock. Managing to right himself, he heard one of the lads on the beach start to screech, a weird high-pitched noise as if his voice hadn't broken yet. And then the sea around him was suddenly churning, spray splashing right up his back and he felt someone grab at him before he fell forward. He went right down, sea water in his mouth and up his nose and felt his palms connect with sand. Hands were pulling at him, and he tried to get away from them, shouting and flailing around, great waves of fear engulfing him along with the water.

It's Alex; he's decided to kill me.

'Get off me, get away,' he shouted, finally getting his feet down and staggering upright, his wet clothes trying to drag him back under. 'It's over for me too.'

Trying to wipe the stinging salt water from his eyes, he waited for Alex's fist to come at him, but saw Jennifer instead, standing up in the water, gasping and pushing her streaming hair away from her face.

'What were you doing?' she shouted at him as she waded unsteadily towards him. She caught hold of his arm. 'You can't do this – your mum, Tess . . .'

When he didn't answer, just stared at her like a lunatic, she shouted the question at him again, and this time he picked up on the worry underpinning the words.

'I was just trying to feel numb,' he said.

'Just trying to feel numb?' she repeated, and then gave a little laugh. 'I thought ...' She looked out to sea and then back at him.

Some time between thinking she looked beautiful wet and wondering why she was here, he noticed she was shivering and tried to take off his jacket, but what with her hand on his arm and the way his clothes were clinging to him, he only succeeded in shrugging it off his shoulders.

'What are you trying to do now?' she said, watching his efforts and still holding his arm. He wanted to believe that it wasn't just to steady herself against the swell of the waves.

'Trying to give you my jacket, you're cold.'

'Oh, Mack,' she said, 'don't do that, it makes no sense, no sense.' Her anguish was unmistakable now, the hand on his arm really gripping him. 'I've wanted to feel numb too, Mack. I've been sick to death of feeling sad and angry. I just wanted to shut down and push everyone away, you most of all. But now, the mirror ... and the note ...' He didn't know if it was the cold or her emotions making her mouth tremble and it didn't matter: he'd caught that hint of forgiveness in her voice and was soaring into the air on it – the sun was on his back, there was a fairytale castle behind him and a beach the colour of her hair beneath his feet and he was going to take a chance. He reached forward and took her face between his hands, feeling the smooth skin against one palm and the rough against the other, dived into the blue of her eyes and kissed her, meeting lips that tasted of salt and Jen. As her arms came up around him what was meant to be a tentative kiss bloomed into something more urgent.

They were both shivering wildly, and he revelled in the way it made her body feel against his. He hadn't thought he was ever going to hold this wonderful, brave, sexy woman again and it made him want to fall into her like he'd fallen into the sea. Remembering the last time they had been here, he pulled away from her, and while she still looked dazed he bent down, put his arms round her hips and lifted her over his shoulder. Slowly, clumsily, he started to wade to the shore.

There were a couple of nasty moments when he nearly turfed them both back into the water, but when they got to the dry sand he lowered her down carefully and just looked at her. The drops of sea water on her eyelashes looked like tears.

'Sebastian and Viola escaping from the sea,' she said.

'Hope not.' He laughed softly. 'I've never kissed my sister like this,' and he pulled her into him again, kissing her so intently and for so long that he was aware of people slowing as they walked past, and of the lads playing football whistling and shouting.

He ignored everything but Jen, intent on showing her how much he loved and wanted her.

This time it was she who pulled away first. Her lips had a blue look about them.

'Parts of me feel as though they are on fire,' she said, her breath juddering, 'but if I don't get these wet clothes off soon I'm going to freeze.'

'Please, please, may I be the one to peel them off for you?' he asked, hearing the shiver running through his own words. He took her hand, intending to move towards the road and his car, but saw a movement near one of the beach huts up on the dunes.

'Come on,' he shouted, pulling her up the beach, but she jerked him back to retrieve her handbag, abandoned in the soft, dry sand.

'What about your shoes and socks?' she said as he set off again.

'Come back for them later.'

'But where are we going?'

'Up here, come on.'

Making any progress over the soft sand was hard in their waterlogged clothes, but they got to the worn, wooden steps leading up into the dunes just as an elderly couple were walking slowly away from the nearest beach hut, the man carrying a large holdall, the woman with what looked like a wet swimming costume in a plastic bag swinging from her hand.

'Excuse me,' Mack shouted and struggled up the steps, pulling Jennifer behind him. The couple turned and it was difficult to tell if they were surprised or alarmed. Reluctantly letting go of Jennifer, Mack reached into the inside pocket of his jacket and pulled out his sopping-wet wallet.

'I know this is going to sound weird, and we look even stranger, but –' he carefully extracted a mess of notes from his wallet and watched them flop and drip as he held them out – 'I don't suppose you'd be willing to rent us your beach hut for a night?'

Jennifer watched Mack as he peeled her jeans and knickers down her legs and flung them on the pile of wet clothes in the corner of the little bedroom, and then they were wrapped in the duvet, his hand smoothing over her shoulders, her breasts, her belly; his lips on hers.

She listened to the thrum of her heart mixing with the sound of the waves outside and let go of those last remnants of doubt holding her back and wound her legs around him.

When she'd been stripping him of his clothes, she had sensed he was holding back as well, perhaps feeling he should be sensitive and not push his luck too far, but that had all changed as his skin had met hers, and she realised she needed that hungry desire of his; needed to know that whatever had gone on over the last few months he couldn't stop himself from wanting to make love to her.

She ran her hands down his body to his backside and fondled and stroked it, before moving one of her hands to his groin.

'Oh God, don't do that, it's too much,' he whispered,

taking his mouth from hers, 'slow down, slow down, I haven't tasted you enough yet.'

He kissed her mouth again and all the way down to a breast, taking such delight in kissing and fondling her there that soon her hips were rising and falling and she was light-headed and breathless with the need to feel him moving over her and inside her. Was it only minutes ago she had felt cold?

'Please,' she said, 'let's get back to where we were, how we fitted together. Before everything.' She heard him make a low noise at that, and his eyes seemed darker and then darker again.

'I need to get my wallet,' he said, sounding breathless, 'there's a drowned condom in there. Don't move.' He struggled out of the duvet, moved a few steps away, came back and kissed her, moved away again and bent to retrieve his wallet. She saw him struggling with the wet packet. 'Fiddly thing,' he said, grimacing at his own impatience, 'I can't get—'

They both jumped as somebody hammered on the front door and Jennifer clawed at the duvet to cover herself.

No, no, this is what happened last time.

'It's all right, Jen,' Mack said, but there was fear in his eyes. 'I swear to God, there are no more lies I'm hiding.'

'Who is it?' she shouted.

No reply. He scooted over to the bedroom window and pulled back the curtain and she saw him squinting towards the door.

No, not that again.

'Can't see,' he said, 'it looks out on the dunes.' He gave another start as the hammering began again and this time did not stop. With worry still evident on his face, he came back to the bed, picked up a pillow and held it to his groin.

'I'll just go and investigate.' He looked so spooked and so sexy that she got out of bed too, wrapping the duvet around herself.

'We'll go together,' she insisted, and they hobbled out of the bedroom, through the tiny front room with its stripy sofa and sand on the floor, and Jennifer positioned herself behind the door as Mack opened it just enough to see who was standing outside.

'I'm sorry,' a male voice said, 'know we're interrupting, but these were just about to float away.'

She saw Mack, with one hand still holding the pillow, reach through the door.

'That's really kind of you,' he said and now, in his other hand, he had his shoes and socks. The man outside said something else and then the woman, but Jennifer didn't catch it, and then Mack was saying, 'Goodbye and thank you again', and reversing back into the room. He did not have enough hands to hold the pillow, hold the shoes and shut the door, and so she did it for him.

'The people from this beach hut,' he said, letting the shoes and socks fall to the floor. He looked a little bewildered. 'That was incredibly nice of them.'

'Well, that's what we're like up here,' she said and saw him give her a warm, brown-eyed look that, as she watched it, sifted into something ruder.

'True,' he said, slowly, 'nice all over. Speaking of which . . . how are you keeping that duvet up?'

'How are you keeping that pillow up?'

With a grin, he showed her before throwing the pillow in a perfect arc across the room.

'Methinks, my lady, you are overdressed now,' he said, lowering his head and looking intently at her and she felt herself reignite from her mouth all the way down to between her legs. She let the duvet drop and they ended up on top of it, him tearing at the condom packet now with his teeth, and finally, finally she had him where she wanted him and he was telling her that he would never hurt her again, didn't ever want to move from where he was right now; laughing at the way they still fitted together.

The light on the beach had changed from yellow to golden by the time they opened the door and sat just inside it, both wrapped in the duvet. Jennifer was resting her hand on the inside of Mack's thigh and thinking about how he had changed under her hands into someone different before. She had to believe he wouldn't change again.

'So, Mack Stone,' she said, 'very like Matt Harper in bed, but better fashion sense.'

He winced. 'Don't, Jen; can we just pretend Matt Harper walked out to sea?'

She laughed. 'Let's hope he was wearing his brogues.'

He pulled her in closer and she settled her head on his shoulder and realised that for the first time since coming home from Manchester her brain wasn't picking away at what she'd lost in the accident. She felt sleepy, but most of all she felt contented that this shoulder was exactly where she should be.

She lifted her head to look at him some more.

'Can you really live with this face?' she asked.

'I can't live without it,' he replied and kissed her on the nose.

A little more kissing and then he pulled her back into his shoulder, carefully, lovingly rearranging the duvet to make sure they were both decent. 'I wouldn't have dared hope today could end like this,' he said, his voice catching. 'I drove here thinking it was all over, that I had to go back to Bath and leave you up here . . .'

'It's all right,' she said, 'shush now. You've done your penance.'

They watched the waves coming in, a couple jogging and then Mack was whispering in her ear, 'Whatever you decide you want to do, Jen, acting, maybe directing, teaching, whatever it is, we'll work out a way of dealing with any morons you'll encounter along the way. I'll make you feel so beautiful anything bad will just bounce off you.' He gave her a squeeze. 'But no more fighting, you've had enough of it and so have I . . .' He trailed off and she picked up on the underlying tension in his voice. He was obviously struggling.

'Jen . . .' he said, '. . . as I'm trying to start with a clean slate, those men in the pub? I confess I went back after you'd gone and, long story, but I wound another guy up so badly he started a fight with them.'

She pinched him hard and was gratified to hear him squawk. 'That's really bad: I gave you brownie points for just turning your back and walking away.'

'I know. Old me, promise it won't happen again. And, while I'm coming completely clean ... the money I got paid for doing the job? I've spent a bit here and there – Phyllida's treatment, some stuff for Doug, the mirror. But I've set the rest aside. I think you should have it.'

Her first reaction was to say it was dirty money and she did not want it, but when she dug down deeper, she found that the thought of spending it did not really disturb her.

'You're right,' she said. 'I think I should. And I know what I want to spend it on: I want to go and see Cress, travel around the States a bit, perhaps get Anna Maria to show me some of South America.'

She saw he was looking out to sea again, and he didn't turn back to her when he said, 'I've got the bank statements in the car, I'll show you how much there is. Enough for what you have planned and then some.'

'Would it cover going to Australia?' she said, suddenly excited by the thought of such new experiences waiting for her. 'We could swim at the Great Barrier Reef, Mack, I've always wanted to do that.'

'We?' he said turning back to her.

'Yes, of course. What? Were you thinking I meant to go on my own?' His face confirmed he had and for some reason that made her want to cry. She kissed the nearest bit of him to her mouth, the soft dip of flesh by his collarbone, and one of his hands came under the duvet to seek out and lace his fingers through hers.

'We *both* need to get away for a while,' she said, 'find out who we are. Recover from a brutal few months.'

She felt him tense up and his fingers hold hers more tightly. 'You're right, it was brutal, what I tried to do to you, Jen.'

'What you were *made* to do to me, Mack. And it was brutal for you too. That's what I meant, we both have to recover.' He was looking as if he might interrupt. 'No, listen. I'd say you're pretty scarred yourself. Dealing with Phyllida all these years; losing your dad so young; all the worry of the Montgomery thing; finding out that . . . that man, was your father . . .'

He brought their hands, still interlaced, out from under the duvet and kissed her fingers and she watched his head bowed over her hand and remembered how Alex had done that in the car coming back from the Henshaws' and how wonderful this felt when that had not.

'You're being way too fair to me, Jen,' he said and then gave a mirthless laugh. 'But I do have one Hell of a set of parents. If it wasn't for Tess . . .'

'I can't wait to meet her,' she said softly. 'I'm so glad you didn't make her up, or Joe, or Fran and Gabi.'

There was such tenderness in his eyes as she finished speaking that she leaned over and kissed him; a soft, warm, loving kiss. The duvet got a bit rearranged in the process.

'After the travelling,' he said, tucking the duvet back

round them both, 'you'll think about getting back into drama somehow?'

The idea made her feel slightly jittery, but she believed now that this jitteriness might be more related to anticipation and excitement than terror. 'I will,' she said, 'and I'll let you help me.'

He nodded slowly. 'Only if you do the same for me, I've no idea what I'm meant to do with my life. I've still got a serious amount of debt, no stomach for journalism and a worrying new tendency to find tramping about the countryside really, really rewarding.'

She started to laugh. 'You know what I'm going to suggest, don't you?'

'Don't . . . don't say I should write a walking book.'

'You should write a walking book.' He was shaking his head, grinning ruefully. 'No, listen . . . you could look at walks from a different angle . . . interview people, find out their favourite ones, what they mean to them, maybe even what they've helped them do?'

'I'm not sure—'

'Sonia, there's an example, I remember her telling me after her first husband died she walked her feet off, you wouldn't think it of her, would you? She just needed to be out and breathing fresh air, seeing rivers, the sea, knowing life was going on . . . and Dad, he's got a walk he does every Sunday with one of his pals, they've done it since they were boys – five miles. Says as long as they can do it and still have enough puff to talk he knows all's right with the world.'

As she'd been talking she had seen him start to really listen, and when she stopped he said earnestly, 'You might just be a genius.'

She leaned back into him and felt his chest do some wonderful jiggling again.

'What now?'

'Thinking about a job offer I got before I left Bath,' he said, 'something at quite a high level.'

'Oh?'

'On a plinth, in fact.' He bent and kissed her shoulder. 'Guy I went to school with suggested I should stand on it dressed as a—'

'Pirate.'

'How the Hell did you know that?' he asked, pulling a little away to look at her properly.

'It's what I thought the first time I saw you, that there was a touch of the pirate there. Something . . . a bit . . . bad.'

Her stomach, or something very near her stomach, did a strange little shimmy and she reached up and tweaked his ear. 'If I asked you to have this pierced, would you?'

'I would,' he said and before she knew it, he had pushed her on to her back and was looking down at her. The duvet was still there somewhere, but whether both of them were covered she did not know.

'I'll have anything pierced if it pleases you,' he said, lowering his mouth to her neck this time. 'But,' kiss, 'I will not,' another kiss, 'paint myself silver to look like a statue. And, while we're on the subject of staying absolutely still, will you stop wriggling about? It's too far for Gregor to make a delivery, so you and I are going to have to be very good and put aside all thoughts of making mad, passionate librarian love.'

'Stop besmirching the library service,' she said in mock indignation, 'we're being chipped away and eroded.'

'Hmm, that sounds nice, I might try some of that on you in a minute, and, about this pirate thing, are you going to insist I wear an eye patch?'

She looked at his brown eyes and the promise they held that if she fell into them all kinds of things would happen to her. 'No, I couldn't bear anything to get in the way of these.' She tried to brush the hair back out of them for him.

'Perhaps I should go for a hook instead then?'

'That'll make writing tricky.'

He laughed and so was unable to make a proper kiss shape with his mouth and when he stopped laughing, he lay down by her side and gathered her into him with one hand on the small of her back and the other gently stroking her neck.

'Jennifer Roseby,' he whispered, 'I really, really love you.'

'Yes,' she said, the waves behind them beating a comforting soundtrack, 'I genuinely believe, Mack Stone, that you do.'

ACKNOWLEDGEMENTS

My thanks to friends Lesley and Martyn Archer for answering my endless questions about libraries and farming; to Changing Faces, the UK based charity for information regarding the issues affecting those with disfigurements to the face, hands or body (please visit their website www.changingfaces.org.uk); to Paul Sanderson, Consultant Orthopaedic Surgeon, for expanding my medical understanding of this subject and to William Pym for his insights into working with hot metal.

Thanks too, as ever, to Broo, Charlotte and Nicola and the team at Quercus plus friends and family who continue to encourage and support. And an honourable mention to my Drama Club, which bears no relation to the one in the book.

Last, but never least, thank you Matt, Kate and Becky. For everything.